Praise for What We Lost in the Fire

In *What We Lost in the Fire*, Wendell Ricketts examines a wide array of characters living their lives without a lot of pomp and circumstance, often just getting by. His gift is to make each examination a poetic journey, as in "The Restless Are Native," in which we are given direct access to the feelings, thoughts, and day-to-day struggles of a waitress named Charlene, who moves through the routines and worries of her life with an effortlessness that seems both self-denying and yet also somehow heroic. Ricketts finds territories where other writers only find interstices, and what results is a collection of stories that uncovers powerful meanings in the most mundane spaces and times.

— **Keith Banner**
author of the short-story collections *The Smallest People Alive* and *Next to Nothing*; the novel *The Life I Lead*; and the anthology, *This is True Love: Essays and Stories*

What We Lost in the Fire is an eclectic gathering of stories about everyday people who discover that their lives are much bigger than the small spaces they are expected to occupy. Through moments of humor, surprising plot twists, and quick-to-the-wit dialogue, Ricketts shows us that such clarity has consequences and isn't always redemptive. Sexuality—as a topic that runs along the spine of many of the stories—is elevated deftly to a more sophisticated arena, away from familiar queer territory and toward poignancy. What impressive storytelling!

— **Rigoberto Gonzalez**
recipient of the Bill Whitehead Award for Lifetime Achievement and of the PEN/Voelcker Award for Poetry and author of *What Drowns the Flowers in Your Mouth: A Memoir of Brotherhood; The Book of Ruin;* and *Butterfly Boy: Memories of a Chicano Mariposa*

Some of the stories in this collection have been published elsewhere in different versions: "Bayonet" (*Jonathan*); "Beef Timeless Fun" (*ImageOutWrite*); "Blood Brothers" (*Blue Mesa Review*); "Everybody Was Kung Fu Fighting" (*Foglifter*); "Financial Aid" (*Blue, Too: More Writing by (for or about) Working-Class Queers*); "Present Company Excepted" (*The Harrington Gay Men's Fiction Quarterly*); "Raspberry Pie" (*The SandMutopia Guardian*); "Roma Termini" (*modern words*); "That Old Dog That Maysie Had" (*Blithe House Quarterly*); "The Mysterious Decampment of Rydel Wents" (*The Long Story*); "The Way it Happens" (*The Mississippi Review*); "Units of Measurement: A Pornographic Morality Tale" (*Velvet Mafia*); "Yard Ball" (*Salt Hill*); "Wasps" (*James White Review*).

Published in the United States by FourCats Press
ISBN: 978-1-7348050-9-3
LCCN: 2021932028

Book design by FourCats Press
First FourCats Press Edition: May 2021
Second printing March 2023
www.FourCatsPress.com
Editor@FourCatsPress.com

Front cover image © Vici MacDonald/The Chronicle. Back cover image, "Untitled," charcoal on art paper by Micheal Milligan.

Acknowledgements

The back-cover art and all of the other drawings that appear in this book are by Micheal Milligan, who died of AIDS on January 1, 1995. Micheal was a dancer, graphic artist, AIDS activist, and "long-term survivor." He was the inspiration for the title story in this collection—and for so much more. My warm thanks go to Dan Postotnick and to Mike Pierce for permission to include Micheal's artwork here.

What We Lost In The Fire

& Other Stories

WENDELL RICKETTS

fourcats press
www.fourcatspress.com

To San Francisco, as you once were ...

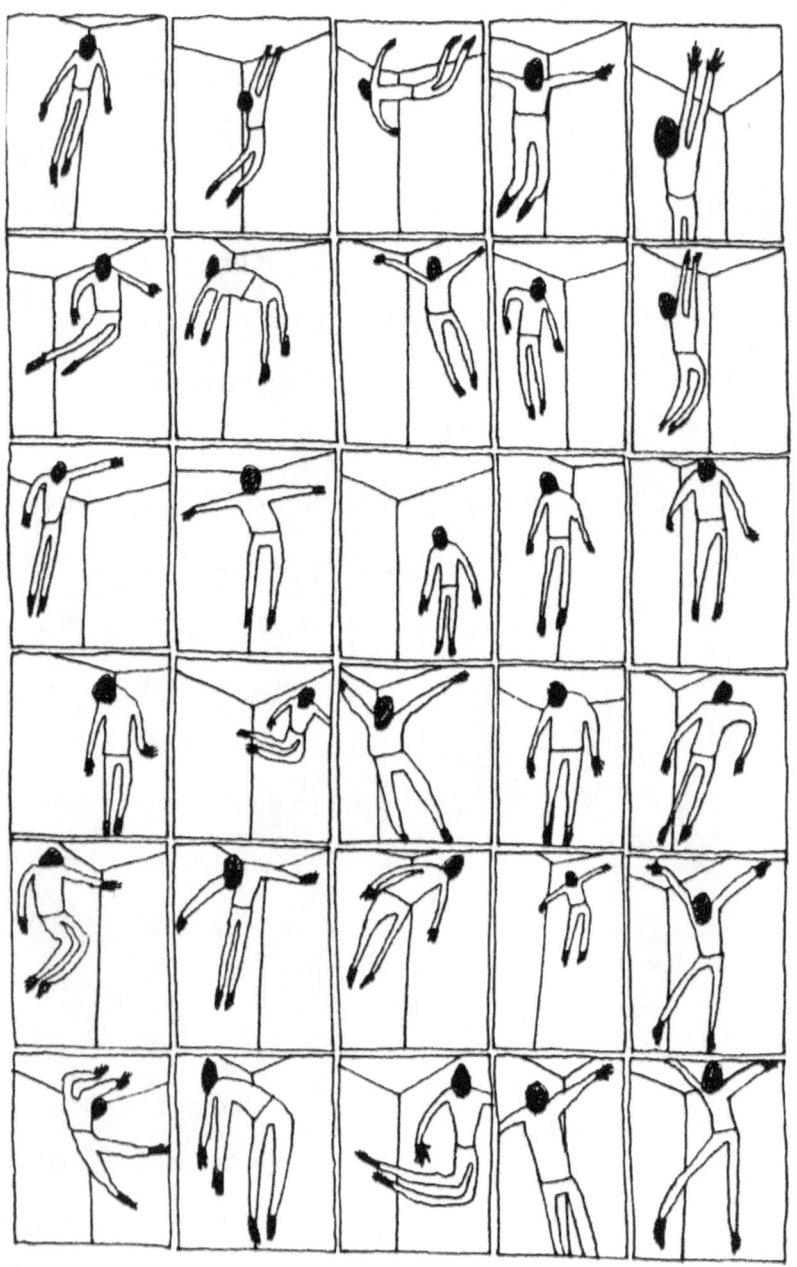

Yard Ball

Tony's on the rec yard, shirtless and sweating in the slantways dusk of a late June evening. He's short, about five-six, but tight, with good definition showing these days, especially on his upper body, which he works on whenever they get a chance to use the weights. Plus he's down to must be eight percent body fat from flat-weeding seven to three and from not eating most of the pig slop they put on your tray at chow.

The weight shed is in the inside corner of the L-shaped rec yard, where the laws can't see unless they get up off their fat, gray-suited asses and walk over there, and so, a lot of the time, that's where guys go to hit it. It ain't cool to be trying to bench press when some dudes are getting down four feet away from you, not that anybody's all that shy. And if it isn't a couple of moes with eyes for each other, say it's somebody turning out a new punk, he's most of the time gonna offer you a chance to knock off a piece, too, 'cuz that's all part of it.

Tonight, though, it's b-ball, and he knows he's moving good. Tony throws both arms out to his side to block the guys closing in on his boy who's carrying the ball. He's concentrating on the game, awright awright, but that doesn't mean he doesn't feel the thickness of a bicep, round and solid, against his forearm, or hard pec muscles rubbing up against his back, the rasp of chest hair.

The best part of getting worked out like this is afterwards. He's lucky; their block gets rec from six to nine, and now that the evenings are longer, there's time for a couple of games, or maybe a game and hit the weights, and then just stand on the strip of grass alongside the double chain link with the razor wire curled on top like some kinda sick ribbon and look out while the sun is still up, let the breeze blow on you, dry you off. You don't wanna put your hands up on the fence, 'cuz that's a good way to get shot, but you can lift your arms like wings, with your fingers laced behind your head, let the wind blow into your armpits, like a warm tongue teasing up and down your sides, until it's ticklish and your nipples pebble up.

Nobody else needs to know, when he's standing there like that, why he's doing it.

Getting ripped on the weights was part of a plan to get respect—that and all the ink, most of which he bought on the inside. When Tony was in the world, and needed some fast cash, looking like a teenage jarhead meant he only had to spend about ten minutes at the bar, pretending to play pool, before he'd turn a date, and most nights he was home in his own bed before one. He was back living with his dad then, near Houston. But when you were on the inside, being twenty-one-years-old and sweet-faced is like blood in the water, and a pretty white boy's either got to catch a ride or get a rep, and he was gonna be dead before anybody did him like some punk in the weight shed.

The hard edge of a voice cuts in. "Yo, yo! Cherokee! I'm open!" That's Vince talking; they call each other litter mates, have matching tats. Tony takes a step left, brings the ball to his chest as if to pass, then jams right and throws around the guy guarding him. The pass flies wild. "My bad," Tony says as they jog down the cement slab toward the opposite hoop.

Part of being hard is having a nick, so most of the guys know Tony as "Cherokee." His dad started calling him that back in the day, he said so Tony wouldn't forget they shared that blood, on his side, even despite the pale skin that came from Tony's mother. The name followed Tony inside, plus the rumor that he'd stabbed some guy to death with a hunting knife, then cut off his scalp. That last part wasn't true, but it was good if some people believed it was true. He had a shank now, because you had to have one to show sometimes and also to keep up with the rumor, but the only way the laws didn't find it was if he left it taped up behind the electrical plate and how was that gonna help him if he ever did need it on the yard or in the showers, which is where they hit you? Anyway, he thought his plan was turning out all right the day he overheard one of the eses say to his homies, "That vato there is firme, man, he's down." If the Hispanics respected you, you could stay pretty safe. They'd get your back against the bloods. Not that they wouldn't cut your throat and spit down your neck if it came to a real race fight, but you knew where you stood then was with your color. There weren't enough Injuns inside to click, so his color was white.

It was Saturday, which meant visits, and Tony's mom had driven in from Normangie. When he walked into the visiting room she was sitting there on a metal folding chair with a wide-ass pair of mafias across her face to cover up that she'd been crying, and the first words out of her mouth were how sorry she was she had to come tell Tony that his daddy finally died. No shock there. His dad had that shit for years, and moving back in with Tony's mom so she could take care of him only slowed down what was coming. "He died in my arms," she kept saying, stuffing a wad of Kleenex in behind the eyeglass frames and pushing at her eyes. That and, "Antonio, I just don't know how he could of got it."

Someone threw Tony the ball, and he caught it and started running. Damn if he wasn't open all the way to the hoop. He was thinking about the year and a half he'd lived at his dad's place in Houston—up until just after he turned seventeen—shooting up, freakin' with the bitches his dad brought home all share and share alike, and being so high and so horny, it didn't always matter which peg went in which hole, so to speak, which was true sometimes even when they were just the two of them, because his dad said there were things he needed that he couldn't get from a woman but he wasn't going to lower himself by going to no stranger. Better keep that in the family, 'cuz we share the same blood, his dad told him. We got the same blood.

All respect to his mom for taking his dad in when he was sick, Tony thought, but she was a clueless bitch. As he ran, he worked the ball into a steady beat—the metallic slap on the concrete, then the softer rebound against his palm. She didn't know how his dad got the shit. The words in Tony's head matched the double rhythm of the ball. They came fast, like fucking: "I do. I do. I do."

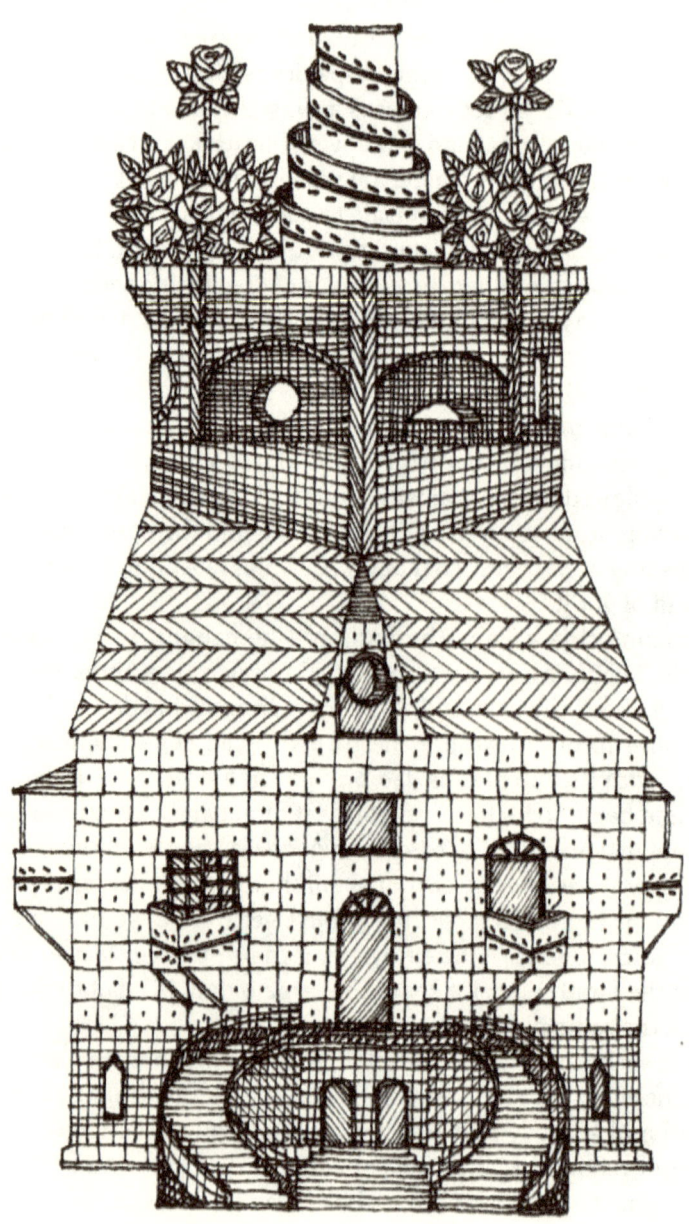

The Restless Are Native

Charlene is sitting in the kitchen, watching the mug of tea on the table before her getting cold. There's hardly any steam anymore coming off the top. She leans over the mug to see if it will fog her glasses, remembering a movie in which a detective held a monocle over someone's nose to check whether he was still breathing. Hercule Poirot maybe.

She thought she wanted the tea, but now she doesn't. The idea seemed good at the time, inviting Jamie over for a cuppa and then, when he actually arrived, all she felt was the slight edge of panic, as though something was expected of her that she didn't completely understand, and she busied herself making the tea, going through with it, as though it were a promise.

Now, at the other end of the kitchen table, Jamie is twisting his mug and talking, such an unbroken stream of talk that Charlene becomes mildly curious about when he's pausing to sip his tea, which is steadily disappearing. She can tell because she's using the transparent glass mugs that someone gave her for a housewarming gift. There are saucers, too, though Charlene tends to use them as sandwich plates. The vanishing tea in Jamie's mug makes her feel hopeful. Maybe he won't stay long. Then she thinks, *What if he wants more?*

Jamie is talking about work. The restaurant where they both have jobs is an inexhaustible source of intrigue: sudden purges and unaccountable loyalties. Jamie never seems to get tired of talking about it, although Charlene would just as soon not think about the restaurant when she doesn't have to be there. But so many people have quit or been fired lately. After less than a year, she and Jamie are old timers.

"We've stuck around through all this bullshit," Jamie is saying. "We ought to go in together and ask for a raise. We spend half our time training all the new waiters anyway, since Frank is never around."

Frank is the owner, and his bad temper and paranoia are responsible for most of the trouble at the restaurant. The place had belonged to his father, and Frank was away in an MBA program when the man suddenly died. His mother insisted that Frank come home to take over the family business, and he doesn't like anyone to forget that running a "chop house"—this is what he calls it—is not what he had in mind for his life. Frank is also young, at least half a dozen years younger than Charlene. But she's older than almost everyone at the restaurant, if that's the issue. The waiters tend to treat her as though she belonged there, just the way the retro, red-leather banquette belonged against the wall near the greeter's station. They, on the other hand, are passing through on the way to better things. Who could know, though? Charlene's mother had been a bartender all her life. When Charlene tells people this, they sometimes respond as though she were revealing an embarrassing confidence.

"Well," says Jamie. "What do you think?"

"Umm," says Charlene. "You're right. I guess you're right."

After Jamie leaves, Charlene cleans up the kitchen and pours out her tea, untouched. She decides to throw away the tea bag, too. She thinks it's better to use them twice, but she usually forgets and finds them later, dried up and dead-looking, the string stiff and brown.

Washing the dishes is peaceful, the steam from the hot water rising up around her face and the satisfying feeling that comes when a rinsed plate emerges from its smear of suds, all shiny and bright again. Minor victories.

There's a chilly breeze coming in through the window above the sink, and Charlene tries to crank the window closed. But it won't shut tight because the ivy planted along the edge of the house has climbed all the way up the wall and started to creep across the screen. The window has been open all summer. It's the first time in months she's wanted to close it. Tomorrow she'll go out with the garden shears and cut the ivy down to the ground, pulling the trailers from the walls.

It's already time to do that again, Charlene thinks with a flicker of surprise, but she dreads it. There's something about pulling the creepers down that bothers her, how they seem to hold on and not want to let go. It reminds her of how kittens are when you pick them up, the way they sink their claws into your sweater and their paws have to be detached, one by one, before you can put them down again. That's how the ivy is, and the creepers leave brown marks against the side of the house, like pieces of skin glued to the wood.

Jamie calls again later when she's already in bed, trying to make her way through what seems like a clunky translation of *The Inferno.* He has a date and wants her to trade a shift with him at the restaurant on Friday. "Sure," Charlene says, "or just let me take it. We don't have to switch. I could use the money." Jamie says that would be great and hangs up.

Jamie has a boyfriend, but he also has a steady string of what he calls dates. They are technically dates, she supposes, in the Miss Manners sense: there is usually some social activity before the sex, but the sex is the point. Or this is how Jamie tells it. Charlene's reaction to all this is essentially neutral, though she can't help but be curious. She doesn't understand how Jamie manages to meet so many people or know he wants to spend time with them, let alone sleep with them. Telling your story over and over again to strangers, even in some pro forma version, being on date-behavior.... Charlene finds that new people tear at her, the way a stiff wind snatches at your hair, at the edges of your coat. She always feels bedraggled afterwards, and numb, as if someone had been slapping her lightly for hours.

When she once expressed bewilderment at Jamie's love life, he was instantly defensive. "I don't necessarily sleep with all of them, you know," he said, because that's what he thought she was saying. In fact, he'd told Charlene enough for her to know that he did, usually, but that wasn't the point anyway. Sex was the easiest part. You could do it automatically and it didn't require much talking. Getting through the sex was always less fraught than getting through supper anyway. Easier than coming up with good reasons for not doing it. She'd had her share of experiences of heading sex off before it got going, but the men always asked—even the ones who took it well—what had made her "change her mind." It was too complicated to explain that she'd never made her mind up in the first place, and at some point she'd just decided to go along, unless she had serious objections, because it seemed to matter more to the men than it did to her. Maybe it was different with two men, she thought. Maybe it matters to both of them.

♒

*T*he next day is Wednesday and Charlene can go shopping. She needs groceries, but mostly it's an excuse not to be in the house. Of course she can go out whenever she wants, but she often feels she needs an errand, a reason to be out, some justification for her presence in public. At the market she pauses in the mammoth produce section, immobilized amid the islands of red vegetables and deep purple fruit, the pyramids of onions, the potatoes with tiny clods of musky dirt still stuck in their eyes, and the cascades of green leafy vegetables in their downward-slanting racks, and over it all a mist rolling like fog. There is a low rumble of fake thunder before the sprinklers come on. Afterwards, the tomatoes glisten with dew.

Charlene feels a little breathless in the produce section—it's like a fruit-and-vegetable museum, the colors arranged in bright blocks like a Fasanella canvas. She's almost surprised that she's actually allowed to touch these vegetables, and she bags her selections carefully, half-expecting a guard to come over and stand nearby, regarding her silently with his hands crossed sternly behind him, the way they do if they think you're getting too close to the Rodins in the sculpture garden. But you keep back even if you don't see the guard—that's how it works.

Standing before what seems a site-specific installation of yellow bell peppers, Charlene removes one and examines the waxy topography of its surface. She begins to turn the pepper over and over in her hands, her mind wandering as she stares deeply into the bin and her eyes cross until the individual vegetables blur at their borders and begin to swim together in a field of bright, healthy yellow that spreads to the edges of her vision.

She looks up, suddenly worried that someone will notice her standing there, transfixed and motionless, except for her obsessive mauling of the pepper. She lifts her hand to pull a plastic bag from the fat roll above her head, snapping it off at the perforation with a quick twist of her wrist. Now that she's been handling the pepper for so long, she feels obligated to buy it, even though they are expensive and she isn't absolutely sure what to do with it. *Take the one you touched! Wait until your father gets home!* Salad, I guess, she decides.

She puts the pepper into the bag, her eyes smarting with the start of tears, then wheels her cart into the corner with the dairy products and stands for a few seconds. She pretends to read the label on a package of cheese while she gives herself a talking to. *You're just tired,* she lectures herself, not out loud, and in a moment she's ready to turn the cart around and finish the shopping, moving down her neat list and ticking items off, as she puts them into the cart, with a careful hand. She likes the look of a checked-off list.

It takes a while for Charlene to get home with her bags—two buses—but she enjoys the special day-off feeling that makes her not care when the bus pulls up, not like the other riders who pace and stare at their watches every few minutes and roll their eyes, trying to involve you in conversations about the way the public services have gone to hell.

The bus service is terrible, but there's nothing to be done about it, and Charlene doesn't like to spend time talking about things that can't be helped. Sometimes you were the victim and got to your destination late and harried, but on those occasions there was no point in saying anything, not even to the bus driver, who only shrugged imperiously or else got surly and passed your stop when he saw you standing at the back door. Nobody was responsible for anything, but everyone needed to take their frustrations out on someone. Sometimes that someone was Charlene, but no more, she thought, than her fair share.

The bus shelter is across from a church, one wide brick wall of which faces a tall office building. The windows of the office tower have been tinted gold. The late afternoon sun reflects off them, sending yellow and orange light onto the red bricks and drawing starbursts and diamonds in the shadows below the severe steeple. It's what Charlene has always thought of as a Methodist steeple, sturdy and clean white, with a no-nonsense New England angularity about it.

The clock on the steeple indicates a little after four, although Charlene notices the way the hour hand is nudged slightly out of position and rests between the four and the five, so that it's hard to tell whether it's seven minutes after five or seven minutes after four. Charlene knows it's nearer four because she'd glanced at the watch on the checker's wrist at the supermarket. The blue digital figures had read 3:52.

She hadn't been trying to figure out the time, exactly, but she had been staring at the checker's hands, and the watch fell into her line of vision. The checker was probably only about twenty-five, but he had strong, wide hands with well shaped fingers. A worker's hands. The half-moons in his fingernails were distinct and white and Charlene tried to remember what her mother had had to say about that ... that half-moons in your fingernails were the sign of a liar or else maybe it was that they started to disappear if you'd been lying.

Charlene had looked at her own hands and noted that the half-moons were visible only in her thumbs, and pretty dimly at that. *I must be lying about something*, she thought to herself, and giggled. The checker looked up curiously, pausing with Charlene's pepper in his hand, but Charlene only smiled, shaking her head absently in response. He had pretty eyes, and long, dark lashes, but not quite as dark as the spray of silky hair that grew across the backs of his hands, cascading down the square edges of his wrists like in pictures of Niagara Falls. She thought he was Italian; the ridge of his nose formed a kind of moraine at the center of his face.

She wondered what they did with the checkers who were left-handed, given that all the checkstands were set up for the key pad on the register to be punched on the right. Maybe her checker was really left-handed and had been forced to learn to do everything over, backwards as it were. She felt a twinge of annoyance at the inflexibility of bosses, and then sympathy for her checker whose job was harder than anyone could tell.

"Paper or plastic?" he said.

"Mmmm ... both, please," Charlene answered.

"Ah, the compromise move," grinned the checker, fitting a paper carrier bag onto the metal rack at the end of the counter and opening a plastic sack inside it, smartly shaping it with his hands and forearms until a white membrane lined the interior.

"Right," said Charlene. "Either way I'm only half wrong."

The checker smiled at her again, his thick lips parting. His eyes are actually twinkling, Charlene thought. I wonder if he's flirting with me. She was wearing her contacts, so maybe it was possible. "You have a real nice day now," he said, handing Charlene her bags.

By the time she reached the bus stop, Charlene had almost forgotten about the checker. The steeple clock reminded her briefly, and she thought of him wistfully, the way she'd imagine an ex-lover, someone she'd been drawn to but hadn't actually ever managed to know all that well. There were a few of those, men who never stopped being strangers, even after she lived with them. It was hard when those relationships ended, months of readjustment, but the experience was never exactly of missing them, individually or specifically. More like the lack of anybody, more like the disappointment of coming home to a house you know will be empty, and yet there's always that moment, just as the key turns in the lock, in which you expect the sound of the stereo or the smell of onions frying, or the gently urgent sensation of warmth on your skin because someone has gotten home first and turned on the heat. Her mind played parlor games with her at these times: "I'm missing something or somebody," it would say. "Can you guess what?"

Charlene didn't really want to go home, but there was nowhere else she could think of to go. She could go to a movie, but that would mean dragging two bags of groceries to the theater or else going home to drop them off first and then riding all the way across town again. Once she got in the door with the bags, though, she knew lethargy would overtake her and she'd never be able to leave again. Her way of doing things traps her.

*T*he following Monday, Jamie is early for his shift. He's on good behavior because Frank has been grousing at him more than usual lately. More than he grouses at everybody. Frank didn't like Jamie's switching a shift with Charlene without letting him know ahead of time. "What difference does it make to him?" Jamie complains angrily to Charlene as he joins her at a two-top in the back of the restaurant, the one they often give to solo diners who come in without a reservation. They're folding a pile of freshly laundered linen dinner napkins, just delivered and still warm, twisting and pulling them into the elaborate, vaguely swan-like structures that will rest pinkly inside the wine glasses at each place setting. "He didn't even come in, did he?"

"I guess he called and Steve told him who was here," Charlene offered.

"Well, fuck Steve!"

"He didn't know any better."

It was a standing rule that Frank wasn't to be told about changes the employees made among themselves, not unless it was unavoidable. True, it didn't change anything in the way the restaurant ran. Jamie and Charlene, especially Charlene, made sure of that. But Frank liked to feel he was in charge. Steve was new and he didn't know all the informal rules yet. He'd picked up the phone in the middle of a rush, when the hostess was seating a difficult party of five who had to be shown three tables before they found one they could all agree on.

Jamie was taking his indignation out on the napkins, pounding his folds flat with the meat of his fist and yanking at the small corners of cloth that emerged from a sort of pocket to form the swans' beaks. The ranks of finished napkins on his side of the table weren't growing as fast as Charlene's because most of his had to be done twice.

Charlene waited, knowing he'd eventually start talking again. After a silence, he did. The topic was his boyfriend, Erick, a story that Charlene knew by now as well as some of her own. Jamie had been nearly through the second semester of his sophomore year in college when they'd met, Jamie's first time away from home and, of course, his first time in an all-male dormitory. He hadn't been adapting so well to life in the dorm, he'd told Charlene. All that noise and aggression and the knowledge that, in the whole four stories of the building, in every room on every floor, there were nothing but men. Their wolfish clannishness had terrified him. He imagined them roaming the halls at night, their eyes yellow and pitiless, looking for strays and loners and culling them from the pack. They could smell his separateness, he believed; even in darkness he stood at the edges of the secret knowledge that held them together and kept him out. And then Erick had come along and, a few months later, the RA had assigned them to room together. Jamie and Erick had been a couple for nearly three years, but there was never a time when their relationship hadn't been stormy.

"We've been together all this time," Jamie was saying, "and for two years I never touched another person. But I didn't have any experience at all when I met Erick, and now I guess I want to sow my oats. It isn't like I want to break up or anything.... I can't imagine being without Erick. I just want to try an open relationship for a while. But Erick goes completely psycho whenever I mention it. I mean, his jealousy is out of control, and I'm starting to resent the feeling that he has possession of me or something. It's my body and my sexuality, and I don't think it's fair of him to impose some inherited heteronormative model on me."

"Well," said Charlotte. "It's certainly tougher to move in that direction than the other—from open to monogamous, I mean."

"But the point is that he's not working on his core issues," Jamie answered, "his insecurity, for one thing. He just keeps talking about how I want to cheapen myself and our relationship by slutting around. I'm finding out that he's actually very sex-negative."

Jamie had been going to Queer Nation meetings and he liked to talk about whether things were sex-negative or sex-positive. "When we're living through this terrible plague," he told Charlotte, "it's easy to start believing that sex itself is the enemy, so it's important for as many people as possible to keep saying that sex is good and natural and that it's our right."

Charlene listens to what Jamie has to say, but she doesn't respond. It isn't wisdom that he's sharing with her anyway, not the juice extracted from something Jamie has lived. Rather, he's simply repeating his catechism; it is, in a sense, a recital of what he would like to believe. Unshakeable convictions, she knows, are what people have when they don't have much experience.

And yet when Jamie goes on to talk about the unpredictability of human existence or the way we never know what might happen or how you could spend years waiting, sad and lonely, never knowing that the right person was out there, groping toward you all that time on a unknown course—when he says these things, Charlene feels a whisper of interest, the pull of a familiar gravity, like the tug of romantic comedies and the love songs in Broadway musicals that she has memorized despite herself, and a certain few novels, some of them quite trashy, whose plots she will never forget. But that is all she feels, this tug. Because Charlene knows there are rules, and one of the rules is that life does not have to work out.

When she was younger, and cynicism seemed romantic, Charlene might have insisted that the true rule was that life was specifically unfair, but she realizes the imprecision of that view now. Because fair or not fair isn't the point; the point is that everything in nature is random. Eight out of ten newly hatched sea urchin larvae will die or be eaten without getting any further in their development. That is the rule. But which two survive? That is random.

Of millions of sperm cells frantically, blindly whipping their way toward some egg that faith tells them will be waiting, only one "wins" survival. From the get-go (and this always makes Charlene smile) at least half must head down the wrong Fallopian tube. Even so, the one that makes it does so at random.

While Jamie is talking, Charlene is thinking to herself—all you need do is to observe the world. Not everyone gets married. Not everyone has enough to eat. Not everyone is happy. Not everyone is beautiful. Not everyone makes it. Babies go to all the trouble of being born—and then die of starvation in their first year. Women survive the Nazi death camps and live to the end of their eighth decade, only to fall under a bus and be killed one sunny, harmless morning in Beverly Hills. This is the kind of thing Charlene reads in the paper all the time.

Randomness. You can make efforts, if you're fortunate, if you have the slightest idea how to begin. And maybe your efforts will make some difference; maybe the right people will notice in time. And maybe they won't.

She doesn't tell Jamie any of this—first, because he would never understand and, second, because he would think she was being fatalistic, when all she was, really, was tired. It honestly didn't make her feel worse to think about randomness. To tell the truth, it often made her feel better, less at fault, less a failure. All those brave, determined, anthropomorphized salmon that populated her fifth-grade science films, most of them never made it upstream. They don't usually tell you that part. They do, on the other hand, like to talk about the ones that die afterwards, after having "made it," after achieving, after giving their all, because that is what they hope you will believe is the natural order of things. But most don't achieve;

they don't go out satisfied—if a fish can be satisfied. Lots die with all of their potential—there's that word that Charlene's teachers had chanted over her like some sort of incantation—all that potential, intact and unfulfilled.

She waits for Jamie to pause long enough that changing the subject won't seem rude. "I hope things don't get too hectic in here tonight," she says.

"On a Monday? Naw. There'll be the usual rowdies watching the football game in the bar, but most of them aren't going to eat."

"Except for about a thousand orders of French fries and mozzarella sticks."

"Right. Except for that."

"I'm going to leave you to finish up the napkins, then," she says, "while I go deal with the fryer."

Jamie nods. Charlene folds her last swan and goes into the kitchen. She finds the twenty-pound plastic sacks of ThinKut Select Potato Strips on a middle shelf in the walk-in freezer and carries three of them into the prep area. She slits the sacks open and dumps their contents into the vat of sugar water next to the deep fryer, a trick Frank says he stole from McDonald's. The oil looks like it's been there all weekend, and she knows she ought to change it, but it's a task she hates. There's no way not to get splashed, and she doesn't think she can face another evening with spot removers and degreasers, trying to get the stains out of her clothes. The food smell in them is bad enough. She goes to the front of the kitchen to peer through the porthole, where she can see that Jamie has almost finished his napkins. Too bad. If he still had a pile to get through, she could probably trade him for doing the fryer. As a compromise, she tops off the fry pot with fresh oil, pouring slowly until the level is right. Dark bits of over-fried potato and breading laze up from the bottom and hover in the yellowish liquid like deformed minnows.

She presses the red switch on the side of the fryer and the digital readout begins to blink "WARMING." *Today and tomorrow and then I'll be off again,* Charlene thinks, and that reminds her about shopping. Things would definitely be easier if she had a car. In fact, she could probably afford a car if she wanted one, but then she's so often heard people remark, "That's too much car for so-and-so," and she thinks she knows what it means. It means you shouldn't allow yourself more freedom than you can handle. If she had a car, she might just get in it and start driving, driving until she ran out of land or her money gave out. And then where would she be?

It was like helium balloons. As a child, Charlene couldn't bear to have one tied around her wrist or even to hold the end of the string in her hand. She was convinced she'd start to rise up with the balloon, unable to let go, and that it would carry her into the sky and then pop or deflate, dropping her into the frigid ocean or scraping her across the jagged rocks. It wasn't the floating away that scared her the most; it was falling, coming down out of control. Driving was like that. Too much freedom was like that. You could reach the end and not know it until you felt yourself going over the edge. It was too dangerous, that much freedom. It fooled you into thinking you'd always be able to tell how far was too far to get back.

Charlene knows there are hundreds of things she will never do, even things she might enjoy: She'll never ride the rapids down the Nile tributaries through the Omo Valley in Ethiopia; she'll never learn to SCUBA dive; she'll never drive alone across Australia in a land rover. And it isn't that she would not be allowed to do these things; it isn't that she couldn't save enough money to afford a trip with an outfitter that took rafters down the Nile. But the fact of the matter is: Her life isn't on that track, and she'll never be the kind of person for whom such experiences are natural.

She has a friend who makes boats in a little country town outside of Oxford, England, and who travels all over the world to race them. Two other friends met and fell in love in the cane fields of Cuba, where they'd gone to help save the sugar harvest. Someone else has supper regularly with Margaret Atwood, whenever she's in town. When Charlene considers things dispassionately, she sees how she is just once removed from these events; she knows the people who know the people. The right existence is only a quantum away.

Charlene can look now and see the arc of her life, the trajectory, so to speak. She knows where it's been, the parameters, and where it's going. Of course anything is possible, anything can happen; but the point is that it doesn't. When she goes back occasionally and digs into the journals she has kept since high school, she is always astonished by how little her life has changed. Well, circumstances change constantly: She moves into a new apartment, she takes a trip, friends visit, relatives fall ill, books are read, there is always some new political outrage, heroes grow old and die. Charlene is busy. The whirl of change, of information that must be accounted for, is constant. But at the center is a hard kernel, a quiet eye, and that, Charlene has come to believe, is who she is. And who she is has said the same thing for a decade and a half: *I am not content. I feel out of place. Love is not staying put.*

That is the house that Charlene lives in, the intact, unflinching structure that is familiar and which goes on and on, buffeted sometimes but essentially untouched, just like the rafts floating down the wild waters of the Omo Valley.

"I'm going to unlock the front door," Jamie calls from the dining room. "Battle stations, everyone!" It was what he always said.

Just get through tonight and tomorrow and then I'll have a nice, calm day off, Charlene thinks again as she washes her hands and checks her makeup in the employee bathroom. Anyway, things weren't as dire as all that. The time she spent waiting tables always went by like a flash, and on Wednesday she'd have a day just for herself. She could start a new book. She could decide to skip the shopping for a week, if she wanted. She could go to the animal shelter and think again about adopting a puppy. Or she could just lounge in bed in her housecoat with glossy magazines and hot chocolate and enjoy the feeling of Autumn coming on.

Really, she tells herself as she hits the batwing doors with the palms of both hands and heads toward her first table, there are all kinds of things I can do. What we're looking at here is an embarrassment of choice.

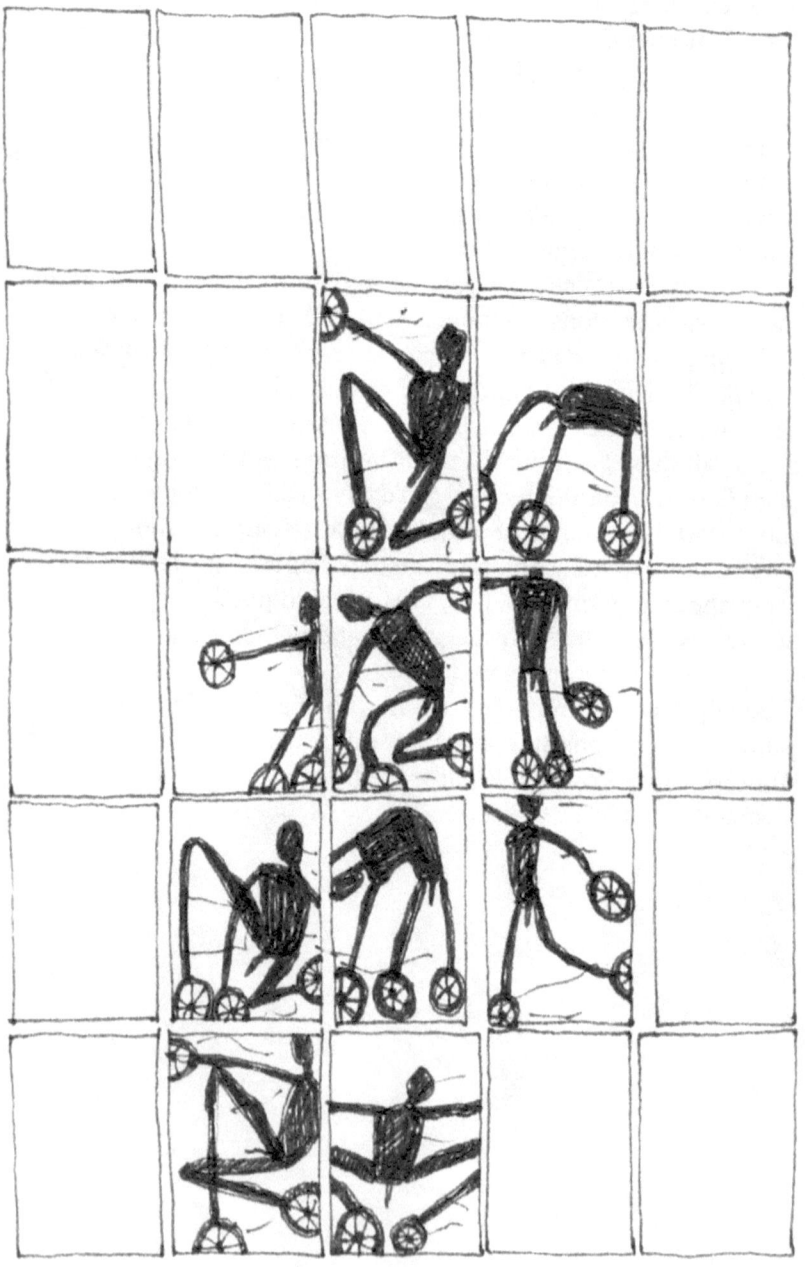

Wasps

"Wasps," she said. "You got wasps right here in under the house."

I bent down to where she pointed, to the small round hole in the wood just below the casement on the cellar window. A line of brown-and-yellow insects flew in and out, vibrating in the thick air. "Sure enough," I said.

"Yep. Wasps."

She was thin and old and bent a few degrees at the waist. The bill of a faded fishing cap was pulled low over her forehead, touching the plastic rim of her dark glasses. Her housedress was a field of flowers once blue, now vague upon the thin, clean cotton. On her feet were crepe-soled blue Keds tied with bright, white laces. And ankle socks.

"It's so godawful hot," she said, "I had to get cleaned up again before I could come out."

She turned and started down the walk and I opened the screen door and followed her.

"Guess I woke you up," she said, not looking back.

My denim work shirt was sweat-stained and wrinkled. "Oh, yes," I admitted. "I fell asleep on the couch. Too hot to do anything else."

I wanted to show, with my off-handed lilt, that I had taken on the local attitude, that I knew we were all in it together, this business of surviving Ohio summers. It was a verbal wink, but she didn't wink back. Barring serious illness, I suspected, she had never in her life been asleep at two in the afternoon. Besides, it was beauty-shop banter, across-the-fence-neighbors idle talk, not the first thing a twenty-three-year-old city boy said to an old woman he didn't know. I saw that now, and I saw that things had already gone hopeless.

We were halfway down the walk. "I'm just house-sitting for a professor, though," I added. "I don't really live here." She didn't answer.

There was no winning with these Ohioans, I silently groused, especially if they were transplanted Yankees. They had stainless steel in them. Over years, their skins emptied out and sagged, but they kept that cattle prod of a core. I thought of the covered bridges that Gare and I seemed to come across on every back road, the ones that went on standing, wrecked and beautiful, through the graying of summer and the crackling thaws of spring, defiant even when the new highways went far around them, leaving them weather-beaten, solid, and obsolete.

"Well," she said, "I wondered if you could use any vegetables today. Got sweet corn, zucchini, tomatoes, cucumbers. Just picked this morning."

We were at the car and the woman opened the trunk: Two baskets of blood-red tomatoes, six immense zucchini. Another basket held plastic bags full of small, pale ears of corn. There was a scale. A pile of paper sacks. A box of waxy cucumbers blotched with yellow. The hot smell of sap and dirt and oil. "Had enough for one basket of pole beans," she said, "but somebody downstreet's promised those."

She fussed a moment in the trunk, shifting the baskets a fraction of an inch, re-stacking the cucumbers. "These Eye-talian tomatoes," she explained, pointing to the smaller, pear-shaped ones. "I peel 'em and I boil 'em and I put 'em up. Later you throw 'em them in the blender and make your own purée." She said "pure-ee."

"These big ones are beefsteaks. They start to break open when they get ripe. See here? I washed everything before I came out. The birds like to peck at the corn but I took a knife and cut all that part away. And these zucchini, I slice them and fry them up in butter. They're real nice that way. Baked, too."

She stopped and looked up at the sky. "I guess I'd better go back in and get my wallet," I said.

"S'posed to hit ninety-one today," she continued when I came out again.

"I believe it must be already," I said.

She opened the trunk. That smell again, rising with the heat.

"It all looks just fine," I stalled, not knowing why I was buying vegetables I wasn't sure Gare and I would eat—why I felt I had to buy them. "How about a bag of corn, one of those big zucchini, and some tomatoes?"

She put three tomatoes on the scale. "Not quite a pound," she observed. "You want a pound and a half?" She picked out a fourth and fifth, larger than the rest, and placed them beside the others.

I examined the zucchini while she arranged the tomatoes in a paper sack with the corn. Finally, I handed one to her; it must have weighed three pounds.

"That it?"

"I think so," I said. I wondered if I were taking enough.

"OK. That's a pound-and-a-half tomatoes for seventy-five, and I'll give you that for fifteen cents." She tapped the zucchini on its broad yellow flank, the side that had lain against the damp ground, out of the sun. "That's a dollar fifty, with the corn."

She lifted the tomatoes out of the bag and put the zucchini at the bottom. "Don't want the tomatoes to get squashed," she said, and lay them back on top of the corn.

"No," I said, "no sense in that."

"Yep," she said as she found two quarters in the pocket of her housedress. "Ninety-one today. That's nothing, though. My daughter lives in Miami and it's over a hundred there every day in summer."

I took my change.

"First went down there twenty-seven years ago when she moved, but I don't go no more. There's too much crime. I know seven people down there, and they've all been mugged. It's bad, all right. One day my daughter was coming home with a birthday cake—her next-door neighbor was having a birthday party and she'd gone out to pick up the cake. So here's my daughter's house, and there's the neighbor's house right next door." The woman gestured with her car keys at places in the air.

"And way over there's an alleyway on the other side." She drew a line in space. "So my daughter pulled up and they mugged her right in her driveway, with the cake still sitting there on the roof of the car.

"She's getting scared to live down there but there's too many folks depend on her. Her husband died a while ago. He had that cancer all through his body. Oh, he was sick for years. They had him in and out the hospital, one kind of therapy and another, even set him up in her living room for a while 'til she said she couldn't take it. They cut out twenty-six inches of his colon and small intestine the first surgery, and then he had to go back not two years later and they took out nearly everything else. He was taking radium for a while, but he died anyway. It was a terrible thing, but we were all relieved when he finally went.

"They had two boys. One's 30 and the other's 34. The older one got married and moved up East, but the younger one's living with me now. He can't decide what he wants to do with himself—but he don't want to live with his mama, that's for sure. So she's in that house down there with just their dogs, and she does for all the old folks in the neighborhood. The man right behind her—Mr. Bell—he's 87, and when his wife died he couldn't drive on account of his eyes were so bad. So my daughter takes him around shopping and to the doctor and such. And she goes over to clean for another lady who's shut in with the cancer, too. She has it all in the stomach and the bone marrow and can't hardly even move at all.

"'Course my daughter's no young woman herself, not with grown sons. And she's got the sugar diabetes. Runs in my family. I don't have it but she does, and now she told me she's got to go in for some tests. I bet it's starting to affect her eyes, like it does, but she won't say. I talked to her last evening and I guess it was today she was going in. That Mr. Bell said he'd go with her to keep her company. He just likes the car ride. I don't know what he'll do if it winds up she can't see nor drive herself.

"She doesn't help things any, though, with the way she smokes. My grandson, he drinks; that's his only bad habit. He used to smoke but he stopped about three years ago. I used to hear him every morning coughing and spitting and I'd tell him, 'You're putting yourself in your grave with those cigarettes.' So he stopped. But my sister smoked all her life and she died of lung cancer. Must be ten years dead now."

She paused and looked up at the sky, watching for something it seemed, squinting behind her dark glasses into the sun. "I see you got two dogs yourself," she said.

"Three," I said, "But they're not mine."

"Oh, yeah, I see the third one now. Well, that police dog's the one you got to watch out for."

"Oh, no," I said. "He can barely even walk anymore. We have to carry him up and down the stairs."

In truth, Thor weighed maybe 80 pounds and could walk the stairs, albeit haltingly, but usually wouldn't. On the airless, sunny days, he made his own way down onto the broad lawn, then sat below the porch at dusk and yawped hoarsely until someone carried him up.

I made only one attempt to break him of what I saw as this habit of laziness. On that night, I positioned Thor's supper bowl conspicuously at the top of the back stairs and tried to coax him up after it. He ignored me, pacing instead in pathetic lurches across the patio. It wasn't long before I was disgusted with my faux baby talk, aware of the thinly veiled hostility behind my "good boys" and my "what a big, strong doggy you ares," and I gave up and went in. But then the moans from the bottom of the stairs started, quickly turning pitiful—and becoming increasingly audible, even when I fled to the study and tried to drown them out with the evening news. In the end, Gare pounded on the wall with his fist, called me a goddamn sadist, and went down to rescue Thor. I felt bad about it, but Gare was never a good judge of dogs.

The very next day, at the end of a desultory excursion to Kroger's, Gare and I were caught in one of those vengeful summer thunderstorms that blow in with no warning. The first we knew of it was a hot spray of gravel through the parking lot; then the first violent drops came, each one heavy and deliberate, a baleful tenor flourish across the hood of Gare's car. We sat for a while, ostensibly waiting it out, while the monsoons crashed around us and the lightning cast its pewter-blue glaze intermittently over the fogged windows. And still we sat, in sudden, private misery, until Gare at last put the key in the ignition, slid the defroster lever to high, and drove silently out into the flooding streets.

By the time we reached the house, Thor had managed to haul himself up to the covered deck above the patio, and that is where we found him, dry and exuberant, his coat bristling with static electricity, his nostrils quivering with the thrill of ozone. I didn't say anything about it, but from then on Gare took over the chore of lugging Thor up the stairs at night. I had the dog down as a malingerer, but in Gare there was a boundless font of pity for the ravages of age.

Now, as if to complete her inspection, the woman moved a few steps closer to the side yard, where Thor lay, shapeless and watery-eyed against the shady wall of the house. "Well," she said at last, "I expect he's got that rheumatism. He should take medicine for it. You got medicine for him?"

"I guess they do," I said. "But he still doesn't seem to be able to walk too well."

"Yep. Well, it won't be long before you'll have to put him down. My sister—not the one that died with lung cancer—she got a bunch of animals. They got six dogs and I don't know how many cats. And some of them got real old and lame and finally had to be put away. But she still takes them to the vet and buys all their medicine and food and shots—and don't think they don't charge you too when one of 'em's got to be put down. I told her, I said I'd have me a nice bank account if I had all the money you spend on those animals.

"They just never had no kids, I guess that's why. And her husband had to go to a home 'cause she couldn't take care of him no more. He was near 80 and in a wheelchair and she's 75 herself. So now she just has the dogs. But it's terrible—she can't go nowhere 'cause nobody wants to watch all those animals. I told her, sometimes I wish they'd all just up and die so's she could get away."

"I used to live in Florida," I said.

"Well then you know. The crime is something awful. One of my daughter's neighbors, Mrs. Stillwell, got knocked down by some muggers and broke her hip and just never got any better. You know how that goes with old people. My daughter went to see her in the hospital, but after a while she didn't even know my daughter. Wasn't but a few days after that, she died.

"And isn't it a shame about that little boy who got killed? They had the funeral this morning, I heard on the radio. But there must not have been much left of him to bury."

"No," I agreed, "he's been dead for three or four weeks."

"June 16," she said. "That's when he got kidnapped and they killed him right after."

"Well, then it's almost two months," I said.

"Found him right after that last big rain," she went on. "Washed him out from under a culvert, but by then the police had been driving back and forth past him for days. Don't ask me why they didn't find him, but of course it wouldn't have mattered anyway."

She looked up again at the sky. "I thank the Lord I'm healthy, though, and I'm 76. Seems like that cancer gets you and you don't have any time left at all. Did you hear about how the homosexuals got their own kinda cancer and it's *contagious*?" she asked.

"Seems I heard something like that."

From inside the house, music came out of the stereo that had gone on playing while I slept. The phonograph was set to repeat automatically, and, as the tone arm reached the end of the record, it paused, then retreated jerkily and began again.

It was opera, a recording I'd found in the bottom of a neglected oak cabinet that also held, on its upper shelves, an assortment of obscure liqueurs and fancy whiskeys in unopened novelty bottles. I wasn't partial to opera, but it was what I listened to whenever I was alone in the house, the windows and doors wide open as an inducement to the breeze.

There was something I loved about playing the records loud on these still and oppressive summer afternoons, as if I could actually see the trills and ornaments of some cascading soprano line reach out to cleave the silence and the heat haze. I tried at those times to imagine how the music sounded from outside the house, from down the block, from fifty houses away, what sensations might be produced by such faint strains of song, heard from deep out of the swelter and distance.

The woman lifted her chin impatiently, tightening the skin over the sharp line of her jaw. "Well, she said, "I really don't have time to talk. I'd better get along before this heat cooks up everything in the trunk."

I nodded. "Thanks for stopping by. Maybe I'll see you next time." I started to turn toward the house.

"Yep. I come 'round every week or so, whenever I got enough to make it worthwhile. My husband and me, we've got a couple acres just north of here, up in Fairfield."

She was in the car, behind the wheel, and I was standing beside her door.

"Just put that corn in to boil for about five minutes," she said. "It won't take any more than that."

"Will do," I said, and watched her car move slowly down the street, black against the shimmering mirage of asphalt.

I was in the cellar a few days later when I heard a commotion from the dogs. I peeped out the half-window that faced the front walk and recognized the blue canvas Keds with their neat, white laces. She may have caught a glimpse of me as I moved the blinds aside to look out, but I stayed where I was, hidden, until I was sure she was gone.

Gazpacho

for Daniel's Judith, on a deck in Chelsea

Back at the apartment he changed into shorts. The heat was unbearable. He felt he shouldn't have to bear it. The windows surrounding the loft magnified the sunlight and cast it into the room until the air was vengeful. Lisa was there, watching television with the sound turned off.

"It's my last day," she said when he came out of the bathroom, although she scarcely looked up. "Mark and I are moving to Seattle."

"We loved your gazpacho," he answered, "even though we didn't eat it all." He shot the woman a sideways glance. She had that look in her eye that told him she was thinking about art. "We ate as much as we could," he continued. "I even offered some to a friend who dropped over unexpectedly."

"We've lived here more than eight years," she murmured. "Perhaps one day it will be said of me that New York was a city that terrified me—in the beginning. But I grew up in Buffalo, in the snow belt. Whenever I meet someone from Buffalo, I can think of only one word: 'kindness.'"

"I suppose we could've eaten the cherries," he groused.

The woman went on. "In November we will be performing my first choral piece. It's based upon a Márquez story (she said Mar-kwez). There are seven women in a room. They can't go outside because it is raining. It's raining quite hard and the water is falling through the roof into containers of various sizes and materials, so that the sound of the water falling is different in different parts of the room, depending upon whether the rain is dripping into metal or pottery or falling into a plastic bucket, for instance, and the seven women are sitting in the room, each in her own chair, not speaking to one another, listening to the sound that the water makes as it falls into the containers and thinking to themselves.... Well, that is that part I will be singing. The thoughts of seven women. My voice and the sound of the water falling into containers from the holes in the roof will be the only accompaniment. And, although the roof will be a real roof with real holes and real water falling through them, the walls will be white lilies. White lilies on three sides. Hothouse lilies."

"Did you know," he broke in, "that there was once a public house in London? Oh, well over three hundred years ago ... called the Enfanta de Castille, because that was the name of the Spanish princess Charles I wanted to marry. But he couldn't marry her because he wouldn't become a Catholic; so her father refused to allow their marriage, and two months later Charles I declared war on Spain. And through the years, as is common in Cockney slang, 'Enfanta de Castille' was transformed into its present name, 'Elephant and Castle.' It's a kind of linguistic trick. Metathesis, I believe it is called."

"Anyway," she said, "I don't really like cherries." She was beginning to annoy him now.

"Those lilies will wilt!" he blurted out. "And how do you intend to hold them up anyway? They will wilt in the heat of the lights from the stage and you will have no way to make them stay put on the walls of the house unless you wire them up there, one by one, and cut off their roots. And how long can *that* go on?"

She turned away and looked out the window without answering. He wondered if he had really said that last thing. Perhaps he only imagined saying it. "I was walking down the street," he began again, trying to appease her now, "just walking down very innocently down the street on my way to get some coffee or dessert, or something, and a man was coming toward me, and he said to me as he passed,

'I am constantly in fear that my ears will fall off.' Isn't that the most extraordinary thing?"

"You're quite right," she said as she whirled around, glaring at him now. "It *is* time for me to go. I've been here far too long."

The man cleared his throat, not certain what he had said to offend her. He suddenly realized she must have discovered that he'd spent the night in the meditation room.

"You see," he apologized, "my analyst says—well, I realize that no one goes into analysis anymore—but anyway he says that I mustn't use these ... *situations* as coping mechanisms. Well, it came as much of a surprise to me as it must be to you. I mean, I always thought one was to *develop* coping mechanisms. After all, there is quite a bit to cope with, isn't there? I mean, the subways break down; there are always a great many loud noises. Sometimes the floor of this apartment trembles as though it were being shaken by a giant hand. And, as if that were not enough, I can be out walking, just walking mind you, minding my own business, saying nothing to anyone, speaking not even to myself, when my path may be crossed by some huge animal or something, with *immense* legs, seven or eight feet tall, sometimes with a tail, sometimes not, but it just crosses the path, it just stands there as I am out walking and won't let me go past. I mean, I have to ask, if you can't cope with a thing like that, what can you do?"

The woman sank into a chair, her back to the man and began sobbing. "I don't think I can finish this piece," she whimpered, "the water piece, the piece with the hothouse lilies. I don't think I can finish it until I learn Italian."

"Preposterous!" he bellowed, stamping his foot against the floor, causing the china to rattle ominously in the hutch. "Everyone knows that grass won't grow unless it rains! These people are really trying to do me in. It's got to have water, I mean it has simply *got* to have water. I've told them that for years, but you can see all the good that did, spring after spring, in with the sod, in with the grass seed, and always, by the end of summer, dead and dried out as a welcome mat."

The woman was done crying now, and she wiped her eyes on a corner of the tablecloth. "It never used to be this much trouble to find a good corned beef sandwich in New York City," she retorted hotly.

He laughed. "But why eat *those* cherries? I'm perfectly certain you can get cherries just as good as these in Seattle. Why, these may even come from Seattle. It rains a lot there, doesn't it?"

The woman stood again and walked to the door. "There's really no reason to go on with this charade," she sighed. "I am not the cook."

"Good God!" he cried, leaping to his feet, "you've got to be more careful! There are *thorns* in that tree. I never noticed them until this moment, but as I look up now I see them clear as they can be against the blue sky. I can see *thorns*. I mean, it must be a lemon tree or something, isn't it?" He sat down. Was she making fun of him?

"'Fear not, the angel said,'" she quoted in a firm voice, her hand fidgeting around the doorknob, "'for I bring you tidings of great....' How does the rest of that go?"

"Now, I am not altogether certain about this," he stammered, hoping she wouldn't leave, "but I believe that yesterday, I think it was yesterday, I gave accurate directions to a couple on the street. They stopped me—I was looking the other way, following the movement of someone down the sidewalk—they stopped me and they asked me, 'How do we get to Broadway?' They were not from here, and I said, well, you go up that way across Sixth Avenue and continue in the same general direction as I am pointing, and you will come to it. Don't stop at West Broadway, I said, but Broadway, if it is indeed Broadway that you want. It is a few blocks past West Broadway. 'Oh yes,' they said, 'thank you.' I think they were Southern."

"I suppose it's true," she shrugged. "New Yorkers wait on line for everything." Then she looked startled. "Did you feel that? Did you feel it? I most distinctly felt the floor move. I most distinctly felt it, right beneath my feet, a vibration, oh for perhaps a second or maybe a second and a half it quivered and I felt it through my whole body. I most definitely did feel it."

"No, it's just the wind," he crooned, wanting his voice to be soothing. "It's just the wind. Why I don't believe there are any leaks in the roof at all, although sometimes the cellar gets into the basement, that is I mean, a *squirrel* gets into the basement and sets up a nest there. My sister had a squirrel in the pantry at her country house in New Hampshire. No one knew anything about it until one weekend they went up and found that a squirrel had emptied an entire box of shredded wheat and then partially filled the box with dried macaroni stars—you know, the little ones you put in soup? It must have been the squirrel that put them there for safekeeping, though no one ever actually saw it. Of course they were appalled. They're the sort who consider squirrels to be rodents. I mean they have children ...

you can imagine." He knew then, even as he was saying it, that he should never have told her.

"There was a woman on the bus the other day, as I was riding through Chinatown," she replied, "an old Chinese woman, and she had just bought a chicken at one of those ghastly open-air markets, with just swarms of flies on everything, and it was alive, and its head was moving. The rest of it was tied up, its feet and wings you know, all trussed, but its head was moving and you could tell it was alive in an orange cellophane bag, and the driver of the bus said, 'You can't get on here with a live animal.' And she said, in her impossible English, 'but it's not a pet, it's food.' And the driver said, 'I don't care. You can't get on the bus with a live animal unless it's a seeing eye dog.' And so the woman—she had the chicken in a bag as I said—she bashed the bag with all her might against the side of the bus, killed the chicken, and got on."

"That reminds me of a funny story," he smiled, "that a friend told me when he came back from Indonesia. He was doing some research in a remote village, quite in the middle of nowhere. One day he was sitting out in this sort of a shanty he'd rigged up, trying to transcribe some notes or whatever, in really the most unbearable tropical heat, and his guide, a native who spoke practically no English, suddenly appeared and began gesturing for them to get into the jeep and leave. The guide was quite insistent. And so my friend, not wanting to be rude, got into the Land Rover and they drove away, with the guide every now and then pointing out the direction. It wasn't as though there were really roads or anything, they drove along dirt paths occasionally and sometimes just through the jungle. They drove for quite a long time and seemed to be far from anywhere. My friend was terribly frightened, as you can imagine. He was with this really rather aboriginal man—and who knows what he thought of Americans—in the middle of this desolate country where he spoke none of the language.

"But after a while the guide made him stop the jeep and they got out and began walking through the low brush, and soon they came upon a clearing. It seemed to be some sort of a tilled field, but nothing was growing there, only turned, brown earth. And as my friend looked into the field he saw that, in the precise center, there was one very tall, very full, round tree with a great many low branches, and that in the air, above the tree, some sort of dark-colored birds were circling, a lot of them, carrion eaters of some kind, dipping and wheeling, and the guide began to pull him across the field toward the tree.

"The guide was very agitated by now, and my friend of course didn't know what was going to happen, until they reached the foot of the tree and the guide pointed up into the branches and my friend could see, in the forks of the branches, particularly those closest to the ground, the tiny, mummified corpses of babies, wrapped in strips of ragged cloth. It was some kind of burial ground. The guide was practically trembling with excitement—of course my friend couldn't understand a word he was saying, and at that point, what with vultures circling overhead, and the heat, and the bodies of babies tied into the tree, why my friend began to get dizzy and finally he fainted. When he came to, he was back in the village. He couldn't ask the guide about what had happened, and he could never find his way back to the tree. To this day, he still wonders if he dreamed the whole thing."

The woman turned slowly and began to feel her way along the wall, moving as if blindfolded. At the window, she stopped and placed her hands flat against the pane. "There was a time," she moaned, "when I could look through any glass and see the ocean."

"Well," the man wondered to himself in the silence that followed, "what was *that* supposed to mean?" But perhaps it was a kind of an opening. Quickly he began to speak. "Then you agree with me about the lilies? I mean I hate to belabor the point, but I just think you haven't thought it all the way through. And then of course there are the thorns to deal with. I mean, all I mean, really, is have you *planned* it all out carefully? I'm sure you get excellent advice from everyone and you certainly don't need me telling you what to do, but I just thought I'd ask, I mean since we were on the subject. Can you actually have given any serious consideration to the thorns?"

"*I* try to think only of Shakespeare," she whispered, not looking at him. "When there is hail and lightning, and the ground shakes and thunder rattles the windows, I think of that scene in *Lear*. That is what has sustained me as I have been composing this piece about the seven women in the room, and the rain water falling into pots of different sizes from the leaks in the roof."

"Well, it is an incredible story," he conceded. "How could Los Angeles have two earthquakes in one day and no one in San Francisco felt the slightest thing? How is that possible? It's a whole different geology out there."

"I once thought of making a dance," she said, "and the only accompaniment would be the recording of a busy signal. You know, from a telephone? But then I realized what a truly irritating sound that is. So instead I had them wear paper sacks over their heads, with no eyeholes cut out."

"I just read a book," he offered, "about a man who killed an awful lot of people and cut their bodies up and put the parts into paper sacks."

She went on cheerfully. "There are just times when creativity cannot be suppressed."

He felt, perhaps, that things were better between them now. He thought she might like to hear something personal from him. "I remember once when I was in first grade," he began. "We were reciting a poem, all of us at once, the entire class: 'Oh how I love to go up in a swing, up in the sky so blue....' And we were acting out the motions—'Up in a swing,' we sang, pumping our arms forward and back with all our might. And that's when I hit my hand on the pencil sharpener that was screwed into the wall at the back of the room and broke my little finger. Of course, everyone had to stop singing. I suspect that was the beginning of my fear of heights."

She nodded. "Have you noticed that you can see through this window directly across the street into an apartment in the next building?" she asked. "There is a man in a green shirt who sits on a bed, and on the bed is some kind of multicolored blanket, it looks like a sarape, or, anyway, something too warm for this time of year, and the man sits, very carefully folding up red squares of tissue paper into small paper carnations and tying each one onto a wire stem and putting it into a box on the floor. Last time I saw him, I thought he was naked, but I think that was more a matter of sun-poisoning. It was dreadfully hot that day."

"Oh, well, *that*," the man said with a sigh. "Of course I have been wondering what it is they sit and talk about. They seem to find enough conversation for hours. You'd surely think they'd have had their fill, after all these years."

She shot him a look. "I am fully aware of who used to live here, you know," she said coldly. "Before us, I mean. I've figured the whole thing out. Her name was Merete. She was Jewish and she was a film student. I know because, after she moved out, there was nothing left in the apartment but a bad reproduction of a Renaissance watercolor of the Virgin Mary and a small, black spool of sixteen-millimeter film. At first I thought it was electrical tape, but it was a film of her and another student in a project from one of her classes. The same take, over and over, two people standing in front of a laboratory table, with one of those wide, glossy onyx tops, and the sink at one end and the metal coupling where you connect the hose for the gas. Did I mention she was Jewish? It took three months to get her name off the mailbox. We still get her mail, though I doubt you've ever noticed."

She was right about everything, of course, and denial was hopeless. "Sometimes I just don't get things done," the man mumbled. And then suddenly he felt angry. What right had she? What right, indeed? He felt his voice rising, strong and full of conviction. "One's teeth begin to fall out," he enunciated clearly. "Quite a number of them at once it seems, three of them from the top jaw alone, fused together like I don't know what, coming out all at once. And then there are the dreams. Dreams in which I open my mouth and spit out shards of teeth, everything broken and ruined and words impossible now, the tongue slashing itself to hamburger in every effort to speak. And is this all because we will not floss? No! I think it is something deeper than that."

"I. Am. Quite. Sure," she retorted, punctuating each word with sharp, angular gestures of her hands, "That. Time. Heals. All. Wounds. There, I've said it."

In the heat of the loft, an ominous trickle of sweat went down the man's back, making him shiver. It was a moment he'd longed for—after so many years he'd finally found the perfect expression of irony, and now she was there to spoil things. But there wasn't a thing for it; he had to forge ahead. "A few days ago I was walking near St. Mark's Place," he said, "and I decided to sit down at a sidewalk café to have a bite to eat. It was ghastly hot; I could scarcely see. I just wanted something cold to drink, I thought. But the array of choices on the menu was dizzying, and I couldn't make up my mind.

"I felt myself growing rather faint, the clouds seemed to be wheeling and circling over my head, when all of a sudden a man came down the street pushing a grocery cart in front of him and saying in the most ordinary kind of sidewalk-vendor sort of voice, 'Two dollars, two dollars,' as if he were selling umbrellas in the rain or something.

Well my dear, don't you see? There wasn't anything in the cart. And that is just how I felt!"

She stopped and stared out the window with a look of tangible contempt. "*He* will never get to Moscow!" she spat.

"There is something to be said for planning ahead," the man admitted, the wind completely out of his sails now. She was like a sponge. For a time, there seemed to be nothing more to say. She was riding out the silence between them like a dare. Yes, yes; it was personal. In his mind, the words went 'round and 'round like a carousel in a madhouse: "The Lord is *not* my shepherd. I *shall* want." She was testing him. And then, the woman faltered.

"I had always thought," she mused, "that I would go before my father. It's the oddest thing."

The man plunged into the breach. "I met them once, you know," he said, his voice a shade too loud at first. "It was quite late but they had phoned me up and asked if I would join them for dessert. They were entertaining someone, a famous journalist, on the spur of the moment. The great man and all. So I went along, expecting the worst, and sure enough, as soon as I got there, the first thing I saw was the reporter, eating a huge plate of pasta with clam sauce. 'Well, that doesn't look much like dessert!' I felt like saying, but I didn't want to spoil it for them. Still, I could already tell things had gotten off on a bad footing. Everyone was very patient, of course, but you just knew he was hoping to make us uncomfortable, the way he kept digging the clams out of their shells with that little fork, and eyeing each one suspiciously before he put it into his mouth. 'Looking for grit,' he said. Well, I was positively riveted by that little ritual, and I didn't hear another word until after the coffee came."

She was at the windows again. "I do believe I saw a flash of lightning," she said. "Though it's rather late for that. The moon set hours ago."

"That's a kind of a bird, isn't it," he asked, "a flicker?"

Blood Brothers

for Kenneth

Lucas and I were the only faggots at Erika's party. Or, at least, we were the only two men dancing together. The room that had been converted into a disco was noisy and hot; it was Erika's back room—the one farthest from the street, located in a cul-de-sac at the end of a long corridor irregularly punctuated by tall doors. The room had perhaps been the original parlor of the house, and the high ceiling still bore the art nouveau scar of some elaborate fixture, the *Acanthus*-leaf design now furry and indistinct beneath stratigraphies of paint.

The occasion was Erika's long-promised housewarming party, an event she had postponed so long that her lease was nearly up and she was thinking of moving again, the idea of a new apartment reminding her that she had never warmed the old one. When Lucas and I arrived, our arms full of refreshments, Erika pointed us to a buffet table at whose center we also found, inexplicably, the wide, flat wedge of a birthday cake. Untouched except for a rectangular gap where the name had been sliced away, the cake looked like a page from a redacted FOIA report.

Among other things, the housewarming was my first opportunity to lay eyes on Greg, Erika's latest conquest. At the moment Greg was kissing his actual girlfriend, whom Erika had christened "Joni

Mitchell," with a certain athletic determination. He was not, so far as I was able to observe, particularly good at it, but much is forgiven of men who look like Greg.

The girlfriend meanwhile, was as plain as Erika's nickname suggested. For the party, she had worn a pair of shapeless blue cotton pants, tied at the waist with a drawstring, like hospital scrubs, and a baggy, short-sleeved pullover blouse with no collar. The material looked homespun; no doubt it was hemp. On her head she had propped a floppy, tie-dyed beret, from under which her fine hair fell humidly, twirling around her face, when she danced, like the fringe of a lampshade.

"Berkeley Nostalgic," Lucas and I joked, but there was no disputing that whatever Joni had used to bind Greg to her was something greater than ordinary household magic. In fact, they were striking in their contrasts—Joni so clearly out of Greg's league—and yet, there she was on the dance floor, his mouth covering hers and the whole surface of her body trying to touch him at once.

As I danced with Lucas, Erika kept leaning over to whisper into my ear how much she wanted to get Greg off by himself, away from his girlfriend; maybe next time he went to the john she'd follow him in and push him up against the wall, maybe sneak up quietly behind him and wrap her hand around his cock, before he had a chance to put it away. Once I had told Erika that straight women should be ashamed of how they wasted men's bodies, and she was determined to convince me she was a connoisseur. It was our way of flirting.

By the night of the party, Erika had already slept with Greg more than once, although clearly not as many times as she would have liked. She said he was a "stud in bed," a phrase whose stilted, porn-movie quality would normally have made me wince, but which Erika managed to imbue with sincere eroticism. For weeks, in fact, Erika had been keeping me entertained at work with stories about Greg, relayed *sotto voce*, whenever we could find a reason to disappear together into the Xerox room.

Erika's sense of sexual adventure was what I admired about her most, or perhaps it was what I envied most, and what I admired, instead, was her ability to combine beauty with a sharp appreciation of irony. Because Erika was beautiful—and what was even more useful, she knew that men found her beautiful. She could, in fact, lay a spell on a room full of men—gay or straight—more efficiently than anyone I had ever known. She could be big sister, cruising buddy, temptress, matchmaker, little girl, or virago, and, if the situation warranted, she could become the most vacant of bimbos. That was perhaps her favorite role, because it was the one that allowed her to tell a man virtually anything without his ever suspecting that she might be making fun of him. Unlike most beautiful people, moreover—and unlike all beautiful men—she knew precisely what beauty was worth, and I had never once known her to miscalculate the rate of exchange.

"Isn't he fabulous?" she sighed as we danced, not taking her eyes off Greg.

"Uh-huh," I agreed. And then, knowing that Erika was expecting a more enthusiastic review, I drawled, "He looks like he has a whole lot going on in his pants."

Erika made her Mona Lisa smile. "Well," she said, "girth is always appreciated."

Greg was a private investigator—a "private dick," as Erika had phrased it, in her Barbara Stanwyck voice, when she had first described the new Adonis in her life. I confess that I suspected her of making it up, a soft-core embellishment, but with his crew cut and his agate eyes, I now saw, he certainly looked the part. Like most of Erika's discoveries, Greg was big and hard-edged, even dangerous, one in the series of soldiers and athletes and low-rent Brandos who were Erika's type, men with masculinity so plentiful it seemed to ooze out of them and gather on their skins like pine sap.

The morning after the first night they spent together, Erika told me, she snuck out of bed early to freshen up before Greg had a chance to see her "a little too *au naturel*." Tiptoeing back from the bathroom, Erika noticed a small pile of Polaroids, four or five in all, tossed casually onto the floor beside Greg's nightstand.

The body in the photos was bloated and bloody, the face pallid and slack. At first, one temple seemed to be crushed, but several of the snapshots showed the area in close-up, even the flat Polaroid colors vivid in the detail: a bullet had torn away most of the left side of the man's head.

"Put those down," Greg growled from the bed, and Erika jumped. "He's one of my cases. Suicide."

She didn't know how long he'd been watching her look at the photos—watching as she went through the stack again and again, returning always to focus on the ruined head—but Greg's cock was already hard when he pulled Erika roughly down onto the bed and told her to suck him, whispering threats and obscenities into her ears.

If Erika thought I was enjoying the details, she was right. "You were being punished for looking," I commented, when she had finished her story.

Erika cut her eyes at me. "Men always want to punish you before they give you what you want. I guess they think it's easier that way."

Barely a week before Erika's housewarming, she and I had lounged in Japanese comfort in her back room, wielding glasses of red wine and carving marbled crumbs from the fragrant, expensive cheese we had carried home from the shop near her house. "This is a goor-rrrgeous cheese," Erika pronounced, mimicking the exaggerated tones of the clerk who had sold it to us. "Absolutely goorrrrgeous!"

Erika and I assembled often in that room, exotic food or drink in hand and a Scrabble board positioned between us on a low table. We sprawled across lumpy harem pillows, imagining a time when we would lead lives of true sophistication and ease rather than simply acting them out in costume balls of the mind. The room where we sat—turret-shaped, with its long, curving wall of wide windows—seemed always on the verge of detaching itself from the house and shooting into space.

As Erika and I considered our racks of tiles, I leaned back to stare thoughtfully at the ceiling, brooding on the umbilical wound at the center of it, the chandelier scar, drifting until an unexpected word bobbed to the surface of my thoughts—"cicatrix." The word came to me like some fantastic ocean creature, floating upward from the depths the way the fortunes did in a "Lucky 8 Ball"—a hollow, black sphere painted to resemble an oversized billiard ball. Inside, a small octagon drifted in a murky, green-black sea, a different future printed on each of its surfaces. You shook the ball and asked a question, then turned it over and waited for the answer to rise into view through the porthole at the bottom. "All Signs Point to Success," you read, or, more often, "It Doesn't Look Promising."

I must have been musing on this memory more intently than I realized, because Erika could finally take it no longer. "And you wonder why people think this is a boring game," she snapped.

I smiled and began to lay out my tiles. I moved deliberately, pausing dramatically before revealing the final "x" and savoring the triumph of the word: *cicatrix*. That chandelier-scar, Lucky-8-Ball word gave me enough points to beat her that night, one of the few times I ever did.

~~~
~~~

But now, buoyed by waves of congenial noise and the thick, changed air, more and more guests were drawn toward the back room. Erika went around throwing open the windows, helping the heat of bodies to seep out into the night.

Someone kept switching the lights on, and someone else kept flicking them off. Finally, a girl in a hooded sweatshirt stood on a friend's shoulders and unscrewed the light bulb, pitching it out the open window. Except for the soft, radar-green glow that came from the front of the stereo then, and the brighter, yellow halo that fidgeted around the base of a single candle, the room was almost completely dark.

We had all had too much to drink—exactly the right amount too much, I would say. People who had recently met were touching each other for the first time on the dance floor. Some of the men took their shirts off; a few of the women did, too. The room was full of sweaty, swaying bodies, pressed together. Something prickled through the air, some electric, invisible sense more primitive than taste or smell, some flutter of the old brain that registered the purely animal significance of skin, sweat, and touch.

Whatever it was, Lucas and I were more than pliable to the influence. I put my hands on Lucas's ass, on his hips, and hauled his body against mine; I held his face in both hands and kissed him, sucking his tongue into my mouth, and we kept dancing. His shirt was wet; it was the blue silk one that he wore untucked, the one that made him look like a cocky college boy on Spring Break. I wanted to unbutton it slowly while I looked straight into his eyes, daring him to blink or turn away. I wanted to suck the sweat out of his armpit, tracing the rivulets across his skin with my tongue.

But that was too much, even for that party. So I pressed my cheek against his and told him what I was thinking about doing. At the same time I closed my hand around the warm bulge of his dick and squeezed it, hard, until I felt it jump against my fingers.

We were being obnoxious, but I didn't care. There was a lot of cock in that room that wanted sucking, including mine and Lucas's. They weren't all going to get what they wanted that night, but we were. So let them be jealous, or curious, or pissed off, I thought. It would only make us hornier.

"Maybe you'd like me to take you into the bedroom right now," I said to Lucas, my mouth on his ear so I didn't have to shout above the music. "Your cock feels like you can barely wait."

I felt him shudder. "I love you," he said.

By one a.m. the crowd at Erika's party had started to thin, and Erika was nowhere to be found. Lucas, too, had wandered off, and Greg and his girlfriend were slouched across the sofa in the living room, still kissing heroically. I watched for a while until I saw Erika appear out of her bedroom, trailed by a young man whose chest I had admired for most of the party. He wore a pair of baggy overalls with one strap undone and, so far as I could tell, nothing else.

"It's not nice for the hostess to walk off with the best party favor," I stage-whispered as they went by.

"Shut u-up!" Erika sang in falsetto, slapping me lightly on the cheek. The boy in overalls gave me a sweet, stoned smile, and I reached up and gently tugged on one exposed nipple. "I taught her everything she knows," I told him.

And then all I wanted was Lucas. When I found him, his face was flushed, and I could tell that he had only just extracted himself from one of those random circles that form at parties, inexplicable groupings in which people who don't know each other stand and pass a joint from hand to hand, smiling like wind-up monkeys, until the butt of the joint is the size of a match tip and is soggy with collective spit.

"You look to me," I said evenly to Lucas, "like a person who very much needs to get his butt fucked. Let's go home." He took my hand, but made no movement toward the front door. "Are you sure you wouldn't rather have him?" Lucas asked, jerking his chin toward the boy in overalls.

"Well," I teased, "I think Erika plans to spend the rest of the night parked on his face, and she'd only be in my way."

Lucas was giving me the look that stoned people get: tight around the mouth and eyelids, as if conscious effort were the only thing keeping the muscles from succumbing to gravity. "Ha," he said without humor. "Ha."

I put one hand up and cradled his face. He pushed back, giving me the weight of his head against my palm. "Come on," I said, leading him to the entryway, "You can wrestle me for the bottom of the bed."

∿
∿

*T*hree months after our first date, Lucas announced that we needed to talk, a phrase that means the same thing in every human language: trouble. He had insisted on driving all the way to the beach to tell me the particulars of his news, although I had already guessed the arc of the revelation—guessed he would say that he was leaving or, at least, that what seemed to be happening between us wasn't going to be possible after all, although I didn't yet know why.

I wasn't surprised. Love made sense to me mostly in metaphors—perhaps only as a metaphor: an exotic continent that one could visit, perhaps even for an extended time—like something out of a glossy travel folder, slick with promises not just of destinations but of states of mind. But then the rest of life called one back, implacable. Summer was over, vacation was done, the heady resins of tropical sweat and wind-borne sea spray were diluted in the drizzle and fog of one's indigenous skies.

In the car, we rose and dipped, rose and dipped along the road to the coast, silent all the way, Lucas's hand heavy on my thigh, my fingers tangling themselves in and out of the dark hair that fell, shining and fragrant, across his shoulders. As we drove, Lucas moved his arm to shift and then brought his hand back to the place above my knee, shocking me each time with its warmth.

When we stopped, we walked onto the sand near a group of teenagers in wetsuits who were plunging into the restless waves, their fiberglass surfboards decorated in shiny, neon colors: lightning bolts, checkerboards, and the rays of fantastic suns. They paddled doggedly against the wind into the deeper sea, past the forests of swirling kelp into the dark water beyond. One thought of the taste of salt on skin. One thought of sharks.

The long, narrow beach, stingy and windswept, was littered that day with the brittle corpses of By-The-Wind Sailors, a cousin of the Portuguese Man O'War. Like Men O'War, the Sailors had no natural means of locomotion and relied on the wind and currents to ferry them about, aimlessly, while they waited for tiny shrimp and minnows to blunder into their inescapable tangle of beautiful, paralyzing tentacles.

They were, for all that, helpless; and the wind pushed them relentlessly onto the shore and then to the desiccating sand beyond. Pale lavender when freshly dead, the Sailors bleached transparent and blew like autumn leaves into drifts that crackled when you walked on them. I told Lucas, who had by then taken off his shoes, to be careful where he stepped, since their tentacles were probably still capable of giving him a sting. They were never really alive, these colonies of adapted cells, and now they weren't entirely dead.

Lucas and I walked parallel to the gray line of the shore break, bent slightly against the wind, our bodies touching, randomly it seemed, as we lurched in the sand giving way beneath our feet. After a few moments, Lucas found a way to introduce his topic.

"You know I've been applying to graduate schools," he began.

"No," I said, "I didn't."

Lucas nodded. "I've been looking at music programs where I can get my master's. And a credential, so I can teach music. You know, in high school."

I stared at him owlishly. "You want to be a high-school teacher?" Lucas nodded again.

"This is definitely not what I expected," I said.

My own high-school music teacher, Mr. Jane, with his feminine surname and his prissy manners, had been the butt of all our cruelty. We took every chance to say that Mr. Jane had better never try to get one of us alone in his office on the pretense of a student conference, though such a meeting would probably have been Mr. Jane's idea of hell.

But Lucas would be no Mr. Jane. At his core, Lucas was still a tough boy from a small Ohio town whose main employer was a factory that made kitchen matches. He was a regular guy—aside from being queer, of course. That and his obsession with Ravel song cycles.

Lucas, too, would always have his disarming playfulness, that quality I craved when I needed delivery from myself and which I called "childishness" when he refused to be as serious as I wanted him to be. Lucas could always see the game in what he did, the foolishness behind it, the way nothing mattered much anyway. So he forgot to put gas in the car, or he gave his bosses fits because he never came back on time from lunch, or he rarely had money in his pocket to pay for his supper when we went out. "I'd be happy eating at McDonald's," he'd say. "You're the one who wants to go someplace more expensive." Or, "My god, we live in a city. How far do you think we'd have to walk even if we *did* run out of gas?"

He would always have his blue-collar pride. He'd escaped to the West from his incestuous hometown with whatever confidence came from a hundred bucks in his wallet and a sweet face. He'd slept on the floor of a friend's closet for six months until he could rent a studio of his own, barely larger. After that, the possibility of having nothing ceased to be frightening, and the prospect of having a little bit more seemed magical. And wasn't that just the kind of ambition it was to be a high-school teacher? A little one, a cozy one? I could have imagined life with a high-school teacher.

"You'd be great at it," I said. "Kids take to you right away. And you play the piano, and you have a beautiful singing voice...."

"I got accepted," Lucas interrupted. "At Humboldt."

"Humboldt," I said. "Humboldt is nearly three hundred miles away."

"I know that," he said. And then the words began to tumble out. "They'll give me a master's *and* the teaching degree," he said. "There aren't even that many programs in the whole country. This one is the closest. I tried to get in last year, too, but I didn't make it...."

Lucas went on, using words like "direction" and "purpose," unconsciously adding a tiny caesura before and after, like audible quotation marks. I thought of the maddening habit some people had of hooking their first and second fingers into the air, a pair on each hand, like cocktail shrimp suspended from the rim of a dish, to indicate that what they were about to utter should be taken with a grain of salt: sic, *soi-disant*, some say.

School wasn't really that far away, Lucas went on. He could take the bus and study on the way. He'd spend every weekend in the city. Unless you have to work, I thought, or log hours in the practice rooms, or finish a project in the library. But I waited while he laid it all out, realizing he had rehearsed these thoughts, but had never spoken them out loud; realizing, as I listened to his enthusiasm abandon him, that he was himself becoming aware, for the first time, how hopeless it really was.

"We can at least try," Lucas offered finally, after a silence. "We don't have to give up."

I looked down the beach. A small group of gulls fought over something lifeless in the low surf, ripples of gray froth dogging their feet. *This is big*, I thought. *This is a big tragedy.* The wind ebbed and came back strong, and I watched the gulls clambering soundlessly up and down its invisible steppes. We had until September.

"I'm getting cold," I said. "Let's go back."

For weeks we didn't speak of it, this form sleeping fitfully between us in the bed, this cadaver in the parlor, sidestepped and ignored, not a word about Lucas's leaving, although I knew he had driven north at least twice to look at rooms. Our careful strategy disintegrated the day we took what was meant to be a restorative drive in the country, quarreled bitterly, and rode the entire distance home in a hoarfrost of silence.

The moment we were through the door of my apartment, I dropped cross-legged on the floor and broke into tears, gasping out that the thought of Lucas's leaving was—what cliché did I use? Tearing me apart? Breaking my heart? The moment was right for fixed phrases. At times, what one needs is not to be unique in his story, but rather to fall back on every soap-opera fantasy and Hollywood romance, every Harlequin moment and Hallmark sentiment, every cultural commonplace of normal, ordinary, *sanctioned* love. One needs their weight and history. That was, in fact, the day when we first mentioned love, a heady and dangerous subsidence—dangerous because it skewed reality. Were we suddenly able to say we loved each other only because the time was artificially short? Or had the actual press of time given birth to an artificial need to make declarations?

So often it happens that life is constructed in this way, pieced together out of the meaning we try to make after some unexpected event has blown us off course. So fully do we trust these moments of epiphany, in fact, that it almost seems that this, *this* is our real life, not that other one at all, and we feel such relief at being able, at last, to distinguish our voyaging, careening, *living* selves from the selves otherwise so mired in everyday vagaries.

Lucas and I were not ready for any possibility to be foreclosed upon. Perhaps we hadn't known exactly what we felt or wanted, but now—when our future was suddenly condensed—no, now that Lucas was going away, everything *was* different.

And then Lucas didn't go away. Or, rather, he did, but within a week he was back. The house he had rented was un-rented; the boxes and furniture we'd loaded into the U-Haul came back in another U-Haul; he wrote a terse letter to the Chair of his department explaining that, for personal reasons, he couldn't stay in the program.

"When somebody pushes my 'on' and 'off' buttons several times in a row," I told Lucas the night he called to say he was coming home, "I get real cranky."

"No more 'off' buttons," Lucas said.

"And no more secret plans I should know about?"

"I promise."

"Is this all just because I told you I loved you?" I asked.

"Why? Do you want to take it back?"

"I don't want to take it back."

"Then that's it," Lucas had said. "I'll be done here in a couple of days."

∿∿
∿∿

*E*rika's party behind us, Lucas and I are barely in the door before I shove him down onto our futon and sprawl over him, rubbing my crotch in his face. The bedclothes are still in chaos from the morning, wadded on the floor like a collapsed parachute. When I let him come up for air, he says, "You don't have any idea how many times tonight you almost got raped."

"Yeah?" I say. "So how come you chickened out? Maybe all those straight boys would have gotten off on watching."

"Maybe," says Lucas, "I wanted you all to myself."

He's leaning over me now, our eyes locked on one another, his face so close I can feel his breath on my cheek, and he parts his lips slightly as if he's going to kiss me. But he doesn't. He hangs there, his mouth inches away, until a trickle of spit spills over his lips and begins to fall onto my lips, into my mouth. Then he does kiss me, and it feels like we're trying to crawl into one another's bodies. We pull our clothes off like shedding skins. We've made love like this before. I know how much need it takes to get there.

"You were flirting with that boy at the party tonight," Lucas says suddenly, his eyes gone flat in the light from the streetlamp outside. "I saw you."

He isn't kidding and, as always, his jealousy frightens me. I'm an idiot, I think to myself, realizing too late the significance of the tight look he'd worn as we left the party. When I don't say anything, Lucas rolls away and lies on his back, a meaningful distance between us.

"Lucas," I begin.

"It hurts my feelings. You know it does." The petulance in his voice is clear. He's spoiling for a fight.

I try again, rolling over to look into his face. "Lucas. You're the only man I want to be with. If you don't know that, you should. Yours is the only body I want to lie down with and wake up next to. You're the only man I want to make me come. I need you, Lucas. Only you. Please."

He's sulking, but I can feel him soften. Still, I know this is serious and I don't take it lightly. What Lucas wants is an exchange of vows. However ordinary the words may seem, it is important that I say them. It's as close to being married as Lucas and I are ever likely to get.

"Lucas. Are you listening to me?" I'm sitting on top of him now, pinning his shoulders down, shaking them.

"Open your eyes, you little fucker." When he does, I look into them to see how far gone we are, how much is play at this point and how much real.

"Lucas. Please. I'll do anything you want. I love you. I need you."

"Prove it," he says at last.

I hold his eyes a moment longer, making sure, and then I reach under the pillow and pull out the knife. We sit up naked, face to face, our legs entwined, our cocks touching, and I silently unsheathe the blade and put the knife into Lucas's hand. Now that my eyes have adjusted, I can see his face clearly, those eyes I never tire of staring into; his long, black lashes; the soft, nearly transparent fuzz around the edges of his ears and across the bridge of his cheekbones, where his razor never reaches. I open my palm to him (give me your hand on this), and turn my head away, leaning into the angle of his shoulder.

"Ready?" he whispers, and I nod. "I love you, too," he says, and then I feel the sharp, shocking pain at the end of my thumb. Even though I've been expecting it, a spasm goes through my body like electricity. My thumb begins to throb.

In the half-light the blood oozing from the wound is nearly black. Lucas gives me the knife and I have difficulty holding it because my hand is trembling from the adrenaline rush. My fingers are sticky with blood. "Does it hurt?" Lucas wants to know.

"Yes, baby, it hurts," I say, and he gives me his hand. "Okay?" I ask. He nods, eyes shut. As I circle his thumb with my free hand, I can feel his pulse, rapid on the inside of his wrist. "It's all right now,"

I say, and then I cut him. The only sound is a long sigh as Lucas lets out the breath he has been holding.

That's the worst of it. We hold our fists out, thumbs up, bloody and wet, and press the wounds together like slender mouths. Our blood mingles, his and mine. Blood brothers. I take Lucas's face with my other hand, palm against the soft-rough plane of his cheek, and pull his lips against mine. Our tongues meet, swimming in one another's saliva; our blood meets, and I imagine that Lucas is already entering my heart.

$$\approx$$

In the morning the sun shines through the window and falls hot across the bed. Lucas begins to sweat, and the heat tugs him out of sleep, like surfacing. This is one of the times when I like Lucas best, in the morning, when we have slept all night together after making love. The sweat leaves him sticky, and he throws his arms wide, unselfconsciously opening his body. His smell is sharp and strong. He smells like the ocean. I can smell sex on him, too, and his cock is almost always hard. If I move gently, I can have it in my mouth before Lucas is completely awake.

This morning my thumb hurts, and I stare into the wound. The skin around the edges has dried out and drawn back slightly, transparent and cornified. The valley of the cut is dark purple. Down there, running deep at the bottom of the gorge, is my blood, our blood. Lucas is in my body.

I watch him sleep and I think: I could kill him. The knife is still there. I could throw his body against the wall. I can deliberately fuck him too hard or when he doesn't want to. I could lie to him or cheat on him; I can betray him by telling other men that he doesn't mean that much to me. Once Lucas was a stranger, and now I have such awesome powers.

The cuts in our thumbs will heal; we are always surprised by how quickly. I doubt there will even be a scar. But we each have untouched fingers left, and there are other places on Lucas's body, on mine, that can still withstand the knife: the moment of agony as the blade parts flesh; the throb then (my heartbeat in a fingertip); the days of soreness afterwards (whatever I hold in my hand a reminder); the itch and pull of healing.

Yes, baby, it hurts. Lucas always asks. But he and I are familiar with this magic. There is pain before we give each other what we truly want, before we take what we long to be given. And so the knife waits under the pillow, where either of us can reach it. After years of discovering what lies deep and secret in each other's hearts, I know that it is easier this way.

That Old Dog That Maysie Had

L ong about a year ago, I shot Maysie's dog one day when I went up on her front porch and it humped my leg. I'd already told her if the damn thing did that again I'd put a bullet between its weepy little eyes and so, when it started in before I'd even got to knock, I fetched the pistol out from under the seat of my truck, went back up the stairs, and fired point blank. Maysie's brother, Raymond, came busting out the front door then, took a look around, and asked me was I the one who'd shot the dog. Not too bright, Raymond isn't, because, except for the gun and the dog, still twitching but well on its way to dead, I was the only thing on the entire falling-down porch. Since their daddy died, ain't neither one of 'em lifted a finger to work on the house. "Sure am," I said.

"Well," Raymond said, "I never much cared for the animal myself, but Maysie was attached. I expect you ain't heard the last of this."

"Maybe not," I said, "but just in case Maysie takes a mind to go out and get her another one, you can tell her that I'll shoot that one, too, if she doesn't show it how to behave right." Raymond just raised his eyebrows up like they was trying to run for it and went back into the house. But I noticed he closed both the screen door and the inside door, and I heard him click the bolt shut before I walked on back down to my truck.

The next day, I was working at my Uncle Jake's shop, winching the engine up outta some rusted-out ole pickup, when this fancy-looking man come in and asked me was I the one had a reputation for shooting people's dogs on their front porch without so much as a "Don't mind if I do." I gave him a look and didn't say nothing.

"I'll take that as a 'yes,'" he said. "Reason I ask is I'm wondering how much it would cost me to get you come out and put down my sad ole pig."

Now I'm not saying that this town's so small anymore that you know every single body on sight, but the rich folks who live in the new developments out on the west edge don't come around here much. And don't nobody come to Jake's shop wearing a tie, not in recent memory, and anyone that does is probly a bill collector or some kind of police. Anyway, that's how I figured it, and I wasn't trying to be friendly before I knew what he wanted.

"I don't shoot pigs," I said. "Besides, I didn't do Maysie's dog for fun nor money. I did it because Maysie's dog was having an unnatural relationship with my shin bone."

"But speaking hypothetically," the man went on, "if I could come up with a figure you found attractive, would you shoot my pig?"

"Why don't you shoot it yourself," I asked. "Or slit its throat?"

The man got a tight look on his face like he was trying hard to swallow down a dry biscuit. "Pearl's been our pet for years," he said finally. "I couldn't bear it."

"You got a pig for a pet?" I said. That wasn't the strangest thing I ever heard, but it was damn close. The man just nodded and looked sad.

"Well," I said. "Well." I couldn't think of anything else I wanted to know, so I went to finish cranking up the motor, still dangling the way it was up in the air like a side of beef on a meat hook. Ain't hardly anything sadder-looking than a vehicle when you got the hood off and the engine mounts, and you've pulled out the motor and everything so there's nothing left but the empty carcass and a hole up front to where you can look straight down and see dirt.

The man started twisting the toe of his shoe around and around in a little hill of sawdust that was left over from the last time we tried to get the oil stains up off the garage floor. "So will you do it?" he asked after a while.

"She sick?" I said, wiping my hands on my coveralls.

"I think she's got cancer," the man said.

A pig with cancer. Now that's an unusual fact. "Whyn't you take her to the vet and have him do away with her?" I said.

"She's too big to fit in the car and, besides, they want a hundred and eighty-two dollars to put a pig down."

I took a glance at his shiny tie and his sport coat that had some kind of design sewed in above the pocket looked like a coat of arms. "Seem like you might could afford that," I snorted.

"I'll pay you seventy-five," he said, "plus gas out to my place and back."

I didn't like to show it, but I had started in to be pretty curious to see this pet pig with cancer that was too big to fit inside the car, never mind what kind of a house the man that owned it might live in. And seventy-five dollars was about as much as I made in a whole day at the shop. "All right," I said.

"You have to come over during the day while the kids are at school," the man said. "I don't want them to be there when you do it."

"How's tomorrow lunchtime?" I asked. Next day was a Wednesday and I figured that ought to of been all right.

The man took a skinny spiral book outta his coat pocket and turned the pages. "Make it Friday?" he asked. "We need some time to say good-bye."

"Friday, then."

He scribbled on the back of a small white card and held it out to me. "My home address and phone number," he said, "in case you have to reschedule or anything." I flipped the card over, leaving a black thumbprint right where he'd wrote his address. Hailey Monroe, it said in fancy script on the printed side, Counselor at Law. Well, that figured.

"Laird Sutton," I said, and stuck out my hand. I hoped he got grease on him.

When Friday morning rolled around, I woke up early to clean my gun. I went into the chest at the foot of my bed, where I keep the guns, and the cleaning oil, and a real World War II Jap bayonet that my Uncle Jake gave me, and pulled out a new box of shells so as to have plenty of extra rounds to carry along. If the pig was as big as the man said, one shot might not be enough. At about a quarter to noon I hollered to the guys in the back that I was taking lunch away from the shop, and I drove out to the address on the card.

"Mr. Monroe," I said when he came to the door.

"Oh, you're right on time," he said. We stood there for a while, him not asking me in, and me trying to look pleasant but not like my spirits was too high, on account of I knew the man thought of this as a solemn occasion.

"Pearl's out back," he said finally, smiling at me kind of nervous and showing a lot of big, square teeth like two rows of hominy. He stepped back from the door and held his arm out, the way the junior crossing guards do when they direct traffic down at the public school, and I took that to mean I was supposed to go ahead on in the house. He walked about eight steps and just stood there, so I came up behind him and waited for him to show me the pig. I figured this was more emotional for him than it was for me.

"Nice place you've got," I said, but really it wasn't as fancy as I thought a lawyer's place would be. They had a lot of space though, or anyway just the living room by itself seemed half as big as the whole trailer where I lived with Alice, or did until she left out of there for a place in the city. That was a while ago now, some time even before I met Maysie.

He had one of those TV sets with a screen the size of a front window and a lounge chair across from that with the plastic wrap still on the footrest. There was a fireplace, of course, and pictures all stood up across the mantle like soldiers. I didn't want to pry by actually walking over to stare at them, but I could see well enough from where I was that there was the same woman in a lot of the pictures, sort of pale and neat-looking, like a librarian or maybe a dental hygienist. I guessed that was the wife because she and him appeared to be in most of the pictures together. Them and a couple of regular old kids, the kind you see anywhere, a boy and a girl, I guess, but really I just made that up on account of it wasn't that easy to tell. Coulda been two girls or a couple of long-haired boys, the way rich folks leave their children because don't lice ever break out in their schools.

"Nice family," I said. "What're your kids' names?"

"Uh ... Jaren and Chris," he said. "They're twins." Which that didn't help me any figuring out who was what, so I just gave up.

"Well, come on outside," the man said, and we walked through the rest of the living room and down a little hall to some glass doors off the kitchen. He slid the doors open and made that "after you" signal with his arm again, so I went out first. He had a cement slab out there, just off the house, about eight by ten with one of those barbecue grills on it that don't take charcoal, and the rest of the yard was grass. Nice regular grass, too; not a yellow patch or a dandelion in sight. He'd fenced off the yard pretty solid with about three rows of bricks for a foundation and then wood planks looked like redwood set into that so the whole thing was about almost ten feet tall. Good and private.

Only thing was, I didn't see no pig.

"Mr. Monroe," I started to say, "where is it you keep...," when out from the side yard came this big, ugly woman the size of a linebacker. She just ambled on out in no particular hurry, all the time fixing me in the eye with a look that was damn unfriendly. She had a man with her wasn't no prettier nor no smaller, and behind the two of them, looking a little grim about the face, came Maysie.

"Hi, Maysie," I said.

"Don't you 'Hi, Maysie' me," she said, "not after you just walked up on my porch and killed my dog."

Now, I was still trying to get the lay of the land and see what this was all going to come to. I had about figured out there wasn't no pig, of course, but I was getting my first good look at that woman Maysie had with her, and frankly, she was more worrisome to me than the fella. She had on a man's shirt with the sleeves torn off up high on the shoulders, and from the ragged edge of the seam all the way down to her wrists wadn't hardly a space didn't have some kind of tattoo on it. In another situation, I might have wanted to look more closely at her designs or ask who worked on her, but I was surely not going to try any of that now. Anyway, she must of outsized me by a good eighty pounds and more'n a few inches. She had biceps on her, too, the woman did. On her bottom half she was wearing some tight, raggedy old pair of greasy blue jeans with her ass hanging off the back like an air conditioner, and black stompin' boots on her feet must have been as big as mine. I ain't never been in the service, but I thought if I did go, she'da probly been who I got for a drill sergeant.

I was still feeling a little bit of indignant because I didn't like being tricked that way, and I was gonna say to Maysie that I'd done told her what I'd do if she didn't fix that dog, and that I was within my rights to keep my word after she'd had fair warning, but right at that time, I didn't exactly see the advantage to bringing all that up. So I just said, "I guess Raymond told you, then."

Maysie made a noise that sounded like "Schaaw!" and stood there with her hands on her hips and her breasts all kinda mashed down inside her overalls. I always thought Maysie woulda done better for herself if she didn't dress like a man half the time.

"This is Earl," Maysie said finally, pointing to the man standing next to her that looked like Paul Bunyan. "And this here's Skee. And you already know Hailey." I just stared around at everybody—didn't seem quite the right time to be shaking folks' hands. Besides, I was busy having a revelation. I knew Maysie had taken up after me with some fella named Skee who I'd never laid eyes on, but now it turned out Skee wadn't no kind of fella.

"Did you bring your gun," Hailey said.

"Yeah," I said, though the way he asked didn't make me feel none too good to be telling them about it.

"Then give it here," he said.

"I won't, neither," I said.

Maysie threw me a look of pure disgust and said, "Skee," and Skee reached around into her back pocket and drew out a switchblade. She flipped it open and started for me.

"Now just hold on here a minute," I said, backing up until I was pressed against the glass doors to the kitchen. "If ya'll got some kind of sick John Wayne Bobbitt shit in mind, you just remember that this is all over a damn dog. And you don't want to be putting a dog's life over a human's. Anyway, Maysie, you always got some old mangy, broke-down, worthless animal or other around your place, usually more than one, so I don't know why you've taken on so about this one. But it don't matter. If you want another dog, I'll get you one. And I'll even buy you the feed for the next six months," I added, on account of Maysie didn't give me the impression she was finding my offer all that sweet. In fact, she was shaking her head at me like I was pitiful. But the good thing was, Skee wasn't coming any closer.

"First off," she said, "he wadn't technically my dog, he was Skee's. Well, Skee give 'em to me, but he was hers first. Skee's been staying over to my place quite a little bit during the last few months, which you'd know if you ever bothered to come around 'cept when you want something."

Now, I knew what she was talking about, even if maybe everybody else didn't. Maysie and I used to go out together for about a minute, but we broke up on accounta she said she got fed up with me showing up past dark, after I'd already been out drinking, and wanting to crawl right into bed with her. Far as I could tell, it didn't matter much to Maysie how or when I crawled into bed with her, she just didn't like it. So I didn't figure what difference it made if she got her a movie and a Dr. Pepper beforehand or if she didn't. My way, the whole thing was over quicker anyhow. But Maysie wouldn't hear nothin' but that we had to break up, and so that's what we did. Things didn't change much between us after that, to tell the truth. I'd still stop over when I was out of beer money or dope, but to be fair, you'd have to say that I also did sometimes ride her up into the next town when she wanted to go to the CostCo and buy a bunch of stuff, 'cuz I had a pickup and could hold more than a sack of groceries like that piss-ant MG ragtop she decided to start tooling around in like she was a damn movie star.

"Second," Maysie was saying, "you want to watch whose animals you're insulting, because I am the only reason you're here instead of saying howdy to Skee and Earl when they showed up at your door all unexpected with a baseball bat. When Skee found out what you done, I had the devil's time convincing her to do this my way. So you'd better thank me for making things a whole lot easier on your sorry ass than you even deserve."

"Uh, thanks, Maysie," I said. "But what're you gonna...."

"And then you can apologize to Skee for shooting hers and my dog in the first place," Maysie interrupted, "'cuz you still got that to account for."

"I know it," I said, "and Skee, truly I am sorry for what I did. I surely didn't ever want to bring a third person into this."

Skee glared at me and spat, hard and loud. The place where the gob landed left a wet crater in the dust the size of a half-dollar. But she put the switchblade back in her pocket.

"Well, that'll do for now," Maysie said. "All right, let's get this done. Laird, give Hailey your gun. And don't make me ask again."

Whatever they had in mind, I didn't much like my chances of gettin' out of it. I thought about running, but I knew I'd never make it over the wall in the yard before they caught me. And wadn't any way to get back out through the house without going through the sliding-glass doors Hailey had closed behind him. I hardly had a minute to think about all that, though, before Hailey come up beside me and held out his hand. I put my gun into it.

"Now," he said, "you take this." He hitched up his pants leg to where he had an ankle holster and he pulled out this little ole Nancy Reagan-sized pistol with mother-of-pearl grips.

"Meet Pearl," he said. "Now you take it."

I took it, but then I just stood there, holding onto the gun by the barrel and goggling down at it in my hand like he'da just passed me a cold, dead chicken neck. When I raised my head again, Maysie, Skee, Earl, and Hailey were staring straight at me, the four of them looking about as warm and helpful as those faces on Mount Rushmore.

"What am I supposed to do with this?" I asked.

Well, that was the first time Skee stopped frowning and started in to look almost a little bit cheerful. "Shoot yourself in the foot," she said.

I paused a minute to let that sink in, then I said, "I don't think so." I tried to hand the gun back to Hailey, but he wouldn't take it.

"Laird, don't be a stone fool," Maysie sighed. "This is fair and you know it. Besides, if you won't, I can't be responsible for keeping Skee and Earl from coming for you. And you know that's gonna be worse. You wanna be foot shot or beat to hell with a bat? You know I ain't trying to shit you, neither. Skee never liked you from the get-go and she's mad enough now to put a hurt on you you'll not soon forget. Do you believe me?"

"Maysie, I surely do believe you," I said, "but this is some crazy shit. You can't just tell a man to shoot himself in the foot and expect him to go ahead and do it."

Maysie ignored that. "Here's how it's gonna go," she said. "After you shoot yourself, I'ma drive you to the emergency room in your truck 'cuz you sure ain't gonna feel much like doin' it yourself. That way, you'll be able to go along home when you want after they look at you. You might as well give me your car keys now, too. Meanwhile, Skee'll come behind in her truck and pick me up. Now you tell 'em whatever you want at the ER, but I advise you to say you shot yourself by accident. You'll sound like a damn fool, but you'll get over it. If you ever try to say anything different, I'm gonna tell 'em you stalked me here to Hailey's house and picked a fight when I wouldn't leave with you. You pulled your gun and Hailey wound up having to shoot you in the foot with his own gun to keep you from hurtin' anybody. It's gonna be four people's word against yours—and one of 'em a lawyer. Don't forget, neither, that you're the guy just blew a pet dog's brains out when it was tied up on the porch, which ain't exactly the actions of a sane and healthy man.

"Holy Mary in a Cadillac, Maysie Diane," I said, "who'd ever a thought you had such a devious mind."

"Well," she said, "one of these days I aim to get the hell out of this town and become a writer, and it's good to have an active imagination."

"Maysie," I said, "you keep on doing shit like this, ain't gonna be a man in this town'll go with you."

When I said that, I saw Skee start to come forward again, but Maysie put her hand out and giggled. "Oh, Laird," she said, "you 'bout as bright as an old penny in a mud puddle. Now get on with it. Skee and I both got jobs we got to get back to some time this afternoon."

"Right or left," I asked.

"Both!" Skee snarled, opening up her big ole mouth and making a nasty, snaggly smirk. I swear to God, seemed like that woman had more tattoos than she had teeth.

"Left," Maysie said, smiling a little herself. "You ain't gonna like it when you have to clutch, but at least you'll be able to step on the gas without breaking down and crying like a girl."

I bent down and put the muzzle of the pistol against the top surface of my left work boot. I had the barrel angled over toward the edge, thinking I might get away with just blowing the tip off one toe, but Hailey brought his face down right next to mine and said, "Tsk, tsk, tsk." Then he covered my gun hand with his and slid the barrel back up toward my ankle until the muzzle was nestled right in there where the bottom of the laces starts. "Better," he said.

Now, I ain't one to say I never did a crazy thing on a dare, but in all my time one thing I never once had the urge to do was to jump off one of those cherry-picker-type things like they have at the county fair with a rope tied to my leg. Still, if ever I did get drunk enough to want to do such a foolish thing, I guess the moment right before I pulled the trigger must have been just like how it is when you step off the edge. You know it's probly not going to kill you, but you ain't too sure how much it's going to hurt before you're through. All I knew was, Skee wasn't never gonna know me to scream in pain, I didn't care how bad it got.

So I fired, and I screamed, and the last thing I heard before I passed out was Skee making a sound like a dull saw blade going through wet wood. I guessed that musta been what she called laughing.

I woke up later at the hospital, with my foot propped up in some kind of a clamp, and a hole in the middle of it like Jesus H. Christ, and I was sure I could spot a little bit of daylight coming through on the other side if I held my head just so to look. They give me something for the pain, but my foot was still throbbing, and each toe felt like it had its own little separate heart inside, and all five of them pounding as if I'd run all the way to the hospital from Hailey Monroe's house. Not that I'd of been able to do such a thing in my condition.

Some doctor came by in one of those baggy suits look like wrinkly green pajamas and said, "Lucky for you it was just a .25 caliber. Your basic Saturday Night Special. Could have been a lot worse. We'll have you out of here in a bit. You had a tetanus shot lately, by the way?"

Well, so that's how it happened. I wasn't sure how I was gonna get home that day on account of I was feeling pretty woozy by the time they wheeled me into the lobby, but damn if Raymond wasn't there waiting for me with the keys to my truck. I was suspicious at first, him being Maysie's brother and all, but he took me home and got me into bed, and that night he slept on the couch, saying he felt responsible and did I mind if he stuck around to make sure I didn't want for anything.

Turns out he was a lot of fun to talk to and not nearly so slow as I took him for at the start, and he started sleeping over even after I was well on account of he said things got awful noisy at his place whenever Skee stayed the night. The way he rolled his eyes when he said "noisy," I knew just what he meant.

Since then, me and Raymond have gotten to be real good friends, and a couple of months ago we just went ahead and moved him in here to my trailer. Skee had quit her place and was living up with Maysie anyway, and I had plenty of room for the two of us. Ever once in a blue moon we go out drinking with Skee and Maysie, but not all that often 'cuz Skee still makes me some nervous. Still, when I decided to get rid of all my guns, Skee bought 'em for a fair price and didn't hand me no attitude about it either. She and Maysie got themselves a new dog not long after that afternoon at Hailey's—some evil-looking mutt with Rottweiler and German Shepherd mixed in it, I think—and that's the main thing keeps me from going over to their house. I'm happy to wait in the truck while Raymond goes inside, but I won't walk up on the porch. Skee went and called that new dog Butcher, and I can't help but think she named it with me in mind.

Raspberry Pie

for D.H.G.

Over lattes at Café Flore, I told Ehan I'd just been to my first whipping. He was eating a piece of raspberry pie, the filling splooging out the sides and onto the plate. I pointed to the loose, crushed berries, oozing syrup. "The guy's ass looked about like that when they got done," I said. Ehan made a face like he'd tasted something foul, which was just the reaction I was hoping for.

It isn't that I like shocking people; I just like shocking Ehan. For the entire four years we were lovers, the thing I hated most about him was what a white-bread prince he was.

Not long after we moved in together, Ehan came home with a bright red Macy's shopping bag. Inside was an omelet pan that hinged in the middle. "Look," he said. "Now we can make omelets without breaking them in half when you flip them over." He was referring to the fact that my omelets usually ended up looking more-or-less like scrambled eggs.

"Oh, that'll be good," I said.

A few weeks later I needed to take something bulky to work and Ehan got out the Macy's bag, which he had carefully folded and put into the cupboard with the broom and the lemon-scented bleach. "I'm not carrying that thing around," I said.

"Why not?" he wanted to know. "It's a great bag and it's got handles." He held it up by the thick strings that grew out of the stiff, red paper at the top, overlapping into an "M" like the golden arches.

"Because I don't want to look like someone who shops at Macy's," I said. "I don't want to look like some fag who just popped over on his lunch hour to try on sweaters."

Offended, he put the bag back into the cupboard. "It's just a bag," he said. "Sometimes I don't understand where you're coming from."

The way Ehan is, if he came to your house, you'd hardly be able to suppress the urge to offer him tea. In a cup, with a saucer. I once heard someone describe Ehan as "patrician" and I couldn't get the word out of my mind. It bobbed around in there like an apple in some great galvanized washtub of language, bumping up against all the other words just like it: patriarchy, patrimony, patriotism. All the words that start out sounding like "father" and end up somewhere else entirely.

"Charming," my mother said, the first time she met him. Ehan complained later that she'd never asked him any questions about himself: But that's the kind of guy he is. The kind that prefers to be interviewed. Hardly polite to volunteer the Oberlin education, the Junior year aboard, the Fulbright. You have to be asked, so the information can leak out modestly.

But my mom's no fool: She doesn't "ooh" and "aah" any more sincerely than I do. I'm sure she took one look at that blood-in-the-face complexion and the parochial chin that won't hold up past forty, and she decided she didn't want to play. Though it isn't like she missed anything essential. Forced to improvise, Ehan found plenty of ways to work in all the important information he liked people to know about himself. Later, when we got back home, I said to Ehan: "Did I tell you that my mother dropped out of school when she was in eighth grade?"

Ehan blinked at me. "Oh," he said. "Oh."

Ehan knows people who own lofts, which they call "spaces"; he goes to parties thrown by Herb Ritts. I go to garages painted black where people piss on each other and when someone screams it is because he is in actual pain. Stirring a third sugar into my coffee, I tell Ehan that the whipping was like theater.

"Why is this turning my stomach?" he said, pushing the pie aside.

Because you're a fucking coward. Because you can't stand the sight of blood. Because your castration fear is so immense that all I used to have to do to make you beg me to stop was to read you a squib out of the paper about some logger who chopped his foot off with an axe and later got it reattached. You would never have been able to discuss poor old John Wayne Bobbitt.

Because I loved you for years during which all you wanted was for me to throw you across the bed and fuck you until it hurt, and all I wanted was to do it; and rather than get what we wanted, we tortured each other, day after day, for years. If you do it the way we did, it's a relationship; if you get someone's consent first, you're a freak.

You'd lie beside me, jerking off, and talk about how you wanted me to fuck you in the shower, forcing you up against the wall and banging your head on the white tile with each thrust. You'd say you wanted me to gag you when I screwed you in our big, wide bed so the neighbors couldn't hear you screaming.

But fantasy isn't reality, is it? You liked to be screwed all right, but gently, sweetly, so it felt like love. You always had to be on your back, where you could see me. You didn't want to be treated like a dog, you said. And you never screamed, not once; instead, you'd groan politely when I finished you off with a greasy hand. After you left me, it took months until I could stop feeling embarrassed about the noise I made in bed.

I remember a day when we fought—one of the hundreds of extravagant, passionate, Talmudic arguments we had instead of good sex. All my words seemed to be tumbling off a cliff and into some deep, cold sea, as suicidal as lemmings. In my frustration, I punched you so hard that a cut opened up in the center of your chest, above your heart. I wasn't proud that I had hit you, but the blood thrilled the shit out of me. It was just your body, bleeding in silence—a reaction that even you couldn't filter through your bullshit and your reasons and your rational explanations.

I was transfixed, watching that dusky red stain spread out across the white field of your thin T-shirt. Here is my guilty secret: I loved you so much I would have licked the blood up and wrapped myself around you later in gratitude.

This is what I wanted to say in answer to Ehan's question. What I said instead was nothing. Ehan was looking at me as though I were an object he couldn't quite identify. I had entered a room he couldn't get into, a place where the atoms of sex and love were so profoundly fissioned that the danger of contamination must have seemed infinite. But it's in the Vedas, baby. Agni may have seven tongues and hair like flames, but he's also the guardian of humanity. If you want the healing, you've got to take the fire.

We stared at each other until I realized that, during all the years I had known Ehan, I had wanted him to understand only one thing: *I am not like you.*

∧∧
∧∧

O n my way to meet Ehan at the Café that day, I had been angry. This is something else I realize: I am angry all the time. Even when I'm happy, I'm angry. I walked down the street hitting parking meters and pounding on the lids of trash cans, all puffed up with anger, swaggering with it, feeling invincible and doomed. My face falls easily into a frown, with no conscious effort on my part, and I was frowning. My shoulders felt huge and able to carry anything; my chest felt thick and strong enough to endure anything. I wanted to pick a fight.

When I am horny and want someone to want me, I am small and furtive, and I look at people out of the corner of my eye, and I am full of envy. When I am horny and angry, I don't want anyone, and I don't care if they want me. I stare people in the eye, and they always look away first. In fact, I glare at them, especially straight boys, and one day I know I'm going to find myself in a world of hurt. I take up space.

In this mood, the men I'm attracted to are bad-asses and punks; they look like Axl Rose or else like lads from the NLF. They're often skinny and have jail tats or a drug habit. But they strut. They are also angry and full of hate, mostly directed at themselves, and when we fuck those are the only things I want from them. I suck anger out of their armpits. I honor their suffering by rationing my tenderness with military discipline.

> *"I been tryin' to get my life together,"* one man says to another on the bus, *"but it's a struggle out there."*
> *"Yeah,"* says the second man, *"it's a hellified struggle."*

I'd like to write about love. Believe me, I would. But rage is all I have to go on.

~~~
~~~

O ne of the few things Ehan and I did well together was go to movies. We always had a lot to say to each other afterwards. I think we used movies as a way to show off for one another—how smart we were, how much notice we could take of subtleties. Having such a convenient excuse to talk—without the fear of saying anything that might come close to the bone—what a relief! Most of the time, I liked the movies he liked. He rarely liked the movies I liked.

Once, and only once, I convinced Ehan to go with me to the kind of movie I usually had to see alone, one with gruesome murders and lots of blood: blood seeping from the trunk of a car where a headless corpse has been stashed; blood welling out of the disemboweled body in the upper bedroom, spreading like a tidal bore across the floorboards and pooling on the stairs.

I don't know what made Ehan agree to go, but he did. It was early enough in our relationship that he was still in his anthropological mood: still visiting me to catalog the manifestation of all the things he feared and wanted. Later, he'd turn missionary on me and make a project of rooting out my primitivisms, one by one.

In that respect, Ehan was playing out an age-old routine—what I sometimes teased him by calling the racial memory of his people. At first, the naked breasts of native women fascinated the missionaries and turned them on, but their desire quickly became disgusting. In the end, they covered up their shame by covering up the breasts: Mother Hubbards as a symbol of the inability to tell the difference between what is out there and what is in here. The whole history of nineteenth-century Western civilization can be described as the refusal to look inward.

By the time we got to the movie, I felt like some sadistic teenage boy who had finally succeeded in dragging his girlfriend to *The Texas Chainsaw Massacre*—partly because he hoped she would bury her face in his chest whenever the movie got gory, and partly because he wanted to scare the shit out of her. They would leave the theater having had completely different experiences, the boy and his girlfriend—and she would say what Ehan always said to me when I suggested that we go to a film with rabid dogs or psychopathic killers or satanic ritual murders: "How can you stand to watch stuff like that?"

What Ehan didn't know—or perhaps what he did know but couldn't acknowledge about the person he loved—was that mayhem turned me on. It didn't necessarily make my dick hard; it wasn't *Schadenfreude*—joy in the suffering of others, which is the kind of thing Germans ought to know about. This sensation was entirely different. A kind of connection, a vibration full of savage intuition.

It was more like: I want to see these things because they look like how I feel inside. Cut up, howling, disintegrated, chaos, pain, raw flesh, pierced by knives. Eaten up. In that famous scene from *Aliens*, when that creature—the one that looks like a turkey neck with teeth—chews its way out of John Hurt's chest, didn't everyone shiver with the same sense of recognition I did? At last, proof of what I had always suspected, that something else besides me was *in there*.

In the movie I convince Ehan to see, a psycho killer kidnaps this guy and chains him between the bumpers of two semis, arms manacled to the front bumper of the truck parked behind, his legs fixed to the back bumper of the truck in front. The psycho has kidnapped the guy's girlfriend as well, and he has her handcuffed in the cab of the first truck. He gets in, starts the engine, and unlocks her handcuffs. He puts his foot on the clutch and then he hands her a gun.

"I'm going to count to ten," he says, "and then I'm going to take my foot off the clutch. Or you can shoot me before I get to ten. It's your choice."

Of course she doesn't shoot him, and of course he lets the truck roll forward, and of course the boyfriend gets ripped in half. I was disgusted with her: she couldn't save her boyfriend, but she could at least have had the satisfaction of shooting the asshole's balls off, or at least his kneecaps, before she blew his brains out. But she took no action at all.

I don't know how the movie ended because that's when Ehan got up and walked out, and I had to go after him. On the sidewalk, with the green and red neon of the marquee lights playing on our faces, Ehan screamed at me. People stared. I tried to calm Ehan down, but he was on a tear like I'd never seen before. When he walked away, I tried to follow, but he told me to get the fuck away from him. Later, when I got home, Ehan was already there, and we picked up where we had left off. That was the fight when I hit Ehan on the chest and made him bleed.

Let's face it: in the movies, blood is Karo syrup and food coloring. It's always too thick and too red. But the attempt to represent a kind of impossible reality is mesmerizing. There's a scene in *Cat People*—the Nastassja Kinski version—where a leopard pulls some guy's arm through the bars of its cage and chews it off. Completely gratuitous violence. I rented the movie and watched that scene again and again, a frame at a time in slow motion, trying to figure out just when they had substituted the fake arm.

But the cut on Ehan's chest wasn't fake, and I've played that scene over and over in my head as well. And now I'm watching Ehan toy with the remains of the raspberry pie that he isn't going to finish, pushing the mangled pieces of crust and crushed berries around the plate with the edge of his fork, staining everything purple-red. We need something to talk about; the silence is starting to menace the fragile peace we've stitched together in the years since the breakup. And I take a deep breath and I say, with comic exaggeration, "So-o-o, Ehan ... seen any good movies lately?"

Speedos and a Sweatshirt

for Mike Lyons

Yes? Okay? I should go ahead? Sure, I'm ready. What's not to be ready? We sit and we talk, and for once I have the perfect excuse for no one else being able to get in a word. But to tell you the truth, I am a little nervous. It isn't every day I get interviewed for the sake of history! Besides, I know you want me to tell you all about Jim, and there's so much to remember. Sure, sure—about me, too.

Your little machine is running? You know, when I was your age, these things were the size of a suitcase—not like now, a pack of cigarettes. All right, let me just take a minute to organize.

You have all of Jim's papers, hm? I gave everything that wasn't personal to your friend, the one who came from your gay museum with a dolly and with that other boy who looked like an advertisement for nutritional supplements. They took away Jim's office, practically intact. They even took the empty filing cabinets—six of them. What was I gonna do, use them for planters?

Anyway, probably there's something you can do with them, hm? In your office? Do they give you an office for going around and talking to old queers?

Of course I know what's an archive.

Jim's letters to me, souvenirs, most of the photos—those I kept. You can have all that, too, if you want, only wait a little until I'm too dead to miss it—please! That was a joke.

Jim kept a lot of news clippings over the years. You might find that useful. Also the papers or whatever they give you from when he went to legal conferences. The manuscripts from his books I'm sure are also in the files. You know he wrote two textbooks for law students about queer people, right? The constitution and civil rights and all that. And about sodomy. He was big on sodomy.

Ha! I made you smile. Good. "Just another day advancing the radical homosexual agenda." That was Jim's joke when I asked him how his day had been. Also speeches—like when they asked him to talk before the Democratic Convention when it came to San Francisco in 1984. I don't know all what else is in there. I had a friend go through and put aside whatever he thought I might want to look at again. All the rest, away it went in the van to your history project.

You know what else I have—somewhere, anyway. The suit Jim wore when they swore him in as judge. Who would keep such a thing, hm? Believe me, I didn't do it because I thought either us was going to wind up famous. Although that was Jim's big warning later when I would try to throw away so much as an old letter—*Think of the biographer!* What I had in mind, though, was that there might come a day when Jim was feeling maybe not so ai-yi-yi, and I'd get out the box with the suit and say, "Remember the last time you had this on? Aren't you glad now you ignored me when I said wear the taffeta?" And it would cheer him up, hm?

But you probably wouldn't want old clothes anyway—they can tear it in shreds and make a reliquary! Or better—they could bury me in it, it should get one more wearing. Someone can make money with the alteration so it'll fit.

Sure it was a big deal, Jim's swearing-in. The first gay judge in the state—in the country! Well, the first one who wasn't a secret, anyway. The closet cases you could tell because they came to the party afterwards just long enough to gulp one glass of champagne, shake Jim's hand, and suddenly have to scram for a pressing engagement.

Real momzers, some of them, who for years Jim had to look out for them so they didn't stab him in the back.

But I have pictures with the mayor and all sorts of other San Francisco bigwigs. The governor—Jerry Brown—even sent a telegram with congratulations for Jim. That I know I gave because we had it in a frame, and I was just noticing this morning that I need to put something else on the wall where it used to be because you can see the outline. Anyway, I thank god for Jerry Brown, because he's the one who made Jim the appointment, and after him it was sixteen years of asshole Republicans. Not that they're not surrounded by us up in Sacramento—fags, but at least Republicans.

Yes, I think it *was* brave when Brown made Jim a judge. And of course it was news. But it also wasn't as though Jim didn't earn his appointment, is what I'm explaining. He was qualified, sure, but he also raised a bundle of money for that man's campaign for governor, and a judgeship is the least Brown should have given him. Besides, when you're the first one, it's not enough to be as good as everybody else—you have to be better. Otherwise, these people—the ones that make such decisions—they wouldn't give you the steam off their piss. So don't think they had made for him some special gay slot out of the goodness of their hearts. Jim deserved. He earned.

After he retired, you know, we just moved everything here and piled it into Jim's office in the house—whatever didn't need to stay in his chambers in City Hall for the next guy, I mean. He was always saying he'd go through it one day because he was sure there was a lot of rubbish. I guess I should have cleaned out myself, before your friends came, but I was no good for that. The worst was not the papers, though, it was the clothes—can you imagine? And I don't mean just the swearing-in suit. The ordinary clothes. With all the people in this town living in rags, could I make a simple trip to Goodwill so Jim's things could go to someone who needs them? No. The socks and undershorts I could wear myself—I won't have to buy for years. Probably never again, to tell you the truth. But the rest—shirts and coats and slacks—they don't fit me. Maybe a shirt or two I could wear for pajamas.

Still, do you know what a selfish thing I did? Ha! I moved all of Jim's clothes out of our room and into the walk-in closet in the guest room, and that's where they sit even as we're talking. Every once in a while, I go in and shut the door behind me, and I just stand there in the dark and smell Jim. Nothing by itself smells much like him anymore, but when they've all been shut away together like that for a while—that wonderful smell, the one that used to get into the sheets and pillow cases—it comes back strong as ever. A few times after he died, I even tried wearing what was left of his favorite cologne, you know, as a way to remember. But it didn't smell good on me. So I put the open bottle way up on the closet shelf. I never thought how fast it would evaporate! But that cologne-smell, too, is mixed in there a little with the other. Faintly. If you know what you're smelling for.

You'd think, after almost a year, I wouldn't get so emotional, hm? Forgive me. I wanted to have things more pulled into a good shape by the time I lit candles for Jim's yahrzeit, but I'm thinking now maybe it won't work out like how I imagined. I don't know why a year seemed such a big deal—an arbitrary date, after all. But I wanted to make everything tidy for Jim, who always wished tidy would rub off on me. And a year, that's tidy, hm? Like bookends.

I don't know how I got started on that anyway. You must have guessed an old guy would ramble on, hm? I hope you brought extra tapes!

So. I guess when people make these kinds of reminiscences, they usually start by saying something like, "I remember as if it was yesterday," hm? That's how it is in the movies. So organized. My memories are a little more jumbled. Poor you, who has to sort it all out! Me, all I have to do is live with them, and I was never one to mind a messy house.

Yes! Good thinking. How I met Jim is the best place to start. And that day, in my mind, is very clear. Crystal clear—ha! Clear like water, I could say, if I wanted to be poetic. Wait a minute and you'll see what I mean. It's a motif!

But I must also tell you that this is not a memory that seems like yesterday. No, this picture I have of the day I first spoke to Jim—though, I should add, this was not the first time I saw him—is nearly sixty years old, and I have to admit, that's exactly what it feels like: an almost-sixty-year-old memory. Some days it feels even older than that, which means, I suppose, that I do. Old man, old memories.

Oh, I'll be eighty-one any day now. It's true what they tell you: As you get older, time does go by faster. Whole weeks seem to disappear while I'm not paying much attention. There I am, in my usual muddle, wandering around the bedroom trying to remember where I put my glasses. And then I look up and it's time for my doctor's appointment again or Teddy is on the phone, asking what time I want to meet him for the ballet. "My God," I say, "I thought that wasn't for weeks yet."

Don't look so concerned! Losing time isn't as frightening as it sounds. Actually, it has a way of softening the edges. And sometimes we need a break from having everything too present. Too much with us, eh? A little literary allusion.

I better explain first about Teddy, who is by now so old he could be in one of those capsules they used to bury under Times Square so the future should know how we lived back in the day. Ha! Teddy's joke, not mine.

Teddy has been my regular theater partner for five decades, give or take—but to be honest, he's been my partner in practically everything. Even after Jim and I got together, I still insisted on my nights out with Teddy. Jim didn't go for it much at first. But Teddy and I were never anything more to each other than best sisters. And with such a lifelong friend everyone should be blessed. So take my advice—start cultivating already. Out of all the friends you have now, you never know which ones are gonna stick.

Teddy was the kind of guy, we used to say, who knew how to pour the tea. You know that phrase? I didn't think so. Someone who could pour the tea was a guy who collected all the best gossip—who knew where the bodies were buried, hm? And he should. Teddy was in San Francisco since before dirt!

Ha! Another line of Teddy's.

Teddy and I met at university. He was in one of my classes and we took one look at each other and that was that. Teddy was what you might call "high strung" in those days. The nervous type. You couldn't make him be still, no matter what. Sometimes you just wanted to say, "Teddy, sit on your hands for God's sake!" In other words, what I'm saying: If you wanted to stay in the closet, you couldn't be seen with Teddy. He didn't exactly pass, hm? But what did I care about that? I just needed a friend. You have to remember, at that point I knew exactly one other gay man for sure.

Well, of course you suspected others. Some of them, it was more than a suspicion. But I'm talking someone who you knew what he was and he knew what you were and, when you were together, you didn't have to talk about the girlfriend you didn't have or how you went "all the way" with some coed you'd met or pretend to be interested in football or, God forbid, hockey. With Teddy and me, it was tits on the table right from the start. In other words, no bullshit. Teddy knew things about me that even Jim didn't know.

No, I don't mean that how it sounds. I didn't keep things from Jim, but you have private reactions, right, that you don't just blab in your lover's face. You have a worry about what's going on in the bedroom, say, or the holidays are coming up, and, okay already, you're going to his sister's, but you've got to tell somebody that you're dying to drown her two little darlings in the bathtub. That's what I'd tell Teddy. And he, of course, had his own tales of loves pursued and loves lost. Mostly lost. Teddy didn't have luck that way.

Anyway, after Teddy and I started hanging out together pretty permanently, Jim and Teddy fought a lot. Not fought, really, more like they'd snipe at each other across the table. "All I'm saying is, why do you have to be such a goddamn flit just because you're a homosexual?" This is Jim talking. Mr. Establishment. See, later on he's defending drag queens in his legal practice, but then, no, it was different.

And so Teddy, who could leave nothing alone, shoots off his mouth about how if Jim thinks the people at his work are fooled by the butch act, he's got another think coming. Both of them drinking too much, of course, because in those days there was no such thing as too much, and it was hard liquor, too, highballs. Even piss-elegant queens weren't yet serving three kinds of Napa Valley Merlot with their supper. Meanwhile, I'm the one in the middle balancing the platter of crudités and trying not to have my lovely dinner party turn into a fucking Edward Albee play!

Oh, terrible, they were. Maybe they were jealous of each other, a little. Maybe Teddy was worried I'd take sides with Jim and leave him out in the cold, because it wasn't so easy for a guy like Teddy to make friends. But there was no danger of my dropping Teddy. After a few years they calmed down and we enjoyed many long truces between skirmishes.

But anyway, the reason I'm telling you this is that, about fifteen years ago, Teddy finally decides to go to the shrink and the guy says he has anxiety-something-or-other, and for this they now have pills. So Teddy is suddenly mild as milk and, for more than the last decade of Jim's life, he and Teddy were best pals. In fact, the last time Jim ran for reelection before he retired, Teddy cashed in some policy and donated to Jim's campaign a thousand dollars. How's that for irony? Of course, Teddy showed up in drag to the swearing-in, but Jim had long since stopped minding Teddy's outrageousness. He just gave Teddy a huge hug and a kiss and said, "You look like a float in the goddamn Rose Parade." And Teddy says, "Honey, let's face it. I'd paint my eyeballs if I could!"

And no one was crying harder at the funeral than Teddy. Always the drama queen—dressed head to foot in black with a veil, no less. Later on he said he was crying because he realized he was stuck taking care of me from now on, but I know he was missing Jim.

So what I was saying—Teddy and I have always kept our supper dates, our dish dates, our theater dates. I bet we've seen literally thousands of operas and ballets in our time. Jim, he never cared much for that sort of thing—dance performances, plays, what have you. He liked sports, if you can make sense of that. I never could! I teased him about it constantly—it was a joke we had between us, you understand: the jock and the bookworm. It's ironic how life turns out. When you're young, you think things are always going to stay the way they are. And if you're a skinny, uncoordinated Jewish kid, how many options do you have? You study. You get smart. You hope for the best.

Still, between you and me, I secretly admired Jim's enthusiasm for sports. He always had something to talk about with the straight men at cocktail parties—and that's not nothing. Straight people don't mind you so much if they can convince themselves that, deep down, you want the same six boring things out of life that they do.

But it was nice having a lover who sat around on weekends watching football or basketball on TV. I would putter around in the garden—replanting my goddamn azaleas or something—and when I came back inside he'd still be there, usually with friends over. Lesbians, mostly, if you want to know—you try to find four queens who want to watch the Super Bowl!

Well, sure, guys *your* age, maybe, because even fags today expect each other to act like frat boys. But what I'm talking is Jim's and my peer group—a different story.

So anyway, I'd make them popcorn and put the beer glasses in the freezer so they would frost up nice when you poured—just like my mother did for my father. It felt—I don't know. Normal, somehow. Wholesome.

Every once in a while during the summers, when he really twisted my arm, I'd drive with Jim across the Bay to watch the baseball games or, more often, we'd go here in the city to Candlestick Park. It was usually freezing there—the fog you know, and the wind lashing off the Bay like little ice darts—and I'd pack blankets and thermoses full of Irish coffee.

That was before they started searching everyone like you might be a member of the goddamn IRA or something—and they take away your booze. Mind you, they meanwhile sell booze at the park, you just can't bring your own. Anyway, we'd get all bundled up and snuggle together—well, later we did, when it seemed safe enough to be seen like that in public, not during the early years—and Jim would watch the game and I'd read the *New York Times*. With white knuckles, too, I can tell you, from trying to keep the wind from blowing the pages all over the stands!

Personally, I always found baseball to be the most boring game on earth, but I liked being there with Jim, and every so often he'd call my attention to something that was going on in the game, and I would be interested just because of how it felt to have his breath on my ear as he patiently explained why everyone in the stands was standing up and yelling like crazy persons. But I still don't think I could tell you the difference between an "RBI" and an "ERA."

And Jim. Jim didn't know a plié from a pile driver. And of course then it was his turn to tease me about my "culture vulture" friends and about how he hadn't counted on his husband turning out to be an opera queen. Well, that I was, but I think Jim also got a secret kick out of my conversations with Teddy and the others who we'd have over for an early supper sometimes before we headed out in our little flock to the War Memorial. That's where they held the opera for all those decades—before the earthquake closed it down, I mean.

We'd sit around kibbitzing and eating some cheese that cost eight thousand dollars a pound and no one had ever heard of, least of all me, and I would try to make Jim laugh with little jokes—you know, involve him in the conversation.

Oh, mostly we made very bad puns. Like, for example: "Vesty the Jew Boy." For *Vesti la giubba? Pagliacci*, hm, the one with the crying clown? Or like calling Elizabeth Schwartzkopf "Betty Blackhead" or saying "Monster Rat" when we meant Montserrat Caballé. Birgit Nilsson—she was The Swedish Meatball. They all had their nicknames.

No, these were not operas. These were opera *singers*. Famous sopranos. Those were the old stars, of course. Later it was people like Kiri Te Kanawa or Kathleen Battle, who you were more or less forced to hear on CD as often as she could get a booking in this town. Now everybody's mad for Cecilia Bartoli—don't ask me why. A lovely girl, but with a voice still green and hard like a piece of fruit you shouldn't have picked yet. Too soon she'll be sorry what they made her do before she was ready.

I don't know why we liked the sopranos. Maybe because they almost always die in the end—but gorgeously! Or could be because it was easier for us to imagine being the one in love with a man than being the man pursuing a woman. Anyway, was it our fault that composers wrote the best parts for sopranos?

I suppose it was a kind of a private language, yes. There were all kinds of abbreviations and code phrases that would have been mysterious to the uninitiated. Mind you, no less incomprehensible to the outsider than the language of baseball—but it was terribly important to us. Terrence McNally even wrote a play about it: *The Lisbon Traviata*. All about an opera queen who murders his lover because of an insane obsession with Maria Callas. Frankly, I don't know how straight people ever understood that play, but I suppose there are plenty of straight opera queens. You don't think we ancient queers keep opera afloat all by ourselves, do you? Though you might get that impression on opening nights in this town.

The opera scene wasn't always so outrageous, but in San Francisco it became quite festive. A real clash of cultures. Oh, you know: On one side of the aisle you'd have the Herb Caen crowd—"old" San Francisco, so to say, though of course there isn't really any such thing. But having a pile of money can buy you an awful lot of heritage, believe me. So there would be these filthy-rich women with wattle necks down to here, but decked out in these godawful dresses that cost ten thousand dollars, you know, with pussy bows the size of box kites or some dreadful plissé fabric that looks like they slept in it. And—on the other side of the aisle—these A-List Pacific Heights queens in head-to-toe leather that cost almost as much. And everyone mingles at intermission, wielding their little glasses of five-dollar champagne like scepters.

Because the leather queens are on the fucking Housing Commission and the scary-hair matrons are married to the guys who give the opera half a million dollars every year!

You never went? You should see it sometime. It's genuine San Francisco. They have standing room still for less than a movie ticket.

It was a different world then, hm? I got interested in opera because it was what you did. You found other people like you and you were introduced to the arts. You know, we thought being gay was the royal road to culture. We scoured Ackerly and Forster and Maugham and Cavafy for all the hidden meanings. We read Proust—at least, we said we did. We made it our business to study classical music and to know about painting, and, if you could speak well about those things, you got an invitation to the party, so to speak. It was all about a sensibility.

And it didn't hurt to be pretty. Many's the time I endured the deadly conversation of some handsome boy who hadn't read anything since *The Boxcar Children* but had gotten in on the arm of one of our friends.

Oh God, yes, it was pretentious! Insufferable is what it was. But we were, many of us, still in the thrall of Oscar Wilde—the salon, the idea that style and wit were more important than almost anything. Or maybe it was just overcompensation—we were queer, but at least we were cultural, hm? And the rest of the world was full of Neanderthals.

Still, I was sorry to see it all go, as it eventually did. Because, my God—is anyone witty anymore? Is anyone urbane? We certainly had more entertaining dinner parties than I remember attending in the last ten years. I mean, there you would be at table with someone who was an expert on Japanese netsuke, a man who had just come back from safari in the Australian Outback, a poet who was translating Villon, a woman visiting from the Seychelles, and someone whose photographs were on exhibit at the art museum that very moment. And now—who do I eat with? A window dresser at Macy's, a therapist, and somebody who writes grant proposals for an AIDS organization. And what's the conversation? Whether Madonna is any good in *Evita*!

I'm sorry. I know how I must sound. But you wouldn't have come to see me if you didn't expect me to tell you that the world was sledding into hell with a blindfold. Isn't that what old people do? Reminisce about the good old days, kvetch about the present? So, I'm true to type. And I'll tell you flat out—all the interesting people are dead.

So.... Maybe a little break, hm? I have some sesame crackers and a nice schmear I picked up at Holey Bagel. Chives and who knows what. No? You're fine?

Maybe some tea, then? It sat all day yesterday in the sun—very delicious with ice. That you will have! Good. I'll be two minutes. Can your machine hear me if I talk from the other side of the pass-through?

Okay. So now, what was I saying? Oh yes, about Teddy and me and the opera.

Jim would go with us now and again, sort of a trade for my going to the baseball with him. He said he thought of himself as Margaret Mead, taking field notes among the savages. I wanted him to go more often—not because I cared if he ever learned to like opera, but because the sight of him in his tuxedo used to take my breath away. Even when he was well into his seventies, he cut an imposing figure. And when he wore a hat! My dear, the crowd would part.

What? No! No, of course he didn't wear a hat with his tuxedo, but he often did when he went to work—just with his three-piece. I thought he must be one of the last twelve men alive who could make a hat look sexy. Well, he was so tall—6'2". And he always had that mane of hair. He never lost a single strand—God how I hated him for that! Even when it started to go gray at the sides his hair was as thick and full as when I first touched it. So a hat never made him look like someone trying to cover up a bald spot.

Here you go. Let me put down a napkin. Sugar? No sugar.

After we met I tried wearing hats, too, for a while; they hadn't yet gone completely out of style. And there was something I liked about two men walking down the street together with hats on and overcoats blowing open in the wind, just looking like two ordinary businessmen and no one having any idea who they really are to each other. It seemed more fun to have that secret back in the days before everybody stopped having secrets about anything at all. Pre-Charles and Diana.

But I never really carried hats off very well anyway. My hair was already thinning by the time I was thirty, and I just stopped trying. Jim was so sweet about it. When I first started going bald, he began making a special point of touching my head and ruffling my hair—what was left—not just when we were making love, but even when we were alone at home together, sitting around doing nothing. He'd come up behind me in the kitchen and put his arms around me and kiss me right on the top of my bald spot.

At first I was so self-conscious that I'd push him away or tell him to stop, but he kept on, in that ineffable way of his. He never tried to argue with me or tell me I was silly to be worried about it, which would only have made it worse. Instead, he'd wait a few days, then he'd be at it again, holding me against his chest as we lay in bed and leaning down to kiss my head, very casually, so that eventually it seemed natural for him to touch me there, just as he always had. As if it were any other part of my body. And I stopped caring about it—at least as far as Jim was concerned. For that I don't think I ever thanked him, not specifically, I mean, for giving me that one place— which was anywhere he was—in which how I looked didn't matter.

Yes, I suppose people are more obsessed with their looks now than they used to be. But when I met Jim, what we cared about most was appearing straight—not being "obvious," you know? And it was harder for some of us than others. But it was a matter of life and death in some cases. I mean, it depended where you were or what you did for a living, but people we know lost their jobs. A young attorney at Jim's firm even killed himself. It wasn't so many years after McCarthy when Jim and I started living together, and the mentality was still very much alive, even in San Francisco. And of course we all knew about the Boise witch hunts.

What Bosie? You mean like Oscar Wilde's Bosie? Boychik, I'm old, but I'm not that old. No, it's a town—Boise, Idaho? Around 1955, someone started the accusation that a group of queens was preying on young boys—"a ring of prominent older homosexuals" was how the papers said it. Of course it was ridiculous. There was no sex ring, as everyone later found out, just a bunch of desperate closet cases and some teenage hustlers who didn't object to getting a blow job in exchange for pocket money. Some of them from surprisingly good homes, which just goes to show—sex is the great leveler.

It leveled a lot of those men in Boise, anyway. Several went to jail and many others had their lives ruined by the accusations and the rumors—they printed people's names in the papers before anything had even been investigated! The Idaho police actually came all the way to San Francisco to arrest people who were suspects. Jim told me he had a friend who worked in a restaurant and the police came and pulled him out right in the middle of a shift one day and shipped him back home to Idaho.

The Boise story was all over the local grapevine, and Jim and I didn't know if it could happen again, or something like it. We were worried about the age issue anyway because he was more than ten years older than I was. I mean, I was twenty-one by the time we got together officially, but Jim was in his thirties and already successful in his firm, and you never knew what conclusions people might draw.

But I do remember thinking that I wished I had known about a place like Boise when I was seventeen or eighteen, because I would probably have found some way to go there.

Why? Because I was desperate to find someone who would prey on me! During the time when I was figuring out what I was, gay life was almost completely underground, and of course I was too young to get into bars anyway. Legally, that is. If some nice older man had approached me in the right way, I would have gone with him in a minute. What I would have done afterward, or how I would have kept it a secret, that I don't think I could tell you.

You've got that look again. You don't approve of men getting together with boys of that age? A lot of people think like you—and maybe things have changed today, hm? I mean, anything you want, you can find it, so maybe if you haven't found it, that means you really don't want it, right? Me, I'm not so sure. You ACTUP types, you seem to think that gay exists in New York, San Francisco, Los Angeles, maybe three or four other cities, where everyone is free and happy and able to find his people with no trouble. You forget that out there in the middle—in the "land you fly over," as Jim used to call it—the closet is still spacious.

Go live in rural Missouri or some damn place and be amazed! Suddenly there's a lot of "bisexuals" running around, hm? And "discreet married man seeking same." Ha! Quite a surprise. It's not so nice like here where you can spit out the window and hit a gay person. And you want to know something else? Not just out there in the savage middle, but right here, too, even on this block probably, are homosexual-type people who would have nothing to do with your so-called community if it came with free checking and annual dental. Bars, boutiques, and bodybuilders—believe me, shana punim, are not for everyone!

So. Hear what I'm saying. A lot of people are looking for someone to help them out of nobody-will-love-me land, and they're maybe not so picky that it should be a pre-approved, card-carrying, liberated urban homosexual. Sometimes the man down the street—the *boy* down the street—will do. I'm telling you this not because you should now search my house for NAMBLA literature, but I want you to understand that meeting Jim saved me from such loneliness—the kind that so much liberation has not destroyed—and if he had met me when I was seventeen, I would only have been luckier.

Okay. A breather, hm? I have to rest a minute I shouldn't get a heart failure.

You think I'm not being fair. You could be right. I don't know you, you don't know me—so we look to each other maybe like people who stand for something more than just ourselves. It could happen. But a lot of what I see today, I must tell you, I don't understand. You have the world and look how you act. I don't mean *you*, you. Generic you. Like me: generic old fart.

But I'm saying: the people who made the first movements in this country, they had politics, they believed that we were here to do something good—for each other, yes, but also for the whole world. Okay, so maybe it was schmaltzy, idealistic even. But if you're idealistic, at least you have ideals, hm? Today, they call it progress when the Stolichnaya company puts a full-page ad in *The Advocate*. Now we are accepted! No, now we are a marketing niche, and gay money is just as good as anybody else's—only, please, don't ask to get married. For this, only the straights may apply.

Jim and I talked about this many times—what was becoming of the gays. You have to take the wide view, he said. Everything else is just a passing style. He might have been right. Life was not exactly perfect for us back when.

Of course I discovered the bar scene, which was a meat rack, just like now. Or so I'm told by my young friends, because God forbid anybody should get a breakdown because a guy on social security walked through the door.

Anyway. First, you were lucky if you could even find them—it wasn't like listed in the phone book! No name on the door, usually not even an address number. And the entrance was down some side street. That was the back entrance, what you used, because the front, the official entrance, was reserved for when the cops showed up and tried to herd everyone off to jail. Or, more often, just beat the shit out of you, which was the favorite off-duty exercise for San Francisco cops. They'd leave their hats, guns, and badges in the trunk and just hang out in their cars, drinking out of open bottles—they wouldn't always come inside—and biding their time to lay into anyone who wandered down the alley alone. Saps, brass knuckles, whatever. And what were you gonna say afterwards? I was at a queer bar and a cop I can't identify broke my jaw? Not likely. So we'd get the signal that the cops were outside in the alley and we'd try to file out the front, all orderly-like and quiet. Sometimes it worked and you made it, sometimes not.

But the bars weren't much for me, anyway. I never felt good-looking enough to go for the gorgeous guys, and they certainly weren't falling all over themselves to pick me out of the crowd, either, such as it was. And I was so painfully shy in those days that I found it hard to meet anybody. And of course that was on top of wondering whether somebody you met might be a vice cop or a prostitute—or maybe just a bouncer ready to eighty-six you for not being old enough to be there in the first place, like I wasn't—and, if you were certain he was none of those things, figuring out whether you were compatible.

In bed, I mean. Which one of you was going to be the boy.

Well, I never really had a preference, but everyone assumed I was the nelly because I was small and because there was no question of my pretending to be a stevedore or something, which is what people seemed to want in those days. Rough trade. You've heard the phrase? Though I wasn't exactly flitting around in a ball gown and a tiara either. I guess I was what people nowadays call a nerd. Bookish, we said then. And I didn't care what we did in bed. If you managed to get through my shyness, and you got me home and got my glasses off, I was just enthusiastic about sex, any which way.

That was one of the wonderful things about Jim. Even though everyone assumed he was the "man" and that I was the one who always got—that I was always the one on the bottom of the bed—it wasn't true. Jim liked to be taken care of as much as the next guy—as much as me, anyway, but he also liked doing the care-taking. I could be rough and I could take it when he felt like being rough. But we never had any problems in that area. Even toward the end, we still made love a couple times a month—not that I was keeping track. Which I think is not so bad when you consider that Jim was on his way to ninety.

You find it hard to imagine a couple of wrinkly old guys having sex? I certainly did at your age. I never would have imagined that it would be possible for Jim and me to do what we did, long after our bodies had lost all charm for anybody but each other.

Jim was expert that way, at making whatever we did together seem right. And I don't just mean sex. Sometimes—and I'm talking about all those years we spent together before anyone thought of being liberated—the feeling would just come over you that what you were doing was wrong somehow, even sick. Two men keeping house together—me at the stove scrambling eggs and Jim sitting at the breakfast nook in his bathrobe and asking me if I thought I wanted new carpet in the den. That wasn't what men were supposed to be doing! Even if all the other straight couples on the block were sitting at breakfast having the same conversation, you just felt that yours was different, that you'd have to get up and hide in the other room if the paperboy came to the door collecting.

I don't know if Jim experienced moments like that. If he did he never told me about them, and I think he would have. But I had them. A lot at first, then less as the years went by. I suppose I almost started to feel militant, to use a word that became popular. Our home, our friends, the things we lived through together—that carried weight. I started to feel that I could defend Jim, that I could defend what Jim and I had made together, even if I couldn't always defend myself. I mean, you nurse a man through enough years of hangovers, bouts with the flu, and shitty moods when his work is driving him crazy, and you feel you have a right to be there.

And Jim was a man who was always going forward. He never bedeviled himself with "what ifs." Our life was our life, and there was no other. Ergo, it was the right thing to be doing. And that was the end of it. I found it maddening at times, if you want the truth—that certitude. In fact, that was probably our most frequent fight. It's so cliché I can hardly bear to tell you, but I'll just give you the opening line and you'll get the gist. I would say, "Damn you, why do you always have to be right about everything?" And away we'd go.

Oh, sure we fought.

I guess you could say often. He was the most stubborn man I've ever known and he could be an absolute tyrant. Ironic, yes, for the man everyone now thinks of as the great mediator? Well, home is home and public life is public life. And I, meanwhile, had a hot head of my own, especially when we first got together and I was embarrassed about Jim's money and the fact that he was older and so well-educated. And had a better job. Such a pill I was! Always trying to assert my independence, always trying to be a man. Don't let anyone ever tell you that gay men don't worry about their masculinity. Especially when you have a lover, it's worse. You're the husband *and* the wife. And you wonder: If you're the one who is doing most of the cooking or you're taking care of the home, or—God forbid—you're the "artistic" one, maybe the other guy sees you as less of a man. This is what you think. Certainly people outside the house see you that way. So you're always trying to measure up. Who can make more money? Who has the more settled career? If you don't get hold of it, the competition will gnaw your insides out.

Of course I calmed down as I got older. I suppose I learned to pick my fights. Age ought to give you something in exchange for taking away your muscle tone, hm? But no one ever made me angrier than Jim. He was forever canceling dates at the last minute because he was staying to work late, or he wanted to put in an "appearance" at some event or political fundraiser—always his damn career! What I realized finally is that Jim adored his work. Even as a child, he wanted to be a lawyer. When he was in fifth grade he wrote an essay about the law that won a prize. For the introduction, he wrote a poem—like an epigraph. And a lousier poem never existed. Stilted. Self-conscious. I'm sure he was trying to copy that tight-assed Brit-ish-boarding-school style that everyone was affecting for a while. Kind of like John Betjeman later on.

John Bet—B-E-T-J-E-M-A-N. A crummy writer who became the British Poet Laureate in, um, 1972, I think. But you don't have to put that in. Who cares what I thought about him? He's dead anyway. You weren't alive in 1972. Probably not even your father was alive in 1972.

Well, at least the Brits have had Poets Laureate for three hundred years. We didn't get an official one in this country until 1985. And thank God for Bill Clinton—he helped get Rita Dove appointed. You know, sometimes you could think he was queer just because of this thing he seems to have for colored women! Remember Maya Angelou at the first inauguration? Another terrible poem if you want my opinion.

All right. You're getting a little tight around the jaws, so I'll change the subject. But something I don't understand—you kids today are forever utzing each other over who's a racist, but the minute anyone passes an innocent comment you get nervous. You're so enlightened you didn't notice maybe that Maya Angelou was colored?

Okay, I'm sorry. I was talking about Jim's awful poem, anyway. I used to have it somewhere. His mother, God rest her soul, saved it and gave it to him—in a gold frame no less—when he got sworn in as a judge. But that was what impressed them at his grade school, I think, the poem. Jim's father, too, had been an attorney—and so Jim was following his heart's desire. How else can I describe it? And later, when he was appointed to the judgeship? Forget about it. He was in heaven. Jim's career, it seemed to come so naturally for him. He worked hard, sure, but he was never busting his balls to be somebody, you know?

Me, I never knew what I wanted to be when I grew up. I've held so many different jobs, and I never had anything like a career. But, you know, another way to look at it, my career was Jim, and I'd still be doing it if he hadn't died. Anyway, when he was at the office or wherever all those nights, it took practice not to let my imagination run away with me. Not to see every missed dinner as a sign that he loved me less. Oh it got better, of course it did. You don't stay with a man for sixty years and still wonder every day if he loves you. Of course Jim loved me. And even when I would have one of my fits I would get over it quickly. As soon as I saw him again, as a matter of fact. I'd hear his key in the door, and I'd be sitting in the living room in a huff, with the lights out and tapping my shoe. Already I had rehearsed everything I was going to say and, boy, was he going to get it right between the eyes. So I'd start out, "You'd better have some good excuse for yourself, mister!"

And he would just say, "My baby, you're right, I'm a terrible husband. Will you let me make it up to you? Please?"

Was I supposed to stay mad after such an apology? Am I made of stone? I always forgave him, pushover that I was. But you learn to make accommodations for the things about the other person that make you want to scream like fingernails on the blackboard.

Accommodations. Did you ever hear that story about John Cage and Merce Cunningham? All the years they were together, John thought Merce was a terrible driver. And so, instead of having fights about it every single time they had to go someplace in the car, they put some nice, comfy pillows in the rear seat, and John would lie back there and take a nap while Merce drove.

Yes, it is a sweet story. But you live for stories like that, hm? Because, straight or queer, no one tells you how to do the simplest things. You're always looking for some advice or some guidance, and then you get to be a couple of A.K.s like we were and suddenly everybody is turning to you and asking you the same questions you always wondered what the hell the answers were. Go know. Life bites you in the ass that way.

So. To tell you the truth, I'm getting a little pooped. I think maybe I should tell you the story of how Jim and I met like we said at the start, and then we can make it a day, hm? You want to come back another time, if you think you can stand it, I'll tell you more.

Okay: Here's how it happened. Though I should first explain that there's the "company" story—the one we tell ... told, I mean, to people who didn't know us that well or Jim's colleagues from work. That sort of thing. And then there's the gay version, which is the true one. Or, at least, it's the complete one. Even among our good friends, not that many people know it. Teddy does, of course, because he was there.

When I got out of Europe with my sisters—a brucha on their souls—I was a boy in high school. We stayed for quite a few years by relatives in Brooklyn, and that's where I learned English. But it took a while because I wasn't what you would call quick. Meantime, frankly, my family was more interested I should attend Shul, and also I worked, because everyone worked even at that age, so I didn't get through public high school quite so fast as the American kids. And in the middle of all that, my father himself got out and took us right away to California because the whole world was moving to California. He got a job at the university in Berkeley. Groundskeeping and maintenance at first. He was lucky, because by then the war was over and everyone was looking for work, but he was a kind of genius at fixing things, and they gave him a position in the machine shop. So he stayed, and that's where he retired twenty-five years later.

When it came time for me to think about college, of course he would hear nothing but that I should go to Cal. He could keep an eye on me he said, and it was cheap. In those days, remember, they had this revolutionary idea that a person should get an education if he wanted, so they took in anyone. Not like today where we have policies to weed out the nogoodniks who we already know they're stupid because they didn't have the sense to be born with money.

Anyhow, I went, and it wasn't bad. In fact, I realized I wasn't such a dummy after all. I discovered a new kind of status, I guess you could call it, which was being the person in class who often knew the answers. Still, as my father used to tell me, "If you are such a smart person, why are you not rich?" But he was proud of me—God forbid he should actually have said it. I liked it so much I took six years to finish my bachelor's, with my father standing behind me pushing the entire time.

Now at Cal, in those days, they had a beautiful gym, and in the gym was a huge swimming pool, also beautiful. The old-fashioned kind that looked like from a Roman bath, with hand-painted tiles on the edge and on all the areas around the pool where you walked, and marble benches against the walls. And the roof they had made with panes of glass the size of picture windows, each one beveled so the whole thing curved, like a giant hothouse, and the sun came right down on top of you.

My father was the one who sent me to the gym—poor man, never knowing where it would lead. "You're such a nebbish," he said. "You better put some meat on those bones or no girl is every going to marry you." Well, I already knew a girl wasn't what I wanted, but I also realized it wasn't out of the question that I would have to get married—I was the only son, and I was sliding through marrying age like I didn't care. Anyway, it was easier to go to the gym than fight with my father. Besides, to obey your father is a mitzvah, I told myself. But what my father had in mind was I should lift weights or go out for a sport, and this I was never going to do. I mean, a mitzvah is a mitzvah—I didn't have to be a saint. So swimming became our compromise.

Anyway, I went, and I loved it, much to my surprise. I started going almost every day, early in the morning when it was less crowded. Also the "serious" swimmers went then, and I, who was never good at anything athletic, I liked considering myself serious. And, as you must by now have guessed, Jim was also swimming at that hour. He was already working as an attorney, but he had taken his law degree from Boalt Hall and so, afterwards, he kept his alumni privileges at Cal. Of course, I didn't know any of this until later.

At the time, what I did notice about Jim—let's just say it wasn't his intellect, hm? No, it was his bathing suit—a very skimpy thing for those days. All the essentials were covered up but also not much was left to the imagination. The only time you saw suits like that was pictures of foreign swim teams—and even then not so much. Judging from the suit, I thought he must be European. But he wasn't—not

Jim and not the suit. His Speedo, I found out after, came from Australia—that's who made them first—but also they were starting to catch on pretty big in the states around then. Very clever, those Speedo guys—they outfitted the Australian swim team for nothing in the '48 Olympics and all the free advertising did wonders. And Jim, he was just a big, healthy California boy who took a vacation to Australia and came back with a suitcase full of fancy-schmancy bathing suits that he sold to his friends. This, also, I don't know until later.

Meanwhile, back at the pool, after a few weeks of seeing each other we had gotten to the point where we waved or nodded hello and goodbye. All very butch, the way men do at the gym. But nothing more than that. I thought he was straight. Of course I thought he was straight. By me, the whole world was straight.

Anyway, one morning, I'm standing at the edge of pool and waiting for the lifeguard to blow his whistle to open the free swim—I'm shivering wet from the shower they made you take before you got in, dripping and hugging myself. And out of the corner of my eye, I see that Jim—who, all I know is, he's some guy who I have now carefully arranged my schedule to be sure to be there whenever he is—has come to stand beside me. And my first reaction is: I have now got a giant neon sign lighting up my ass. Suddenly, I'm convinced that every single person there can tell I'm queer and that I have a crush on this guy I don't even know. That's the worst thing when you're leaning halfway out the closet door—the anxiety that you can't control who knows about you. Years went by before I realized that nobody gives two shits because they're too busy worrying about whatever makes them feel self-conscious. But who knew that at the time?

And then Jim spoke to me. Just a few words about nothing, but the point is what he *didn't* say. He didn't try to involve me in some slap-you-on-the-back jock bullshit or ask who did I like in the World Series or had I noticed the tsitskehs on the co-ed at the check-in desk. Which is the kind of talk, even today, you get into an elevator with a straight man and unless you're wearing a wig and a dress, he will mention these things to you. But the important thing is, Jim had broken the ice, and so after that I had permission—that's how it felt—to talk to him when we ran into each other, though what I said couldn't have been too engaging because, when I wasn't speaking in words of one syllable, I was stuttering like a moron.

What I'm remembering is the water. Or, I should say, Jim in the water. I liked to watch him especially when he swam laps underneath—you know, for breath control. He'd push off from one end and wriggle through the water like a sea snake. He knew when I was watching, too, because sometimes he would get to the other side and not come up for the longest, knowing that I'd get nervous. So I would peer over the edge and there he would be, hanging just beneath the surface and smiling up at me, the little waves in the water making his face split into pieces and then come back together again.

When the hour was over, he'd haul himself out of the pool, pushing up on the edge so his triceps made upside-down Vs on the outsides of his arms, and the water would run down his body, leaving furrows in the hair on his legs and his forearms, like when wind blows through a wheat field. I thought I had never seen anything so beautiful. It wasn't even erotic—well, of course it was erotic. But I mean, seeing him like that didn't make me suddenly horny. I guess what I felt more than anything was that I wanted to touch him, just to see what he felt like.

Naturally, Jim acted as if he didn't even notice the attention or the way I looked puppy-dog eyes at him. And he was afraid I was jail bait—or this is what he said after. I'd go sit on the bench with my towel wrapped around my legs so the marble wasn't so cold, and he'd pull a gray sweatshirt out of his bag—one of those oversized, long-sleeved, crew-necked ones made out of brushed cotton—and throw it on, just like that, still wearing his Speedo, and saunter over to where I was sitting, and he'd stand there, waiting to talk. Sometimes he'd put one foot up on the bench right beside me and lean down, with his forearms crossed over one thigh. For me, who had never in my life been so close to a man—how can I explain. He might as well have been showing me pornography.

And this is how it went for months. We'd chat—about school, about his job, about California, about swimming. But never anything revealing. He never dropped any bobby pins, as we used to say—never let on he was queer, is what I mean. So why was he spending time with me? I made myself—and Teddy—crazy.

"He's obviously flirting with you," Teddy would tell me, and I would insist it couldn't be so. Because why would anyone? This is what I was thinking of myself.

The frustration, meanwhile, was killing me. So near and yet so far, hm? I decided, if I couldn't have Jim, that I was at least going to have sex with *someone*, because the mornings I spent staring at Jim's chest were making me very edgy, if you follow me. I had heard about this bathroom—a tearoom, hm?—in one of those department stores on Union Square, and so that's where I went. Also I was hoping that if I went there I might learn some great homosexual mystery—I don't know, from osmosis, maybe—that would tell me what was what about Jim. A secret signal or something, because you know, in those days you heard things. Like, homosexuals wear green socks on Thursdays. Or you could ask someone, "Do you like seafood?" and, if he said yes, you would know he was also that way. I wish I could tell you I was making this up, but this is how naive I was.

In any case, I got myself immediately arrested for groping some red-headed guy with a crewcut who turned out to be a security guard. He's standing at the urinal jacking off, mind you, but still, he carefully zips up and then he pulls out his handcuffs and arrests me. You can hardly imagine how convinced I was that the world had come to the end. My father, my school—everything ruined. So I call the only person I can call—Teddy—and Teddy calls a friend, and the friend says he knows an attorney who is taking queer vice cases, and Teddy makes the appointment. Meanwhile, he comes and bails me out and I don't leave the house for the three days until we have to go to the lawyer's office. My father, to whom I cannot even show my face, is convinced I'm in my room preparing to die. Which, in a way, I was.

So the day comes and Teddy takes me to downtown San Francisco to a fancy office on Montgomery Street. I've never been in such a place, with the wine-colored leather sofa and the mahogany coffee tables, but who can pay much attention to the surroundings since all I'm thinking is, I'm about to go in and tell some stranger that I was caught trying to get laid in a men's bathroom and could he please keep me from going to jail for the rest of my life. Because what do I know about what they can do to you?

So the secretary comes and says Mr. So-and-So will see you now, and Teddy and I walk into this kind of swishy office with an enormous desk with a black marble top—and who should be sitting on the other side but the man from the pool. And I don't know which one of us—Jim or me—looks more like he's ready to plotz. Teddy has by now figured out that something isn't right, and he's hopping around, getting more nervous with every second that Jim and I stare at each other and don't talk. "What? WHAT?" he's saying.

And Jim, he suddenly undergoes a transformation and turns into Mr. Cool As A Cucumber. "Won't you gentlemen please sit down?" he says to us—gentlemen, yet. And he tells Teddy, "You must be Mr. Harris. We spoke on the phone." Teddy, who is speechless, sits. I sit. And Jim, he starts doing his lawyer schtick, explaining what I have to do and what's going to happen next, just like we were any two clients off the street. I don't say anything about seeing him at the pool, and he doesn't say anything. For the next month, until my hearing, I don't go near the gym, of course, and whenever I talk to Jim on the phone or see him in his office, the whole thing is completely professional.

Well, to make a long story shorter, the hearing is over in about ten minutes, the judge throws out the case for entrapment or some damn thing, and I'm out the door without so much as paying a fine. No record, no nothing, on account of Jim convinces them that I'm so young and upstanding that it wouldn't be right. What I don't know until Jim later tells me is that there's dozens and dozens of these cases because the whole Bay Area is going crazy with vice crackdowns, and almost all of the cases are getting thrown out. The police don't even really expect convictions, they're just out to harass queers and embarrass as many people as possible. Which, they were doing a good job.

So we're outside on the steps of the courthouse, and Jim offers me a ride back home. At this point, why the fuck not, I think, so off we go. And he says to me, "I don't think you should be going to places like that."

"I know," I tell him.

And he asks me, "What were you doing there?"

Hello Mr. Lawyer! I'm thinking to myself. Was it perhaps not you who, less than twenty minutes ago, heard the security guard tell the world that I tried to grab his dick while he was standing at a urinal? So I say, "What do you think I was doing there?"

"No," Jim insists, "I mean, what were you *really* doing there?"

And what am I going to tell but him the truth? "Looking for someone like you," I say.

So he sighs to himself. And then he reaches over and squeezes my knee and he tells me, "Well, you don't need to look any more."

And that, my young friend, what I just told you—that is *not* the company story, hm? Jim never repeated it because it was a story on me, and I never did ... well, who knows why? We usually said we just met at the pool. But now you have the whole megillah on tape, all out in public, and I don't have to worry about it anymore.

You know, in a way, I guess you could say that my mess had something to do with the direction Jim's career took, because after that he accepted more and more gay cases until he eventually opened his own firm with some other gay lawyers he knew—very hush-hush at first—just to deal with civil rights stuff. He started to get involved in the bar raids and liquor-license suspensions that were going on—like that one famous case in the late fifties where the state closed two gay bars, one a very popular bohemian hangout in North Beach called The Black Cat where all the poets and the wannabes went, and then another one in Oakland—Mary's First and Last Chance. An awful name, hm? The police said the bars were a resort for prostitutes and sexual perverts. And Jim said everyone had the same right to gather together in public places as long as they weren't breaking the law. He won that case on a technicality, but a win was a win, especially then.

And Jim's career more or less just went from there. It's a small pond, San Francisco—not to take away from what Jim did, but what I mean is that a person who is determined can make his mark here. Or could, when Jim was coming up, because so many people were still terrified to be known, and Jim, he just stopped caring. I think maybe being in a couple made things look different to him.

Being single and hiding is one thing; the only person you're lying to is yourself. But when you have a partner, being in the closet also means acting like your lover is just some school chum you happen to room with—who of course doesn't mind giving up his room to sleep on the couch when the other guys' parents come to town. And I'll tell you this: In all the time we were together, Jim never once asked me to pretend to be someone I wasn't.

After Liam sent the transcript of the interview up to the house—and, please God, never have I heard such a WASP name as Liam—I must have read over it a dozen times. At first, I wasn't going to. For quite a while, the transcript sat in the envelope, torn open at one end, and I told myself I wouldn't look. But eventually I did. And from the very first time I was amazed at how much I left out. No surprise to anyone who knows me—I talked too much about myself and not enough about Jim. But everything about his work is in his papers, and a lot of people know more about his professional life than me. If Liam wants to know, he'll go ask them.

In his cover note, Liam said they plan to put my interview into their gay archive with the rest of Jim's materials. So, it's official: I'm a museum piece. How's that for information guaranteed to make a person feel not so young? But, if that's the case, then I think maybe it doesn't matter so much that I rambled the way I did. The words of the widow. Helpful for establishing context.

Liam also asked me if I want to correct anything.

And I did have a correction to make—a big one, too. I wanted to correct the part about Jim's death. I wanted to take my pen and a ruler and make a perfectly straight, black line through every place where I mentioned it. I thought, if I take my scissors and carefully cut out each time those words are said, will he come back?

He wouldn't come back. And what I would have left is what I have now: A story with holes in it, each one of them the outline of a place where someone used to be.

So how's that for no way to run an interview, hm? I am interesting to them only because of the holes. Did they come when Jim was still alive and could talk for himself? They didn't come. The young think there's so much time. But I don't blame them. I don't blame anybody. Maybe I blame Jim's parents for bequeathing him such a lousy heart it should give him trouble all his life and mess up big stretches of his retirement, too. I thought I'd finally have Jim all to myself with nobody else wanting anything from him when he retired, but no: there were surgeries and physical therapies and relatives weaving in and out of the house like ants! And if it wasn't his work calling him to come in, it was his doctors.

But such a polite boy in his leather jacket and his Nazi shoes. Nobody thinks what they wear on their bodies anymore. And tattoos! Everyone has tattoos nowadays. In my time a tattoo meant something a little different, I can tell you that. But he meant nothing by it. And this is perhaps what bothered me most of all.

Jim had a tattoo, from being in the Navy, right on his shoulder, his deltoid I think you call it. I sometimes wanted to cover it with my hand when we made love. When Jim and I went back east to see my relatives in the summers I dreaded those times when someone would suggest we go swimming and they should see his tattoo. Some of them had tattoos of their own—on their wrists. I was old enough I might have one, too, but by God's grace I got sent to America as a teenager instead. My parents stayed behind—why, I never asked. And, by the time I saw my father again, he wasn't in the mood to talk.

What I know is what my Saba was willing to explain: One day my father is late coming home from work, and when he arrives through the door he sees the furniture is broken, the windows are full of bullet holes, my mother is gone. Even if the signs weren't so clear he would know what an empty house means. They were Communists, after all, when it was bad enough just to be a Jew. So, he runs. Well, you call it running, but it was much quieter than that—sewer pipes, neighbors' cellars, buried and half-smothered under rags and old clothes in the bed of a draper's truck. Somehow he gets out. What was he supposed to do, stay and look for her?

I didn't want to be angry at him. Just like I didn't want to be angry at Jim, either, for going ahead without me. But what are you going to do: These are the kinds of thoughts you have. Maybe my mother asked herself, too, why my father didn't save her, but maybe nobody saves anybody, hm? Still, it's shameful to make comparisons of this kind. I have no right. My personal grief against what my parents must have gone through? Am I living in hell? No, hell this is not.

No one should hate life. If there is any sin, that must be one of the big ones.

And every once in a while, small miracles occur.

A couple of weeks after my interview, Liam calls to ask would I mind some follow-up questions. What's to mind, I say, because my appointment book is not exactly drowning in ink.

So he comes over, we have a little nosh; it's more like a visit than an interview, but I'm still waiting for him to start asking questions. Only he isn't getting around to it and he's so nervous he's making me nervous. Finally he spits it out: "I want to do something for you."

But I don't need anything for me, I say. I was glad to do the interview, and it was very pleasant to have permission to talk so much about me and Jim—almost like I had him back here for a few hours. By now, you can imagine, most of my friends are up to here with my reminiscences.

"Wait," Liam says, and he jumps from the table and runs into the bathroom, looking like he's about to toss up the nice sandwich I just made. But I don't hear unpleasant sounds coming from the bathroom, and a few minutes later the door opens and he comes out. And this is the part, may God strike me dead if I'm lying: The boy is standing there naked like a jaybird.

I am, of course, with my jaw on the floor—to say the least. What is a twenty-three-year-old boy doing in the doorway to my bathroom with no clothes on? I think, is he going to rob me? Stupid thought because, if there's one thing I know, it's that he's not carrying a weapon.

But I'm looking—of course I'm looking. He's a beautiful boy. One of those black Irish types, sturdy with good muscles, but thin and wiry, like the old Dorothea Lange photos you see of field workers in the West. Furry legs and arms, but straight hair, not curly. And mostly smooth on his chest, with one thick line pointing down from the middle of his stomach to the woolly patch around his privates. And white, white skin, so the dark hair shows up even more. You can see the veins in his arms and hands—worker's hands, I always thought of them. He's tall, like Jim.

"Liam," I say, "is something the matter?" Another person might have been more clever.

He's not moving from the doorway—in fact, he's gripping the door jamb on both sides so hard I can see that the top of his fingers are turning red and white from the pressure, and he says, again, "I just wanted to give you something." And so, being that old age has apparently rotted out most of my synapses, I finally begin to understand what should have been obvious.

Now Harvey Kivel, my dear old friend, he assures me that there are young men—younger men, I should say, which at this point is everyone—who go for older guys. Even guys Harvey's and my age. Gerontophiles he calls them. Antique dealers, I say. Anyway, maybe someone who wanted you for your wrinkles might be more comforting in the end than someone who wanted you for your muscles. Muscles you can lose, but God continues to be generous with the wrinkles. And no use raising your arms up to heaven and crying out, "Thank you, God, for all the character you've given my face, but please, I have more than I deserve. Dayenu!" Because God doesn't always know from dayenu. Still, I don't think this is Liam's story.

So I go to him and I reach gently around behind to the hook on the bathroom wall where I hang my robe, and I take it down and wrap it around his shoulders. "Here, sweetie," I say, "put this on and then come sit over here with me on the sofa, where we'll have a little talk, hm?" I hold his hand, which is ice cold, and we go sit.

Immediately he throws his arms around me and burrows his head down against my chest, practically trying to crawl onto my lap, and so I fold him up against me as close as I can and we sit that way for a long while. Being there like that with him, which incidentally I'm not minding at all, makes me think that I haven't touched another human being in almost a year. Oh sure, quick hugs at the funeral and some afterwards, but not like this.

Finally he says, "I feel so bad about Jim."

"Yes?" I say.

"How could you stand losing someone you loved so much?"

"Well," I say, suddenly wise, "I only lost him for a year. I had him for almost sixty before that. That's what I have to keep remembering."

"Are you sad all the time?" he wants to know.

And I tell him the truth: "Not all the time."

Then we stay quiet again for another while, still cuddling. I put my face down into his head of thick, black hair, rubbing gently against the masses of it tumbling all across his shoulders, just soaking up his smell, until Liam gives out such a sigh, and he says, for the third time, "I wanted to do something nice for you. "

"I know," I say. "And you have. Plus, I have an idea, if you don't mind."

"You can do anything you want," he says.

"Shh," I say. "Wait."

In the guest bedroom I go to the closet with all Jim's clothes, and I take down from the shelf one of his old gray pullover sweatshirts. This is one of my favorites—frayed around the collar and torn on one sleeve. I've washed it so many times the cloth is soft as flannel. Thank God Jim never lost the habit of wearing them. We must have bought and worn out dozens and dozens of them over the years, although I can say it became a challenge to find the ones made only of cotton.

In the dresser, meanwhile, I still have one or two of Jim's old Speedos. He wore them, still, but not so much in public as he got older. He said he didn't want to look like one of those ancient German tourists on vacation in Rio, with a belly like a brown leather basketball hanging over the waistband and, behind, an ass like a flat tire. But sometimes, when we would go up to the hot springs, just the two of us, or when we were among old friends, he would still wear them to swim because they were comfortable.

Me, I never thought he looked so bad, but like all of us maybe, he sometimes found it hard to love such an old body, hm? Jim was hardly one to be vain, but he was definitely not pleased when the gray pubic hairs started coming in. Gray hairs on your head, he said, you're distinguished; gray hairs on your chest, you're experienced. Gray hairs on your balls—baby, you're old!

Anyway, these two things, the sweatshirt and a pair of Speedos, I take out to Liam, who is still curled up on the couch. I wonder would you put these on, I say. For a minute he gets a look on his face like I'm about to suggest some necrophiliac fantasy, but I put up my hand. "Don't worry. Nothing kinky. Besides, a pretty boy like you, I'd be dead in minutes."

That makes him laugh, and I'm glad because I know he's been thinking to himself that maybe the problem is I don't find him attractive. He puts on the clothes I'm holding out to him, and everything fits, more or less. He has a nice schlong, this Liam. Of course I noticed. I'm old, not dead. Symmetrical and perky, with I would say a lot of character. Not that I've seen so many, but you could tell a lot from a man's pischer.

Pretty soon, though, he's got everything covered up again, and he's just standing there, waiting for me to talk. "You look very handsome," I tell him, which is true. I never knew Jim at Liam's age, but, if I did, it's not so crazy to think he should have looked a little like Liam.

Now that I think of it again, though, there might be some photos. Jim would have been—what?—almost done with law school when he was Liam's age. More or less. I'll have to go dig through the albums and see, though the family pictures might all have gone to Jim's sister. The ones from before I was in the family, anyhow. We had a stack of those old albums, with the stiff black pages like cardboard and that sheet of almost transparent tissue in between. And those little white corners you had to glue into place, by some miracle of God, in the right position to fit the picture so the photo would be straight on the page. Too much for me: My photographs, I kept in boxes.

So Liam asks me, "What do you want me to do?"

This embarrasses me, even more than sex would have embarrassed me, but it's what I want and, anyway, the whole idea of his being in my house like this has been strange from the beginning, so why not?

I say, "I wonder could you go over by the window and stand in front. Also, maybe you would push the sleeves on the sweatshirt up to your elbows, hm? Yes, like so."

And I sit on the sofa where I can look at him nice and clear. Not so close I'm right on top, but enough to see what I want to see. The sunshine coming through behind him lights up the edges of his body, catching the fine hairs on the nape of his neck and on his arms and giving them highlights: gold, red, and some color that isn't really a color, it's just light. Liam is touched all around by this glow, from the sun, so bright that his face seems to move in and out of shadows, as if there were ripples in the light. I think: This must be how it is when you see an angel—so bright, so overwhelming that you have to remind yourself to pay attention to the details.

When Jim stood over me beside the pool, on those days when I waited on the cold bench to talk with him about nothing, the sun came through the window panes in the ceiling, filling in the space behind him and outlining his face in gold—like an aura, like later when I saw for the first time Kirlian photography, and Jim explained to me that your skin has light on the inside that not everyone can see.

And suddenly I am laughing, because what is happening to me is what I can only call joy, though I also feel the tears fill up the corners of my eyes and spilling down. Joy so big my body seems to be stretching to hold it in, and I'm taking breaths huge enough to fill up my new lungs and to make new spaces in my unladen heart.

Liam, too, is laughing, his head thrown back, and his face—as it wavers in and out of my focus, disintegrating for a moment into the warm sunlight behind him and then surfacing again so that I can see again the clean, clear features I already find so familiar—that face that reminds me of my Jim, waiting beneath the water for me to peer over the edge and catch him, unharmed, happy, opening his entire self into a smile that he has hidden there for no one else but me to find it.

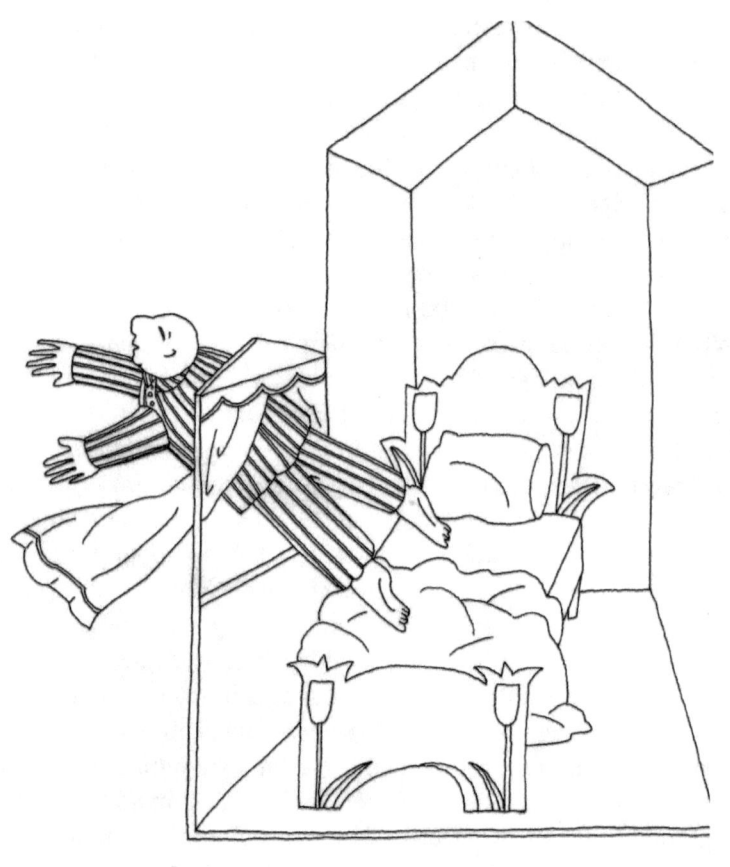

The Mysterious Decampment of Rydel Wents

for S. G. & N. C. Tuell

"Time is the longest distance between two places."
Tennessee Williams, The Glass Menagerie

W hen Rydel Wents disappeared one sunny, late-Winter morning from the town of Louisa, Ohio, no one was more surprised than his colleagues at Astarte Senior High School, where Mr. Wents had, for some fourteen years, taught American literature, English grammar, and, when there seemed to be some call for it (which was rarely), a two-semester Latin "intensive" that satisfied the graduation requirement for students who wanted something more exotic on their transcripts than the customary Spanish or French. In point of fact, there was no one beside Mr.

Wents' colleagues—and, of course, his students—who were in a position to have noted his disappearance, let alone be surprised by it. Apart from his fellow teachers and a few of the parents of his students, with whom he was formally acquainted but rarely socially engaged, Mr. Wents was friendly with few adults in Louisa.

Not that Mr. Wents was unpopular—quite the opposite. Near the middle of each May, for example, a few weeks before the school year closed, Mr. Wents hosted an eagerly anticipated graduation party at his home. The event was well chaperoned by parents and by other teachers, which was, indeed, the point: Mr. Wents' graduation "bash" was, as he put it to his students, "your first adult party," and they were expected to mingle with the adults (as much as the adults with the students), and to participate in conversations of genuine substance that did not involve television shows, sports, or popular music. Though the annual parties were officially held on behalf of graduating seniors, they were open to any student who was willing to abide by the few additional rules: no smoking, no standing in the corners talking to people you knew before you came, and no alcohol.

The latter rule was officially broken each year by Mr. Wents himself, who, precisely at nine o'clock, poured every adult and every graduating senior a half-glass of champagne (ginger ale for the rest or for those who declined) and proposed a toast. Though Mr. Wents was not known to be a garrulous or outgoing man, his toasts were invariably held to be both eloquent and warm, even touching, with no hint of the cloying sentimentalism that students, parents, and teachers alike understood would befall their lot when graduation day itself rolled around. But perhaps the fulsome prognostications and tearful farewells of graduation ceremonies were needed for their ritual qualities, and perhaps Mr. Wents' party was equally necessary for the balance it provided in the proceedings, which, in a way, it unofficially launched.

In any case, the graduation party was not the sole reason for the high esteem in which Mr. Wents was held. As a teacher, he was also well liked, if not necessarily beloved, by his students, who considered him neither "fruity" (allowances being made for the fact that he was an English teacher) nor prone to giving unexpected quizzes or salting his exams with vague and deliberately deceiving questions.

For his part, Mr. Wents found his students, with a certain few exceptions, ill prepared, crude in their humor, and rather sadly unambitious, though on the whole a good deal kinder in spirit than the general impression of teenagers provided by the television specials on "modern youth" that he so often saw advertised during prime-time programming.

If Mr. Wents had an eccentricity, it was his obsession with rooting out laziness. He ruthlessly flunked cheaters and he detested plagiarizers. He had, in fact, recently made an impression on his peers by publishing a paper in a little English journal that told teachers how to use the internet to track down essays either forged outright or purchased from one of the term-paper factories that Mr. Wents considered his personal windmills. In his classes, he railed against such offenders, often saying more than he intended about intellectual dishonesty and the moral bankruptcy of treating knowledge as though it were a commodity that could be bought, sold, or bartered like so much barley.

Mr. Wents' passion was largely lost on his students, unfortunately, who believed that a commodity was precisely what knowledge was, and who considered themselves, though they would perhaps not have phrased it this way, to be purchasing, with their six-and-a-half hours per day of comparative obedience, a certain useful chunk of it that could later be exchanged for something they wanted more.

Although there were two foreign students at Astarte each term— one from Taiwan, the Winter Mr. Wents disappeared, and one from Argentina—and though the owners of Louisa's four motels, all of whom were from India and all of whom were named Patel, usually enrolled at least one child in Astarte each year, Mr. Wents' students were rarely anything other than white or black. Race and national origin were not the major dividing lines in Louisa, however—many of the white students affected black speech anyway, or a certain stylized, MTV-quality version of it, and not infrequently chanted rap lyrics to the rest of the class when Mr. Wents asked, on the first day of his senior Am Lit survey, whether anyone knew any poems by heart. What assigned students to groups was money, their parents' occupations, and the colleges they imagined attending, if they imagined attending college at all.

Mr. Wents overheard their conversations about clothing and cars and computers and their slurs against students who worked for minimum wage at McDonald's or whose mothers had been seen leaving a thrift store. He tried to be especially gracious with his classes around prom and graduation time because he recognized how these events threw students' social standing into brutal relief.

When Mr. Wents failed to appear on campus that certain March morning, the natural assumption was that something terrible had happened to him. Were he not seriously ill (or worse), Mr. Wents was not a man who missed work without phoning. In fact, he was a man who scarcely missed work at all. Mrs. Piontkowski, the typing teacher, recalled that Mr. Wents had once had strep throat and had stayed away from school for three days, mostly out of concern for exposing his students and colleagues to infection. Other than that, Mr. Wents' attendance was perfect.

The principal's secretary, Ms. Tyler, phoned Mr. Wents' house as soon as the morning tardy bell had rung, but reported that there was no answer, a bit of information that only fueled the bleakest speculations. As Coach Lytton had a free hour immediately after the brief homeroom period, he volunteered to drive to Mr. Wents' home, a small, two-story house in a subdivision, red brick like virtually all the other houses on Mr. Wents' and surrounding blocks, but, unlike those others, outfitted with touches that expressed a certain sense of individuality, even of irony. Mr. Wents' storm shutters, for example, had been custom-crafted in the colonial style, with the header and footer rails, as well as the styles, whimsically scalloped, the hinges and catches cleverly recessed, and were carved all over in a series of bas-relief scenes that might have struck certain observers as vaguely Renaissance in inspiration. The shutters were painted a deep forest green; the house trim was otherwise a glossy black. Coach Lytton was to remark, later, that the shutters made the house look like Hansel and Gretel's cottage. The witch's cottage, Mr. Wents might have corrected him, though he would have understood that a man in Coach Lytton's profession could be expected to remember his Grimms' tales in only the most general sense.

In any case, Mr. Wents' shutters were naturally pegged back on such a fine day, and Coach Lytton walked the perimeter of the house twice, peering through the sheers and calling Mr. Wents' name, but was forced to return to Astarte with the news that nothing at Mr. Wents' house struck one as out of the ordinary, leaving aside, of course, the fact of his absence. Coach Lytton was unable to tell for certain whether Mr. Wents' silver-blue Acura were still in the carport (the rolling garage door had been fashioned without external windows), though he said he doubted that the car was there because, having called loudly through the door, he felt certain that the sound that returned to him was the hollow echo of a large and empty room.

As the hours passed, several teachers stopped at the administration building to see whether Ms. Tyler, whose day was now given over entirely to the mystery of Mr. Wents, had uncovered any new information. About mid-morning, she placed a call to Mr. Wents' sister, Nathalie, in St. Louis, Missouri, who was listed in his employment file as his emergency contact. Nathalie Wents was, of course, not at home in the middle of the work day, and Ms. Tyler left a message on her machine that was as bland as possible under the circumstances. As she had been instructed, Ms. Tyler also left the principal's home phone number in the message she recorded, as well as the number of the school office. No one was particularly satisfied with this action, however, as it brought to the matter neither a conclusion nor any new clues. Unfortunately, what little personal information they possessed about Mr. Wents was, with the call to his sister, entirely exhausted.

At first lunch, Coach Lytton suggested that the police might be called to break into Mr. Wents' house to make sure he wasn't still in there, and it was a credit to Ms. Tyler's charm and persuasiveness that the dispatcher with whom she spoke eventually agreed to send an officer to check on a man who had, by that point, been officially missing for only a few hours. In the event, it was the paramedic unit of the local fire house who responded to the dispatcher's call. Though they were able to remove Mr. Wents' front door with minimal damage (but only after canvassing his neighbors to ensure that Mr. Wents had given no one a key for use in emergencies and after carefully checking for a spare copy beneath each of the terra cotta flower pots along Mr. Wents' front walk, empty now of the snapdragons, *Salpiglossis*, floss, and other annuals they held after each season's final frost), the information they relayed to the police dispatcher, who in turn phoned Ms. Tyler, was that neither Mr. Wents nor "a body" were inside the house proper, the basement, or the garage, and that there was no indication at all that any trouble had befallen Mr. Wents inside his own home. There was nothing resembling a note (suicide had not been mentioned explicitly, but it was understood that a note was the sort of thing they might find), though they acknowledged that they hadn't spent a great deal of time going through Mr. Wents' personal effects. The only odd thing, the dispatcher said, was that the paramedics had found the beds neatly made in both the master and the guest bedrooms, which led them to wonder whether Mr. Wents (whose Acura was, by the way, in its customary place in the carport) had spent the night elsewhere.

Were that to have been the case, the mystery would only have deepened, because Mr. Wents' disappearance was first noted on a Tuesday morning, the day after Mr. Wents had arrived as usual for the start of the school week, and his students and the other teachers were firmly convinced that he had said and done nothing to suggest that he planned to be away for the evening or—more to the point— that he did not intend to return the following day. In fact, his senior literature students reported, on Monday he had shown them parts of a video of *The Glass Menagerie*, the play they were to study in the coming weeks, and asked them to read the first four scenes overnight for homework. The scenes, he assured them with perhaps a trace of weariness, were quite short.

Emmett Mattox, a student in that class, said that Mr. Wents had promised they would see the entire video in time, but had spent Monday fast-forwarding to various scenes, in order, as he put it, to introduce them to the major characters. After they had watched several speeches and discussed briefly some of the ways in which hearing an actor deliver lines was different from reading the same lines on the page, Mr. Wents had proposed that they begin their study of the play by focusing on two linked questions: Did they think that Amanda Wingfield, the mother in the piece, was crazy? And, Did they believe that Tennessee Williams thought that Amanda Wingfield was crazy?

It took no longer than the end of the first day of Mr. Wents' absence for Mr. Acevedo, the drama teacher, who subtly resented the fact that Mr. Wents taught plays in his literature classes, to forge a series of connections between the play and Mr. Wents, upon all of which he declaimed in the teachers' lounge to those who would listen, a group that grew smaller as the days of Mr. Wents' absence wore on.

Mr. Wents' sister lived in St. Louis, Mr. Acevedo pointed out; *The Glass Menagerie* was set in St. Louis. There is a central disappearance in *The Glass Menagerie*—that of the father—a correlation that was clear on its face. In one scene, Tom Wingfield, Amanda's son, claims that he is at last "waking up" to his life but adds, archly, that all the signs of it are "interior" and, thus, invisible to others. There was, in addition, Mr. Wents' crucial parting question to his class: Was Amanda Wingfield crazy? What could that have meant other than that Mr. Wents, on the very eve of his disappearance, had begun to distrust his own sanity?

Finally, according to Emmett Mattox, who became Mr. Acevedo's principal informant regarding Mr. Wents' behavior during that final class, Mr. Wents had taken pains to explain to his students that he had chosen to show them a video of the more famous Katherine Hepburn version of the play, which had been made for television in 1973, rather than of the original 1950 film version; the nearly forgotten 1966 version with Shirley Booth; or the 1987 version, some of whose stars his students might actually have recognized, because the play had been bludgeoned near to death in that incarnation, Mr. Wents had opined, by the techniques of so-called modern acting.

Emmett had carefully recorded these details in his notebook, though it struck Mr. Acevedo as strange that he had bothered to retain so much of Mr. Wents' obscure Hollywood trivia, information that seemed unlikely to interest a boy such as Emmett, inward and stick-thin as he was, with inchoate personal tastes, an ambiguous intellect, and a propensity to stutter when he was nervous.

Mr. Acevedo had nonetheless determined, by peering into Mr. Wents' personnel file as it lay open on Ms. Tyler's desk during the early confusion about whom to contact on the missing teacher's behalf, that Mr. Wents himself had graduated from Astarte in 1973, at the point when the school was called "high" but not yet "senior" because the seventh and eighth grades were still taught there. Clearly the impact of the Hepburn film on the impressionable young Rydel Wents in the very year of his graduation had been more profound than anyone had realized. In fact, Mr. Acevedo considered this last his greatest insight, coming as it did as the result of something like detective work, though he was vague on what the details meant, taken all together, or what light they shed upon the situation of Mr. Wents. That notwithstanding, Mr. Acevedo was later known to comment, with studied equivocation, that he had all along believed that the key to the entire episode lay in *The Glass Menagerie*, if only people would read it carefully.

What Mr. Acevedo didn't tell, in part because he feared something might be revealed in the telling that he had not himself grasped, was that he had specifically discussed *The Glass Menagerie* with Mr. Wents on an afternoon not long before the latter's disappearance. Knocking shyly on the door of Mr. Acevedo's classroom, Mr. Wents had asked whether the drama teacher felt inclined to pass along any insights into *The Glass Menagerie* that might be helpful in teaching it. It was no more than a polite gesture, Mr. Acevedo believed, but the two men had talked.

Mr. Acevedo, in fact, never taught *The Glass Menagerie* because he found it static and maudlin, and he said as much to Mr. Wents. "It's a play about immobility, about characters whose neurotic attachment to the past ruins them for living in the present," Mr. Acevedo had begun, speaking in the tones he normally reserved for lectures. "It's about failed dreams and past glories, the way almost everything Williams wrote was. In other words, it's an ancien régime bore, and there's nothing in it that teenagers know about or care to know. If I tried to teach it, I'd never make myself heard above the snoring."

Mr. Wents had taken a seat at one of the student desks, and he looked up at Mr. Acevedo, who stood before the blackboard, the base of his spine pressed uncomfortably against the chalk rail. "Well," Mr. Wents said after a moment, tapping a pencil against the edge of his shoe, "perhaps you're right. I mean, my first reaction is that you're being a little hard on old Tennessee, but you may be right.

"My thinking is that *Glass Menagerie* speaks to the way we each create our own fables, our personal creation myths, if you will, out of whatever we've experienced—why we went to school where we did, why we chose this and not that career, a happy childhood or a grim one, what our parents were like. And we piece it all together into a more-or-less straightforward narrative and we tell our stories. That's what we call social success, if you think about it—you go out and you tell your story and are expected to be a receptacle for the stories of others. But in *The Glass Menagerie*, the characters' stories have become, so to speak, fossilized.

"Amanda, for example, is almost a kind of Ancient Mariner, condemned to repetition. And her children know it's wrong—they even know it's deadly—but no one knows how to fix it. Tom leaves, but he's merely reliving his father's desertion. And Laura, of course, is doomed. I think that's what teenagers might see in it—the danger of being trapped, perhaps without knowing it, in the wagon ruts your parents have laid down. I only think of that analogy, I suppose, because I happened to see them a few summers back, when I drove out through Kansas and Oklahoma with my sister. And there they were, left over from the days of the great westward push—these thin, tan grooves where grass still won't grow that point straight out across the prairies. Over the decades, as people traced the same routes again and again, the ruts got deeper and the mud hardened like cement, until it was actually dangerous to travel in the old tracks. They'd become grooves in stone, and they could splinter a wagon wheel or make the animals lame. I imagined they were what you might see if you could take a photograph of time passing.

"So I was thinking that students might see that in it—a caution about the importance of knowing when it's time to escape from whatever was planned for you by someone else, or maybe about stepping out of the paths that seem most obvious."

Mr. Wents paused while Mr. Acevedo regarded him. "Well," Mr. Wents chuckled, "I'm not making a lot of sense. Anyway, I guess it's unusual, my being here."

Mr. Wents' sister arrived just over forty-eight hours after Ms. Tyler's tentative phone message, though Ms. Tyler found herself, for several days more, in the position of continuing to be considered the official clearinghouse for information regarding a man she barely knew. Making a disappearance struck Ms. Tyler as a highly private act, and the role into which she had been thrust, more or less by circumstance, was distasteful to her.

As a consequence, she was eager to refer all inquiries regarding Mr. Wents to his sister, and began to do so immediately upon the latter's arrival. In a small town like Louisa, however, where nascent mysteries so frequently metamorphose into ordinary exaggerations, an event like Mr. Wents' disappearance fed the need of individuals to feel implicated in grander crises, and, by the time Ms. Tyler had said for the dozenth time, "Well, his sister is here now. You should probably ask her that," she was less cordial than she had originally planned to be.

The appearance of Mr. Wents' sister, of course, meant that someone was on the scene who was more-or-less authorized to go through Mr. Wents' personal effects in search of clues that no one else had been positioned to uncover. Nathalie Wents did her best to understand (indeed, to forgive) the extreme curiosity of those whom her brother had taught and with whom he worked, but she was not, herself, an inquisitive person and she found that the pressure to produce answers made her jumpy and impatient.

By the time she arrived, the police were ready to open an official missing-persons case on Mr. Wents, which meant that Nathalie Wents spent most of her first two days in Louisa in the company of detectives, trying to answer their questions and making a genuine effort to investigate each of the avenues they suggested (stacks of mail, credit card receipts, address books, journals) for information that might help them find Mr. Wents.

As far as Nathalie Wents was able to determine, however, her brother's mail was neither exotic nor revealing, and, if he had kept diaries or datebooks of any kind, she did not find them. His lesson plans, meanwhile, were located in folders in his desk at school, but were of no more help in determining whether Mr. Wents did or did not imagine a future for himself in Louisa. If the lesson plans had advanced no more than a week or two and then stopped, well, that would have meant one thing. If they had gone all the way to the end of the year, that might have meant another.

As has been said, however, Mr. Wents was virtually never absent from school, and he had never been called upon to prepare the kind of detailed notes that substitute teachers find so helpful. His course outlines were dog-eared Ditto sheets, their purple ink faded to near illegibility, upon which a few cryptic marginalia had been added, from time to time, by a hand wielding an almost impossibly fine-tipped pen. "Week One," "Week Two" went the headers, all the way to "Week Eighteen," which marked the end of the semester and which had evidently been "Week Eighteen" for more than a dozen years. Though none of his students reported finding Mr. Wents' lectures dull, the obvious inference was that he had taught his courses in the same way year after year, unvarying, unwavering.

Nathalie Wents began her stay in Louisa at one of its motels, perhaps imagining that her brother might yet return home to find her there, officially uninvited. Out of respect for Mr. Wents and for the troubling events that had brought Nathalie to Louisa, the motel keeper declined to charge her for her room. After a few days, however, and after being encouraged by Mr. Wents' colleagues, she elected to move into the house that her brother had—and there seemed no other word for it—abandoned. His was certainly a more comfortable and commodious home than the one she had left in St. Louis; she was, in particular, grateful for the small, virtuous garden and the neat, green lawn that stretched out from the house on four sides like a picnic cloth. On the advice of the police, Nathalie consulted lawyers, whose talk of petitions to the court, declarations, and administrations of probate struck her not so much as confusing but as beside the point. She and Mr. Wents had no living relatives, and there was no one but him to object if she took over the house.

As the days passed and the end of the school year drew near, each dilatory sunset represented for Astarte's students another turn of the wheel that brought slowly into focus the ten thousand possibilities of summer. For their teachers and parents, summer's approach held another promise: If only summer managed to arrive, the problem of Mr. Wents would be rendered temporarily moot. Teachers effectively disappeared between June and September anyway, burrowing into seasonal hibernation like African frogs beneath the mud. Even for a student to spot one at the market in the interim seemed shocking, like the sighting of a movie star in public.

Time's passing, of course, also helped to transform shock and sadness into resentment, as may sometimes occur even after a death. Mr. Wents had really left them in the lurch, hadn't he? Several of Astarte's teachers were working hard hours to cover Mr. Wents' abandoned classes, the principal having decided against hiring a new teacher to cover the remainder of the semester, and Mr. Wents' lack of documentation now struck them as deliberately unhelpful, even uncollegial.

To show their disapproval, they remarked to one another and, occasionally, even within hearing of their students, how out of character it was for Mr. Wents to have left so suddenly, forgetting his responsibilities. But what else might they have said? Sudden disappearance is in no one's character, with the exception perhaps of escaped convicts or witnesses to gangland violence. Since few rumors are more enticing than those involving a secret past, however, there were those who imagined that Mr. Wents might well have been at least the latter if not the former.

Other semi-fictions grew like pearls around a grain of possibility: Mr. Wents had gone to Cincinnati and been murdered by a prostitute, perhaps even a *male* prostitute. (Mr. Wents' fondness for Tennessee Williams and Katherine Hepburn were reconsidered in the light of this new conjecture.) He had somehow been struck on the head and rendered amnesiac, and was even now wandering the streets of some nearby town, a stranger to everyone but especially to himself.

May came, and with it both the thick Ohio heat and the cicadas, full in the bloom of their seventeen-year cycle. In the overgrowth that encroached upon the narrow county roads and in the woods surrounding the banks of ponds and creeks, they buzzed tirelessly, a camouflaged army wielding angry rattles.

Emmett Mattox, too, had marked the days of Mr. Wents' absence, though he did so only in private, such as when he lay awake in his narrow bed in the pre-dawn hours, pondering his worries the way a child will harass a loosened tooth, prodding it relentlessly with his tongue to gauge degrees of pain. When asked questions about Mr. Wents, Emmett had told what facts he knew, but volunteered no theories of his own. Because no one expected him to be the sort of person who had theories, he was largely ignored once Mr. Acevedo had been distracted from his initial inquisitions.

For Emmett, as for all of Astarte's seniors, graduation day loomed, and, inasmuch as Mr. Wents was not available to host his annual party, another teacher had offered her home a few weeks before the event would otherwise have been cancelled. Emmett had planned to go—had, indeed, promised his few friends that he would meet them there. On the evening in question, however, he sat on the edge of his bed, fully dressed and staring down at the dully glowing surface of his just-polished shoes, until the pale orange light in his room had descended the scale of shadows into darkness. Because it was a Friday, his parents had driven down street for their weekly canasta game immediately after supper, and Emmett was alone in the house.

When the faint light from the face of his wrist watch showed that the hour announced for the party had passed and that another had taken its place, Emmett rose, removing his tie and looping it over the clothes rod in his closet. He replaced his church slacks with blue jeans and, locking the front door quietly, walked into the night.

Emmett felt stealthy, though there was no need for stealth. And he felt he should leave his parents a note, though he could hardly imagine what he might say in a few lines, scratched onto the back of an envelope and attached with a magnet to the refrigerator door, that would make clear to them the state of his mind. Besides, if his parents returned home before him, they would assume he had gone to his graduation party and would not worry.

The walk to Mr. Wents' house was not far, less than two miles, and the night air was bathtub-warm on Emmett's bare arms. He walked slowly, tracing the ascent of the tapioca-colored moon above him, watching the stilted movement of bodies beyond the lighted windows of houses, the gray-blue light show of television screens. He heard laughter, the bark of dogs, music, crickets, the punctuations of silence.

When Emmett rang Mr. Wents' bell, the porch light came on almost immediately, though a few moments passed before Nathalie Wents opened the door. The two stared at one another, balancing curiosity, surprise, disappointment. "I'm Emmett Mattox, ma'am," the boy said when Nathalie didn't speak, "I was one of Mr. Wents' students. One of his senior students."

"One of Rydel's seniors?" Nathalie repeated dimly. In a moment she recovered herself. "Well, forgive me for standing here like a fool," she said. "You surprised me, is all. It's nice to meet you, Emmett. But tonight's your graduation party, isn't it? Shouldn't you be off celebrating?"

"Yes, ma'am," Emmett said. "They invited me, but I decided not to go."

The corners of Nathalie's mouth lifted slightly. "They invited me, too," she said, "but I guess I didn't go either." In the overhead light of the porch Emmett saw that her face was kind, like her brother's. "Won't you come in?" she asked. She stepped back from the door and the boy passed into the living room.

Nathalie followed him, returning to the armchair where she had been reading before Emmett's arrival. A hardback crime novel lay cracked open, face-down against one of the chair's upholstered arms.

"Mr. Wents used to have the graduation parties here," Emmett said.

Nathalie nodded. With an upturned palm she gestured toward the loveseat opposite her chair. "Please," she said.

Emmett sat, his eyes searching the objects in the room. Books filled built-in cases on three walls, and a collection of black-and-white photographs were displayed in elegant metal frames above the fireplace. Emmett could see that two of the photos depicted mountain landscapes, but the rest were abstract compositions of light and shadow that Emmett couldn't assemble into coherent forms from his place across the room. The comfortable, unremarkable furniture told him nothing about whether it reflected Mr. Wents' original arrangements or had been brought from St. Louis by his sister. Across the back of Nathalie's overstuffed armchair a lace antimacassar was splayed like a spider web. Perhaps that item was more to a woman's taste than a man's.

"You've been here before, then?" Nathalie asked.

"No, ma'am. I was just a junior when they had last year's party. I mean, juniors could come, but I...."

"It's so much better when the celebration is in your honor, isn't it?" Nathalie said.

Emmett nodded.

"Well, I've been told more times than I can count what a tradition it was for the graduation party to be held here, and I wondered at first whether I should offer to let them do it again this year, but it just struck me as ... grim. Everyone would be thinking that Rydel *wasn't* here, and I felt it couldn't possibly be...."

"The same."

"That's right. Not the same.

"No, ma'am. I don't expect it would be."

"So then, when the party was to be elsewhere, there seemed no reason for me to show up at all, though they were still so thoughtful to ask." Nathalie marked her place in the novel with a playing card and closed the book, laying it on the table beside her chair. "Still," she continued, "no reason for you to stay away."

"No, ma'am. I just wanted to be ... here," Emmett said.

"Did you?" Nathalie said. "Well, I'm glad for the company." She plucked a mote of lint from the upholstery. "You'd drink a Coke, wouldn't you, Emmett?" she said. "Or orange juice. It's freshly squeezed. I'll give you some ice since it isn't cold yet. Or I could make some coffee. Do you drink coffee?"

"Orange juice," Emmett said. "Thank you."

When Nathalie returned with the juice, Emmett propped the glass between his knees, rubbing his thumbs lightly against the rim. He took a sip. In the glass, a cube of ice calved with an emphatic pop.

Emmett looked up and saw that Nathalie was smiling at him, her eyes patient and warm, her eyebrows raised in an expression of comic alarm. Mr. Wents had done a similar trick, waiting through Emmett's silences, soothing him with insignificant jests until Emmett's self-consciousness fell away, pointless.

"I'm glad you decided to come tonight," Nathalie said at last. "On this occasion, I mean. I know Rydel would have been proud of you and would have wanted to give you his congratulations."

"He helped me a lot," said Emmett.

"You helped him, too. I mean, I'm sure you did. That's the way it is with teachers, you know. It's not just a one-way street."

"I guess not," said Emmett.

Nathalie folded her bifocals into their soft leather case, and began to tap the case against her knee. "Emmett," she asked quietly, "are you here because you have something to say about Rydel? About what happened to Rydel?"

"Oh, no, ma'am," the boy said quickly. "I don't know anything about that." In fact, now that he was actually sitting in Mr. Wents' home, Emmett realized that he never had speculated much about what had become of his teacher. Mr. Wents was gone, and Emmett had accepted the fact as permanent: the way it would be from now on. Others may have wondered whether Mr. Wents might one day reappear, but Emmett did not.

Nathalie allowed her eyes to remain on Emmett's face, not as a challenge but in anticipation that Emmett would continue. If not for that look, Emmett would probably have run down to a stop, not because he had no more to say, but because he was accustomed to being cut off before he was done. He didn't always say things right, he guessed, or people got tired of waiting on him. Still, he recognized that it was curious that he should feel so comfortable sitting without speaking in what was, in reality, the house of a stranger, as if he'd been there a hundred times before, and he wanted Nathalie to share his sense of ease.

"I guess it's unusual, me being here," he said.

Nathalie's burst of laughter surprised him. "Emmett," she said kindly, "you have a dramatic gift for understatement."

No one who doesn't fit in ever escapes being aware of the fact, and Emmett was no exception. He knew he was an improbable person, even without knowing all the reasons why. He understood that people found him odd and that some, more than others, let it show how much he unnerved them. But Mr. Wents, and now his sister, seemed to take him in stride. Emmett tugged the brim of an imaginary Stetson. "Ma'am," he drawled.

"Sir," she replied, ducking her chin and unfurling the edges of her skirt against her chair in an imitation of a curtsy. "But I'm sure you came here with something on your mind," she said. "I guess I'm not quite as good a listener as Rydel, but I expect I'll do."

Emmett leaned forward to set his juice glass on the coffee table. Then he picked it up again and held it. He let out a slow breath. After a few beats he spoke. "I have been thinking some things. Not that it's any kind of an explanation. It's just some ideas."

"Tell me," said Nathalie.

"Well, there were a lot of days when I would go to Mr. Wents' room after school instead of going straight home. It's not far to my house, and I like the walk anyway. I mean, I'd just let the school buses go on without me—they're pretty crowded, and the drivers don't see much of anything that goes on...."

"I can imagine," Nathalie said.

"So I'd go by and peek in his door, and he'd usually be putting papers away or writing grades down in his book, and he'd say, 'Well, here's my friend, Emmett,' and I knew it was okay to go in."

"And he was always there?"

"There was a few times when the room was locked up when I'd go by, but most always he'd be there. And then we'd just talk. About what happened in class that day, or anything. And there were certain things that Mr. Wents liked to talk about. More than others, I mean."

Nathalie shifted in her chair in a way that made Emmett pause. "You're describing a part of Rydel's life I know nothing about," she explained. "What he was like with his students. I mean, you know that someone is a teacher, but.... What *did* you two talk about, Emmett?"

"Well, one of his favorites was time," Emmett said. "He liked to talk about time. Like, kind of philosophical, but not so you couldn't figure out what he meant. I remember this one day, I went by and Mr. Wents was fooling around with his film projector. Some teachers have these certain kids who always work the films, you know? But Mr. Wents, he liked to do that himself. And he said, 'Oh, Emmett, you'll enjoy this.' And he turned the projector on and let the film run for a minute, and then he ran it back a little and played it again, and he said, 'Look at that.'

"Now, I didn't know what I was supposed to look at, because the only thing on the screen was just some guy walking across a room. But Mr. Wents slowed it down as much as it would go, so you could see every frame by itself, and he said how each frame was like a single moment in time, captured by the camera. But also how you could tell that the man moved a little bit between frames, you know, so it looked all jerky. Which means that the camera missed something.

And even if you got the fastest camera in the world, one that took a picture every billionth of a second, which isn't even possible, the man would still be walking *between* the frames, in some place you can't exactly measure with time."

Nathalie's face contorted briefly, her eyes and brows furrowing in a small, tight motion. "All right...," she began, "so Rydel was saying— what? That motion keeps going, but that time ... can't follow?"

"Yeah. Or no. Or, I don't really know either. I think he was saying something like that, though, that we think we understand time because we give names to it—minutes, years, decades, whatever. But it's all just pretend, in a way. Who's to say a second is a second? Or did the moon still take a month to go around the earth during all those billions of years before there was anyone to say it was a month? See what I mean?"

"I'm not so sure," Nathalie said.

"Well, it's all only ideas, anyway, just things to stretch your mind. I'll tell you about another time, when Mr. Wents got on the subject of mountains. You look at them, he said, and they seem completely still and permanent—like they've been standing there forever looking just exactly the way they look when you see them for the first time. But really, they're always either sinking or rising, but so slowly no one can ever see it. So, if you were a mountain, people might be moving around so fast in comparison that you couldn't see *them*. You'd be going along at your normal mountain speed, but people are moving a trillion times faster or something, and they'd be invisible. He said it was like if you could imagine catching time between your fingers like a piece of bubble gum, and pulling it apart further and further, until, at the two thin edges, time started going either really slow or really fast, and things could disappear."

"That doesn't sound much like any English class I ever took," Nathalie said.

"He didn't only teach us English," Emmett said. "I mean, not just what the books said. He talked about anything you wanted to. He told us that people wrote stories and plays or whatever because they were trying to figure something out about life, so you had to talk about life if you wanted to figure out about the writing."

Nathalie nodded. A moment passed, and then she stood and went into the kitchen. Emmett heard the thwack of the knife against the cutting board as Nathalie halved oranges, and then the drone of the electric juicer. When she returned, she carried a fresh glass for each of them. They sat together in the companionable quiet of the room.

"I'm trying to add up what you said, Emmett," Nathalie began, "and if I'm understanding you right, your idea is that Rydel.... I'm not even sure how to put it. That he disappeared because he somehow ... *went into time*?"

"I don't know it for a true fact," said Emmett, "but Mr. Wents, he used to say that there were all these streams of time flowing around us, an infinite number, even though they're invisible. And that made me start to thinking that maybe, if you could only figure out how, a person could just put his foot out and step into a different stream."

"Would you want to do that," Nathalie asked quickly, "even if it meant you couldn't step back?"

Emmett chewed the edge of his thumbnail. "Some days," he said.

Nathalie stared at her hands, folded in her lap, her head down. Emmett wondered if he'd upset her, and yet the stillness between them remained elastic and smooth. He closed his eyes and imagined coming to a complete stop. In the quiet, Emmett could hear the rhythmic *sit-sit-sit* of his wrist watch, the whisper of the second hand marking the moments.

"Let me show you something," Nathalie said at last.

She led Emmett to a large, square room whose entrance was nearly hidden by the stairwell. As Emmett entered, he saw that dozens of clocks in ornate wooden or marble cases clustered on every horizontal surface. More hung on the walls in carefully balanced groupings, and, in each of the four corners, a stately grandfather clock stood upright against the commissure.

"This is Rydel's clock room," Nathalie said. "There are forty-three of them, almost all of them antiques. He started on clocks as a hobby when he was about your age, going around to junk shops and farm sales and picking up broken-down clocks he could get for next to nothing. He'd buy them and he'd fix them up again. If you can believe it, I actually recognize a few of these clocks from when Rydel and I were still young enough to be living with our parents. Anyway, it took him months sometimes to get them looking new—he'd repaint the dials and fill in the slightest dents in the wood. Very exacting work. More patient than I could ever have been."

She opened a wide drawer in a cherry-wood console table on which two large tambour clocks stood on squat pedestal bases, their fat, round faces the unblinking eyes of an owl, the cases themselves tapering, toward the edges, like the ends of a bell curve. The bottom of the drawer was subdivided into dozens of compartments, in which lay an assortment of nearly invisible springs and gears, a set of magnifying loupes, a collection of dwarf screwdrivers, a pair of pliers whose slender nose was as narrow and sharp as a sewing needle. Several small bottles of paint shared a niche with a clutch of artist's brushes whose tips had been sheared to leave only a few sable bristles. From the drawer came the faint, spicy odor of varnish.

"Rydel's clock tools," Nathalie said. She took an envelope from the drawer and held it open so that Emmett could see the wafer of metallic paper that rested inside. "Gold leaf," she said. "The manufacturers sometimes etched the face glass with this. Rydel used to say you had to hold your breath the whole time you were working with gold leaf, or it would fly away like milkweed fluff."

Nathalie followed Emmett's gaze around the room. "But all the clocks have stopped," the boy said.

"They have," Nathalie agreed. "By the time I got here, they'd run down. Or most of them, anyway. Some are the kind that are set to go eight days or more without winding. But they all stopped eventually, and I just let it be."

"Let's wind them," Emmett said.

Nathalie hesitated. She had more or less decided to have nothing to do with the clocks, which seemed to belong so intensely, so privately to Rydel's life. "There really are quite a few...," she began, but Emmett wasn't listening. He'd begun to walk the perimeter of the room, running his fingers lovingly over the surfaces of the still, silent clocks. Nathalie watched him, dreamy and tenuous in his transit. He was smiling for the first time since he'd entered the house, and Nathalie felt eagerness, even joy, surge out of him, an emphatic blossom in a landscape that had seemed so bleak. "Well, why shouldn't we?" she said after a moment. "What time is it, then?"

"Just about twenty of ten," Emmett told her.

"If we hurry, we might be able to get them all done before they're due to strike."

They began to work on the clocks, winding them with decorative, nickeled keys, urging heavy pendulums into action, or pulling on delicate chains to raise counterweighted finial bobs and set mainsprings in motion again. They unlatched glass doors and undid miniature hasps on brass bezels in order to reach the clocks' hands and carefully nudge them into position. Emmett called out the minutes so they could synchronize their efforts. "Nine forty-five," he said. "Nine fifty-two." They finished their task just as Emmett declared, "Nine fifty-seven."

They stood just inside the room, Nathalie at Emmett's back, waiting out the final moments. When the clocks at last struck their discordant carillon of chimes, bells, gongs, and chirps, a passion of shivarees, cannonades, and random harmonies spilling from their dormant throats, Emmett began to laugh, his clean, high sound climbing above the gamelan tumult. As the last of the clocks fell silent, and Emmett's laughter, too, remained only as a kind of oscillation in the air, Nathalie spoke from behind the boy. "I think my theory of what happened to Rydel is simpler than yours," she said. "What I think is that he just got tired of being who he was, and he went somewhere to try being someone new.

"The ironic thing is that his going away made it possible for me to be someone new, too. I don't think I even knew that's what I wanted until after I was already here, where nobody knew me, and suddenly I could see a possibility I hadn't ever imagined."

"You didn't like St. Louis?" Emmett asked.

"I wouldn't say that, exactly. It's just that.... Sometimes, Emmett, you find yourself on a path, and it isn't even a bad path, but you just don't remember choosing it, and you can tell it doesn't fit, and you want to step out of it but you can't see how."

"You won't go back, then?"

"No," she said, "I don't even think of it."

Nathalie moved closer to the boy, pulling him against her and enclosing him in the circle of her arms. Emmett's body seemed to stretch to fill her embrace, as if he had been waiting for her touch, and, against her body, Nathalie felt the thin bones of his shoulders, of his chest, light and hollow as a bird's. Emmett looked down and watched the two hands clasped together against him, realizing that these familiar hands had waited patiently to pass their comfort on to him.

Nathalie leaned into the angle of Emmett's neck and spoke against his ear. "And you can do it, too, Emmett, if you ever want to. You don't have to take only what people say is meant for you, if you don't feel it. You can decide to be someone new, if ever you decide. If ever you really need to. I think you know that. I think you've known that for a while."

They stood together in the doorway, surrounded by Rydel Wents' clocks now whirring and ticking and beating again in their renewed life, and listened as his clocks counted out, for their pleasure alone, all the time in the world.

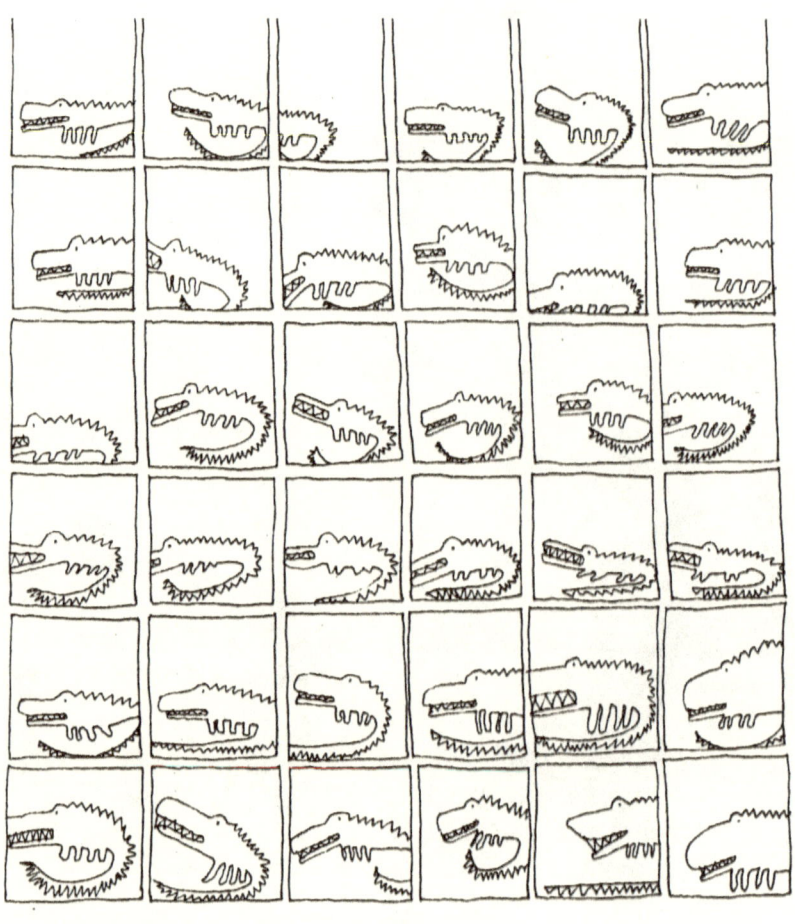

Present Company Excepted

for William J. Mann

Eddie's invitation to supper was what Marcus was on about. As soon as he had retrieved Eddie's phone message from the service—and made Ross listen to it twice for nuances—he began to plan an emergency brunch. They all needed a chance to brainstorm before the night in question.

"Why are you making such a big deal about this?" Ross asked.

Marcus picked up the phone and began punching in Victor and Tim's number. "I do not happen to be aware of making a big deal out of anything," he said. "What I happen to be aware of is calling my friend, Victor."

Ross rolled his eyes. "Like I said."

Marcus arranged his face into an expression that was officially unimpeachable but which, he knew, made Ross grind his teeth: eyes vague and long-suffering, brows elevated in faint interest, lips an inscrutable Maginot line—a gaze that said, "While *you* are being impossible, *I* am mature enough to hold my tongue."

"Excuse me while I go start dinner," Ross said.

Marcus watched Ross disappear through the bat-wing doors into the kitchen. He chewed his lower lip and waited for the sound of a connection at the other end of the line. When Victor picked up, he barely had time to form the word "Hello?" before Marcus blurted out, "He *cannot* be serious!"

"Oh, God," Victor said, "you got your invitation, too. Did he *explain* anything?"

"Eddie does not explain, doll. All he said was 'Please come for supper Sunday evening so you can meet Angel.'"

"Does he think we don't know where this one *came* from?" Victor squeaked. "I mean, I've heard of working the streets, but this is ridiculous."

"Which is *precisely* why I am calling. We need to meet up and get our stories straight before we show our faces on Sunday and make the mistake of saying something we mean. Can you and Tim have brunch this Saturday?"

"Ah, clever girl. Yes. We'll strategize over brunch. Who else do you think Eddie has invited?"

"Seth and Adam-the-lawyer, no doubt, though I'm sure Adam plans to be out of town, which means we'll have the incomparable pleasure of listening to Seth star in his favorite role as grass widow. And probably Joel, his new deputy assistant something-in-accounting. He's Eddie's excuse to play Dolly Levi these days."

"Do tell."

"Age-old story, darling. Eddie's determined to see Joel married—or, as they say, know the reason why."

"*I* know the reason why. Because he keeps inviting him to supper with friends who are already married."

"Personally, I'd rather he didn't even *have* single people to these little parties," Marcus grumbled. He lowered his voice dramatically. "It's too much temptation for Ross."

"Of course. For *Ross*. I gather Miss Gypsy Feet is at home, otherwise you wouldn't be trying to sound like Brenda Vacarro."

"You gather correctly. Oh, God, who else? Eddie's message said he thought there'd be ten of us. So do you think that means he's counting Seth-minus-Adam plus Joel as one pair and he's invited another couple, or does he think Adam *is* coming and he's invited a date for Joel?"

"Oh, I'm sure he's got someone in mind for Joel or he won't get to sing 'Matchmaker.' Oooh. But if Adam *isn't* coming, it'll be an odd number, and you know Eddie won't be happy about *that*."

"I *hate* it when Eddie does this. All right. Well, we can't ask Joel to brunch. He's Eddie's friend and he'll tell him everything we say. You call Seth and see if Adam is or isn't going to be around for Sunday night—and get them to come to brunch. Can you do that? That'll be six out of ten, anyway."

"Aye aye, Cap'n."

"You're a god, Victor, honey. The usual place, hm? Say eleven in the a.m.?"

"Righty-o."

"Perfect. You know, I've never understood why everyone says you're so hard to get along with. I've *always* found you so very, very cooperative."

"Fuck you, too."

"Bitch."

"Cunt."

"Bye."

The "usual place" was The Piccolo Gardens, a brunch spot in Pacific Heights that featured overpriced Eggs Benedict, handsome waiters, and a fountain in the outdoor garden whose centerpiece was a group of putti who stood, shoulder to shoulder, urinating into a clam shell below their feet.

Marcus had been right: Adam wasn't expected back in San Francisco until Wednesday of the following week. As a result, he wasn't at brunch; Victor, too, showed up without Tim in tow. "He decided he needed to go into the office," Victor explained, but Marcus strongly suspected that they'd had a fight and that Tim had bowed out of the brunch at the last minute. Tim, in his opinion, didn't always try very hard to fit in with the group.

Ross, Marcus, and Victor were already at the table when Seth arrived.

"So Seth," Victor began when they were settled and mimosas had been ordered all around, "are you missing Adam much?"

"I missed him a little this morning when I woke up," Seth replied, "but he just left the day before yesterday. I'll miss him more in a few days."

"Oh, but by then you'll be much too busy to miss him, won't you, dear?" purred Victor. Marcus and Ross laughed. "I still have that little email missive you sent me last time Adam was out of town."

"I specifically remember telling you to get rid of that," Seth said.

"Did you? Oh, you probably did, but it seemed much too useful to throw away. Did you tell Adam about that time?"

"I tell him whatever he asks," Seth replied.

"Which just means that the poor mooncalf didn't come up with the right question," Victor said. He turned to Marcus. "Can you imagine anyone being so clueless about his own lover?"

"It isn't like that," Seth said. "Adam...."

Victor gave a little hoot. "*Trusts* you?" he trilled. "That's so sweet. Marcus, isn't that sweet?"

"You know what they say about queens who live in glass casas," Marcus said.

Victor ignored him. He turned back to Seth, "Anyway," he said, "I'm sure he'd be fascinated by this note. Seth asked me to take him to a well known, not to say infamous, park—"

"Where I'm sure you terrified a troupe of Brownies who were there on a field trip," Marcus broke in. "Look, there's my friend, Darryl. Yoo hoo! Darryl!" He waved across the garden to where Darryl leaned against the outdoor waiters' station, talking with Roman, one of the restaurant's two owners. Roman was standing in that morning for an employee who had called in sick and he wasn't happy about it. As he complained, the thick bundle of oversized menus wedged beneath his arm threatened to burst from his grasp. Darryl waved back, then waggled a finger in the air to indicate that he would need a few minutes to join the group.

"You invited Darryl?" Ross hissed under his breath.

"Good Lawd!" Victor drawled. "I don't wants ta alarm y'all, but somebody done let a *colored* woman up in the place."

"Ssshhh!" Marcus said. "He'll hear."

"Is he invited to Eddie's?" Seth wanted to know.

"Well, sort of," Marcus said. "I invited him. Oh, knock it off," he added, gauging the expressions on his friends' faces. "I *told* Eddie. In fact, I said I knew someone who was just dying to meet Joel, and of course Eddie said he was delighted to have him."

"So he's a party favor for Joel?" Victor asked.

"He's a guest like the rest of us," Marcus answered. Ross snorted into his napkin and said nothing.

"Wait a minute," Seth whined. "That's you three plus Tim makes four. Eddie and Angel are six, Joel and Darryl are eight. And I'm number nine. That's an odd number. Eddie wouldn't have been 'delighted' unless you went and told him that Adam was coming after all. You did, didn't you?"

Marcus looked exasperated. "Oh, for crying out loud," he said. "If it's such a big deal, why didn't *you* tell him that Adam was going to be away?"

"When I RSVP'd, I *did* tell him," Seth sputtered. "But now you've made it sound like Adam changed his plans or something. How was I supposed to know that you'd decided to appoint yourself the ... the ... the *cruise* director?"

"Exactly how I would have put it," Victor broke in, "except I would have said 'control queen.'"

"Oh, get over it," Marcus said. "Eddie will be fine."

Ross sighed. "Don't you think it's going to be a little obvious to Darryl that the only reason you've invited him is because Angel's black, too? I mean, Darryl barely knows Eddie. He barely knows *us*, while I'm at it."

"Angel is not black. He's from Central America or something."

"The Dominican Republic. And he's black."

"He speaks Spanish."

"Yes," Ross said. "And he's black."

"Well, whatever," Marcus said. "If there's someone there for Angel to relate to, what's so wrong with that?"

Victor laughed. "Well, I guess we're just gonna have to put your little ole name into the hopper for the Politically Correct Fagolah of the Year Award, aren't we?"

Seth, who had been silent during the interchange about Darryl, spoke up again. "I can't believe you told Eddie that Adam would be back in time for the dinner party," he said.

"Look," Marcus snapped, "if I promise to buy the next round of mimosas, do you think I might have even the slimmest chance of getting the three of you to shut the fuck up?"

"Geez," said Victor, a sly smile on his face. "Tina Testy."

Marcus glared at him and would have spoken, but Darryl chose that moment to take his seat at the table.

"Hey, everyone," he said.

"Darryl! Darling!" said Marcus. "Welcome, welcome! Let's see. You know Victor and Ross. And this is—"

"Seth," Darryl said. "We've met."

"Really?" Marcus said, blinking stupidly. "And how do you two know each other?"

"Uh ... well," Seth stammered. "We met at—"

"Not another word!" Victor interrupted. "And you get an 'F' for hostess etiquette, little Missy," he continued, shaking his index finger at Marcus. "Don't you know you're never supposed to ask gay men where they met? Anyway, it was at the gym, right? That's where all gay men in San Francisco who, if you're not sure where they met each other, that's where they met each other. Now, Darryl, won't you join us in a mimosa? Marcus was just about to buy us a pitcher."

Some two hours later—and despite the shaky beginning—brunch ended on a positive note. The five men left the restaurant in good spirits, aided in part by the half-dozen pitchers of mimosas they had consumed and in part by the bright conversation, which had included Darryl's hysterical imitation of Jack Nicholson as a drag queen (they had all recently seen the new Patrick Swayze movie, *To Wong Foo*, and amused each other at brunch by seeing who could recast the movie's three cross-dressing friends with the most outlandish group of straight male stars).

To Marcus's frustration, however, the topic of Eddie's dinner party resurfaced only briefly when Darryl asked for a rundown of the other guests.

"Well," Marcus had begun, "the five of us, plus Victor's partner, Tim, and then there's this guy, Joel, a friend of Eddie's whom you don't know—"

"We're assuming," Victor interjected.

"And Angel, Eddie's new boyfriend—"

"Whom Marcus doesn't approve of," Victor interrupted again.

Marcus shook his head vigorously. "That's not true. I don't really even know him."

Victor leaned toward Darryl and spoke in a conspiratorial whisper. "Marcus thinks Angel is NOKD. You know, 'Not Our Kind, Dear.'"

The table broke into giggles, and Marcus pursed his lips until his companions' laughter had run its course. He decided to try again. "I will admit, there are some things about their relationship that concern me," he began.

"Like Serbia concerns Bosnia," Victor quipped.

"Like O.J. Simpson concerns Fred Goldman," Ross added.

Marcus held a hand up, fingers splayed. "Skip it," he said, trying to give his voice a threatening edge. The table moved on to other topics.

Later, the men stood outside the restaurant, preparing to say their good-byes. "I'm telling you," Victor was saying, "Dustin Hoffman had the balls to play *Tootsie*, and suddenly that made it safe for every straight boy in Hollywood who was itching to put on a dress."

"I don't know whose idea it was to use the hetties in *Wong Foo*, anyway," Seth said. "It's not like they couldn't have found a real drag queen or two in Hollywood, like they did in *Priscilla: Queen of the Desert*."

"You mean, like Eddie Murphy?" Victor giggled.

"I don't think he is a drag queen," Ross put in. "I think he just *does* drag queens."

Victor began an imitation of Eddie Murphy. "I sweah, officah, dat girl was jes' as real as me!" Marcus shot a look at Darryl to see if he was laughing and, observing that he was, joined the others in applauding Victor's impression.

"I feel like walking," Seth said. "Anyone want to come along?" Victor and Marcus were agreeable, but Ross excused himself, saying that he hoped to spend some time sunning on the deck and wanted to get into position ahead of the late-afternoon fog. Darryl, too, declined. He planned to drive to El Cerrito to visit a friend who was ill, he explained, and wanted to be on his way back before the end-of-the-weekend traffic completely shut down the Bay Bridge.

So it was Marcus, Seth, and Victor who began the slow climb through Pacific Heights to the top of Fillmore Hill, which was the destination Seth had in mind, and to the expansive view of San Francisco Bay that could be had from that vantage point.

"All right, sis. Spill," Marcus said to Seth as soon as he was satisfied that Ross and Darryl were out of earshot. "How do you know him *really*?"

"Rita Relentless," Victor said.

Seth sighed. "I met him at Gregg Johnson's going-away party."

"He was at Gregg Johnson's going-away party? I didn't see him there," Marcus said.

"Well, it was a big party. And he wasn't there for long."

"You mean you—"

"No! He left with Bill ... Bill ... what's his name?"

"Let's see," said Victor. "Gay man in San Francisco. Named Bill. Can't think why I can't narrow it down to a face."

"*Enn*-ee-way," Seth said.

"Oh, wait," Victor continued. "It's Bill Sloan, right? Big shoulders, long hair, sort of Fabio-looking. From Vallejo or some damn place?"

"That's the one," Seth said.

"Oh, please, I've talked to him. How many esses in 'vapid'?"

"Gee, Victor," Marcus interjected, "I've never known you to be so discriminating. In fact, I believe it was you who once offered me this bit of bedroom philosophy: 'You don't have to talk to them—just push their face into the pillow.'"

"I am *speaking* here," Seth said. "So, anyway, I was chasing him around Gregg's apartment, trying to keep him away from Bill Sloan, but the most I could get out of him was his phone number before the two of them took off. And you know how depressing it is when the two cutest boys at the party go home together. Anyway, I'd heard that Bill was, so to speak, one of San Francisco's towering figures, so I thought maybe I was just out of the running."

"Poor Seth," said Victor. "Some men are show-ers and some men are grow-ers. And then there's you."

"Like you would know," Seth snarled.

Marcus waved his hand as if shooing a mosquito. "From what I've been told," he said, "once you get him horizontal, there's nothing towering about it. And I have that from two separate authorities."

"Who?" Victor and Seth asked in unison.

"Scotty Burisima and Jim Fall."

"No! Scotty Burisima slept with Bill Sloan?" Victor asked.

"Jealous cause he never slept with you?" Marcus countered.

"I never said I was interested."

"You didn't have to, darling. It was all in the drool coming down your chin when you asked him to spot you at the gym last week. This time," he added, patting Seth confidentially on the arm, "they really *did* meet at the gym."

The three men laughed. "So like I said," Seth continued, "I had Darryl's number and I called and one thing led to another."

"So is it true what they say about black men?" Marcus teased.

Victor feigned annoyance. "Can we *please* elevate the conversation," he said, "and get to the important details?" He took Seth's elbow. "Now be honest, Sethela. Darryl didn't know you had a lover, did he?"

Seth shook his head. "It didn't exactly come up at the party. I mean ... Adam was out of town ... and then when I called Darryl, I meant to tell him, but he kind of just came right over and then it was too awkward to blurt it out."

"Post-coital confession," Victor giggled. "Very malapropos."

"I did tell him finally," Seth continued. "And it wasn't like he freaked out or anything. He just said, 'You probably shouldn't call me again because I don't do married men.'"

"I wonder why," Victor said. "We're ever so much more discreet."

"And grateful," Marcus added. "Don't forget grateful."

"They should have some kind of club where guys with lovers can go and meet other guys with lovers who just want to fool around," Seth said. "You know—no strings attached."

"They do," said Marcus. "It's called San Francisco."

Victor smiled and pointed across the street. "I know the queen who lives there," he said, indicating a three-storey yellow Victorian situated some distance from the sidewalk. A driveway lined with pencil-straight cypresses led to the front entrance. "He throws a big bash every year, some AIDS benefit thing with three hundred rich fags in tuxedos, and he always has Tim do the flowers."

"Tim's a florist?" Seth asked.

"Yeah, like Mother Theresa was a nun," Victor answered. "You've seen his shop in the Castro—believe me, you have. They've got this huge front window right on the corner, and the display is always something bizarre like five enormous *Protea* upside down in a fish tank, and underneath them there's a little pile of shiny black river rocks, varnished of course, with one huge red anthurium poking up out of it. It's sort of like ikebana meets kitsch. Very post-modern."

"Yikes," Seth said. "That's Tim's shop?"

"That's my Timmy," Victor said. "Exotic plants in bondage. A hundred and seventy-five dollars a bunch. Anyway, I met Eartha Kitt once at one of those parties."

The men were silent for a few moments as they walked. "So ...," Victor asked Seth at last, "I take it that you and Adam are having an open relationship?"

"An open relationship," Marcus sniffed. "That means one guy fucks around and the other guy is miserable, right?"

Seth looked uncomfortable and said nothing, but Victor's and Marcus's determined silence made it clear that an explanation was expected. "Yes, I guess it's 'open,'" he said, "if you want to use such a seventies word. I just don't see what the big deal is if I occasionally see someone when Adam is out of town."

"Well, of course not," Victor said. "Personally, I think it's very clever of you to find a husband who's a lawyer and who travels so much."

"Well, he's very junior now," Seth said. "The firm has this big out-of-town case and they're making him pick up the witness interviews and stuff that other people don't want to do. When he's been there a while he won't have to run all over the place all the time."

"Now there's a style-cramper," Marcus said.

"Besides," Victor went on, "how do we know Adam isn't doing the exact same thing in—Where is he?"

"Denver," Seth said.

"In Denver. Land of cowboys and four-wheel-drive vehicles."

"Oh, yes," said Marcus, "Ex-ta-*reeem*-ly butch!"

"Victor, sweetie," Seth said, "please don't make me murder you in public."

Seth's tone held just enough of a hint of "I'm not kidding" to convince Victor to change the subject.

"We still haven't figured out what we're doing about Eddie," he said, "which I thought was the whole point of this morning's tête-à-tête. I mean, besides eating Eggs Florentine beneath the twin shadows of Waiter Raúl's granite-like pectorals."

"Why do we have to do anything," Seth asked. "We've been to a hundred parties where somebody's showing off his new boyfriend. Let's just go and be casual about it."

"You do not grasp the situation," Marcus said. "This is not just some 'come-meet-the-guy-I'm-fucking-now' party. Angel is.... Angel was...."

Victor filled in the missing word. "Homeless," he said.

"As in recently," Marcus continued. "As in Eddie literally picked this guy up out of a squat on Polk Street and brought him home and set up house."

"Polk Street!" Seth shuddered. "So Eddie is paying him?"

"Well, for God's sake, I don't know if any actual cash is changing hands," Marcus said, "but Eddie buys his clothes and feeds him, and he's living there rent-free. So I suppose you could say Eddie's paying him. The kid barely speaks English."

"The kid barely speaks," Victor said. "Eddie told me it took him weeks to get the guy to tell him his real name. At first Eddie thought he was a little bit crazy, but now he doesn't think so anymore."

"My God!" said Seth. "How long has he been living there?"

Marcus stroked his goatee thoughtfully. "It must be three or four months, wouldn't you say, Victor?"

"Sounds right."

"Well, wasn't he afraid of getting some disease?" Seth continued. "Isn't he afraid of getting robbed?"

Marcus was nodding energetically. "This is why we need to talk. I think Eddie's making a big mistake. This kid could be a drug dealer or some kind of psychopath. And Eddie's just a meal ticket. He's gonna wake up some day with a knife between his ribs, you mark my words."

"Well *that's* a little dramatic," Victor said. "Eddie's not stupid."

"Eddie is being led around by his dick and you know it," Marcus retorted.

"Is this kid really cute or something?" Seth asked.

Marcus made a face. "If you like that sort of thing."

"Yeah," Victor laughed, "that young, café-con-leche skin, tight buns, baseball biceps, uncut pinga sort of thing."

"Scamming, lice-ridden street trash."

"Affection-starved, sweet-faced, open-twenty-four-hours-a-day boy toy."

"What-*ever*," Marcus said.

"How old is he?" Seth wanted to know.

"Oh, I'm sure he's barely twenty-one," Victor answered.

"Is he even really *gay*," Marcus said. "That's the question. Or is he just one of those Hispanic kids who'll do it for money as long as he's the one putting it in, if you know what I mean. Because if that's the case, Eddie could be in real danger if he unwittingly does something that threatens this guy's machismo."

"Knowing Eddie's tastes," Victor smirked, "I doubt that will emerge as a problem."

"Laugh all you want," Marcus groused. "This guy's an illegal, for Christ's sake. For all we know he was a mercenary or something back wherever he came from. There could be a death squad after him."

"Yes-s-s," Victor hissed. "That's *much* more likely than that he just likes Eddie."

Marcus narrowed his eyes petulantly. "I *thought* you were on my side," he said.

"Of course I'm on your side, Marcus-kins," Victor said. "I just think we shouldn't let our imaginations run away with us."

"Maybe he's just desperate for affection since Jack died," Seth offered. "And he has let himself go a little. Physically, I mean. This might have been the only way he could find someone."

"He *is* pushing forty," Marcus agreed.

Victor snorted. "He's thirty-six. *I* am forty."

"He isn't getting any younger, is my point," Marcus said. "And I think Seth is right. Eddie is using Jack's death as an excuse to withdraw. When Ross and I asked him to stay with us for a few days last spring when we had that cabin in Guerneville, he wouldn't come. The only time any of us see him now is when he throws these suppers. He never calls, he's stopped going to the gym, and—"

"No River *and* no gym? Can he be far from suicide?" Victor said.

"I'm going to ignore that," Marcus went on, "because I'm sure you were trying to be humorous. I, on the other hand, am *seriously* trying to keep a friend's best interests in mind. In addition to everything else, Eddie's obsession with this boy has trapped him in that apartment. He can't exactly take him anywhere. I mean, think about it: this kid's probably never even seen a mall or a grocery store. He doesn't speak English, so Eddie can't take him to the movies or to the theater...."

"Eddie is learning Spanish, I understand," Victor said.

"So is this guy a lover or a hobby?" Seth asked.

"*Precisely* my point," Marcus said. "What's wrong with Eddie finding a nice guy his own age, who shares the same interests, who he can talk to, and who there's some future with? He doesn't have to settle for some whore off the street."

"Well, you know Joanne Woodward's line in *The Long Hot Summer*," Victor said. "'The last, desperate resort is strangers.'"

"Well, everyone's a stranger before you meet him, right?" Seth offered.

"Say-eth honey," Marcus said, affecting a syrupy accent, "Miss Victor is quoting Mr. Faulknah and is not to be contradicted. Moah impo'tant, he is speaking regarding a mattah on which he is perhaps our foahmost authority."

"Oh," said Seth. "But when you think about it, it *could* be kind of romantic."

"Yeah," Marcus sneered, "if you think a *Pygmalion* complex is romantic."

"Well, *Pygmalion* was romantic," Seth said. "Or *My Fair Lady*, anyway."

"Seth, darling," Marcus began, "you are twenty-five years old. Officially, you're still a twink. You and Adam have been together for approximately fifteen minutes and you have no idea what is at stake here. I'm sure a little brown on the side seems fun and exotic to you, but Eddie doesn't have that many dating years left. He is, as you say, letting himself go, and I have seen this before, even if you haven't.

Some pathetic, middle-aged fag hooks up with a hustler, the hustler milks his new sugar daddy for all he's worth—but, of course, he's still turning tricks or dealing drugs on the side for spending money—then he ups and leaves one night because somebody has offered to put him in pornos in L.A. and, and, by the time this all plays itself out, Eddie's turned into a troll."

Victor had allowed himself a few giggles during Marcus's speech, but, now that Marcus had paused, he let go with a full-throated burst of laughter. "You *must* write screenplays, Marcus," he said. "That cinematic imagination is wasted on us."

Marcus pretended to ignore Victor's last remark. They had reached the crest of the Fillmore Hill, and he walked to the middle of the deserted street and stood looking out across the Bay, brilliant in the sun. Sailboats dotted the water like tufts of cotton blown across the surface of a lapis mirror. "It isn't right," he said to no one in particular. "One of us ought to do something."

The following evening, seven guests arrived at Eddie's penthouse apartment in the complex on Potrero Hill. As Seth had predicted, Eddie was perturbed to discover that Adam's absence reduced his table to nine, but he was too hospitable to make a fuss about it in front of company. "There are so many lovely people I could have invited to round things out," was all he would allow himself to say.

The guests each met Angel, shook his hand, and then politely ignored him. Perhaps they weren't trying intentionally to shut him out; rather, they were working hard at pretending that Angel's presence in Eddie's apartment was so ordinary that no mention of it was required. Moreover, since they could barely talk to Angel, they were at a loss for ways to include him in the conversation.

Tim, who had a little Spanish, asked Angel some questions about where he was from, but the boy refused to do more than nod or shake his head. In fact, his response to all attempts to communicate was similarly nonverbal. He did, however, meet each of their gazes with a frank, trusting expression, and he raised his eyebrows slightly as he listened to the conversation, opening his wide face in good-natured bemusement. If he was bored by the stream of words he couldn't entirely follow, he wasn't rude enough to show it. Too, he smiled easily, though he did so most readily when Eddie squeezed his hand or touched him on the shoulder. Still, Marcus noted with some annoyance, he wasn't smiling any more warmly or often at Darryl than he was at anyone else.

Once, when Darryl excused himself momentarily to duck into the "little boys' room" and Eddie was trying to get rid of a telephone solicitor, Marcus seized the opportunity to stage-whisper to Ross, "I don't understand why Angel and Darryl aren't hitting it off better. I thought they'd, you know, *like* each other."

"Darryl and *Joel* seem to like each other," Ross whispered back. "Have you noticed?"

"I didn't bring him for Joel!" Marcus said. "And keep your voice down."

"Well, why should Darryl and Angel hook up?" Ross asked. "Darryl doesn't know any Spanish."

"What difference does that make?" Marcus snarled under his breath. "Angel isn't talking to anybody—in Spanish *or* in English."

"I thought that was your point," Ross said.

"No shit that's my fucking point," Marcus muttered crossly, chewing his lower lip.

When they sat down to supper, Eddie had insisted on a toast. "I want to drink to Angel's official 'coming out,' so to speak," he said, "and to the first chance the two of us have had to spend an evening together with my friends, and—I hope, now—*our* friends. Please raise your glasses."

Marcus turned to face Ross so that Eddie wouldn't see him cross his eyes.

"Please do go ahead and eat," Eddie continued when the toast was finished, indicating with a gesture that his guests should begin circulating the platters filled with salmon steaks and bulbs of roasted fennel, "but I wanted to say one or two more things. I know that you've been concerned about me since Jack's death and I appreciate it. And I know, too, that some of you have worried that my new relationship ... that Angel"—he paused to take Angel's hand in his—"that Angel and I.... Well, we're sort of the odd couple, aren't we?"

"I'm sure we'll all drink to that," joked Tim, lifting his wine glass into the air, "but don't blame Angel for being odd." The other guests tittered politely.

Eddie returned a grin. "So all I really want to say is, just be happy for us. And wish me good luck with my Spanish lessons, and Angel with his English lessons, so that pretty soon we can fight with each other in two languages instead of just one. That's all!" He leaned over to Angel and kissed him loudly on the cheek. Angel blushed and nuzzled against Eddie's shoulder. When he spoke, the sound was muffled, "*Salud, dinero, y amor*," he said.

Victor couldn't help himself. "He speaks!" he blurted out.

"Well, of course he speaks," said Eddie. "Now let's eat."

The rest of the table conversation was the usual: travel (Adam and Seth had discovered a small, family-run resort on the Snake River that rented rustic rooms for a reasonable weekly rate and were planning to spend Adam's vacation there in the Fall, despite the five-hour drive to Mendocino County); new restaurants (there was general consensus that the tapas place that had recently opened in the Mission was wildly overrated); and electoral politics ("I'd vote for David Duke for mayor," Joel had said, "if the city would come up with some more parking places").

Marcus, however, was uncharacteristically quiet during the meal. Ross noticed and tried to jolly Marcus into the conversation by poking him playfully in the ribs and, when that didn't produce the desired effect, by whispering baby talk into his ear. That was often enough to draw Marcus out of a dark mood. But it wasn't until the conversation turned to the upcoming Gay Freedom Day Parade that Marcus allowed himself to be distracted for a few moments from his scrutiny of Eddie and Angel. "What's the theme this year, anyway?" he asked. "Does anybody know?"

"Unity Through Diversity," said Eddie. "I saw it in the paper the other day."

"Well, that's deep," Tim said. "But what's it mean?"

"It means," said Victor, "that a Filipino lesbian single mother with environmental illness and a speech impediment shall lead us."

"Wait," Marcus quipped. "Didn't we elect her to the Board of Supervisors last November?"

That broke everyone up and, when the laughter had subsided, Marcus continued with a derisive tone in his voice. "Last year it was 'Strength Through Community.' Who comes up with these Wonder Bread slogans, anyway? I bet we could invent better ones just sitting around this table."

"More realistic ones anyway," said Seth. "How about 'Victory Through Bitching'?"

"Weight Loss Through Purging?" Victor offered.

"Career Advancement Through Promiscuity," said Darryl.

"Better Living Through Chemicals," Ross tossed in.

"Drive Through Banking."

There was a pause, and then laughter rumbled around the table once again. The final contribution was Marcus's, and it turned out literally to be the last words on the subject, as Tim and Eddie both threw up their hands to signal that they didn't intend to enter the competition.

The evening drew to a close not long afterwards. As the men stood in Eddie's narrow foyer, rooted to the spot by the ritual of final good-byes, Marcus leaned in close to Eddie's ear and said, "We can talk about this more later, but I'm friendly with the guys who own Piccolo Gardens. You know that restaurant on Sacramento that Ross and I like? And they're always looking for help in the kitchen. I don't know if Angel would be interested in that kind of work, but I could put in a word for him if you like."

Eddie opened his mouth as if to object, and Marcus aborted the interruption with a gesture. "I realize they'd have to pay Angel in cash, if that's what's worrying you," he continued, "and I don't think they would have any problem with that. In fact, I know they wouldn't. You should keep this between us, but Angel wouldn't be the first. Anyway, it's just until he finds something else."

"Oh, well," said Eddie. "That's a thought. That's definitely a thought. Let me see how Angel feels, but it might be a good idea. I think he'd like having his own money. You know how men can be about pulling their weight."

"Exactly," said Marcus. "I'll call you."

Victor and Ross were already standing in the outside hallway, looking impatient, and Marcus finished the rest of his farewells quickly. "Isn't Darryl coming?" he asked as they made their way to the bank of elevators.

"Uh-uh," Ross said. "He's getting a ride from Joel."

"I'll bet Joel's giving him a ride," Marcus said, irritation apparent in his voice.

"Green is the *best* color on you," Victor said.

"Remind me to say something snappy to you tomorrow," Marcus yawned. "Right now I'm too exhausted."

Some three weeks after Eddie's dinner party, Seth invited Marcus and Ross to join him and Adam at the movies. "It's that new science-fiction thing," Seth had said. "And it's got that hot guy in it, you know—what's his name? With all the biceps? He was on Jay Leno the other night, pretending to be straight."

"That narrows it down," Marcus said. "What time?"

They agreed to meet for the bargain matinee, but, as Marcus and Ross walked down the sidewalk toward the crowd already lined up outside the theater, they were surprised to see Seth standing to one side, by himself in the damp wind, his hands jammed into his coat pockets. Seth seemed to be scanning the street anxiously, and, as soon as he had spotted Marcus and Ross, he started toward them. Marcus imagined that Adam must be having the usual difficulty parking, and he intended to say as much. They were still twenty feet apart, however, when Seth nearly shouted, "You won't believe what happened!"

"Adam finally left you for the priesthood?" Marcus quipped.

"Angel got arrested."

"Oh, good lord," Ross groaned.

"That's terrible," Marcus said. "Eddie must be a wreck." He looked at his two companions, their dumpling faces swaddled in scarves. "But come on, you guys," he continued. "I mean, I don't mean to speak ill, but you can't be surprised, given where Eddie found him."

"It wasn't like that," Seth said. "He got picked up by the INS. They pulled a raid at the restaurant and they took in four other guys."

Ross frowned slightly. "Angel was working at a restaurant?" he said.

"Piccolo Gardens ," Seth replied, his words coming in a rush. "It just happened, like, two hours ago. Adam's down at the INS right now. He doesn't know a thing about immigration law, but Eddie called us and was freaking out, so Adam said he'd meet him and try to figure out what to do."

"So Eddie's really upset?" Marcus asked.

"He's a mess," said Seth. "He's convinced they're going to send Angel straight back to the D.R."

"Should we all go downtown, then?" Ross wanted to know.

"What good would that do?" Marcus asked, a little too loudly. "I mean, we'd just be in the way." His friends' silence hurried him on: "Unless you two think it would help, then of course we should go right now."

"Well, Adam says not to," Seth said slowly, his eyes on Marcus. "He said that having a lot of people show up might even make it worse. Like, they'll figure all of us knew Angel was an illegal or whatever."

"I just think someone should be with Eddie," Ross said.

"I told you *Adam* was with Eddie," Seth said, a hint of peevishness in his tone.

"And he'll let us know immediately if Eddie needs anything, won't he?" Marcus asked, putting a conciliatory hand on Seth's forearm.

Seth nodded. "That's what he said."

"Then the important thing is for us to be available in case that happens," Marcus said. "So I suggest we—"

"There's no way Piccolo Gardens got raided," Ross interrupted. "It can't be on the regular INS beat. It isn't exactly some 16th Street burrito joint."

"No," said Seth. "Eddie talked to Roman, one of the guys who owns it, and he's convinced that someone dimed them out."

"Not necessarily," Marcus said. "They do have sort of a reputation. Remember, Ross, they had that French guy working there for a long time, the one Roman was dating?"

"I think he was from Quebec," Ross said.

"Quebec, then. But I'm saying, if *I* knew they were paying people under the table, other people must have, too."

"Right," said Ross. "Other people must have."

"Look, " Seth said, "I couldn't reach you guys on the phone, so I just decided to show up and find you. But I don't really feel like going to the movies. I'm worried about Eddie and I want to be home when Adam calls."

"That makes perfect sense," Marcus said. "What if we all go over to your house and wait together?"

Seth, eager to get to his apartment, agreed quickly and all but ran to his car. As Marcus and Ross began the several blocks' walk back to their own parking place, Marcus sensed a heaviness in the air between them. "This is very upsetting," he said finally. "Poor Eddie."

"I didn't even know Angel was working there," Ross said.

Marcus made an unspecific noise in his throat. "About two weeks. I helped him get the job, actually."

"*You* did?"

"Don't sound so shocked. I do good deeds occasionally. Anyway, Eddie preferred to keep it quiet and I just thought the fewer people who knew the better. So I didn't mention anything to you. It *is* illegal, you know."

"Evidently," Ross said.

"Well, I thought it would help," Marcus went on. "But now.... Look, don't take this the wrong way—because you know I'd be the last person to wish something bad on Eddie—but I'm already starting to wonder if maybe this has at least the possibility of turning out for the best. In the end, I mean. If they do send Angel back. Not that it seems that way right now."

"So Angel's being arrested has a silver lining?" Ross asked.

"No! Yes. No. Look, I just mean, if things turn out for the worst—and I'm not saying they will—Eddie can still get his life back to normal."

"I'm betting Eddie would say his life is *already* normal."

"Okay. That didn't come out right. All I'm suggesting is that things might seem different after the fact. Looking back on them, I mean."

When they were at the car, Ross went around to the driver's side but didn't unlock the doors. He leaned against the roof of the car and stood staring at Marcus, who waited with his hand on the passenger-door handle.

"What are you looking at me like that for?" Marcus said. "Open, please." Ross didn't move.

"Spare me the *Murder, She Wrote* moment," Marcus said. "If you've got something to say, say it."

Ross lowered his forehead against the car's roof. He could see, through crossed eyes, the glaze of condensation his breath made on the teal blue surface. When he spoke, his lips touched the cold metal. "Tell me you didn't do this."

"What?" Marcus demanded.

Ross raised his head, and Marcus could see water in his eyes. "Tell me you didn't do this."

"What do you mean? Snitch on Angel? What possible reason would I have had for doing something like that?"

Ross nodded and opened his door. He pressed the button that released the lock on Marcus's side.

They made their way to Seth and Adam's house in silence. Marcus tried curving his left arm around Ross's shoulder as they drove, but he felt Ross tense his back muscles and hunch forward slightly in the seat, perhaps without meaning to. Marcus turned to look out the window. He put his hand back into his own lap.

The Way It Happens

To start things off, she gets mugged. Afterwards, she's lying on the sidewalk. Doesn't know what hit her—that's the cliché, but it's also the truth. There's a lot of violence around. You can't always help the police make a sketch. Anyway, even if you do, it's approximate. They can't get inside your head with tiny cameras and see what your mind sees. Not yet, they can't.

She was walking and then she was down, one shoe off, the sack of groceries burst open and the contents fanned out across the grungy sidewalk: a bag of cat litter, three small containers of vanilla yogurt, a *New Yorker*, some peaches, and cans of soup—tomato, cream of mushroom, broccoli cheese. From this perspective the fissures in the broken cement take on geological proportions. She can see slender, sickly yellow leaves pushing up through the cracks like Carboniferous ferns. That and cigarette butts and the blackened crusts of chewing gum.

The lid of one of the yogurts has popped off and white globs are leaking onto the street. In the moment before people's ankles and shoes start appearing around her head like thick, leafless stalks, she has time to think: *How pathetic. It's bad enough being a crime victim without everyone seeing your cat litter and your single-serving yogurts.*

Her backpack is gone. The man—she guesses it was a man—yanked it off her shoulder and ran. The most expensive thing in it was her new *Norton Anthology of Poetry*—nearly fifty bucks, including tax. Unfortunately, she needs the book for the class she's just been assigned to teach. The ferret-mouthed department secretary made it clear she had no intention of trying to wrangle a desk copy out of the publisher at this late date, so Paula had no choice but to buy one. Now she has to buy two.

When she tells the cop about this later, he repeats his question in a polite, official voice as if she didn't understand the first time: *Did she lose any valuables?* "That was valuable," she insists. "If it was a fifty-dollar watch, you'd consider it a valuable."

The cop looks at her, then writes a few lines in a palm-sized notebook with leather covers—or they look like leather. Just like on television. She wonders where you would get one of those, whether there were cop-supply stores somewhere like art-supply stores. You probably stick with the ones with paper covers for a while when you're a rookie, then you get serious.

The cop asks her a few more questions—he's efficient but bored. He wants to know her driver's license number and she tells him. The mugger took her license, too, long since expired. She'd used her Radiograph to alter the date to make it valid for another two birthdays. She figures they're going to figure this out eventually but she doesn't volunteer. She only uses it for identification, anyway. She's never actually owned a car and she hasn't driven in years. In the city, you don't really. Funny how you could tell a cop that you'd just been robbed and that your wallet was gone and he'd believe you were who you said you were and that you lived where you said you did. Any other time they demanded proof. Now they seemed to understand she couldn't produce any.

But none of that happens for a while and she's still belly down on the sidewalk, just starting to notice that her right knee is stinging where the skin has been scoured off. She sits up and examines her knee, turning back the torn flap of jeans to get the full picture. There's not much blood after all, just some lymph tinged with red oozing out in neat rows where pebbles dug into her flesh. There'll be a bruise.

People help her up, and now all the ankles and pant legs have faces and voices. They're asking her if she's hurt, if she feels dizzy, does she want someone to call an ambulance. Mostly she feels conspicuous and embarrassed; so she answers no to all the questions. She's read about this: It's part of the psychology of being a victim. You feel guilty. You wish you could be invisible. People's sudden pity and concern flood in like someone's turned the hose on you. Poor you: But don't you look ridiculous with your pants ripped and one shoe still AWOL and your sad groceries strewn across the pavement for everyone to see. Glad it isn't me.

The worst of it is, she knows there's no fast way out. Someone assures her that the police are on their way and another voice is saying that he saw the whole thing and won't mind being a witness. She tries to smile at him. "Thank you," she says, interrupting him in the middle of one of his sentences. "That'll help. That'll be a help."

A runty, gray-haired woman in a brownish-green old-lady coat is already starting the post mortem. Her blocky coat is made of some thick cloth that looks sturdy enough to stand up by itself, like an old-lady exoskeleton. "It's getting so you can't even go to the store," the woman in the carapace-coat is saying. "You take your life in your hands."

That's when the guy in the gray NYU sweatshirt comes running up. He's in his twenties, impressively tall, with close-cropped blonde hair and a single gold stud in his left earlobe. "Paula?" he asks. "Are you Paula Brandt?"

She's confused for a moment. Is he with the police? His haircut makes him look like a cadet of some kind, that and his athletic shoulders.

"I think I found your wallet," he says. "The guy threw it behind a dumpster." He holds up her library card. "This is almost the only thing left in it—that and some photos. But it's got your name on it."

"Yeah," she says. She needs a couple of beats to figure out that he's expecting more of an answer, so she adds, "I mean, yes—it's mine. I'm Paula." She hates saying her name in front of people. It sounds dull; it's a fat-girl name. "You ran after him?" she asks, because she can't think of what else to say.

NYU-boy smiles and looks proud of himself. "Yeah, but I came along too late. He was long gone. But purse-snatchers almost always drop what they take within a few hundred yards of the crime scene. I just looked in the obvious places on my way back." He's still smiling, holding up her wallet. *He isn't even out of breath*, Paula thinks.

She extends her hand and he puts the wallet into it gently. "How do you know?" she asks. "About the obvious places?"

"Criminal Science major," the boy answers.

People are looking at her expectantly, waiting to see what she'll say next. She's aware that she has a role to play here. "Well," she says, "I guess that makes you my hero," and several people laugh. The boy puffs up like he's going to bust out of his sweatshirt. He's got a good face, wide across the cheekbones, almost Slavic, with big eyes and dark lashes. *In spite of everything*, Paula thinks, *I still notice that.* The woman in the heavy coat pats him on the arm. "See," she says, "there's still some good guys left in the world."

Paula likes that he's taking attention away from her. She wants him to have this moment. She wants him to be able to tell his buddies how he came to the rescue of some woman who'd been mugged and that he chased the bad guy down the street. *It's a good one*, Paula thinks. *A story to dine out on.* She can probably dine out on it, too. People love to hear their worst fears confirmed. Everyone gets an urban tale to tell.

For a while, Paula's the center of a little storm, better diversion than television. Then a patrol car is pulling up alongside the curb, and Paula is starting to see an end to all this.

By the time the police are done, most of the crowd has melted away, a layer at a time from the outside first, like a snowman. The police make it less interesting to be a voyeur; their presence takes the vicarious fun out of being a junior crime-spotter. While Paula is talking to them a man walks up and hands her what's left of her groceries. Everything has been repackaged: someone went home and got a new plastic bag and collected her things off the street. It's an overwhelming gesture of kindness that makes Paula shy all over again. When she can finally leave, one of the cops asks if she wants a ride home. *Must be a slow crime day*, she thinks, and says no thanks.

As the cops drive off, the one who questioned her leans out the window to say they'll call if they dig anything up—like earthworms, she imagines. He tips his leather-covered notebook at her in a parting wave, and Paula starts down the block. NYU-boy is waiting for her, propped against a No Parking sign. "Hi," he says.

"Hi," says Paula, and keeps walking. He falls in beside her.

"Do they think they'll find the guy who did it?" he wants to know.

"I doubt it," she says. "I mean, this must happen fifty times a day. And nobody saw anything very helpful. They said I was lucky not to be hurt. And to be sure to cancel my credit cards." She laughs and the boy looks puzzled. "I don't have any credit cards," she explains.

They keep walking and Paula realizes that he means to escort her home. She wonders if a more cautious person might not want him to know where she lives. Maybe a more cautious person wouldn't have gotten mugged. "You don't have to walk me," she says.

The boy smiles shyly. "I want to."

"I'm not likely to get robbed again, you know," she says, self-mocking. "Statistically speaking, I'm probably safe for at least the next eighteen months." But she doesn't actually mind his presence; she wasn't scared while she was getting mugged but now it's nice to have company. Someone who was there, someone she doesn't have to explain it to. She thinks about telling her friends what happened and then decides she doesn't actually have to. Nothing shows—it isn't like she's going to have bruises too visible to hide—and she can keep it a secret if she wants.

"Well, I've never been mugged," he says, "so my number might come up at any time. Maybe you'd better walk *me* to make sure *I'm* safe."

He's charming, Paula has to hand him that. But still young enough to be naive about it. He isn't smarmy; he doesn't seem to know how cute he's being. "How old are you?" Paula asks.

"Twenty-three. Just turned twenty-three. How 'bout you?"

"Older than twenty-three."

"You don't look it."

Paula laughs out loud. It feels good, a genuine laugh. She takes in a big breath of clean air and feels lighter. "Who taught you that you were supposed to tell women they didn't look their age?" she asks, turning to look at the boy's face for the first time. He blushes and stares at the sidewalk.

"Well, you don't," he mumbles.

"It's okay," she says, not wanting to hurt his feelings. "It's sweet. Thank you. It's just ... I don't know. Chivalrous."

"I like that," he says, brightening. "Good crossword-puzzle word."

"You *like* crossword puzzles?" she asks.

He smiles again, showing two rows of white, uneven teeth. "You don't think I'm the type, huh?" he says, picking up Paula's teasing tone. "I'd challenge you sometime, but I'm pretty good."

This is okay, Paula thinks. This is not odd. All I'm doing is having a conversation with a guy I ran into on the street. In some places in the world, it's still considered normal to talk to strangers. It's like striking up a conversation with someone you sit next to on the plane. Some people actually expect it and are pissed off if you stick your head into your book and refuse to trade details with them about where you live and why you're traveling. "So do you have a library card?" she asks the boy.

"What?"

"You know, a library card."

"Yeah...."

"Let's see it."

He's shaking his head as he pulls out his wallet. "It's my student ID," he says, "they use it as a library card." He hands her a blue laminated rectangle with the predictable mug shot, his square, handsome face bearing a look of surprise as if he was expecting something other than the camera.

"Okay, Brian Burke Mitchell," she says, handing the card back, "now we're even. Although I have to tell you that my mother told me never to trust a man with three first names."

Even before they get to Paula's building, Brian has asked her to have supper with him. *Does she feel like getting something to eat?* is how he puts it. Paula isn't hungry, but she says yes. She makes him wait downstairs on the stoop while she drops off the remains of her groceries. At first she thinks of dumping the whole thing down the garbage chute, just to avoid dealing with it again later, when she imagines she'll be feeling less stoic than she does at the moment. But the canned stuff is still okay, and, by some miracle, the cat litter didn't break open. That's always the heaviest item walking back from the store. Why do that again if she doesn't have to? Besides, tossing everything seems ungrateful to the man who went to the trouble of salvaging her groceries. Only one of the peaches made it, she observes as she empties the bag, and she puts it into the refrigerator where it shares a shelf with a crusted jar of chutney and nothing else.

She changes out of her ripped jeans and combs her hair. She debates whether to put on lipstick. It's almost dark outside, and she is dressing for the evening after all, though that seems a strange way of putting it. She decides against it, but does put on a different sweater, a heavy one of thick maroon wool, one that makes her feel like a grownup. Then she goes back into the bathroom and washes her face. Before she goes down to Brian again she reaches for the lipstick anyway.

"Nice sweater," he says as soon as she appears from behind the ornate street door.

Paula smiles. "I put on lipstick," she says, "so I want to go some-where where they don't have napkin dispensers."

Brian takes her arm and leads her in a direction. "You look good," he says, so sincerely that Paula has to stifle another laugh. She doesn't know where they're going and it's nice not to care. She thinks of another word: *squired*. She's being squired to supper. As they're stopped at a corner, waiting for the light to change, Paula maneuvers ahead of him a half-step so she can see more of his face. She wants a better look, now that they seem to have entered a new phase. First, he was just someone helping her home after a mugging. Now, they're sort of on a date.

He catches her watching him and smiles backs. She's amazed all over again by the whiteness of his teeth. The two in front on top are serrated on the bottom edge, she notices, like a teenager's. Healthy teeth are a sign of money—but maybe not that much money because his are also slightly out of line. He's never had braces. Good thing, too, or his face would be too perfect, almost blinding to look at. If his eyes were only brown, that would soften the effect, but of course they're blue—sky blue—and lovely. As it is, he reminds her of a Marine recruiting poster.

"I've never met anyone this way before," she says. "I mean, I've never needed to be rescued."

The light changes and he starts them across the intersection. He's focused diligently on getting them safely to the far corner, but she sees the angle of his mouth turn up.

"I didn't rescue you, remember?" he says. "I came along too late, after it was all over, and helped pick up the pieces."

"Oh," Paula says, "so I guess that makes me just one of the pieces you picked up." After it's out, she cringes. She didn't mean to say something with that much innuendo in it.

But of course he recognizes the double meaning. "No!" he says, a little too loudly. Then he says, "I just mean that I didn't do anything heroic." *Shucks, ma'am. Twarn't nothin'.*

Paula decides she'd better steer them to neutral ground. "Well, let's just *tell* people you rescued me," she says playfully. "It's a better story. Anyway, I *feel* rescued. And it could have been a lot worse. The only thing I lost was a book—a very expensive book that I will have to replace, unfortunately, but still just a book."

"It wouldn't have been worse," he says. "I mean, it probably wouldn't. A lot of people dwell on that—what might have happened—but you shouldn't. These guys are pretty much strictly hit-and-run. Anything that takes more than a few seconds and they're outta there. Too easy to draw a crowd if you make a big production out of it. Someone's gonna be a hero and try and stop you or at least winds up with a better shot at recognizing you later. The percentages are bad."

"Criminal Science major?" Paula teases.

For a moment Brian looks uncomfortable, even annoyed; a flicker of something that Paula's gut identifies as anger plays over those reassuringly preppy features, then he's back to normal. *As if I know what normal looks like on him*, she thinks.

"Actually," he says, "the reason I'm in school is I want to become a profiler some day."

"One of those guys who gets inside the minds of criminals and figures out what makes them tick?" she asks.

"Something like that," Brian says. Then he pauses. "Italian?"

"No," Paula says. "Jewish." They've stopped in front of a restaurant and she doesn't realize her mistake at first. "Oh, God," she says, "that wasn't about me, was it?"

Brian is holding the door open and grinning at her so kindly that she decides not to kick herself too much for not taking his meaning. "Thank you, Sir Brian," she says, and steps down into a large square room noisy with diners and smelling aggressively of garlic and bread. The walls, a stark, cream-cheese white, are decorated with bright, pastel watercolors, reproductions of great works that strike Paula as more or less familiar. Brian sees the question on her face and points to the ceiling. She looks up and finally makes the connection: two beautifully muscled male arms stretch toward one another, the fingers nearly touching. God gives life to Adam. The entire ceiling is an enormous copy of the famous fresco, and now she can put the walls into context as well.

"It's the Sistine Chapel!" she beams, surprised at how delighted, even giddy she feels to know that.

"Yeah," says Brian, "that's what this place is called—La Cappella."

A waiter motions them to an empty table where wine glasses in two versions—what she always thinks of as the Laurel kind and the Hardy kind—stand alongside water goblets in a dignified grouping. Brian touches her elbow to guide her. She realizes that he never waited for her to say whether or not Italian was okay, then she decides she kind of likes Brian's assumptions, his good-natured, masculine pushiness.

He's still playing at being gallant. Men her age don't bother anymore, either assuming she'll be offended or just because it isn't done between professional people, which is who she dates, if she dates. Brian doesn't see her as a peer, for better or worse. Turns out it's a nice change.

The first few minutes after they're seated are awkward. They're face to face and completely still for the first time with nothing to do except talk to each other. The waiter brings a bottle of Asti, which Brian has apparently ordered when she wasn't paying attention, and she gratefully takes a first sip, holding the tart flavors against the roof of her mouth before swallowing. A number of possible topics of conversation have occurred to her, and she weighs the options. She could remark that the actual *Creation of Adam* seems much smaller in real life, almost lost among the overwhelming colors and the hundreds of figures that surround it. She could mention a friend's observation that the *Creation of Eve*, just one panel over and at the true center of the Sistine ceiling, is virtually unknown, while the Adam fresco winds up in car commercials and on the labels of bottled spaghetti sauce.

In the end she says neither thing because she doesn't want to sound pretentious. Perhaps Brian hasn't traveled, and, of course, she has only been to Italy once herself. Besides, she isn't sure what Brian might say about the Eve situation, and she doesn't want to be unpleasantly surprised. She settles on a safer subject. "So, Brian," she says, "where do you come from? Originally, I mean?"

He ducks his chin and puts his hands over his face, a palm against each eye. Paula isn't sure if he's laughing because he finds the question banal or if she's unintentionally upset him. If so, she wouldn't be surprised. She generally finds people to be something of a minefield. Brian raises his heavy, blonde head to look at her, and she has the sensation that she's watching the lid go up on a rolltop desk. "You don't want to know where I come from, Paula," he says finally. "You want to know if I find you attractive."

Paula barely gets out her word of protest before he's reached his two wide hands across the table and taken one of hers between them—all without jostling the flatware or spilling anything, she's self-possessed enough to observe. "And I do," he says, half-whispering. He's holding her gaze, like a cobra. "Paula, I think you're beautiful."

After supper, he insists on walking her home. He holds her arm the entire way in the crook of his, and she lets him. They make small talk on her stoop until she invites him up for coffee, and, a half-hour after the coffee is gone, they end up in bed. Paula doesn't pretend to be shocked, not even to herself, because these things happen, but she knows they don't generally happen to her. In fact, that's the remark that got him upstairs in the first place: Just as the chit chat was reaching the stage of semi-long pauses and self-conscious grins, he had simply said, "Invite me up for coffee?" It was a question, but there was a demand in it.

"I don't usually ask people I've just met to visit my apartment," she tried, not wanting to seem coy, aware, too, that she wasn't exactly saying no.

"You don't usually get robbed," Brian had answered, "and I don't usually chase muggers. Maybe this is a day for doing things you don't usually do."

After he spoke, he ducked his head again and kicked her railing. *He's embarrassed himself*, Paula thought, and that was his ticket in: All of a sudden she wondered what it would be like to kiss him. When he looked up she was holding her hand out, reaching for him just like in the painting at the restaurant, and that was that. Maybe the charm was a little self-conscious at this point, but what the hell. She was flattered that he was making the effort.

Charm wasn't the only thing he was good at, as it turned out, and, after Brian went home, she surveyed the happy wreckage of the bed, the sheets tangled into damp, aromatic bunkers, the pillows long since lost over the edge of the mattress, the cat beneath the sofa who would refuse to emerge until morning. *It's true what they say about younger men*, she thought, thrilled because she felt wicked—*it's all about stamina. Stamina and tight skin.*

While she tidied up, Paula let herself try on the role of Older Woman, a possibility she hadn't entertained before. It was a niche, certainly; it implied a fair exchange. There was even some grace and dignity involved. Better than simply being an *aging* woman. And he had pursued *her*; that was novel. She sat up in bed for a while after that, feeling worldly and wondering whom she could tell.

*P*aula is falling asleep about the time Brian reaches the downtown apartment he shares with his lover, Anthony. He unlocks the deadbolt and rolls back the security bar as quietly as possible, but, once inside, he can see from the entryway that a light is still on in the rear of the apartment. He hooks his coat over a doorknob and goes to stand in the doorway of the bedroom where Anthony is propped up in bed, a book spread open on his lap.

"I told you she wasn't going to have anything worth taking," Anthony says.

"Whatever," Brian shrugs, and turns away. He heads for the shower, shedding clothes as he goes. He doesn't bother to close the bathroom door because he knows Anthony likes watching him dry off. If he's in the mood he gives Anthony a show, putting one foot up on the edge of the tub and bending over while he dries between his toes so Anthony gets a good look at his ass. "Big lush jock butt," is how Anthony likes to describe it. Tonight, though, Brian doesn't feel in the mood, and, anyway, Anthony comes in to sit on the toilet while he's still in the shower.

"You were gone a long time," Anthony says.

"We ate supper."

Anthony makes a snorting sound that Brian detests. If he were to push aside the blue vinyl curtain and look out, Brian knows, he would find Anthony with his head cocked at a disagreeable angle, his lips set into a thin, prissy line. He'd be sitting with his legs crossed at the knees, one hand anchoring the edge of his robe so that it fell elegantly above his ankles—a brittle figurine. When Anthony gets like this, all Brian wants to do is smash his face in with a brick. So he doesn't look outside the shower.

Instead, he turns the water up as high as the flow-control nozzle will let him and says, over the noise, "You didn't have to hit her so hard, you know. She practically went skidding. You always hit 'em too hard."

"It's supposed to look like a real mugging," Anthony replies coldly. "And I thought you liked them a little banged up. Makes for a more dramatic rescue. Anyway, I'm not taking any chances that one of these bitches has mace in her pocket. Or a gun."

Brian doesn't disguise the sneer in his voice when he says the next thing: "She strike you as someone who makes a habit of walking to the grocery store strapped?"

"Believe me," Anthony sniffs, "she didn't strike me as anything. But what people look like is deceiving—isn't that right, darling? That's how come you can pull off these little capers."

"Fuck you," Brian says.

"No," Anthony spits back, "fuck you!" He stalks out of the bathroom, slamming the door behind him. Brian takes his time finishing his shower.

When Brian gets to bed, the lamp on the night stand is on and Anthony is still awake, his arms folded across his chest. He stares reproachfully at the ceiling, barely blinking. "So was she a tight little fuck?" he asks in his nasty voice. "Does she suck as good as me?"

Brian sits on the edge of the mattress and begins toweling his hair. "I don't even know where that's coming from," he says. "This was your idea, remember?"

Anthony ignores that comment, but the silence between them gets as thick as plaster. After a while Brian says, "She wanted to see my ID card."

"I hope you weren't stupid enough to show it to her."

"Why not? It's four years old and I'm never going to see her again."

"It's a small city, sometimes."

"She's not the type to make a fuss in public if she runs into some guy she screwed who never called her again."

"I guess you'd know about that," Anthony says. He puffs air out through his nose. Not quite the snorting sound, but close.

Brian grits his teeth. "Maybe I'll take her book back to her tomorrow," he says.

"And how the fuck do you propose to do that?"

"I dunno. Maybe I'll drop it off at her building, leave her a note saying I went back to look around one more time behind the store and I found it. Or I'll say I just decided to buy her a new one."

"She'll know," Anthony says.

"She won't know."

"Oh, she won't know," Anthony mocks. "No one's ever smart enough to figure your shit out, are they? She probably even fell for that crap about being a Criminal Science major."

"I was a Criminal Science major."

"Yeah, baby, was. Right up until they caught you fucking one of your professors on his office divan. I keep telling you, they don't like fags in law enforcement."

"I'm not a fag," Brian says quietly. "We've had this discussion."

"Why don't you just admit you want to see her again? As if I'm so stupid I can't tell that's what's going on."

Brian goes into a fit of hair-drying, whipping the towel around his head and shaking the bed like a wet dog. When he's done he flips the damp towel across the room where it hits the closet door. He slides beneath the sheets.

"Come on, Brian," Anthony whines. "You fucking promised." He sits up, twisting the blanket between his fists. "You told me it would be just one time with these bitches and I didn't have to worry about repeats."

"Yeah, okay, so I promised," Brian says.

"You prick. Okay. Fine. That's what you want? How's this: I'm not doing it anymore, you sick motherfucker! Chase down your own pussy from now on!"

"Jesus," Brian says, "calm down. I said I promised, all right? Look, here—just wait a sec." He throws back the covers and goes to bathroom, where his jeans lie in a heap on the floor. From one pocket he takes the card from La Cappella on which Paula has written her phone number. "See?" he says, holding it up so Anthony can take note of the unfamiliar handwriting, full of loops. He folds the card into a crisp V so that it stands by itself in the glass ashtray on the night table. In the drawer is the disposable Bic he keeps around for lighting blunts, and he uses that to set the card on fire. When all that's left is a fragment of ash, he climbs back into bed and flicks out the light. "Happy now?" he says.

Anthony waits in silence for few dignified minutes before he rolls toward Brian and throws one arm across his chest, nuzzling his neck. He lowers his head to kiss the hollow below Brian's Adam's apple, and then, when Brian doesn't push him away, he moves down to encircle Brian's left nipple with his lips. As Anthony slides his mouth farther down Brian's stomach, darkening the line of blonde hair with saliva, Brian wonders whether he'll still be able to smell smoke in the morning, however faintly.

Brian finds it appeasing, even comforting to watch the back of Anthony's head as it makes its way down his torso, and he tangles his fingers gently among the glossy curls. Anthony's good, most of the time, he decides. Still, Brian's not sorry he took a moment, while he was riding home on the subway, to copy Paula's number onto the second card from La Cappella, the one that's still tucked into his wallet. He'll have to be sure to hide that better before they go to sleep, in case Anthony wakes up with the urge to snoop.

Always just a few jumps ahead, Brian thinks to himself, and then what Anthony's doing, down between his legs, becomes so distracting that he decides to stop thinking about anything at all for a while.

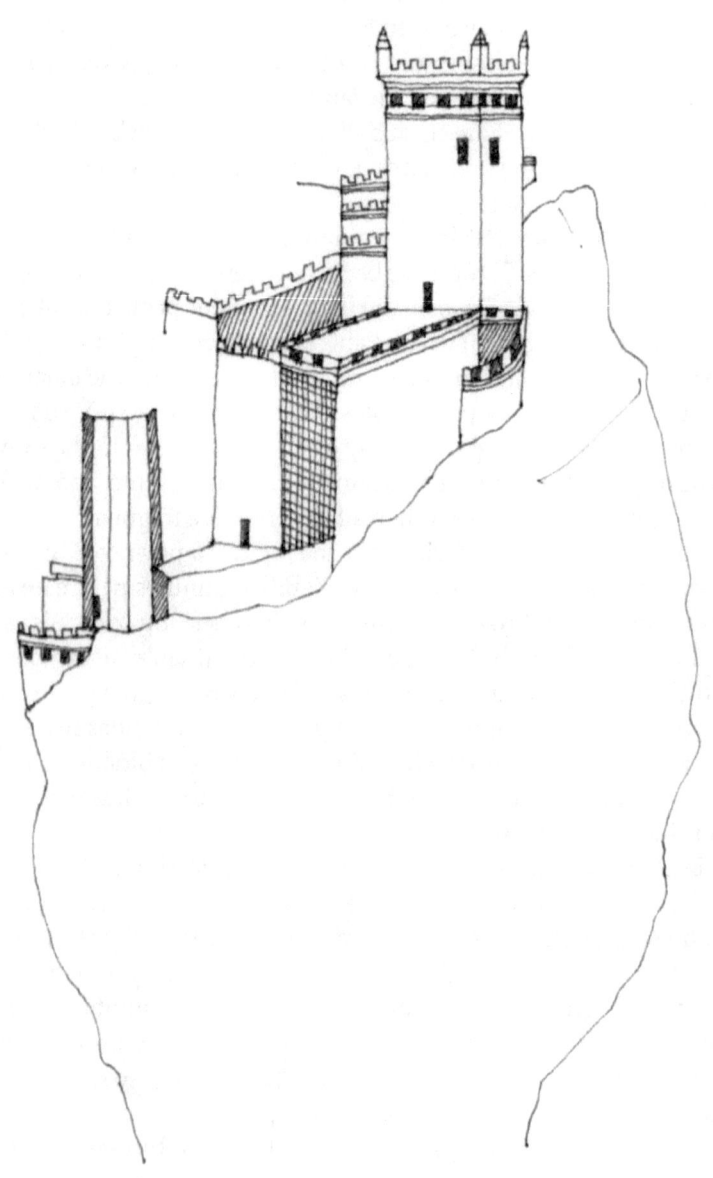

Roma Termini

D arren Wien was in Rome the day he realized he was out of the running. A moment of self-reflection that was, even at the time, full of clichés: An American homosexual just beyond forty; sex, of a sort, in a vividly squalid theater south of the train station where subtitled straight porn showed on a pocked and fraying screen; a boy whore named Massimo; the fact that Massimo was originally from Sicily and had decided to stay in Rome at the end of his compulsory military service. Massimo had been a *bersagliero*—literally, a target shooter. And what is to be done when life hands you metaphors no better than that?

Take, for example, the Indian Summer evening a few months earlier, when Darren had attended a friend's pool party. In the blossoming quiet after the boisterous children had finally, mercifully been ordered to bed, Darren noticed that a large, blow-up beach ball, patterned like a globe, had been left to glide across the surface of the empty pool, ferried by invisible breezes and by the currents of the pumps working away below the surface. *The planet adrift in space*, Darren tried. *The floating world.*

But really what he experienced was a rather garish plastic ball with a phallic white plug jutting from one end, a scummy pool turned a milky and urinary shade of chartreuse, an evening in which the mosquitoes promised to be fierce. He'd have liked to have done something with all that, but he couldn't manage. The trouble with life is that it is sometimes too specific for art.

Darren had paid for sex exactly twice in his life. The first time was in 1979, during a trip to Tijuana. He'd driven south across the border from Laguna Beach, where he was staying with a friend who had insisted that a week's holiday in Southern California was just what Darren needed. Darren was barely installed in the guest room, however, before his friend began talking up the idea of a side trip to Mexico.

"We'll call Bob," the friend had said, speaking of his ex-lover, a middle-aged college professor who dressed as though he might be asked at any moment to step into a golf game. "Bob will go to Mexico at the drop of a hat."

Perhaps it was just a way to get Darren out from underfoot for the weekend. Darren's host was in high demand in Laguna Beach, in the way handsome boys once were, before beauty turned brutal. He had other fish to fry and a bungalow with very thin walls.

So, in the end, the trip was rather suddenly arranged. Bob drove into the driveway one afternoon and honked his horn, and he and Darren went to Tijuana. The boys they picked up on the street that night didn't mention money until after they'd put their clothes back on, at which point the older one began to threaten them without conviction (police involvement, eviction from the hotel). Bob rolled his eyes at Darren. "This is so '50s!" he laughed. He handed over twenty dollars and told the boys to beat it. Darren and Bob could hardly wait to get back to Laguna Beach to tell their story.

Massimo was the second time, although what Darren paid for was not the sex, officially speaking: He gave Massimo money so he could change the oil in his Vespa, with which he took Darren from and returned him to the rear edge of the train station, where the creosote-soaked yards began, because the smoking, hiccoughing scooter so clearly needed it. Darren might have had stand-up sex with Massimo in one of the stalls in the bathrooms alongside the tracks, but that wasn't Massimo's style. He liked to get to know a person, he said, to be a little friendly.

Salvatore, another Sicilian, had approached first as Darren leaned against the wall outside the reeking bathroom, its floor slick with a viscid paste of spit, piss, and greasy soot from the platforms. But, like Cassius, Salvatore had a lean and hungry look that put Darren off.

Darren wanted to be enthusiastic about the sleaziness of Salvatore: his obvious desperation, the way his half-hard cock was outlined, pornographically, in his tight, filthy jeans; the fact that he, as he put it, "did everything," which meant that you could have fucked him if you wanted to. Later Darren thought he should perhaps have taken Salvatore up on his offer—more straightforward and, ultimately, cheaper than Massimo. (Salvatore's final demand, before he walked away in disgust, was that Darren accompany him into the *gabbineto* for just under three bucks American.)

But Darren had already seen Massimo and that was whom he wanted. Massimo was butch. He looked as though he'd showered recently. Darren didn't imagine he'd find his foreskin rancid and stinking of ammonia. These are the sort of details a person thinks of when he thinks of paying for sex, however distasteful they seem in other contexts.

When Salvatore smiled, he looked like a vulture. When Massimo smiled, he looked liked a wolf. Wolves are good luck in Rome—*Romolo e Remo* and all that—and if a Roman wants to wish you good luck, he'll tell you "*in bocca al lupo.*" Who knows why being in a wolf's mouth is good luck. Perhaps because the wolf cares so tenderly for its young, carrying the pups gently between jaws that have the power to shear and tear. Maybe it's just a perverse phrase that means its opposite, like "break a leg" in English.

Anyway, Darren liked Massimo *il lupo* better than Salvatore *l'avvoltoio*, though he was confused at first whether Massimo was working the station or just hanging around, the way boys of his age hang around all over Rome, draped picturesquely against statues and fountains, stationed in haphazard groupings along the pied, peeling walls that line the piazzas. What are all these boys, many of them so beautiful, waiting for, a person might wonder, but that's a mystery as eternal as *mamma Roma*.

Disoccupazione breeds trouble, certainly—not always big trouble, but idleness, a listlessness of spirit. People who are not Italian like to say that Italians don't work hard, but the fact is that they fall largely into two groups: people who hold jobs they know they cannot lose and who are bored as a result, and people who live in ceaseless fear of unemployment and who are, therefore, obsessed with their jobs. Then there are boys like Massimo who slip between the categories.

They have little chance of finding legitimate work; their only income is "black money."

Having sampled a few of Rome's gay clubs, with their perversely invisible entranceways, their dogged air of furtive anonymity, Darren was tempted to say that homosexuality was the one thing Italians didn't do well. When he tried the quip out on his traveling companion, however, the retort came back instantly: "But they've had so many centuries of practice!" And that observation, more clever and more spontaneous than Darren's, made him decide to abandon his witticism for use at post-vacation dinner parties back home.

Still, you needed some way to talk about how it was between men in Italy, some way to make sense of what anyone could plainly see—not the easiest task without sounding like a guest on a daytime talk show. Because you tended to start using terms like "behavior" and "roles" and "identities," which is the way we talk about sex in America.

In Rome, it's like this: *"If I'm going to sell my body, it has to be with someone I can talk to. Who understands that I'm not desperate, a drug addict or something. Who won't see me on the street two days later and refuse to look me in the eye or, worse, laugh up his sleeve. Because I do nothing to be ashamed of. And it has to be someplace better than a bathroom at the train station—a private house, for example, or at least the cinema."*

Which explains how Darren got to the cinema, since he didn't have a private room. Normally he would have had, but he had broken his own rule on this trip and agreed to travel *in due,* accompanying an old friend who, having no Italian, was convinced that scoundrel gypsies and thieving cab drivers would ruin his long-anticipated vacation. Thus was Darren pressed into service, shouldering his duties as translator *cum* guide in exchange for airfare, which he could scarcely have afforded on his own, and becoming in the process what the Victorians quaintly called "a paid companion." Under the circumstances, the term was particularly ironic. But even if Darren had been alone, the difficulty would have remained of getting Massimo past the Signora at the front desk.

The earlier declaration was Massimo's, of course. His speech sounded very sincere in Italian, with gestures, intonation, and that magnetic rhythm. One of the problems with Italian is that it's a language that makes anything seem reasonable. In other words, if you heard the same lines from an English-speaking whore on Polk Street, you'd be inclined to disbelieve him, as Darren was not with regard to Massimo. Or you might suspect it was just part of the fantasy, the setup. A cynical form of foreplay: the hooker with a heart of gold.

A cliché, you see? But maybe you're willing to pay a bit more for this—for someone, if you believe him, who doesn't "go" with just anybody, who exercises discretion in his partners, because, even if it's only by a whore, we still love to think we've been chosen. At least Darren did. *Does.*

Two days before they were to leave for Rome, Darren flew to JFK, then cabbed to the uptown apartment his traveling companion shared with one of those New York roommates that no one ever sees. They'd decided—the friend had decided—to put themselves on an Italian schedule and were forcing themselves to stay awake through the nights. If they succeeded, the friend argued, they'd arrive in Rome in the third morning fresh and ready to begin the day. While his friend went out to an all-night bookstore to buy last-minute travel guides, Darren drank take-out espresso in the tiny living room, leafing through magazines and trying to make the hours pass before he could safely go to bed without deranging his circadian rhythms.

In one magazine was an interview—a minor character actor who was suddenly, perilously famous for being queer or for coming out or for having AIDS, or maybe for some combination of the three. "I was the whore of Babylon," the actor told the interviewer.

Great line. Unless you know who the Whore of Babylon actually is. But isn't it interesting: He meant that he'd been promiscuous. Though that's not the word. Promiscuous means utterly indiscriminate—that you go with everything, like the color taupe. But the actor wasn't promiscuous; he had types, he had to experience desire in order to have sex, which implies discrimination, no matter how wide the swath you cut. No one is attracted to an entire gender.

Massimo, of course, or those of his profession, are officially supposed to be promiscuous, meaning indiscriminate, indifferent. But they are neither. Darren had known a few whores in his time. His most recent ex had even become one briefly on the occasion of his thirtieth birthday, his mechanism for proving to himself that he was still attractive. And not just attractive enough for people to want to have sex with him, but attractive enough for them to want to pay for it. Because money, after all, makes attraction more sincere. Though what Darren's ex didn't account for is that a man will pay a male whore for all kinds of reasons, physical beauty (or dick size or Abs of Steel) being only part of the package. Convenience is another part, availability. So is the likelihood of never having to see him again. So is the belief, general all over the world, that you can ask a whore for anything and that he either won't make you feel ashamed for wanting it or that he's seen much worse.

Massimo did that: made Darren feel that what he wanted wasn't shameful. Afterwards, as the two rode back on Massimo's scooter to the train station, Massimo asked Darren several times, "Did you like that?" (He had.) "That's a fat cock, isn't it?" (It was.) He even shared his philosophy that only a healthy man could produce semen as fine-tasting as his. Bitter cum is what you get from guys who are sick, Massimo explained. "*Sborro amaro.*" The pronunciation is difficult for the non-native speaker—the alveolar trill, the lax vowels.

Cum is always bitter, Darren wanted to tell him, though it is an acquired taste, perhaps like grappa. Would anyone believe that Darren remembered a time when people used to joke about the flavors of cum as if they were vintages of wine? That fellow obviously smoked, that one was a vegetarian, the other one was taking medication of some kind (but not *that* kind, not then).

The man in the interview, the Whore of Babylon, had said he wanted the accomplishment of his later years to be to put an end to secret lives. Private lives, if you like a Noel Coward pun. So he was using the interview to tell everyone about his former sex life, about his legions of tricks, about all the "husbands" he'd gone through, as if he were some great, cannibalistic female spider. The shadow woman: the Whore of Babylon. Given the caliber of the man and the caliber of the magazine, Darren didn't think he really had any idea what he was talking about. Other than obeying the urge toward memoir. Toward the need, ultimately, for confession.

When Massimo was ready to come, he asked Darren whether he wanted it "*dentro*" or "*fuori*." No question, really: Darren wanted it *dentro*. He thought Massimo was polite to ask; it showed a kind of sophistication on his part. In fact, that was one of the things he appreciated about Massimo: Though Massimo was unlikely a connoisseur of cocksucking himself, he was philosophical about Darren's interest in it. He wanted to give Darren a good cock, because he knew he'd like it. He'd offered Darren his cum because he thought Darren might like that, too.

Dentro or *fuori*. All the same to Massimo probably, though perhaps he, too, got an extra fraction of thrill out of being "accepted" in that way. Men do: It's a fact of life. But nobody wants to talk about what cum actually means in the sex lives of human beings. The unaccounted-for factor in the teenage-pregnancy statistics. The "reason" behind barebacking, behind so-called risky sex. Men like you to take their cum. And a lot of people are eager to oblige.

But maybe you tell people they can't do that anymore and maybe you're even right and maybe they go along with it, grudgingly or pragmatically or perhaps with the missionary zeal that characterized the late '80s and limped on until the end of the '90s, when more likely than being asked for spare change as you walked on certain streets was to be accosted by a blankly handsome boy with a concerned expression on his face who wanted you to attend a meeting where you could confess your safe-sex failures and promise never to do them again, as if having unsafe sex was vaguely like abandoning your AA schedule, and renewing your commitment to it was all that was necessary to climb back on the wagon. It was "healthy" to make this commitment, one learned, and not just in the obvious physical sense. Rather, "healthy" became a code word that implied, darkly, the idea that other kinds of sex were shameful, morally wrong, addictive—addictive, in particular, being a favorite word of the end of the millennium. Along with *appropriate*: Talking about why Darren wanted Massimo's cum wasn't *appropriate*. Isn't. Not while everyone is soldiering together against the epidemic, the scourge, the plague, the chaos, the troubles, the unpleasantness, the genocide, the blight, the end of the world, the horror, the Pandemonium, the catastrophe, the Holocaust, the outbreak, the pestilence, the pandemic, the curse, the contagion, the disaster, the cataclysm, the devastation, the calamity, the extermination, the apocalypse, the fall of Wormwood, Armageddon. The Whore of Babylon.

But whatever you do, you can't pretend you don't know that people feel they're missing something important. And that's why Darren wasn't going to let Massimo's cum go wasted. Although, had he been able to get words out of the end of Massimo's plantain-shaped dick, instead of semen, he might have been just as happy.

If the project is to put an end to secret lives, of course, the part that's hard to tell isn't picking someone up outside the bathroom of a train station or sucking him off in a straight porn theater, or even giving him money afterwards. The part that's hard to admit comes later.

When Darren and Massimo parted company, they made a date for that evening, agreeing to meet again on the Spanish Steps at six p.m. Darren wasn't sure what he was going to do with him—one thought was to bring Massimo back to the *pensione* to be shared with Darren's traveling companion, and there, perhaps, to discover whether Massimo might possibly, if persuaded sufficiently by affection or by *lire, prenderlo in culo*, since Darren suspected he had an ass—like ninety percent of the boys in Italy, high and tight and shaped like two halves of a melon—that would have made him pant.

By the time they left each other at the back of the train station, Darren and Massimo had already discussed the question of *maschio* versus *femminile*. Italians appreciate the distinction, but don't go to the extreme of the Mexicans, who practically turn it into a religion. Tijuana whores who know no other English know the phrase, "Doan' tosh my ass." Massimo asked Darren which position he preferred, and Darren explained that, in the United States, it didn't matter so much, that you pretty much did whatever you wanted, assuming an agreeable partner. *Everything in America is wonderful*, Massimo said; Darren thought he was too guileless for irony, but you could never tell.

Darren stood on the Spanish Steps—*La Scalinata della Trinità dei Monti*—for half an hour. If he looked to his left, he could see the pastel, unprepossessing entrance to the house at 26 Piazza di Spagna (from which the steps take their common name), the rooms where Keats tried in vain to stave off consumption.

Darren had expected Massimo to be late. Massimo was the man and Darren was the woman, after all—that had been established at the porn theater—and women wait for men. But, as soon as the minute hand edged past 6:15, Darren started to know he wouldn't show up at all. In situations like these, you feel that everyone who looks at you—and the Steps were mobbed that evening—knows that you've been stood up. Or, worse, that you've been stood up by a whore. They don't have to suffer such indignities: they have homes, families, spouses, lovers, dates, girlfriends, partners, mates, counterparts, marriages, mistresses, boyfriends, assignations, people who expect them, places to be, places they belong, places.

They do not have secret lives.

Or this is what Darren thought as he stood there, watching the hands of his watch clasp together over the Antarctic of the dial: 6:30. Why had he bothered to put on a clean shirt, he wondered. Did he really need to bathe; brush his teeth; fish out the last pair of socks that were actually clean, not just rinsed in the bidet and hung across the radiator overnight; think about where they might go for a piece of pizza afterward; make *plans*? Much of what Darren had done was in the service of a private, unspoken agenda whose demolition left him stranded.

And of course what you feel at a moment like that is not so much that you've been fooled or cheated or even stood up. Because some genuine arrangement would have had to have been established before it could be disarranged. And it was never like that. In Massimo's existence you were never more than a contingency plan—what he might do if nothing else materialized. He didn't reject you; he held you in abeyance. A quantum worse. You see that now.

But it reminds you that the attributes, elements, charming qualities that you used to believe bound you to others are no longer working so well when it comes to ... that certain arena of sex and love. Certainly you have friends. Some of them of significant long-standing.

But now that you're waiting for a whore on the Spanish Steps in Rome, you have to admit to yourself that the whole adventure had a purpose you'd hidden even from yourself. You wanted to be different from the others. Sure, you gave him some cash (the equivalent of ten dollars and sixty cents, if it really matters), but you wanted him to come back not for cash, or not solely for the cash, but for you. Because he was interested in your attributes, your charming qualities, your elements. Perhaps the worst part is going back to the hotel room alone, because your friend never believed your whore would show up and silently watched you getting dressed and brushing your teeth and putting on deodorant, knowing it all the time, and when you come back in the door, your friend won't say "I told you so," because he won't have to.

You'll bring back bread and cheese instead, you decide, for which you'll need to walk some distance from the Steps, though that's all to the good: some time ought to pass before you reappear at the *pensione* (your friend might consider, at least for a moment, that perhaps he was wrong and that Massimo had shown up after all) and anyway you want to give the impression, as you return, laden with packages, of someone with less impeachable reasons for going abroad in the Roman night. You'll get some expensive cheese and some of that chocolate fondant you've been looking for, and pasta to take home on the plane—bucatini, which you can never find in American markets—and, oh, on the way back, you'll stop by the Scalinata to see if your whore has shown up yet.

What you can't stop thinking about are the specifics of intimacy that are, paradoxically, impersonal: the softness of skin under your fingers when you run your hand beneath a lover's shirt; the pleasantly painful turgescence of overkissed lips; the feathery, almost liquid texture of hair; the way hair smells.

So much revolves around exactly that, you think—what you're allowed to do with another person's body, what you have access to: putting your feet in the other person's lap, being able to lay your palm flat on the skin above his heart, the fact that it's not strange when you reach beneath the covers and hold his cock. Little by little you're granted the right to occupy, even if only temporarily, territories on another person's body. Miraculous, really. The kinds of things a stranger would never allow, would call the cops if you tried. Little by little, of course, those same rights can be revoked—the easements previously granted are not renewed; passage is denied; new boundaries are drawn. But you never think it's going to be for the last time, even if, one day without your knowing it, it necessarily is.

Ironically, buying Massimo gave you access to his cock, to his balls, to his armpits, his tiny nipples, the optimistic line of hair down the middle of his chest. What you couldn't buy was Massimo's mouth, his tongue willingly in yours, his hands in your hair, the time it would have taken for the smell of his body to become familiar. No, your lease restricted you to the adjacent lots, and yet acquiring the rights to those was no more complicated than buying a loaf of bread.

And that's how you come to the realization: You're out of the running because you quit; you settled out; you can't handle the competition; you're all wrong for it; there's always someone younger and more handsome; playing the game is exhausting; the game told you to get out and you pretended not to understand; you are ridiculous; sex is ridiculous; love at your age is humiliating; you had more than your share of chances and you threw them away; you've stopped caring; you never meant it to be like this, but now you can't figure out a way to turn things around; you couldn't help but notice the moment when you started to become invisible.

What does it meant to have no more secrets or, at least, to entertain no more secrets about sex?

The forty-year-old gay man at the dawn of the third millennium is an ironic figure. You are pleased, you think, to have survived, but now that you're out of the game—*hors de combat*, so to speak—what did it matter, really? Maybe you were never popular in the first place, which is *why* you're still alive, because isn't it often said of the dead what great beauties they were and how everyone desired them? But maybe that was better. If you were the Whore of Babylon, at least you'd have a past.

Now that you're still alive, on the other hand, all that's left for you to do is to pick up what you left behind while you waited for the plague to end: like bags stored for years in a bus-station locker. You find the long-lost key, you make your way downtown, you retrieve from the depths of the chrome-colored box shaped like a cremation chamber the barely remembered items that once were yours. But you've lived without them so long, you hardly recall their function. And, anyway, you've proved, by all the years, that you were capable of doing without: a certain insouciance and a sardonic wit; your game face; great, peppery handfuls of longing that you can't do much about anymore. That's what you chose instead of a past.

You don't like to complain, but you feel you can't fail to mention what almost seems a kind of a broken promise. You've always known what people thought about your kind, what fears your parents had for you: Queers are fixated on youth and beauty and disregard anyone who has neither; to grow old is to live past being desired. But you liked the new rhetoric you were hearing, and you spouted it along with everyone else. You said: *It just isn't true. It's an ugly stereotype. People never see what our lives are actually like because we're invisible, so they're misled by propaganda.*

But now you want to ask: Excuse me, but when we were saying those things, was there any reason to believe they were actually true, or were we just saying what we *hoped* was true—what we thought, at the least, might one day *become* true? You could handle being an unlucky exception, the one that proves the rule, if that's all it was. If what the rhetoric told you held true for others, even if you hadn't seemed to get your share of it. The people who were there at the time, the ones who marched with you, meanwhile, they're either dead or as disappointed as you are, so no sense asking them.

And now, with Massimo, you've become a stereotype: the middle-aged faggot who pays for sex. The first time it was a game. This time it ...

wasn't. But that's another of those clichés you were told represented a reality that was as dead and gone as child labor. One of the things that couldn't happen anymore. Because of social progress and all. Because you'd been liberated. From everything but desire.

And meanwhile there is such desire. The nearly boundless geography of what you long for is staggering. Wanting things you cannot have, of course—or, at least, that you do not have—is virtually an element of patriotism. If you're not wanting enough, you're barely holding up your end of being American. But now you see the cost of that. You have to be parsimonious with longing, you have to parcel it out—not because there is a limited supply of it (far from it), but because it's like eating puffer fish. A little poison is what you want: enough to numb the lips, to make the tongue tingle. You've got to take it in controlled amounts. Too much and you're comatose—or worse.

So let us put it this way: If you are a few days beyond your fortieth birthday; and if you are standing on the Spanish Steps in one of the most beautiful and terrifying cities in the world; and if it is an early evening on which the Steps are briefly deserted because of a sudden rain that came and went nearly without your notice; and if, out of vanity, you have elected not to wear your glasses, a decision you now regret because the reflection of the shop lights on the wetness of the rectangular, slate-gray paving stones has rendered the piazza a teeming blur of unparticular movement, a disturbed anthill awash in fractal light; and if you have nonetheless been searching or rather pretending to search the crowd as it returns from temporary cover for someone in particular, a pretense not because you are not really waiting for someone but because you are not sure you will see him and are more or less depending upon him to pick you out, which explains your unnatural pose against the clammy marble that is even now staining your pants with taxi soot and tourist grime liberated by rain; and if the man—the boy, really—on whom you are waiting is a prostitute to whom you have recently given a certain sum of money; and if you have reluctantly concluded, as his tardiness devolved into incontestable absence, that further waiting is pointless; and if you are contemplating what errand could possibly give dignity to your descent from the stairs, to your return, alone, to the hotel room and to the prim silence of your friend; and if you feel, almost superstitiously, that you cannot risk actual motion until you have hit upon a suitable plan; and if you experience yourself, at that moment, as a sort of shuttlecock in an existential game, juddering between utter anonymity and gut-wrenching conspicuousness—well, then, you can rightly lay claim to having had a kind of epiphany.

God knows you've had plenty of time to think.

Overcoming inertia is the hardest part, and Darren more-or-less hurls himself off the step on which he's standing, falling into the comfortable, purposeful movement of the crowd. Shame is the only enemy, Darren thinks. The embarrassment of being. We're embarrassed to be! That moment when you start to fear that what you simply, finally *are* is no longer good enough. When your presence ever after needs justification.

Nearly hidden in an angle of the Piazza di Spagna is an entrance for the Metro, and Darren let himself percolate through its mephitic mouth. He bought his fare and went down the scabrous passageway to the nearest track. He had no particular destination, so it hardly mattered whether he ended up on the inbound or the outbound platform. When the train came, he got on and sat down. He rode to the end of the line and then he rode back. As the train reentered the Spagna station, Darren meant to get up, but the muscles of his body acquiesced into the seat cushion, and he stayed put. Darren watched sadly as the train left the station for the second time. He'd have to go through the whole cycle again.

At every stop, men and boys entered the subway car or got off. Such astonishing men, Darren thought. From the adolescents to the grandpas, Italy hardly made an unattractive man. Although it is still considered impolite to stare, men in Italy mind less being looked at, and Darren let himself look, nodding respectfully if his gaze was returned. It was just like anywhere: You saw a man who drew you in, and in the flash of a moment you'd imagined an entire existence with him, but he was on his way to something else, and your lives didn't intersect.

Or they did intersect, briefly—for an afternoon, for a year—but the moment eventually came when the door closed, when he walked off, rode off, faded gently out of sight, when, at last, all the potential of him died aborning.

He would have been the Whore of Babylon, Darren decided, if he could have figured out how to go about it. Because even if you set out to be promiscuous, it's not exactly the sort of thing you can accomplish by yourself, is it? But in Darren's life, the truth was that he had counted losses instead of conquests, preserving in his heart the stigmata of each and every parting as raw and fresh as if it had been struck into his flesh only moments ago, a devotion that now seemed to him equal parts heroism and pathos, honor and lunacy. They would never have imagined, the absent men (would it have mattered if they had?), the vast, lapidary, and incorruptible edifice of his fidelity.

But it made no difference now. He was done with all that.

He wouldn't shop after all, Darren thought. As soon as he could, he'd get off the subway and go back to the *pensione*. He was tired, and anyway he'd stopped caring what his friend might think. Worry of that kind belonged to another life, the one he'd lived before his evening on the garish and filthy Spanish Steps. The train would finish out the route it had no choice but to take, and Darren would wait for it to carry him back to his proper stop. He settled uncomfortably into his seat, stung and scorched, over the entire surface of his body, by the contingencies of men.

Beef Timeless Fun

June meant the Alameda County Fair and the fair was the foretelling of summer, so Jake accepted gladly when Pieter-from-the-office suggested they make an outing of it. Jake was the one with a car, but the fair was no fun alone. That was the trade, then. Jake would pick Pieter up at eleven o'clock on Saturday morning.

Pieter was the administrative assistant of the Managing Partner at the financial-district law firm where Jake had worked for nearly three years as a "permanent temp." When Jake filled out his twice-monthly timesheets, he was tempted to write the word "oxymoron" in the space marked "position."

Pieter was the only other out homo at the firm, excluding the categories of "Identifiable But Closeted," "Attends HRC Fundraisers But Who He Sleeps With Is Nobody's Business," and "Queer But Makes Way Too Much Money To Associate With The Likes Of You." In any case, he and Jake had recognized each other with a glance on Jake's first day. Being friendly seemed the natural thing to do, or as natural as any relationship could be with someone you probably wouldn't meet, let alone befriend, in other circumstances. How Pieter described them was "the Lunchables," and he would call Jake on the inside line once or twice a week around a quarter to twelve to ask, "So are we lunchable today?"

Yes, they were lunchable, but they weren't exactly friends. For one thing, Pieter was much too *intime* with the office manager, Alexandra, for Jake's taste. She had a Jayne Mansfield bosom, a Jersey accent, and hair that seemed not so much styled as paralyzed with curare. Pieter called her brassy. Jake thought of her as petty and conniving and he didn't trust her. By extension, that meant he didn't trust Pieter, whose cubicle was directly across the hall from Alexandra's office. Entirely too often someone would leave Alexandra's office and Pieter would leap up, scurry in, and close the door behind him. It was as if they *wanted* their co-workers to think they were the Borgias.

Jake was exhausted by the workplace intrigue, but wasn't entirely free to ignore it. That is, he could choose not to repeat gossip or divulge confidences, but it was nearly impossible not to hear them: who was lazy, who spent all her time on personal phone calls, who left early but submitted a regular time sheet, whose boss let her get away with murder. Refusing to listen was snobbish; it implied an alliance with whomever was being criticized. There was no neutral.

The secretaries' duties were dull and repetitive and often pitched just slightly below the level of outright panic because procrastination slid consistently downhill from the corner offices to the associates bivouacked along the inside walls and, from there, to the cubicle warrens at the windowless center of each of the law firm's floors. There, as elsewhere, location indicated power—or no power at all. But the smallishness of his co-workers was the real millstone. That and the recognition that the spite and insult-collecting were all in the service of nothing of importance. The firm's attorneys weren't overturning death-penalty convictions or fighting to win proper medical care for veterans. Instead, they helped insurance companies sue one another or aided them in paying as little as possible when a client's ship captain got drunk and ran a cruise liner onto a reef or an aerospace company was forced to admit it had spent twenty years pumping toxic chemicals into the ground.

A few times a month, Jake was responsible for arranging six- or eight-person intercontinental conference calls with the help of a relentlessly good-natured man named (naturally) Giles at the Lime Street headquarters of Lloyd's of London. Giles did what Jake did, or so Jake supposed, but the two of them had become entrapped in a gladiatorial contest of manners whose goal was to project the greater degree of sunny professionalism or unflappable competence when Mr. DeVries decided at the last minute to leave early and everyone had to be rescheduled or Ms. Elliot became stapler-tossing irate because her speakerphone fizzled with static in the middle of a conversation. He and Giles were not brothers-in-arms; they never spoke together in low, conspiratorial voices or bonded by referring to the attorneys as self-absorbed monsters. As a result, whenever he had to deal with Giles, Jake felt the throbbing desire to say something mean-spirited and risqué, the way Poe described the perverse urge to leap from great heights.

So that was another issue: Pieter idolized his boss and behaved as though he drew personal cachet from the firm's successes. He dressed exclusively in Ralph Lauren button-downs and bowties, which he omitted occasionally but not reliably on "casual" Fridays. Jake, conversely, wore Ralph Lauren only if he could find it at the Goodwill and considered the attorneys a sociopathic alien species that required regular feeding (stacks of paper still warm from the copier were their favorite fare) to keep them from growing fangs and gnawing the secretaries' limbs off. Secretarial work paid Jake's bills—he knew how to use document-management software, he could type fast, and he sounded capable over the phone; the job didn't require much else—so he kept his mouth shut to the degree that seemed judicious. But no force on earth required him to believe he worked for nice people.

He'd once said as much to Pieter, and Pieter had gone immediately starchy. "Well," he said, "I suppose I can't afford to be as cynical as you. I have to retire here." A period of cooling had followed and a week without lunchables, and then things had picked up again where they had left off, excepting, of course, the mental swerving required to avoid any mention of how Jake felt about his job or his employers. It wasn't as though they didn't have plenty of topics; work just couldn't be one of them.

*T*he fair was in Pleasanton, a city in an eastern angle of Alameda County that Jake would have bet nine out of ten San Franciscans could not place on a map. Fortunately, they almost never had to. If the Midwest was "the land you fly over" for those shuttling between the West Coast and New York, Pleasanton was part of "the land you drive past" on the way from San Francisco to Los Angeles. The fact that Pleasanton affected a laconic, Gold Rush air and that downtown store owners favored cowboy fonts for their window signage helped disguise the number of millionaires who lived there, including Pieter's boss. Maybe they would run into him at the fair, Jake joked. Pieter frowned ambiguously: either he vigorously hoped not or he could imagine nothing so outlandish.

On the drive to Pleasanton, Jake learned that he and Pieter had both spent time as children on small, barely successful farms, and that the experience had given them an appreciation of the difficulties of raising livestock and of the innocent earnestness of 4-H Clubs. But neither of them liked pigs, not even prize-winning pigs, and they planned to steer clear of those paddocks. Once they arrived, though, they realized there were more pigs than anything else, and they were hard to avoid, by sight or smell. They did see some good steers and lively horses as well as a large group of rangy-looking goats, the kids all head-butting hunger, the testicles of the adult males dangling like obscene breadfruit.

In an adjacent, fetid hangar, half a football field's worth of hens and roosters, some of them quite robust, were crammed into cages the size of bachelor-pad microwaves. The hens jerked and croaked, and the roosters puffed their feathers, shifting menacingly from foot to foot and regarding passersby with hostility. The rabbits fared about the same for space, but their stunned immobility made them seem less like live animals and more like incarcerated plush toys.

An anteroom housed the "Exotic Animal" exhibit: a skink; a pair of hill mynahs; an aquarium with a half-dozen orange-and-white clownfish (which children kept terrifying by slapping their palms against the glass with cries of "Nemo! It's Nemo!"); a boa constrictor; and some baby chicks. Jake wondered whether the chicks were near the boa constrictor for an unpleasant reason.

Neither Jake nor Pieter was interested in the rides, not the roving nuclei of loud, belligerent children that gathered at their entrances nor the sullen, jail-tattooed men who took tickets indifferently and cinched down safety bars with brusque movements that implied a capacity for violence. Once they had made their way through the livestock, they shared an outstanding corndog and a passable funnel cake and drank small bottles of water for $3 each. Finally, they settled in for plates of barbecue under a makeshift restaurant tent where picnic tables had been arranged end-to-end to create family-style rows. Spools of paper towels and trays of ketchup, hot sauce, and other condiments were spaced irregularly along the length of the tables. Behind a line of portable steam tables, a rank of male servers hacked into knots of smoked sausages and slabs of fatty, glistening brisket, messily filling plates which they shoved down the counter toward two women who ladled out the baked beans, cole slaw, and other sides. In the barbecue tent, a strict gender-division of labor seemed to be the rule.

"This is meat pornography," Pieter said happily once they'd found a place to sit. He unrolled his silverware, which had been swaddled in a paper napkin like a mummy, and laid his knife and fork out on the fake gingham tablecloth. "This is a gauntlet flung down at the feet of vegetarians!"

"A gauntlet in the shape of a hot link," Jake said. Then he added, "You know, I realize I'm not sure what a gauntlet is."

"A glove," I'd always assumed," Pieter said. "But now that you ask, I may be getting it confused with something about jousting."

"If it's a glove, then what does it mean to run the gauntlet? Or whatever it is, how can you both throw one down and run one?"

"An excellent lexical query," Pieter said. "Why don't we ask one of these fine folks?" He made a sweeping gesture with his knife around the room.

Jake's eyes following the contours of the invisible semicircle Pieter had outlined. He knew what he was supposed to see and, to an extent, he did see it: the straight boys who came to the fair and turned into Wyatt Earp, hooking their thumbs into their belt loops and walking with a swaggering affectation of bowleggedness, as if they'd been riding the range all day. The young women in T-shirts with elaborately frayed hems and spike heels, their hair ratted or shaved on one side or mulleted ("Why don't they ever come to *our* barbers?" Pieter had quipped earlier as they crossed the midway), and their exposed skin so pale and mushy that it seemed ready to slough off at a touch.

And he knew what Pieter was getting at. Every year at Pride Parade time, TV crews would come to Market Street to film 300-pound transvestites in leopard-skin spandex, but no one came to Pleasanton to film 300-pound straight guys with "Bikini Inspector" T-shirts and beer bellies avalanching toward their knees. If the media were going to make a spectacle of half-naked gym boys on floats, they ought to come to the fair and give equal time to the twenty-something suburban girls with hysterical makeup and pink shorts roughly the size of a deck of playing cards ("a pubic hair away from being illegal," as Jake's mother used to say). And there was no doubt that straight women in their late-40s looked no better in bandeau tops and daisy dukes than men in their late-40s looked in buttless chaps and spandex. No one was allowed to age with dignity.

"It's all drag, I guess," Jake said.

"It's all drag, but some of it *is* a drag," Pieter observed.

"Well, anyway, we're here, too," Jake said.

"True," said Pieter, "but this isn't our world. We've got one foot in and one foot out, and that makes us different."

Jake was thinking about worlds and who belonged in them. "Either that or it means we're going to dance the hokey pokey," he said.

∿∿
∿∿

After lunch, Pieter wanted to visit the "textiles," which turned out to be scores of quilts, many of which were quite pretty, but just as many of which were not. "If you were going to spend hundreds of hours making a quilt, why would you piece Leonardo Di Caprio into the center of it?" Jake asked, but Pieter had wandered away and the woman nearest to Jake shot him a dirty look.

From there, they moved on to the display of "fine arts," where amateur photographs, oils, water colors, ceramics, and other creations had been paired with what were apparently the winning poems in a writing contest. Jake knew he would probably be sorry if he read them, but he was both touched and distressed by the effort to present these meager efforts with such formal dignity. The last poem he read concerned a failed marriage; the second line spoke of "lonliness," and somewhere near the last stanza a "sillowette" made an appearance. "Don't these fucking people even have a fucking spell checker on their fucking computers?" he wondered out loud. Too loud, evidently; Pieter appeared at Jake's elbow and suggested it was time to go.

So they meandered back toward the Blue Gate, in the general vicinity of which they had parked (for $10.00), passing, on the way, the karaoke competition and a collection of "vintage" engines.

In one display, the winch from a turn-of-the-last-century fishing trawler sputtered and clanked, winding a massive capstan that must originally have hauled nets full of thrashing, terror-crazed fish from the sea. At the moment it smoked and leaked oil, managing to seem simultaneously indestructible and on the verge of exploding. A rickety lean-to called "Bob's Pump House" held a steam-powered tractor with iron wheels and a machine whose only purpose seemed to be to cause jets of water to squirt from a pipe that extended into the meadow on one side of the structure. Six levers protruded from a casing that resembled a giant stenotype machine and, if several people got going on them at the same time and in the right rhythm, the water shot as high as twenty feet in the air, cascading down onto a small mob of children who scattered, squealing, as if any fate were preferable to being drenched in the artificial rain before rushing back to be doused once more.

The last display before the gates was a booth sponsored by the Alameda County Cattlewomen's Association. As Tanya Tucker songs played in the background, the association's members hawked free rides on a mechanical bull and promised prizes to anyone who could last at least three minutes. ("Come on, fellas, I'm sure your wives would say some of you can last at least three minutes, wouldn't they?") Jake and Pieter were already at the turnstiles at the edge of the parking lot when an enthusiastic cheer went up for one of the bullriders. Jake turned to watch and noticed, for the first time, the red-and-white banner that waved above the Cattlewomen's booth. "BEEF TIMELESS FUN" it read. He would have asked Pieter what he thought it meant, but Pieter had already gone through the stile and was moving purposefully toward Jake's car.

A half hour later, Jake dropped Pieter back at his apartment where they said their goodbyes.

"Well, thank you," Pieter said. "That was a lot of fun."

"Yes, it was," Jake said, "and I'm glad you asked me. I'd never have gone by myself."

"Yessss," Pieter said, in the campy voice he sometimes used. "We'll do it again next year."

Pieter closed the car door, gave Jake a last wave, and disappeared under the portico that led to his elevator. He lived, Jake knew, in the penthouse of the building with a man he didn't love—or even particularly like—but the rent was controlled and the guy wouldn't move out, and Pieter had no intention of abandoning such a prime piece of real estate. When his ex dozed off in front of the TV one afternoon and let a fire start that all but destroyed the kitchen, Pieter had wavered, but then the man had stayed. After all, that's what renters' insurance was for.

Jake turned off the engine. There was virtually no chance, he realized, that he would know Pieter next year when County Fair time rolled around. Jake was going to quit his job at the law firm. The decision had been accruing, if that was the right word, all afternoon long, and now he felt the comfort of it settle over him like a crisp, clean sheet.

Pieter would say he was wrong. He'd say that the firm was likely to take Jake on permanently before the year was out. There would be insurance benefits and paid vacation. He'd say it whether or not it was true. His conversations with Alexandra made it possible that he knew about the firm's plans for Jake, but Jake would never be certain. Maybe Pieter was lobbying on Jake's behalf. Maybe he was lobbying against him. Things could go on like that for quite a while, and perhaps that's what work was: an endless variation on the prisoner's dilemma. Timeless fun. Unless you were the beef.

He wouldn't forget one thing Pieter had said, though. About the fair, he'd been exactly right. The fair was both familiar and alien: the cheesy entertainments, the rough boys and the tragic girls, the smell of overused deep-fryer grease and of goat urine in the hay, the American flags and the Confederate patches on jean vests, the dazed silence of the caged rabbits, the "sillowettes," the arc of Pieter's knife as he gestured in the barbecue tent. When Jake was a boy, he wouldn't have been a tourist at the fair, but something had happened and now he was. No matter where he stood, he only had one foot in.

"America is the scariest place on earth," he said out loud, even though he knew Pieter was far above him and could no longer hear.

Everybody Was Kung Fu Fighting

for Ryan R.

"... here comes the big boss, let's get it on ..." (Carl Douglas)

or some reason we were talking about Chinese New Year, about whether, if you were Chinese, you just called it "New Year" instead of Chinese New Year.

"Once we were at this Chinese restaurant?" Dorflex was saying. "And they were having, like, a celebration? And I asked what was the occasion? And this Chinese guy told me it was New Year's? Just New Year's?"

Burke was nodding like a hula-dancer doll in the back window of a Camaro, the signal that he wanted to be next in line to hold the Talking Stick.

"It's like if you ask an American what's the 4th of July, he's not going to tell you it's American Independence Day," Burke said. "He's just going to say it's Independence Day."

I can't stand it. "What if the guy was Chinese and American?" I ask.

"What?" says Dorflex.

"You said 'this Chinese guy' like he wasn't American. They're not mutually exclusive, you know. Anyway, American is a nationality and Chinese is a race or ethnicity or whatever. So the guy in the restaurant was probably Chinese-American and it doesn't prove anything, what he said."

Adam goes, "Everything is hyphenated," riffing on the title of that stupid film with that little bulge-eyed faggot from *Lord of the Rings* that's supposed to be all deep about memory and shit but just ends up being a Euro-trash wannabe. Adam is one of my housemates. He has the biggest room and pays the least amount of rent, which he considers fair because the lease is in his name. He also claims to be a socialist, which don't get me started.

Dorflex was giving me her super-intense, my-eyes-are-lasers stare to let me know I was pissing her off. "I'm just saying, the guy was Chinese? And they were celebrating Chinese New Year? Only he just called it 'New Year?'" Ever since Dorflex and Burke got together, she's been talking like that: Everything she says is a question. If I had to sleep with Burke, I'd be full of questions, too.

"Oh, sorry," I say, "I didn't realize you asked him to show you his passport before you started interrogating him about holidays."

"I don't see why you have to get all politically correct?" Dorflex says. "I'm just making a point? About what they call New Year?" Next to her, her roommate, Ziva, was helping Dorflex glare, working like a repeater station to intensify the contempt emissions. Ziva used to be bi, but six months ago she announced she was a lesbian separatist and would no longer respond to male-oriented language. Now, if you want to ask her anything, you have to say it to Dorflex first, and then Dorflex translates. I don't understand why Ziva keeps showing up to drink with us, but I imagine it's because none of us has the nerve to tell her in male to cough up her share of the bar tab.

Dodging Ziva's hostility vectors, I stare right back at Dorflex. "It isn't even Chinese. They celebrate it in a bunch of places in Asia, anywhere they use the lunar calendar." I don't actually know if this is true, but I figure Dorflex doesn't know either. "So, yeah, if your point is that people in China don't go around saying, 'Happy Chinese New Year' ... but the guy in the restaurant was most probably American and so it doesn't have anything to do with whether Chinese people say Chinese New Year or whether Americans say American Independence Day. It's a stupid analogy."

"God, you're such a little bitch," Adam says.

"I'm going to get a beer," I say, and I very pointedly get up without asking if any of them want anything. "Get a pitcher," Burke says to my back, but I act like I don't hear him.

The bartender is kind of cute, but then they're always kind of cute. In a queer bar, it's part of the job description. Possibly it's the entire job description. Anyway, we live two flights up from this place—in the asshole of SOMA, just blocks from where they turn the streets into open-air pissoirs during the annual Dore Alley freak show—and I have zero interest in being the guy who tricks out of the bar that's downstairs from his apartment. I don't cruise here at all, as a matter of fact. First off, everyone is so jaded, and second, all this leather-and-hankie drag is seriously over. I'm not saying I'd mind if some big, hunky Daddy carried me off and had his way with me, but then to find out he's a union-busting lawyer at Littler Mendelson or something and that his leather pants go to the cleaners in the same bag with his suits from Nieman's—I mean, just imagining who he really is, is like, the anti-Viagra.

Anyway, I order a gin and tonic instead of a beer. I decide not to go back to the table because right then I hate all the people who are supposed to be my friends. I carry my drink down to the end of the bar, where there's plenty of open space. There are a few hot guys playing pool, but right at the moment I pretty much hate hot guys, too.

Four evenings a week I work as a waiter at Chevy's, which is a Mexican restaurant for people who don't know what a Mexican restaurant is. It's very popular with off-duty Wells Fargo tellers and with tourists who want to eat enchiladas in California without having to deal with any actual Mexicans. In fact, we do have real Mexicans, but they're all dishwashers and no one in the dining room every sees them. When I get home, I smell like tortilla chips and the juice from canned jalapeños.

For a queer kid from the dwarf-fescue-lawn-and-ornamental-citrus-tree burbs of Sac, this is supposed to be the shit, right? A Victorian flat with the bathtub in one room and the sink in another, two floors up from a famous leather bar that's listed in all the faggot travel guides. A job that officially pays crap but gives me sixty bucks a night in tips, easy. Big-city life in Oz and safe-sex sluts everywhere you look.

Not long after I got here, though, I had a revelation: I'm just not that into it. The provinces are still the provinces, and the fact that you can see some independent Afghan film that only opened on about twelve screens in the entire United States or have a queer mayor or Maoist roommates or eat Vietnamese food one night and kosher vegetarian the next doesn't make the place seem less small, even if there's 800,000 other people to share the culture warp with you. Anyway, it's not San Francisco's fault. It's me.

I don't want Dorflex and the others to get the idea that I'm just pouting because then one of them will come looking for me and I'll end up back at their table, wasting another night of my life talking about random shit that doesn't matter to anybody, like how, if you read *War and Peace* at the rate of one word per hour, every day for the rest of your life, you still wouldn't be able to finish it—which, in recent memory, is something Adam actually did want to talk about. So I gulp down my drink (not difficult: once you get past all the ice, it's about a half-dozen dainty swallows) and then, when three drag queens come gabbling through the entrance, I take advantage of all the dust they're raising to slip through the black leather curtain and out the door. Normally, I love hanging out with drag queens. If you feel the need to fade into the background for an evening but you don't want to just sit around alone at home, they're your best bet. You're a portable audience, and the only thing they ever ask of you is applause.

I decide to walk. Basically, walking is boring, but boredom is sometimes all you can stand. There's a catch, though. I can never just come to the end of the walk, turn around, and go back the same way. It's too depressing. If I end up in a blind alley, it's dramatic: There's that moment when you've got no choice but to retrace your steps, and you feel like an idiot, because if you had any business being there you'd have known it was a dead end, and people start to give you those "get your punk ass outa my neighborhood" looks. Anyway, once you get south of Market, the streets are arranged pretty much in a grid, and the blocked-off alleys tend to be short so you can see before you turn that they don't go anywhere. You can keep walking until you hit water, more-or-less, and even then you can always skirt around it.

I pass my favorite Thai restaurant; a bunch of bars with door-ways that look like slits gouged out of the sides of buildings with a router; a piercing parlor; an outlet for discount leather jackets that smell like cat pee; a by-the-hour motel painted cantaloupe orange; the studio of this famous S&M photographer who looks like some species of flightless bird but who we're supposed to be all grateful to because he's this, like, sexual-liberation icon; and a store that sells bustiers and edible panties for women who weigh more than 200 pounds. This is where I live now, and all of this is here all the time, whether I want it to be or not.

I start walking toward the freeway, to get beyond that thin slice of the "south of the slot" area that's crammed with loft "spaces" and unsold yuppie condos and designer bars dying like cycads in the wake of the asteroid that killed off the dot-com millionaire. A few blocks away, you start to see the industrial skeletons of a previous extinction: warehouses, loading docks, and rust blooming like lichens on metal surfaces. It's a place made for first-year photography students at the Design Institute, the ones who like to take slightly overexposed black-and-whites of train tracks and the busted-out, crossword-puzzle windows of abandoned factories. It's also one of the cheaper areas—relatively speaking—left in San Francisco, partly because it's ugly and partly because there's no parking or grocery stores and not much in the way of bus lines, either. It's all very, like, gritty urban realism. When I first moved to this part of the city, someone broke into my truck and ripped off a box of paperbacks I was planning to drop off for the library sale. In San Francisco, even the petty-ass thieves are literate.

The closer I get to the freeway, the more the traffic starts to sound like waves breaking in the distance. Down here, below the elevated highway, the drivers in the few cars on the street turtle their necks to keep an eye on me as they pass, as if I could reach in and scoop them out of their metal shells with one claw. The look on their faces is both knowing and disapproving: Doesn't take a genius to guess what *you're* doing here at this time of night where practically nobody lives and the industrial printers and the "direct to the trade" designer-lighting store have been locked up for hours.

A cop car approaches from the opposite side of the street, slows down, then rolls into a lazy U-turn. I keep walking, but before I've covered half the block, I can hear him coming up behind me. Three more steps and blue flashes pulse like summer lightning. I stop and he pulls up beside me, his passenger-side window already rolled down.

"Where you headed?" he asks. My first reaction is to think he's offering me a ride.

"Uh, no thanks," I say, "I'm just walking."

"You live around here?"

"Eleventh Street."

"That's in the other direction," he says, extending his thumb from his right fist like a hitchhiker and pumping it back and forth a few times alongside his ear. It doesn't seem to be a question, so I just look at him. He makes me feel I should be doing something more to demonstrate my innocence, but the fact is, I *am* innocent.

"Not much to see at night in this part of town," he says. Another nonquestion-question. Whatever speech pathology he's got, it's exactly the opposite of Dorflex's.

"So can I go?" I ask.

A smile ignites on his face. He's got recruiting-poster features: dirty-blonde hair with lashes several shades darker and so thick they seem to outline his eyes in kohl; a jaw line that shows the whole, clean length of the blunted V of his mandible; an assertive chin; and museum-grade lips—not the usual white-boy mouth like the edges of a two stacked dinner plates. "Hop in," he says.

"Hop in?" I parrot back at him, stupid with disorientation. "Are you arresting me?"

"Of course not," he says. "Hop in."

"But I'm not going anywhere," I say. "I'm just walking."

"So just ride instead." He pats the passenger seat.

When I still don't move, he adds, "Hey, didn't your mom teach you you should always obey a police officer?"

"She told me not to get into cars with strangers, if you really want to know what my mother taught me."

"Right. Except if the stranger is a policeman. Because policemen are your friends."

"Are you serious?" I say.

He pats the car seat again. "Hop in. Friend."

The theories to consider are basically two. Theory One, he's a maniac on the Son of Sam/William Bonin/Leonard Lake tip. Point against him: driving around late at night offering rides to people who haven't asked might reasonably be defined as abnormal. Point in his favor: the patrol car and uniform lend him an extreme amount of cred. Point against him: He doesn't *seem* crazy or dangerous but then again, someone who really was crazy and dangerous would probably be doing his best not to show it, including going to the trouble of stealing a cop car. Point in his favor: This is San Francisco, which leads directly to Theory Two. In most places in the world, a guy inviting another guy he doesn't know to get into his car at something like ten at night might arouse suspicion, but here it's what sociologists would call normative. Plus, although SF certainly has more than its share of whack jobs, there's still bound to be more guys trying to get laid than there are serial killers, statistically speaking. In any case, I do what he says.

"Ever been in a police car before?" he asks once we're moving. "In the front seat, I mean." He gives me a wink that's the equivalent of an elbow in the ribs.

"Isn't it, like, against the regulations to have civilians in your car?" I counter.

He laughs. "I'm off duty."

Since I don't know cop rules, I have no way to know whether that makes any difference, but I doubt it. He drives for a while down the nearly deserted streets, guiding the wheel with the heel of his left palm, cruising like someone with no particular destination, his fingers gently tapping the ridged plastic. A couple of times I glance over to remind myself what he looks like. His body seems solid, accessible, with none of those hard angles that remind me of pigeon-spike strips: don't land here. Under his uniform shirt he's wearing a white T, and a curl of chest hair foams past the edge of the collar and into the bay of his throat. He's probably ten years older than me. When I look, he smiles back, casual. We don't talk, but it isn't weird. We're like a couple of old friends, just rolling.

The simple quirkiness of riding in a cop car with a stranger I would probably kiss gives me little breathless roller-coaster moments. Hitchcock or someone like that said human beings love to scare themselves to death. *Right at this precise instant, no one knows where I am*, I think, and the idea sends a sharp, raw shot to my brain like snorting coke: panic and rapture, alarm and weightlessness. *I could disappear!* and then: *Oh god, I could disappear!*

Objectively, there's probably not much to worry about. I've already checked to make sure the passenger door's not locked, and I know this neighborhood. I know, too, that we'll eventually hit the piers and he'll be forced to turn either north or south. North would take us up toward Market Street, where there are busses and street lights. In the other direction—well, I've never been in the other direction. On the map, what's there is a lot of empty, gray-green space.

Maybe getting into the car with him was stupid, but what's impressive is realizing what a strong gravitational pull the fantasy of my demolition exerts, the urge to become one of those "without a trace" mysteries: The Roanokes, Ambrose Bierce, Butch and Sundance, John Anglin and his brother, D.B. Cooper, Joe Pichler, Natalee Holloway, the Ecuadorian guy who worked in a pizzeria near the WTC and, after September 11th, nobody ever heard from him again but no one's sure he's dead either. Most of them probably are dead, but at least a few must have recognized an opportunity to float away, to land like Professor Marvel in an unheard-of world and step off into a new life as if whatever came before was just a navigational error. In unexpected moments, we suddenly sense the weight of what we are, and for scary, euphoric seconds all we want is to get out from under it.

As we're nearing the ballpark he takes a left, spinning the wheel with one hand. He heads toward Market for a few blocks, then turns again on Howard, driving west. "You're at 11th and Natoma, right?" he says.

"What?" I say, my voice too high.

"I'm taking you home," he says.

"How do you know where I live?"

"Face recognition software. You went to the gay pride parade last June, right?"

"So?"

"Don't get hostile, I'm just saying. You went. At big public events, we take routine crowd pictures, we scan them in, and then the software goes to work on matching them with photos from the California DMV database. For events like the parade, where there's a lot of out-of-towners, the hits are only around forty percent. Usually, though, it's a lot higher. We got enough anti-terrorism funding from the Feds to outfit about half the cruisers with these video cams"—he taps a device mounted on a swivel to the right of the steering wheel; a small lens points at the passenger seat—"which are linked to the mainframe."

I think this over for a few minutes. "Bullshit," I say at last.

He smiles again, that klieg-light smile. "Yeah," he says. "It's bullshit."

I stare at him. Men acting squirrelly isn't exactly news to me, but there's enough clutter between us to make me wonder whether I should pull the plug. To his credit, he takes the hint and dials himself down a few notches before he starts to talk again.

"Just a lucky guess is basically all. You already said 11th Street, right? After that I picked a likely corner. Most of the housing on 11th Street is between Mission and Howard anyway."

"Well, since you figured it out, that's as good a place as any to drop me off."

"You're not going to invite me up?"

"Why?"

"Because you want to."

"Because *you* want to, is what you mean. This whole thing, coming up behind me on the street and offering me a ride and everything … that's pretty weird, you know."

"I know, Brad. But isn't it *nice*?" The line comes out in a poncy Brit accent and he bites off the last word just like Frank N. Furter. The shift in his voice is such a shock that I can't help but laugh. Nelly fags can be entertaining, but they're usually so relentlessly desperate about making you think they're witty that you end up feeling lonely. At the other end of the spectrum, there are the guys who act like they're auditioning as stand-ins for Mt. Rushmore and who wouldn't camp even if you offered them free gym memberships for life. So when a normal-acting guy lets the queen pop out for a second or two because she's just right for the part and then puts her away again, there's no way not to be charmed.

"Okay," I say. I give him directions, and he finds parking on the alley side of my building. As I start to walk toward the apartment, I notice he's got the trunk of his cruiser open. He pulls out a long, cylindrical nylon bag and slings it over his shoulder by the straps. He sees the curiosity on my face. "Skis," he explains. "I just had them waxed and sharpened. D'you mind if I bring them inside? Even cop cars get broken into, you know. In neighborhoods like this, especially cop cars."

"Sure," I say.

Once we get upstairs, it's the usual ritual: I offer him a drink, and he paces the living room, trying to find something he can comment on. While I'm still busy with the ice and the glasses, he starts in with the questions. "This is a big flat. You got roommates?"

"Yeah, a couple. They're basically assholes, so don't feel you missed anything." I'm glad no one's home because I don't want to have to be in attendance during their pathetic efforts to make small talk with my friend, or guest, or trick, or whatever he is. Or hear Adam start in about the police state.

I carry the two drinks into the living room, where he's settled in on the upholstered, U-shaped seat below the turret window. The window leans out over the street like an observation tower. It's the apartment's best feature. "You got a name," I say, "or am I just supposed to call you 'officer'?" He isolates one shoulder like a Martha Graham dancer and twists it toward me so I can see the nametag over his right pocket: "L. Valachi."

"I'm guessing Lance, Lawrence, or Louis," I say, "but what I'm hoping is not Leroy or Lamar. Or Lloyd … or Leslie. Oh god, why are all the 'L' names so dorky?"

"The first man I was ever with was named Lamar," he says. "He was from Arkansas and he was very sexy. We did it while his wife was asleep in the next room."

"I've never slept with a guy named Lamar while his wife was in the next room," I say.

"Oh, I bet there are lots of things you've never done," he says. It comes out perfectly flat, like he's saying, "My eyes are gray." His expression arranges itself on his face like built-in furniture.

"Anyway," he says, "I'm Luther."

I tell him my name.

"So how come your roommates are assholes?" he wants to know. I give him the brief version of Adam and Burke and Dorflex and Chinese New Year and *War and Peace* and all the rest. "Last I saw them, they were in the bar downstairs getting hammered," I finish. "Wednesday is 'Leather Ladies' night, so Dorflex and Ziva get to drink for half-price, even though neither of them wears leather. Thank god."

Luther-the-cop just nods and stares out the window. There's a light fog, and the street lamps are surrounded by bruise-colored halos. He takes two slow sips of his drink. "You have no idea how many assholes you come across in my line of work," he says. "Some days you just want to...." Like a kid, he forms the thumb and first two fingers of his right hand into the shape of a pistol, then he snaps his wrist upward in an imitation of recoil. "POW!" he says.

"Yeah," I say. "Pow."

"I mean, wouldn't you do it if you could get away with it? Just to not have to deal with that shit anymore?"

"I ... what are we talking about?"

"Listen," Luther says, jumping up, it's kind of warm in here. Do these windows open?"

I lean over to struggle with the window nearest Luther. It slides up in a series of fits and starts, and the cool night air reaches in for us. "That's nice," he says. "D'you mind if I use your john?"

I point him down the hall. On the street below I can see that people are starting to leave the bar, and the nice-to-meet-yous and see-you-laters begin to float up. It's getting to be that time of night, at least for people who have regular jobs. The bar'll be dead soon, and Adam and Burke will come banging up the stairs, and probably Dorflex, too. She and Burke never sleep at her place anymore, now that Ziva doesn't feel the space is safe when there are men in the house.

I hear Luther making his way back, but my thoughts are focused on the way other people's freedom can begin to close in on you, about how you don't even notice, until it's too late, that you hardly have any room left to move in. He sets the nylon bag on the window seat, sits down beside it, and slides the zipper open. I figure he wants to show me his skis, not that I'd know enough to be impressed.

What's inside the bag is long and black and tube-shaped, and I'm about to say, "That sure doesn't look like skis" when Luther takes out a rifle. He props it across his knees while he lifts other, odd-shaped metal pieces out of the bag. One of them, I realize, is a scope, but I don't know about the rest. He's looking more at me than at the rifle as he screws and snaps things into place. The sounds that come as his hands move are clean, precise.

"What is that for?" I say finally, stupidly.

He laughs. "Well, it sure isn't for hunting Bambis." He shifts to sit next to me, his thigh touching mine. "You take it," he says.

"Why?" I say.

"Just take it," he says again, and I do. I'm surprised to notice that the metal feels slightly warm in my hands, and that the odor it gives off reminds me of my father's workshop in the garage back at our old house.

"Now listen," Luther is saying. "This is an easy weapon to fire, especially at this distance, and the sight is first-class. But I'm guessing you've never done this before, and there's going to be a lot of panic and running around afterwards, so what I'm saying is that you can only get one. So you have to choose. Think about it now while we have time, because you won't be able to re-aim and go again. You have to decide which one you really want."

"What the fuck are you talking about?"

"Look," Luther goes on. "See that guy down there in the green shirt? Just hold the barrel up, out the window, and look through here. Can you see? He looks like he's six inches away, doesn't he? It's a great scope. Get him right in the middle of the circle, where the 'T' is. It's just like taking a picture, really, the same principle."

Luther is standing now. He puts his hands on my shoulders and turns me gently so I'm facing the window full on. I get up on my knees, the barrel of the rifle out the window. I'm looking at the man in the green shirt. Luther walks over and switches off the living room light.

"You've probably heard this before in movies," he says, "but it's true. You don't really pull the trigger, you squeeze it. Want to try? Don't worry, the safety is on, nothing can happen. Doesn't need much pressure at all. You just take a deep breath and, as you let it out, you'll feel that sensation of your chest sort of collapsing in. That'll help you. You're going to do the same thing with the trigger, let it collapse inward toward your body as you exhale. Nice and slow."

Down below, I see that Burke and Dorflex have come out of the bar. Adam is right behind them and then Ziva, who's hanging onto some paper-white girl with hair that's green on one side of her part and chemical-blonde on the other. I stiffen and lower the rifle, but Luther puts a hand under my left forearm and calmly raises the barrel again.

"That's them, huh?"

I don't say anything.

"Okay now. Afterwards, I'll take the bag out the alley door and put it in the car. Then I'll come out front and say I was in the neighborhood when I noticed the commotion. When the cops come, I'll volunteer to canvass the building, so I'll be back up later to talk to you. But just in case someone else gets here first, you're going to say you were in bed, reading. Decide on a book now, whatever's next to your bed. No one's going to twig. Don't worry."

The four of them are clustered at the edge of the curb, where Burke has hooked one arm around a parking meter, swaying rhythmically as he watches Dorflex talk. I can't hear what she's saying, but I can feel her voice reach all the way up to the surface of my skin, snapping at me like a wet towel.

"I'm going to flip the safety off now," Luther says. He does something to the rifle and I hear a click. And then he's pressing against me, his chest against my back, his arms extended along the length of mine, helping me support the rifle. His body is warm and solid and I give in to the pressure and curve forward slightly, taking his weight. His lips brush my ear and I can feel the slight stubble of his cheek against mine.

"Ready to breathe?" he whispers, and I begin my inhalation.

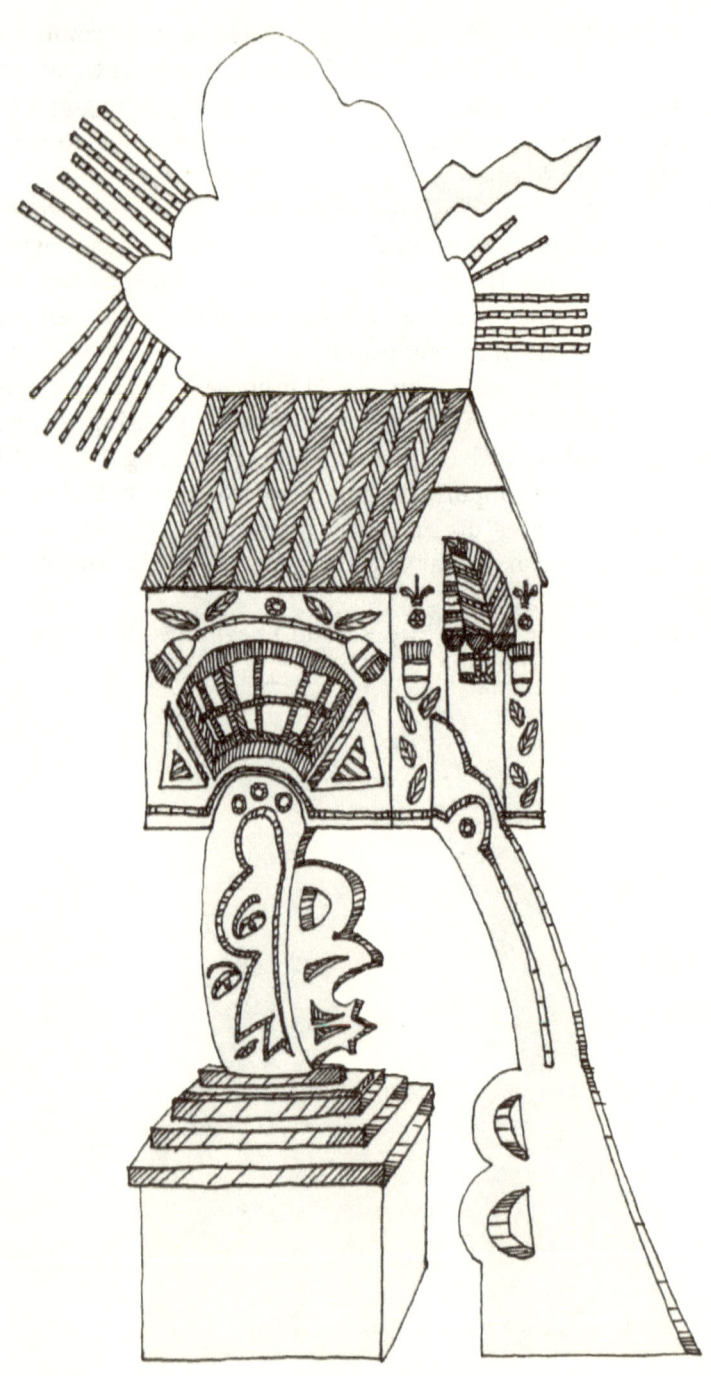

Financial Aid

The guy sitting across the narrow table is a grim, efficient little queen, blinking at me through expensive glasses that feature a tiny YSL logo and stems no thicker than a cocktail straw. His pale green shirt is tight over his bird chest; his voice is tight; on the small card he has just given me, his handwriting is tight, with meticulously formed letters and every dot and comma in place.

I know his type because I've encountered them so many times before. I know he isn't going to let me do what I want. It doesn't matter that he's gay and I know it or that I'm gay and he knows it. I'm not one of his friends, and I'm certainly not someone he's ever noticed out in public, meaning at one of the clubs he frequents with his clique. If I did have the gall to show up at one of their places, I'm the guy they'd be laughing at behind their hands—hair-challenged, they'd say, because mine is long and shaggy and thick, and has never been "styled" in my adult life, unless you count whatever they do for you at SuperCuts. Right now, it's looking more than a little nappy, held down behind a bandana that I'm wearing to keep it from flying all over the place and not as a fashion statement. I worked at the bar until four in the morning, went home for a bowl of cereal and a pot of coffee, rode my bike to campus for my eight o'clock and ten o'clock classes, dropped off my already-late rent check, and then went home again for a three-hour nap before coming to campus one last time today to meet with this asshole. Who kept me waiting for forty-five minutes.

He's younger than me by at least a half-dozen years, but someone has given him the authority to disburse financial aid checks, and he has decided I can't have mine. "You have to have a current university ID," he keeps saying. I haven't gone to get one yet. It's the end of the afternoon on a Friday, and I won't have time to make it across campus, stand in that line, get my picture taken, wait for the photo to develop and the laminator to do its work, and then come back to the Financial Aid building which, for no good reason, closes on Fridays an hour earlier than all the other campus offices.

"But does the ID card really matter that much?" I ask. "If I show up over there, they still have to check my name on some computer record to make sure I'm a student or else they won't give me a card, right? Can't you do the same thing? I have my driver's license." I take out my license and extend it across the table. He ignores the object in my hand the way polite people ignore bad breath.

"Our computer system isn't networked with the admissions and records computers," he says.

"Well, couldn't you call and verify that I'm registered as a student?" I slide my license back into the plastic window in my wallet, massaging the frayed Velcro strips together until the closure holds.

"I'm not authorized to do that."

Now I know, and he knows that I know, that he could get authorized if he got off his ass and asked his supervisor, or he could just be a nice guy and give me the check. It's not like he'd be facing a lot of jail time for breaking that particular rule. But he isn't going to do it. He doesn't *have* to do it, I suppose is the sticking point. Plus the fact that I'm just not his kind. He decided on sight that he didn't like me, which is probably fair because I decided I didn't like him, either. You can never tell, in situations like this, whether the other queen is being hateful because he's attracted to you, because he *isn't* attracted to you, or because he's suspects you have the nerve to be attracted to him.

He's looking at me now with his eyebrows lifted, the tips of his thin, pale fingers tented together. It's time for me to go; there's nothing more he can do.

I glance at the stiff paper rectangle he has handed me. It's an appointment card, imprinted with his name, inviting me to return on Monday at three p.m. to receive my check. *Sean Owens. Financial Aid Specialist.* Who is now calling my bluff. Will I stand up, raise my voice, demand that he find me someone else to talk to, thereby demonstrating that I'm the vulgar prole he thinks I am, or will I slink meekly away, letting him have a victory that means nothing to him but means a great deal to me?

The check he is holding but won't let me have will cover the check I wrote several hours ago for my rent. By the time I get my financial aid award deposited on late Monday afternoon, there's a good chance my rent check will already have bounced, which isn't how I'd prefer to have things go with my landlord, who doesn't know me very well and isn't happy that I've been late with the rent for the last few months. The longest it was ever late was three days, but it might as well have been three years. "You know, we write the late-charge clause into the lease for a reason," he said today, as I held my check out to him.

"I know," I say, "and I'm sorry. You should go ahead and charge me if you need to." I'm holding the piece of paper hopefully between my thumb and forefinger, and he still hasn't taken his hands out of his pockets.

"No," he says, "no, I don't want to do that." He sighs like he's doing me the biggest favor in the world over ten fucking bucks. "But please just try to get the rent here on time, okay?"

"Sure," I say. He sighs again, drags one hand out of his Dockers, folds my check in half without looking at it, and slips it into his pocket along with his fist.

After all that, having the check bounce would be ... inconvenient. Plus my landlord would definitely insist on the late penalty, and his bank and mine will both want their bounced-check charges.

The queen sitting across from me is about to cost me forty bucks, give or take, which is more than a week's food budget. I could tell him this; maybe he'd even relent. But my stubbornness is blossoming. Why should I give him the satisfaction of hearing me explain my life? What right does he have, with his shiny, hundred-dollar, oxblood Doc Martens, to know that I'm broke? No doubt he collects such information, not because any individual piece of it is valuable, but because the accumulated mass of it is a physical souvenir, like an ear, that he can carry in a pouch above the cinder of his heart.

I stare at the floor. My Keds are worn and pretty putrid, even for me—the tip of the right one is nearly black with grease from where I catch it, at least once a day, in my bike chain, which is coming loose around the derailleur. Both shoes are frilled with semi-dry mud: an afternoon downpour drenched the campus as I was leaving the landlord's house, and I'd taken a short cut to the Financial Aid building, riding through the soccer field and an unpaved parking lot next to the dorms in order to arrive on time for my appointment. I slouch down in my chair.

"Look," I say, lifting my head slowly so that my brown eyes are dead-on level with his gray ones. "I know you think that being a fag gives you the right to act like an officious little Nazi, but things are going to go different for you today from how they usually do." As I'm speaking I swing my right leg up under the table between us and prop it on the edge of his chair, placing my heel carefully between his legs. He tries to push back, but I've been watching him as we talked, and his office is small. There aren't more than a couple of inches to spare between the back of his chair and the wall.

"So now you have a choice," I say calmly. "I'm going to count to three, and on three, one of two things is going to happen. Either you're going to hand that check over to me, and we'll go on about our business, or I am going to grind my nasty, greasy, muddy foot right up into your crotch. I realize you may not feel much like giving me my check at that point, but you don't feel much like giving it to me now, so I don't see how I lose anything. Besides, that'll be all right because then we'll be square. I'm going to ruin you a pair of nice, clean khakis, which cost you a lot more than it's going to cost me not to have that check when I leave here today, plus you'll have to go home looking like you had some kind of embarrassing accident, and you don't strike me as the kind of guy who enjoys that sort of thing. I really don't care which one it is."

The look on his face is just what I had hoped for. He isn't scared or even angry, just shocked. *This isn't how civilized people act*, his eyes are telling me. His eyes, and the slight gap that has opened between his thin, elegant lips. I scoot my chair forward a bit for effect. "ONE!" I begin.

Before I can get to two, he flips the check over, stabs at it with a rubber stamp, and shoves it across the desk.

"You still have to sign for it," he snarls. I pick up the check, then casually lift my foot down from the edge of his chair.

"You sign for me," I say. "And you remember something, too, you arrogant piece of crap. You remember that it was another faggot who did this to you. You be sure and understand that it was another queer cocksucking shirtlifting dicksmoking motherfucker who was here today so you don't make a mistake and try to tell people how you were almost *gay bashed* or some shit, because you never were. It was much worse than that." I stand and start to go.

"Trash," he sniffs. I don't turn around. Instead, I kick the base of his hollow-core door as hard as I can so that it flies back and slams into the wall outside, the knob digging a neat, round divot into the drywall. Secretaries in the outer office look up, alarm on their faces, but nobody moves. At the bottom of his door, my filthy Keds leave a brown-and-black arc smeared across the institutional white paint. I know that probably won't be there for long. He'll be on the phone to maintenance as soon as I'm out of sight, screaming for somebody to come and clean it off.

As I walk out to the rack to unchain my bike, I imagine what the janitor might look like when he comes to deal with the stain on the door. I hope he's queer, and I hope he's handsome, and I hope he can sense the vibration left behind in that room from what went on there and decides that Mr. Sean Owens has not even come close to the end of being fucked with today.

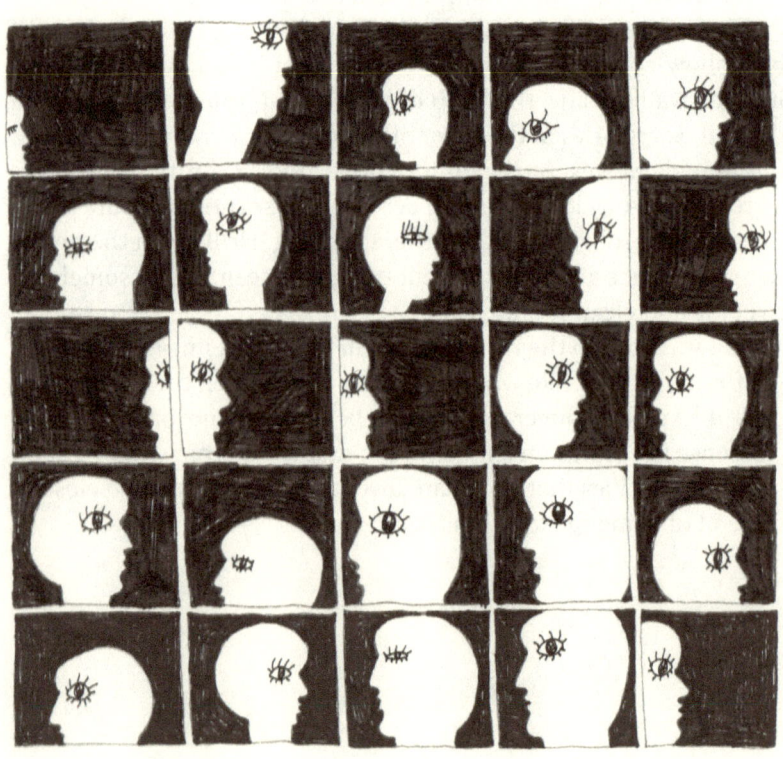

Jeremy

You won't be surprised that I found the cabin empty and silent when I arrived there for the last time, the lights extinguished (of course there was no one to tend the generator), and the savage smell of decay seeping from beneath the rubber seal of the chest freezer. I didn't open it. If I'd rather live in ignorance of certain details, no one could fault me. Besides, someone will look inside eventually, and then the newspapers will compete to print the gruesome details. Except that I will not be among their readers, avid for gore: when I get where I'm going I hope not to see a newspaper for a very long time.

Even without recent events as background, being in the cabin was an odd and unpleasant experience. Can anything be more unfamiliar than the familiar place you've chosen to abandon? Of course there was nothing there to tell me what has become of Jeremy. I don't know what I expected to find—nothing as prosaic as a note, certainly. He couldn't have known for certain I'd be the one to find it, and he wouldn't have wanted to compromise me. Besides, what could he have written under the circumstances? Still, I wanted ... something. A sign of some sort, a clue only I would recognize. Not a secret signal that told me how to reach him—I didn't want that—but an acknowledgement that he knew I knew, and that he understood what my knowing meant. Instead, he vanished. As you know, I've not seen him for more than two months.

Of course I realize, in the end, that silence was the more rational choice, even if the more unsettling one. Stupid people wouldn't understand that Jeremy is supremely rational, that his logic turns out to be more shocking than his violence.

The police showed up only a few hours after the story appeared in the local paper, wanting to know what I could tell them about Jeremy and his "appetites." One of them actually used that word: "Were you aware he had certain *appetites*?" They were back again two nights later, and for weeks they continued to show up with random frequency. They were convinced Jeremy was contacting me, though they couldn't imagine how he was slipping messages past them. The answer is that there were no messages.

The second time they came they brought their search warrant and took my computer, along with other things that made less sense (every last article of Jeremy's clothing, for one thing, though I suppose I should thank them for sparing me that). I was sure they had tapped the phone and were following me whenever I went out. That's certainly what I would have done. Even if I felt inclined to help, I'm quite sure I know less than they do about the only question that really matters to them—where Jeremy is—so my vague and unhelpful answers were painfully sincere.

Their obsession with Jeremy—for that is what it feels like—is surely fueled by the fact that he humiliates them. Yes, he targets them as well, but mostly he makes them look like fools. Even with all their equipment and their computers and their weapons, which they slap against their flanks like science-fiction phalli, they were never able to foresee what he would do or when or, more to the point, stop him.

Jeremy, in the meantime, teased them with his emails and his letters and especially with his videos. I've now seen one of them, thanks to the police. You would have been as disoriented as I, I think. These days, movies and TV show us simulated atrocities of every kind, but most of us see real violence so rarely that we barely know how to recognize it anymore. Your mind tries hard to convince you that the whole thing is staged.

They never told me exactly what led them to Jeremy, though I felt the tumblers sliding into place the moment I heard. No question:

a few of them must have known almost instantly what connected the men that Jeremy chose, but he counted on their silence and their guilt. It wouldn't have taken a brilliant police mind in any case to understand that Jeremy's project was revenge—pure and vicious—even if no one could admit in public the reason for the revenge, his *jus ad bellum*.

For Jeremy, this town meant torture and had done since before he was out of his teens, so I'm sure there's been no shortage of worried consciences. I hope some of those bastards go on suffering in terror. I don't wish Jeremy's literal vengeance on them, but the fear that he might still be out there somewhere—their Moloch, their Monster of Montmartre—could begin to save their souls.

Anyway, it should be they who explain Jeremy to the rest of us. They created him in their hellhole of a small-town jail, in their airless interrogation rooms putrid with the smell of cigarettes and the sweat of men who'd worn the same shirt for days. I wanted to say something like that, but I suddenly felt so deeply, deeply weary, and I sat like a good child, responding as calmly as I was able to their questions.

The police knew Jeremy and I were together, of course—not that we'd have been able to keep that a secret for all this time in a place like this, not that we ever tried—and they had a hundred pointless questions about that. They're convinced the sexual aspect is explanatory, that it was just a short step from one "perversion" to another. I didn't bother to suggest to them that it was Jeremy's love for me that kept him in check as long as it did. I let them fumble through their questions, my enjoyment of their discomfort only partially diluting the chill that comes over you when you're being scrutinized by someone with the power to make disapproval count. Someone able to disapprove on behalf of an entire government: "The eyes that fix you in a formulated phrase."

They wanted to formulate me and they hope to formulate Jeremy; they'd love us excruciated on a pin, but they didn't get that satisfaction from me. I was impassive, straightforward. I admit to some pleasure in shoving it in their faces. They asked me if Jeremy had ever written me any letters, and I showed them the love letters—well, copies, anyway. I had already mailed the originals to myself at one of those private mail boxes. I said something implausible about having donated the originals to an archive years ago, and they didn't even ask which one. Anyway, the letters are rather graphic. You'll recall that Jeremy was quite inexperienced when we met, and he took some delight in cataloguing our private moments together. I find the letters charming for his enthusiasm and his naiveté. So precocious, he even quoted to me those ambiguous lines of Whitman's:

> Give me now libidinous joys only,
> Give me the drench of my passions, give me life coarse
> and rank.

I had forgotten about that.

The one who led the interrogation snorted as he read Jeremy's descriptions of our sex, but they were disappointed if they expected me to be embarrassed. Of course, they took the copies with them as I'd expected, but they'll find nothing there that will help. They were, after all, written more than ten years ago, long before any of this. Still, it's the fixation of the police to collect information, even if they have no idea what it means or how it connects with anything else. They hoard it the way shut-ins hoard plastic grocery bags.

I tried to comprehend that they were men with families and loved ones, with children who sat in their laps and laid blonde heads against their chests, with wives they turned toward for comfort in the night. It was enough to soften them for me, but not enough. I felt the hate nudging me, seductive and so persistent, like a horse after the lumps of sugar in your pocket. It would have been no effort at all to give up trying to stanch the hate and let myself submerge in the red baptism of it. I could taste the intoxication at the back of my throat, a milder version, I suppose, of what Jeremy experiences when he is in rut. I will need to be forgiven for that.

In any case, I got up to the cabin and finished what I needed to do, evidently without their knowing. If I hadn't been so nerve-wracking, I might almost have enjoyed the cloak-and-dagger of it. You know how I love my thrillers. After I went to pick up the packet of Jeremy's letters, I drove south for a couple of hours and spent the night in a town I hadn't even known existed. In the morning, I left the truck parked on a quiet back street about a mile from the motel and then caught a bus west to another town on the banks of the river, spent the night there as well, and finally caught a second bus back to pick up the truck. Two nights in godforsaken motels that want cash and don't ask for credit cards; two nights of free HBO and revolting, watered-down coffee in the morning, jumping out of my skin every time I heard footsteps outside my room. And after that the long drive to the cabin.

I don't know whether any of that was strictly necessary. It's not as though I've done this sort of thing before. But I couldn't risk leading them straight to the cabin before I'd had a chance to see it, and I didn't know another way to gauge how closely they were keeping tabs on me. If I didn't notice anything unusual during all my moving around, I supposed, if they didn't try to stop me from leaving town, I could go ahead with as much of a plan as I'd been able to work out. Forty miles out I bought five gas cans at the Walmart and filled them at the self-service pump so I wouldn't have to stop again until I was done. Turns out all that extra gas came in handy for other reasons.

When they connect the dots and realize I own the cabin, or did until yesterday morning, when I completed my business at the re-al-estate office and caused everyone consternation by insisting on taking my proceeds in cash, I shall certainly be accused of being an accessory, of obstructing justice, or their version of it, and I'll be in serious legal trouble. An *accomplice*. How could I not have known, they asked me more than once. But I didn't.

Well, perhaps that isn't exactly true. Up until I got to the cabin, the only thing giving me a bad conscience was knowing that I'd harbored a vague suspicion that something wasn't right with Jeremy and did nothing about it. There's no denying that I stopped suggesting some time ago that we come up to spend weekends together at the cabin. Naturally I had registered Jeremy's lack of interest—unusual because he'd once so loved the forest there—and in some part of my being I must have considered the possibility that *he was using it*. I had no specific theories, though I can't honestly say I didn't ask myself whether he was bringing tricks there. After all these years, I could hardly have minded that. But the train of thought doesn't bear inspection. If it was just for a little fun, why take someone all the way up there? Four hours' drive each way. Given the price of gas, it wouldn't have cost too much more to rent a motel room here in town. I can't defend myself. I sensed I mustn't press the issue with him, and I didn't. Who knows what might have happened if I had insisted, but I've never for a moment worried that Jeremy would harm me, even to save himself. Perhaps he would just have disappeared sooner.

The police made the same connection, of course, and the interrogator asked why I didn't seem to be afraid that Jeremy would come after me.

"The thought never entered my mind," I said.

The interrogator pounced. "And why is that?"

I answered bluntly: "Because Jeremy's interest is in people who hurt and abused him. I've done neither."

But now I truly am an accomplice. I've destroyed evidence, though I'd like to think it's not evidence that could ever make any real difference.

That's part of the reason for my leaving, too, of course.

By separate mail, I'll be sending the police a list of additional names and disposal sites they may not know about. Jeremy kept meticulous and detailed logs in one of those spiral notebooks you can buy anywhere, right down to the scientific names of bones, so many of which (phalanges, fibula, manubrium) sound like exotic plants only a professional landscaper would recognize. I found the notebook as I was cleaning out the cabin, just slipped in among the books on one of the shelves in the main room. The fact that I didn't miss it is pure randomness. I worried it was disloyal to turn the notebook over—a foolish concern, but that was my first reaction. Ultimately, logic prevailed: They already know more than enough to hang Jeremy ten times over, literally as well as figuratively, and the families of the men named in the list will appreciate, in time, the opportunity to know for certain what they now only dread. "Appreciate" is the wrong word. They would choose to know, if the choice were between knowing and not knowing, though of course what they would wish for most of all is an entirely different set of choices. We have that in common.

I took Jeremy's notebook to a Kinko's in the next town over and copied it on a Xerox machine the size of a Volkswagen. I also used one of their rent-by-the-hour computers to type out a separate list of names and locations culled from the notebook, and I printed out a copy without saving the file. I asked them at Kinko's to FedEx the copy of the diary to *The Star* for me, and I'll put the list for the police in the regular mail along with this letter to you. Even without a return address on the envelope, it'll take them two minutes to figure out where it came from, but I'm not trying to be mysterious. I suppose I took such pains with the notebook out of some last surviving loyalty to Jeremy. I wanted them to have the names and other details but nothing that Jeremy had actually held in his own hands. Yes, I still love him and feel protective of him, after everything, though I hope never to see him again. Does that shock you? It shocks me.

The negotiation with *The Star* was surprisingly quick. I faxed two pages from the notebook, and they offered me $50,000 for the original. In a few days, the cashier's check will be in the hands of Father DeSiard, along with instructions for distributing it to the families of the men Jeremy killed. You know I don't normally have much to do with the papists, but DeSiard is decent enough. Besides, he's a politician, like all of them, and his ego is so huge that the publicity he'll get from this will keep him honest. I realize the money doesn't break down to much for any one of the families, but it's neither absolution nor mitigation and it isn't meant to be. Nor do I relish the idea that somebody's children may end up reading exactly what happened to their father while they're standing in the checkout line at Kroger's, but there are no unmixed blessings in this story. It's what I could do to get Jeremy's story out, and I feel I owed him that.

Which is as much as to say that there aren't any unmixed motives, either, and I'm not convinced there are even any innocent victims. That's not to defend Jeremy, but to say that no one would ever have believed what happened to him otherwise. In fact, for all of his adult life, I'm the only one who ever did, and even I didn't know all of the details. In the diaries, he tells everything: what happened to him when he was seventeen and was kept captive for four nights in the town jail before they decided he hadn't stolen somebody's car. He had no one to miss him or to come get him out, and I suppose they were counting on that, the bastards. They knew what he was, that's for sure, and they used him for every one of those four days, the sheriff, his deputies, the buddies they phoned to come join the party. Some of those are among the dead now, but I'm not sure it isn't fair for their families to know what they did to a boy. What Jeremy did isn't for weak stomachs, either, but he had an Old Testament sense of justice.

In any case, once I found the notebook, I had to do something to discharge the obligation that had suddenly been handed to me, and now I have. At the cabin, I burned the notebook and Jeremy's love letters and threw the ashes in the lake. It all felt very East Indian and funerary, as if I were ritually releasing souls. Including, of course, my own.

I feel a twinge for what the couple who bought the cabin will face once they get there, but I made it clear that the place was a wreck and I gave them a ridiculously low price to take it sight unseen. I got about half what the land alone was worth, never mind the buildings on it or the machinery. Anyway, that ought to salve their outrage somewhat. Nothing too ghastly, now that the freezer's gone, but there were stains on the rug, and the mattress on the guest bed was a ruin. I dragged all that out to the back yard, soaked it in gasoline, and set it on fire along with a few other things. Trash fires are common enough out here, so I doubted anyone would investigate. Later, the new owners might recall seeing signs of a recent fire when they first arrived, and they might tell the police, and the police might find all of that very suspicious. But they won't be able to prove I did it and, anyway, I can't worry about that now. I'm depending upon my intuition that my eager yuppie buyers are fussy enough to tear out everything that isn't nailed down and repaint everything that is. I told them the mantelpiece and some of the moldings were oak, if they wanted to spend the time stripping them, and they seemed to light up. "Original oak!" they said.

By the time the police get around to searching the cabin, nothing of use to them will be left. More protection of Jeremy, I suppose, but also of myself. My life was in that cabin, too, in the years I lived in it alone before I moved to the city and in the summers Jeremy and I had there together after we met. We couldn't get enough of each other.

It's terrifying how much you cannot foresee about your life. As Jeremy and I lay there in the night, naked on top of the sheets because the heat was fierce those summers, even at midnight, I thought I was world-wise and pragmatic because, battle-scarred veteran of other love affairs, I dared to allow my mind to experiment with the idea that I might not always love Jeremy or him me, or that someday we might have to give up the cabin. That was my idea of giving a name to the worst that might happen. Such arrogance, to imagine I could weigh all the possible outcomes, could imagine the worst. I had no idea.

In any case, I felt I didn't dare make more than one trip back and forth to the cabin, and I couldn't manage the freezer, the mattress, and the rug at one go; so I chose to dispose of the first as the more egregious item. I left it at the dump, but someone will notice that the door is still attached, which I believe is against the law, and that will be that. As I've told you, I don't know what's inside, but perhaps it's something someone might want to bury. After plane crashes and so forth you read that relatives are desperate for some physical object and are relieved to sit through a funeral service with a shoe or a swizzle stick or a kneecap resting on the satin cushion inside the coffin in front of the altar. I would find it bizarre and macabre, but grief is always obscene.

I've lost Jeremy, of course, and I grieve for him, though I also grieve for myself. He's dead in every practical sense of the word, but so is what I had of a life, which I must now cleanly amputate if I care to go on with a vestige of autonomy left intact. I can't determine whether I'm doing the right or the wrong thing. I know I have adopted a single-mindedness about myself that I wear like borrowed clothes. It's an odd sensation to operate in the world as though one's actions existed in true isolation. Of course, it's never exactly like that: On the freeway you slow down so as not to run into the idiot who has suddenly changed lanes in front of you; you can't pretend you don't see the other cars. If I want this letter to reach you, I'll have to drop it into a box and depend upon strangers to carry it the rest of the way. We are helplessly tied to others.

But those are small matters, comparatively. By making my disappearance, I've divorced myself from the questions of what others will think of me, what they would expect from me, whether they will have feelings or needs that I might, under other circumstances, bend my actions around. I've become my own moral compass. In the process, I've come close to what must have guided Jeremy, which is to say sociopathy. It's exhilarating and terrifying to cut the rope and push out across the water on your own. There is always the danger that you'll entirely forget the way back to shore.

I don't pretend not to be curious, but for the most part I don't find myself sorry not to know more. I admit I'd prefer not to live out my days wondering if I'll open the door one day and find him standing there. But I don't think he'll turn up where I'm going, and I can't even be sure he's alive. If he went into the deep woods to end himself, no one may ever know of it. If I'm angry about anything, I suppose it's that—and my reasons are completely selfish. Things would go easier for me if there were some way to be certain that Jeremy was gone for good. They'd lose interest in me then, or they might. I've read that it's difficult these days for any living person to truly disappear, but then I suppose everything depends upon how tenaciously someone else cares to look.

Which brings me to my reason for writing: Please do your best to forgive me for winking out like this, my old friend. In time, if it seems I can, I may let you and a few others—presuming there's anyone who still cares—know my whereabouts, but you'll have to leave that up to me. You can't try to find me, and I won't make contact unless I decide it's safe for both of us. I apologize for the harshness of my insistence on this point and for what perhaps seems like melodrama. I have my reasons.

I know you have also grasped by now that you must not keep this letter. I may have over-exposed you simply in sending it, but on balance I decided the greater kindness was to make things clear rather than allow you to imagine who-knows-what scenario. I have realized something, in fact, though I don't know whether you will find it helpful or merely pathetic. I might easily have lost Jeremy under entirely mundane circumstances, as so many of our friends have been lost: betrayals, unbridgeable conflicts, even the plague (literally mundane by now, a thing of this world). But if any of those had occurred, I am convinced I would have felt this same impulse to drift away, the one I am so carefully obeying now. My life with him was a life because he was in it, but I am suddenly balanced upon a stool with two legs. I don't care if the police believe that Jeremy came for me in the end, despite my assurances that he would not, but I couldn't bear it if you wondered the same thing. Let us leave it this way, then. At long last, let us say, I came for myself.

Bayonet

In my bedroom, my mother is sitting beside me at the olive-green desk. She's made me bring in one of the chairs from the dining room, and now we're pulled up next to each other, close enough for me to smell the cigarette smoke in her clothes and the AquaNet in her hair. The bulb in my gooseneck lamp is the only light in the room and, on the other side of the window, moths and flies are beating toward it. As they do, geckos stalk them across the surface of the screen, so motionless they might be plastic toys. Their strikes are invisible, but the results are unmistakable: in the gecko's mouth, legs and wings hang crosswise, pointing in the wrong directions but still twitching. I can look straight into the geckos' eyes, the color of copper pipe.

"You aren't even trying," my mother is saying. She's sick of me. There was no pleasure in seeing her that way, with the light of the lamp on one side of her face and shadow on the other, like the moon. So I focus on the geckos.

I think my mother is beautiful. Some days, when she picks me up after school, she stays to talk with my teachers, and she has a habit of sticking the white plastic stem of her sunglasses into the corner of her mouth, where she sucks on it gently. She stands that way while they talk, her head tilted to the right, but something in her posture suggests she's only half-listening, that she has more important things on her mind. I wanted to be as elegant as that.

She's trying to help me with my math homework—long division. Miss Peterson, my sixth-grade teacher, has been sending home notes. I was doing well in all my other subjects, but I was about to get a "D" in math, Miss Peterson said. In my school, there are only seventy-eight students in eight grades, and a "D" is the same as flunking. We live in the country. In the boondocks, my mother says. The only kids who got "Ds" are the hopeless ones, like Hinano Kalama. He's retarded, but we aren't supposed to say that word. Hinano lives with his grandmother, who teaches Sunday School and bakes every single week, cookies or brownies or cupcakes, if someone is having a birthday, which she gives to Hinano to carry in Tupperware containers. He can do that, at least. She plays the ukulele and sings at the May Day pageant, which is the second biggest deal at my school after the Christmas play. Everybody loves her. They feel sorry for her because she's stuck with Hinano, who's taller than anyone else in my grade and takes about a week to say anything if you ask him a question, but the teachers still give him "Ds." The other person who got "Ds" is Tammy Saito, who stutters and sweats and has an old-lady face even though she's the same age as me. She was also born with a cleft palate, and the scar in the middle of her upper lip looks like the thick, raised seams on my stuffed animals after I pull all the fur off.

If I get a "D" in math, I'll end up like them.

"You're not applying yourself," my mother says. Miss Peterson wrote that on my first-quarter report card, and it had become my mom's new favorite saying, right along with "You just don't have any stick-to-itiveness." She'd signed my report card with the "C-" in math and sent it back without writing anything in the box for "Parent Comments." That blank space was terrible, like the silence when my mom got really mad. The silence before something caught fire. As long as she kept talking, things were okay. Later, she and Miss Peterson started sending each other notes all the time, and I had to carry them back and forth, in sealed envelopes, like a spy against myself.

I try to concentrate on the page of problems on the desk in front of me. They want you to figure out things like: 721 divided by 47. What Miss Peterson called the dividends are housed in neat, three-sided cabins, with the divisor outside on the left. At the bottom of the page there's a printed warning in purple capitals: SHOW YOUR WORK.

That's the whole trouble. I could have gotten the answers if they let us do it the way I knew how. I knew that 47 times 10 was 470. You put the 10 over on the right side and subtracted 470 from 721. So then you had 251 left over. You could try 47 times 5. You put the five over in the column underneath the 10, and subtracted 235 from 251. When the number got below 47, you did the same thing, but added a decimal point. You just kept going like that. After a while, you narrowed in on the answer. I can multiply and subtract okay.

But we aren't allowed to do that anymore. We have to learn the new math. They sent home a notice about it. We have to put the answer on the top of the little cabin now, not on the right side in a column. Now you have to think how many times 47 would go into 72 first, and you have to get it exactly right or the problem won't work out. Then after you subtract, you can bring down the 1. To me, it's a stupid way to do the problem, but you have to show your work, so I can't just do it the old way on scratch paper and transfer the answers. Besides, we always go over the homework in class, and I knew Miss Peterson would call on me to work a problem on the board, and there would be no way to hide.

My mom understands how to do it the new way, but she doesn't know how to explain it. She isn't a good teacher. And I'm not a good student because I'm not going to do the homework. I'm not going to do what Miss Peterson wants, not if we sit here all night. It wasn't my mom's fault, and I was sorry she'd gotten in the middle of me and Miss Peterson, but she doesn't know what Miss Peterson is really like, and I can't explain. Anyway, even if I did, I already know what she'd say. She'd tell me that you don't always like everyone you come across in life, but you still have to get along with them, especially if they can hurt you. "When you have your head in the lion's mouth," she likes to say, "you can't snatch it out. You've got to ease it out."

Finally, my mom gives up for the night. "Fine," she says. "Flunk math. It's your funeral." She picks up the dining room chair and carries it out, turning to slam my door. I can hear the chair bumping along as she maneuvers it down the hall. I feel bad, but also relieved. She won't try that again until the next note. I turn off my desk lamp and sit in the dark until I know she's in the kitchen, making coffee. She's opening a new can of MJB, and I can hear the hum of the electric can-opener. She drinks coffee all day long. My stepfather would be home from work soon, and after she drank a cup of coffee and smoked a cigarette and calmed down from helping me with my homework, she'd fix him a plate. Then she'd start getting ready for work. She works as a bartender from nine every night until three the next morning.

When I hear my stepfather's Pioneer coming up the gravel driveway, I turn the lamp on again and put a record on my record player. One of the teachers who likes me gave me a stack of old LPs without the jackets. My mom looked at them and said, "No wonder she gave you these. No one's ever heard of these people." My favorite is the one called *Rite of Spring*. I turn the white plastic knob all the way down to nothing and then slowly edge the sound up again. I keep it to where only I can hear it, but it doesn't matter because I know the music by heart. I tie a pillowcase around my neck like a cape and I hold a pencil between my thumb and forefinger and I conduct, twirling slowly around my room in the dark until I'm ready to sleep.

♒

*T*he next day is Saturday, and I can spend the day at the beach. I almost always go to the beach after school anyway, but on Saturdays I can stay from dawn until the sun goes down if I wanted. On weekends, I have chores I'm supposed to do, but mostly I don't do them, or I wait until after dark. My mom and my stepfather call me lazy, but if I have to pick up all the putrid mangos that have fallen off the trees in our yard and started to rot, what difference does it make if I do it at night instead of wasting the daylight? My stepfather is paranoid about burglars, so he's rigged floodlights on the four corners of the house. When they're on, it looks like noon out in the yard anyway. What do we have to steal, is what I want to know.

At the beach you can dig under rocks for crabs and what we call sand turtles—not turtles at all but small creatures like white, shiny cockroaches that bubble with foam when you hold them between your fingers. You can snorkel and body surf. There are tide pools where, in the deeper ones, reef fish and even baby sharks sometimes get trapped between the tides. You can hike the old lava flows almost a mile down the coast. I'd done that enough to give me calluses on my feet, and could walk on the lava barefoot. Some days I spend so much time in the water that at night, if I lie still in my bed with my arms spread, I can feel the ocean moving under me, as if I'm still drifting gently up and down on the surface of the sea. It feels like someone touching me softly all along the surface of my body.

As long as I can remember, my mother and stepfather have never wanted to spend much time at the beach, though sometimes my mom cooks a pot of rice and makes potato salad and marinates teriyaki meat in the big Pyrex bowl, and we go for a barbecue at one of those parks where they have built-in grills next to the water. I'm just as glad to go by myself.

The surfing beach, just across the highway at the end of the gravel path that led to our house, is hardly ever crowded. There's no bus out here, and the red mud slicks the road over when it rains, which is a lot of November and December. You have to be coming our way for a reason, because the road doesn't go anywhere else. But the waves are good, and there are usually at least a few surfers in the water. Lately, I'd been spending a lot of time watching them: When they were standing on the shore counting waves before they went in, or after they were done surfing, as they leaned back up the slope of the beach, their boards under their arms and their feet burying themselves over and over in the sand like pillars.

Sometimes a group of haole soldiers comes in a jeep from the army base in Wahiawa, about fifteen miles away at almost the exact center of the island. That's where we go when my mom wants to do a big grocery shop. When the soldiers go into the cinder-block changing room, I park my bike outside and follow behind, pretending I need to pee. I wish I could touch them; I wish I could sit on their laps. I keep hoping they'll notice me and invite me to go somewhere with them, but it doesn't happen. Sometimes one of them smiles or says hello, but that's all. When they leave, I feel out of breath.

Later, alone in my room, I remind myself about the shapes of their bodies, about whether their faces were kind or hard. I picture the beach, and they begin to appear, walking toward the water. I see them in the long light that comes at the end of the day, when the sun is falling over the water. They're beautiful and the beach is beautiful, and no one ever wonders what I do there all day long.

This Saturday, the water is too churned up for snorkeling, and I'm tired of tide pools. Anyway, I'm thirsty, and I decide to stop at the Kamakura I.G.A. to buy an Icee. They cost fifty cents, but you can cut out the red-and-blue diamonds on the side of the paper cup and save them, and when you have ten you got a free drink. I have money because every Sunday night my mom leaves three stacks of five quarters on the corner of my desk: three dollars and seventy-five cents. The quarters come from her tips at the bar. Some of them are colored with red fingernail polish on one side, which are the ones that come out of the jukebox. My mom keeps a beer glass full of red quarters by the cash register so she can sing along to music if the bar gets too quiet, or else she gives them to her good customers so they can play the jukebox for free. They get three songs for a quarter, so they usually ask her what she wants to hear. If she wanted to keep them drinking, my mom said, she'd tell them to put on Patsy Cline. On weekend evenings, she tries to make things seem more lively, and so she asks for that song that starts out, "Jeremiah was a bullfrog, was a good friend of mine." When the man comes to empty the jukebox, he gives my mom back all the red quarters. Some of them mix in with her tips.

Lunch at school cost thirty-five cents. The rest is spending money. I could afford to buy an Icee almost every day if I wanted, but I usually save that for Saturdays. With the leftover money, I buy comic books. Batman is my favorite, and he's the last thing I think about most nights before I fall asleep. I make up adventures for him and me all over the world. We always get into danger, but each one has the same ending: Batman and I fall asleep together, safe at last and holding each other like buddies .

Mr. Kamakura smiles and waves when he sees me. He's pretty old, and everything in his store seemed old, too: the slats in the wooden floor that have been worn down to a soft furriness by years of bare feet shuffling sand across them, the glass countertops, cracked at the corners and repaired with masking tape. "You like one cone sushi?" he asks. "Mrs. K just made fresh."

Cone sushi are thirty cents each. "Okay," I said. "And a cola Icee, please."

Mr. Kamakura presses a lever, and the Icee slushes out of the machine, which is the size of our refrigerator at home. I give him four quarters and he opens a Roi-Tan box to make change. "You be careful now," he says. "Police officah, he come by today, say some bolo-head buggah makin' problems down da beach, nasty man do nasty t'ings. Any kine trouble, you run o'heah fast, no worry, okay?"

"Okay," I say. I take my change and walk back down the road toward the beach. I bite into the cone sushi and there's a splash of tartness as the rice vinegar mixes in my mouth with the sweet juice from the aburaage pouch. There are tiny shavings of carrot in there, too, but you hardly taste them.

I know Mr. Kamakura was talking about sex. On the bookshelf in our living room, my mom left a blue pamphlet with the title *A Doctor Talks to Nine- to Twelve-Year-Olds*. One day it was just there. I know she left it there for me because I'm the only one who touches that bookshelf other than to dust it. But I still made sure to read the pamphlet only when I was alone in the house, and I put it back in exactly the same place—between a paperback copy of *The Sand Pebbles* and a hardback of *Wake Island Command*. When you slid it in, you had to be careful not to rip the paper cover of *Wake Island Command*, which already had a lot of tears in it.

I've read that book at least five times. It has a painting on the front of fighter planes coming through the clouds and tells about a commander who tried to defend Wake Island from a Japanese attack on the day after Pearl Harbor. He was forced to surrender, and he and his men were starved and tortured in Japanese POW camps. When I was in fourth grade, I took *Wake Island Command* to school for one of the book reports we had to give out loud in front of the class. I told about the men having to stand naked in the prison yard all day long without moving. If they moved, they'd get beaten or even shot. To me, that was the most important part of the book. My teacher sent a note to my mother that said she thought I was reading too much "in the adult area." My mother laughed and balled the note into a tight sphere. Every once in a while she did something I never expected.

The pamphlet has phrases in it like, "The man and woman lie together in an embrace that gives pleasure to both of them." It isn't very specific, and the diagrams don't look anything like bodies, but I know what they're talking about. I've memorized all the words for things. I doubt anyone else in my whole school has read a pamphlet like that.

In the last section, the doctor explains that there are people who try to touch children in ways that only grownups are supposed to touch one another, and that if someone ever did that to me, I had to tell my mom and dad or a teacher right away. I think: If one of the men in the changing room tried to touch me, I wouldn't tell anyone.

The next day, we go to church, the way we do every Sunday morning. The church owns my school, so it was the same place with all the same people. It was like going to school six days a week instead of five. My homework still isn't done.

Before services, we kids all attend Sunday School. My teacher is Mrs. Kalama, though I know the next year I'll have to go to Miss Peterson's group, and when we pray, I ask to be able to stay with Mrs. Kalama. The oldest kids, meanwhile, get the minister's wife, Mrs. Powell. There's only one other married teacher at my school, and that's Mrs. Cooper. Her husband got killed in Vietnam. She has a son named Tommy, who's sixteen. Tommy goes to high school all the way in Kahuku. He hangs around after Sunday School during the time when we're supposed to be having snacks and waiting for our parents to show up so we can all go to big church together.

Tommy is tall and has a lot of frizzy blonde hair. He says the bad words that we're not allowed to say, including the really bad word, and he's mean to us kids, especially to me. I complain about Tommy all the time, but nothing ever changes. Mrs. Cooper didn't know what to do with him since his father died. That's what she told my mother.

When Sunday School is over, Tommy follows us to the outside lunch tables next to the playground where the little kids are already on the swing set. He sits at my table. I ignore him and go on reading the book I brought until he sticks the tip of his finger into my last, uneaten graham cracker, twisting the dirty point of his fingernail back and forth like a drill.

"Cut it out, Tommy!" I say.

"Make me," he says.

"Cut it out or I'll tell."

"Girls tell," he says, "so you probably would. 'Cuz you're such a girl."

"I will, if you don't leave us kids alone. Your mom said you had to stop bugging us."

He mocks my voice: "*Leave us kids alone.*"

"Go pick on somebody your own size," I say, which is what my mom told me to say if he bothered me again. Tommy leans over and brings his face directly in line with mine, as if he's going to kiss me.

"Gee, now you are my size," he says. "I guess I should be picking on you."

I shove against his chest to get him away from me, and he steps back, yanking my arm with him. The next thing, we're scrambling on the ground. Someone might have called it wrestling, but it wasn't really. I never learned how to fight and, anyway, he's ten times stronger than me. Basically, he's just pounding me and I'm getting pounded. He isn't hitting as hard as I know he can. If I don't fight back too much, he usually lets me go after a few punches.

He flips me onto my back with his knees pinning my elbows down and leans into my face. He hawks up a wad of spit and lets it hang partway from his lips, drooling toward mine. I can see the place on his chin where a patch of blonde hairs poke out like tiny sand-colored pins. He's wearing corduroy shorts, and the fuzz on his thighs rubs against my cheeks on both sides. I roll out of that pretty easily because he wasn't really ever going to spit in my face. That would have been serious. But then he puts me in a headlock and starts raking his knuckles hard across the top of my skull, which really hurts. The muscle of his forearm is thick against my throat. I punch feebly against his ribs as I try to push away. I can feel the tautness of his body, the way the flesh under the surface of his skin hardens when I struggle and he flexes to keep hold of me. I can smell the sweat of his armpit and the fresh-laundry scent of his T-shirt.

"Say 'I'm a sissy,'" he says. "Say it!"

I'm not going say it. Sissy was what Miss Peterson called me. She made me come to the board one day to do a math problem and I didn't know how and I started to cry. She told me to see her after school, and that was when she said it: "You're quite a little sissy, aren't you?"

"No," I said.

"Then what were you crying about?"

I kept my mouth shut and concentrated on the linoleum tiles laid out on the classroom floor like a green-and-black checkerboard. I wasn't going to cry in front of her again—not ever. But I wouldn't talk to her either. Finally, she sent me home.

"Fucking baby," Tommy says, "fucking baby sissy."

Suddenly, I do something I haven't planned. I reach my right arm down and jam my hand between Tommy's legs, squeezing as hard as I can. My hand is only on him for a second before Tommy throws me off, but I'm astonished by how warm he is there, how warm and how soft. By then a teacher is racing around the corner of the main classroom building, yelling at us to knock it off you two, and Tommy stumbles back a few steps. I haven't hurt him much, but it takes him a moment to realize that and to get over the shock of what I've done. He stares at me, and I like the look on his face, which is almost fear. "Bet that got you all excited," he snarls before he turns and runs toward the koa bushes that grow in a dense wall along the edge of the playground. There's an empty field on the other side and, beyond that, the gravel road to Tommy's house.

When we get home from church, my mom and stepdad change clothes and climb back into the car. They're going to my Uncle Charlie and Aunty Ida's house to help them pull a tree stump out of the yard. My stepfather has a hitch on the Pioneer that you can attach a chain to. My mom asked me whether I wanted to come along, but she knew I didn't. "Don't turn on the stove," she says as they drive away.

My Uncle Charlie was a sergeant in the Army, and a lot of the stuff around our house came from the base where he worked. Mortar casings on the patio that they used for ashtrays. The barrel at the corner of the yard where we burned trash. Even my desk and my lamp. It was Army surplus, he said. When we were broke, Aunty Ida took my mom shopping at the PX, because you could buy things cheaper there. Those were the times when we had pancakes for supper. At the PX, you could get the really big box of Bisquick. My mom acted as though it were a funny idea that had just occurred to her, to have breakfast at night.

Something else we had from my Uncle Charlie was a bayonet from an SKS rifle. It came from Vietnam, where he'd been four times, but he said the Chinese made it. Or else the Russians. One or the other. The blade is slim and about nine inches long. My mom keeps it in the middle drawer of her desk and uses it as a letter opener. Ever since Uncle Charlie gave my mom the bayonet, I can't stop looking at it. I take it out of the drawer when nobody is home and play with it. I like to run the edge across the ridges of my thumbprint and feel them catch. When he gave it to her, Uncle Charlie said it was sharp enough to shred paper. I take the bayonet out of the desk and carry it carefully into the yard.

My mom has planted spider lilies all along the makai side of our house. She put them in right after we moved, ten or fifteen plants in all. With as much rain as we get, they grow fast. The leaves are deep green, long and waxy and sharp at the tips like a sword point. They're almost as wide as my hand, with a ridge down the middle length like a banana leaf. The flowers grow at the ends of fat, fibrous stalks that shoot from the center of each plant, three feet long, rigid and fleshy when you close your fingers around them. The lilies are in bloom, and a circle of narrow white petals arc, then droop from the end of each stalk like a Fourth-of-July rocket.

I lift the bayonet over my head and bring it down first against one of those thick green stalks. There's a satisfying *snik* as the blade passes through. I try again, making a game of slicing so quickly and so viciously that the tops of the stalks hesitate, unaware of being cut, before toppling into the dirt. I begin ripping wildly at the lilies—the stems, the leaves, the pathetically fragile and beautiful flowers. I slit the leaves lengthwise, again and again, then tear at the frayed ends. I move from one end of the garden to the other, rendering it all, stabbing and slashing and ruining whatever I can reach, making particularly certain that not one single white bloom remains; and I hack a second and third time at the ends of the already-cut stalks, weeping their watery milk, until nothing of them is left to protrude above the plants.

While it's going on, I think of nothing, or only of the pleasure of destruction and of the satisfaction of watching the pile of litter spread across the floor of the garden. At some point, I stop and looked around me. I know what I've done, and I understood that I'll have to pay for it. I bring the bayonet back inside and rinse it carefully at the kitchen sink, then dry it on a dish towel and put it back into my mother's desk drawer. If my parents take their time at Uncle Charlie and Aunty Ida's, or if they stay into the evening to drink, I probably have until the morning, but nightfall is hours away. And there are always my stepfather's floodlights. I lie down on my bed to wait.

*I*t's still daylight when the front door slams and I hear my mother surge through the house like a breaking wave. She flings open the door to my room and comes toward me, her arms flailing wildly, just as mine had done, to strike me wherever she can reach. "Why? Why? Why?" she demands with each blow. "Why would you do that?" I raise my hands to cover my head and curl my body away from her, letting the slaps and punches fall. She's angry enough to close her fists, and she's hurting me, but I deserve it and I take my punishment in silence. Finally, she stops, her breathing heavy. "Why did you *do it!*" she sobs at last, collapsing to her knees at the foot of my bed. I've never felt such compassion for her. My mother truly cared about those lilies.

I leave her there and go to the storage shed in our back yard. I take out the big green plastic trash can that I use for picking up mangos, drop the rake and the rusty pruning shears inside, and drag it all to the side of the house. Though I always hose the can out after I use it, the stink of rotten fruit remains. I begin to clean the garden as best I can, piling up the shredded leaves and chunks of stem, fleshy and angled like the celery my mother puts in stew. With the shears I straighten the ragged edges of leaves and amputate those too mangled to survive. I use my fingers to pull the limp white petals from where they had lodged like confetti in the plants' interiors. As I'm working, my mother comes into the yard.

"You tell me why," she says quietly.

"I don't know," I say.

She watches me work for a few moments. "That's only the beginning of what you'll do to make up for this," she says. "You're grounded for two weeks, and tonight your father and I will talk about what has to be done about you."

"My father is dead," I say.

"No beach for two weeks. And you come straight home from school and do your homework. When you're done, you stay in your room until supper is ready. And you're going to start doing your chores every weekend like you're supposed to. Things are going to change around this house!"

I keep working.

"There is something wrong with you," she says, "and we're going to find out what it is." She turns and heads back inside

I take my time finishing up, in no hurry to begin the days of exile in my room. If it's a question of what's wrong with me, my mother is about as prepared to figure that out as I am to learn new division. And in the end, nothing will change around our house or anywhere, least of all my mother. Nothing ever did after these storms, after the threats and ultimatums, after the explosions of anger or even after the few sentences of truth we allowed ourselves to speak, carefully nestled in rage like fresh eggs in a crumpled sheet of newspaper.

But I have changed. If I feel anything about what I've done, it's a strange sense of leave-taking. I've discovered a place that exists beyond their ability to hurt me. It isn't that I think I've become immune, but rather that I am full. They—my mother, Miss Peterson, Tommy—can do no worse now than more of what I already know I can outlive. In the years that follow, every new sadness will remind me that I am fluent in this language.

I finish cleaning up my mess, put away the tools, and go back into the house. The lilies will heal, and the two weeks will come to an end. Until then, I can fall asleep with the visions I have memorized—with the lonely surfers who never see me and the loud and handsome soldiers who are indifferent to me; with Tommy who, for all his cruelty, was the only one who touched me; and with Batman who, for as lovingly as I know he would have touched me, was never real. I conduct them in the darkness like music, drifting in a sea of my making until I have floated far from shore.

Pickpockets

Who steals my purse steals trash.... (Othello)

First thing when Harley and I moved down here to Florida, we started hearing about the pickpockets. An epidemic, people were saying. No one could describe them because no one ever saw them. That was the whole point—you never knew they were coming. But you could say you'd been hit, and no one doubted you. The fact that you hadn't seen anything was your proof.

We'd sit around at our White Mischief meetings—that's what they call the old-queers group—playing Paiute and Crazy Eights, and the talk would eventually get around to who'd been hit lately and how much they'd had taken from them, like it was a contest. Old people competing over who'd been the most victim.

So far, Olly Tansy had the winning story. He was at the Walmart and felt a shove come from behind, hard. He lurched into a lady who was clutching at least a dozen five-packs of Wrigley's Doublemint gum to her chest. The gum scattered like roaches. She fell on the gum; Olly Tansy fell on her. He broke a bone in the side of his hand, not as dramatic as a hip for a geezer like him, but impressive anyway. He had to wear a white plastic splint for a month—a boxer's splint he said the doctor called it. Then he showed up with a tennis ball he had to squeeze.

Anyway, Olly Tansy says all he saw was a head of dirty-blonde hair moving fast toward the automotive department, and he was always sure to remind you, if you didn't know, that anyone could get out of the store from there. "This is how they treat old people nowadays," he said. "They got no respect. They'd stab you as soon as look at you." "They" could be anybody, but especially the pickpockets.

I decided I was going to trap one, just to see what they looked like. I'm seventy years old; I guess I'm good bait. I went to the swap meet they hold every other week in the parking lot of the MCC church, which I guess they borrow from the Lutherans or something, and found an old, scuffed-up wallet for a buck. I took it home and crammed the pockets with losing Lotto tickets and the coupons from the Sunday paper that skid out and fall everywhere when you pick it up.

Harley likes to go out for Chinese, and I have a bunch of fortune-cookie fortunes from past meals saved in a fake lacquer tray on the dresser. I put some of those in, too, including the one I like so much I've memorized it: "Life is the same story retold in endless voices." I keep that one especially because it makes Harley uncomfortable. He says we have to guard against turning morbid in our old age.

To make it official, I decided to try the Walmart first. I wore a pair of yellow, falling-down polyester golf slacks, washed so many times they sag like boob skin. I don't play golf, I want to make clear. But they cost next to nothing at Goodwill, and they're comfortable for taking walks. Anyway, the back pocket gaps open, slack-jawed. That's where I put my fake wallet, letting it stick out just a little for good measure. I thought about telling Olly Tansy about my plan, but I decided it would be more dramatic later, after I'd caught a pickpocket.

I took along a walking stick, which I don't need, but I thought it would help me whomp the pickpocket. Or trip him, if I could get it between his legs. Anyway, it was a good prop. I walked around the store, shuffling, slow, bent over, pretending to be confused about what I came in for, none of which I am in real life, even if Harley, who's ten years younger, treats me like the only reason I'm still alive is that I've got my soul clamped tight in my back teeth.

I went over to the men's department and mauled the packages of socks as if I couldn't remember what they were for. When my grubbing fingers pushed a few over the edge of the bin and onto the floor, I bent way over, slow and decrepit, knowing the wallet was rising up out of my pocket like a Pez candy, waiting for the shadow of a hand.

I was pretending to be an actor, an undercover cop, maybe overdoing it a little. All my concentration was focused on about four square inches of skin at the top of my right butt cheek. I was thinking how the sciatica I have on that side was going to help me, because the area is sensitive and I'd feel the slightest touch.

I admit, I was also thinking about how I'd tell my story. We'd sat and dealt cards so many times that we knew just about everything anybody ever did in his past. When you're young, people take you to supper and slap you on the back because of your promise—all the things you're about to do—but soon enough you spend up all that currency. When you're old, you try to impress folks with what you did before, with the stories of how you made use of all your promise, but you can't dine out on that forever, especially because there's not always so much to tell. All that time gone by, and you could probably get the whole saga on a 3x5 card. The only new material is illness, death, and injuries. So here was the chance for something with a twist, a different kind of potential. I could be a hero. I might even get my picture in the *Penny Shopper*. That's better than a busted finger. If it worked, I could make it my new hobby.

I'd decided to try my luck over in among the power tools when the unexpected happened. A hand on my arm. It was a salesclerk. "Sir? Sir!" he was saying, too loud, like I was deaf, which I am not. "Your wallet, sir. Your wallet." I reached behind me. The sagging pocket was empty. I couldn't believe I'd missed the thing I'd been waiting for, the point of the whole adventure. There was a commotion over by the socks: a group of people, shouting voices, confusion. A pair of security guards push-walked a struggling guy toward the front of the store. They had his back to me, and I couldn't see his face. "We got him, sir," the clerk was saying. "The guy who picked your pocket." He shook the wallet at me like he was thinking of smacking me on the chin with it.

"I don't want it," I said, and I turned away, trying to see the way to the auto department.

"But isn't this your wallet?" the stupid clerk was saying. "I saw him take it from you." He opened up the wallet and started digging around for ID. I could see another security cop coming our way, his polyester uniform as defeated as my slacks.

The clerk pawed through the coupons, the Lotto tickets. There was no quick getaway. Even if I made a run out the front door I'd still have to cross that giant parking lot and stand at the bus stop for a while. An anti-climax. I should have let Harley drive me, but I didn't want to see the look on his face when I told him what I was doing, and I'd never have got him to leave me alone long enough for my plan to work.

"It's not mine," I said, turning in dumb-show circles and looking for a break in the growing crowd. "Some mistake." The pushy clerk's expression of pity was starting the slide into accusation, but I already knew that same face would be smirking later when he told the story. Some old Alzheimer's case who couldn't recognize his own wallet. He'd throw in how I was dressed like bum in falling-off-my-ass pants. But anyway, he'd still nailed the pickpocket.

Some of my worthless paper drifted to the floor. Last to go before the clerk caught himself was the rectangular white slip from the Chinese restaurant, the one with the fortune that I'd long ago learned by heart.

Units of Measurement: A Pornographic Morality Tale

for John Scott

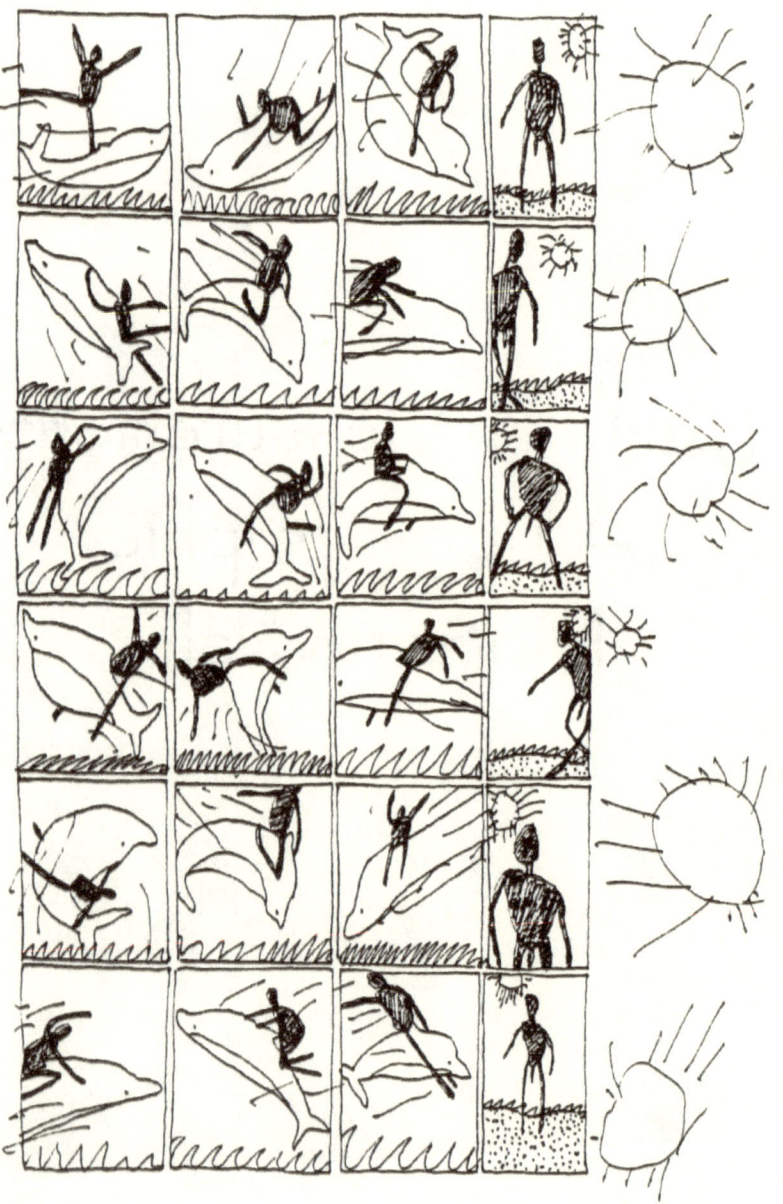

I.

$\mathcal{H}$e and I are sitting in the back of a café, just talking. We're in the patio part, through the rear door and into an open-air garden that strikes me as slightly prehistoric. And yet it is unmistakably a San Francisco garden: whatever will stay green in damp air, won't go pale, or worse, for lack of sun. Hardy things that survive. The café is a popular place. More of a bakery, really, with booths in the front and picnic tables in the back. It's nice on the patio, when the weather's warm enough. When it's not, they have smudge pots.

"AIDS is an occupational hazard." This is what he's saying. That's not the only thing he says, but it's how I sort that day out from all the other memories. It's the pull quote for that time we had the AIDS-as-occupational-hazard conversation. It's a watershed, a word I can't say without remembering the time I drove five hours to have lunch with a friend in the Mendocino forest. After eating, we hiked the steep fire road to the razorback ridge, and I filled my backpack with pine cones the size of footballs. My fingers were muddy with pine sap; the odor of resin rose like an aureole around my head. My friend lifted an eyebrow at the dark, sticky stains of pine tar on my jeans. "You know you're never going to get those out," she said. "That's in there for good." I looked up then and saw the sign nailed to a tree: "You Are Entering A Watershed Area."

He's been making porn movies for a while now, on account of his dick, which is famous. This is the longest period of employment in his life. Not the sort of thing you'd ordinarily put on a résumé, but he's not the sort of person who ordinarily needs a résumé. He's not even the sort of person who ordinarily needs a job.

"Any kind of employment you can name involves risk," he says. "A secretary working in an office could catch her hair in the roller of her electric typewriter and get hurt."

My objection isn't so much that he holds this opinion privately, but he's just given an interview to a reporter for the local newspaper's Sunday magazine insert saying essentially the same thing: some earnest young pup with a seventy-five-dollar haircut and a set of Calphalon cookware at home who pitched a piece on "AIDS in the Sex Industry." She could hardly contain her delight at finding someone eager to admit he didn't use condoms while making pornos and didn't especially care if anyone else did. One person willing to go on the record and you can declare a trend. And he's so eager for attention he doesn't know when he's being played.

Anyway, it's easy for him to say that. He isn't the one getting fucked, at least not on film. In real life, getting fucked is what he likes better than anything. But on film, a dick that big has only one function: it goes in. No one's going to pay to watch some guy fuck another guy whose dick is bigger than his. Don't ask me why; it's the economy of fag porn.

I don't find his movies all that erotic, to tell the truth. My interest is really more clinical: How is the guy on the bottom getting all that *in* there? I asked him about that once, about the guys who could turn their assholes into caverns and make his dick disappear, as if without effort. Had they spent hours getting ready with dildos? Were they, as they usually appeared to be, operating on a fistful of Valium?

"Well...," he drawled, embarrassed, the way he was whenever the conversation turned to sex specifically—his sex life—as opposed to sex thematically. "They have one talent," he said prudishly, "and I have another."

I knew that was exactly how he thought of it—having a big dick—not as something that had simply grown there, a genetic accident, but as a talent, a skill for which praise was warranted. That, of course, was a belief he shared with thousands, maybe millions, and his movies were infomercials for dick-hunger. But don't take my word for it. The principle can be viewed in action, even today—at sex clubs, in the park: The scrawny, pock-marked, balding, or hunch-backed guy with a big dick is transformed, via the removal of a layer of obscuring fabric, into the belle of the ball. It's a Cinderella story of sorts, if Cinderella were an otherwise out-of-the-running homo with decidedly hidden charms. Very democratizing, in fact—the only time body beauty doesn't count for much: Haul out a penis of note and the men circle, mouths agape, like so many lantern fish in the miles-deep ocean where sunlight does not penetrate.

Walking down the path with him one day to the beach at Land's End, I watched a bicyclist ram a guard rail and tumble to the ground because he'd seen The Unit—as we jokingly called it—flopping around in loose cotton painter's pants. The man got up, brushing the gravel from his scraped knees and shaking his head in wonderment: what he'd glimpsed was a vision.

In the end: Arguing with his analogy about the secretary is pointless. When I say that occupational hazards aren't usually deadly, he counters by saying that thousands of people do die each year in work-related accidents. Doesn't matter. Neither one of us has the facts, which is to say *the truth*. The truth, ultimately, is minor. It's just that this is the thing we're talking about, in the back of a café, sipping lattes. He doesn't have HIV yet, or at least he hasn't tested antibody-positive yet. About a year later he's living in another state, and I get a letter saying that he'd started noticing spots the color of grape juice that could only be lesions, so he got tested and now he's officially positive and has decided to tell everyone.

I read his letter, standing at the desk in the post office that is about two blocks from the apartment of another friend who is, at that exact moment, dying: home from the hospital at his insistence, but no one believes it'll be for long. On my way to his house, I decide to stop for my mail. My shift hasn't started yet; I need a few more moments to perform internal alchemy. The letter pisses me off, then I feel numb. But numb isn't the right word, either. I feel like the child with the kite who has been warned to keep a tight hold on the string. A moment's distraction and the spool falls, the kite jerking upward like a freed hawk. I feel the way it feels to watch the kite float out of sight and to understand that the moment before letting go can't be retrieved, that all that's left are recriminations on the ground.

For a while after the lesions started appearing, he kept talking about making more porn films. And why not: He still looked good— slim and blonde, with a body that could have belonged to someone you might actually meet; a dirty ginger wash across his chest; a few stray hairs, thicker than the rest, on his shoulders; tufts of it, darker still, in his ass crack.

When he worked out, he managed to achieve a kind of lanky, adolescent muscularity in about a week and a half: another gift of his genetics. During his non-gym periods, his limbs took on a rounder look, boyish with baby fat. He didn't look like a gymnast or a swimmer, those perpetual archetypes, the assembly-line porn boys of the nineties who seem press-formed out of fiberglass, like surfboards with cocks. He'd grown up beating off to the diametrically different images of another generation—the skinny, pimply boys of twenty years before—which may explain why, in his first appearance in a glossy stroke mag, he dyed his hair orange, shaved it into a Mohawk, and practiced sneering like Billy Idol, costuming himself to look exactly like what he was: a white punk from the back woods of Oregon whose beliefs about America were just as frightening as they seemed. Venerable Oscar was right: Give a man a mask and he'll tell you the truth.

He had some of the first lesions frozen off. One of the perks of private insurance is that you can walk into the dermatologist's office and ask for such a thing and they give it to you and figure out a way to bill your insurer without disclosing the incriminating details. He never even saw the bill—he had people for that.

But his polite, enthusiastic inquiries to porn producers and erstwhile backers went dead-end. Everyone knew he had "it" now; infected porn stars were expected to lie or to disappear. Many of us can name the ones who did one or the other—or both. Later come the revelations: the Brit with the uncut dick, granite jaw, and louche, unsmiling James Dean façade "comes out" positive. Illusions shatter: Maybe he wasn't such a stone Top after all. The boys he was balling on film, presumably, have their own reactions.

Unaccustomed to being refused, he was at first affronted by the resistance to his comeback in a porn film that starred nothing but men with HIV. "People need to see this," he said to the man, a former funder, who labeled the idea "morbid." So he entered a new phase, the closest he ever came to aligning himself with a political principle. He had a tattoo inked onto his right deltoid—*HIV+*—thick and red, like graffiti, as if crudely drawn with magic marker. He let the lesions stay and arranged his clothing to make them more visible. It was a version of fetish sex, like the pictures his favorite photographers displayed in their South of Market garrets: the beautiful man with one withered arm; the young bodybuilder with milky-blind eyes. He was there, too, in the exhibit, showing off a body that had been roughly kissed over and over by a lover who enjoyed leaving marks. Only his dick was spared.

The last time I saw him was during the Folsom Street Fair on a sunny Sunday when most people were, according to protocol, as naked as possible. He was dressed in black leather: vest, chaps with nothing beneath them but a too-small jock strap, motorcycle boots, an aviator's cap. And he was emaciated, sallow, his ass saggy from AZT, the skin on his face stretched across the bones: The high cheeks and Neanderthal brow that had once helped him look sexy, vaguely European, had betrayed him by showing, underneath it all, that there was nothing more than a skeleton. He looked like the queer angel of death.

II.

*T*he worst thing that ever happened to him, if you want my opinion, was winning The Biggest Dick in San Francisco contest. The next step, naturally, was for it to be filmed in action, so he made a few videos in which he can be seen having desultory sex—him and his penis, impressive even at three-quarters mast. There are other people in the films—once even a woman, during that brief period when someone decided that having gay men fuck women brought some sort of bi-kinky, hetero-fetish quality to videos. But the other characters are barely more than props; even he becomes superfluous. If his dick could have appeared without him, everyone might have been just as happy.

The problem is, he's lousy at dialogue—even in real life, his voice is tense and unnatural and he has a way of self-consciously snickering, as if intending to be droll. Being filmed, of course, only makes things worse. The obligate comments that porn Tops spew like verbal tics, "Take that dick!" or "You like that big dick, huh?" and so on—always *that* dick, the disembodied one, never *my* dick—come out sounding like parody, but the film continues to spin because he's not yet bankrolled at a high enough level to allow a lot of retakes. Predictably, he has trouble staying hard when he's the one in the saddle; it's an unnatural position for him, and his greater interest in the dick of the person he's fucking is obvious. That aside, the films have a certain, "shot-in-my-basement" appeal, as porn flicks go. He always grins after he comes.

In any case, his few videos in release, and the few others "in the can" (purportedly his best work) are enough to ensure that he will be called a "porn star" when he's referred to in print after that—and for the rest of his life—especially by white journalist fags by whom it is considered a boon to be on a first-name basis with porn stars. He is a minor celebrity—even a major one in some cosmographies. I know a man, for instance, who is prouder to have tricked once with Donnie Russo than he is to have had an audience with the Pope.

He gives interviews to many local and several national queer magazines in which he's asked questions about literature and gay rights and censorship and government funding for AIDS, because, honestly, who among us could be expected to say, directly into the figurative spotlight of media attention, "What the fuck makes you think I have anything worth saying about that?"

He does jack-off shows at a dive in the Tenderloin, the highlight of which comes when he bends over and puts the head of his own dick into his mouth. The crowd seems to love that, though I don't know why: The act excludes them completely. Besides, it's nothing you haven't seen done by Chinese acrobats.

He invites me to his show a couple of times, and I walk in without paying, full of I'm-with-the-band feeling. When I tell him, later, that I find the whole scene a little sleazy—the audience, mostly older men with an unmistakable suburban furtiveness, masturbating beneath coats and newspapers; the anxious cruising in the back aisle of the theater; the ritualistic, frenzied worship of slim hips, blonde hair, and big dick—he tells me my problem is that I'm full of guilt about sex. "There's no such thing as sleazy," he says. "It's just sex. If you think sex is sleazy, then the theater is sleazy. But if you think sex is natural and human, then that's what the theater is."

"Would you actually have sex with most of those guys in the audience?" I ask.

"I probably have," he giggles.

I have to hand him that: He is the Mother Theresa of sex, the most equal-opportunity dick around. He's the whore you always fantasize about meeting, if you're the sort of person who fantasizes about such things—the one who isn't really in it for the money. Sure, there are men he's more attracted to than others; he has endless passionate, disappointing crushes, all of them on boys who are so fucked up—either by drugs or living on the street or by working in the same "industry" as he does, and somehow not able to rise above the sadness, the way he says he can—that none of his affairs turns out well. More than anything, he wants to be wanted. And, with his dick as bait, he gets wanted a fair amount. I don't really need to spell out the limitations of the process.

The first time I met him was on a public bus in Waikīkī. The year was 1982. I was on vacation with a boyfriend I no longer have and we were making our way to a dance club that no longer exists. We planned to finish the evening off at the local baths—The Steamworks, also called The Lewers Sewers, in honor of the street where it was located. Perhaps I should make a point of saying that there was a time when accompanying your lover to the baths was not shocking.

When my boyfriend and I began to chat with him on the bus, we learned that he was already on his way to the baths—admission was halved for early arrivals, and his famous frugality was piqued. Who remembers how the topic of our mutual destination arose, but cruising was his best kind of talk—anything vaguely salubrious and suggestive, the double entendre. That's when the self-conscious snicker came in handy. But talking about sex was more natural for gay men then; you were expected to know something about it, to have played the game a little. They say that ballet is gay men's baseball, but really sex is.

In any case, by the end of the eighties we had begun to worry that we couldn't talk about anything else; and, in the nineties, we learned to pretend, publicly at least, that our interest in sex had fallen somewhere between our enthusiasm, say, for flavored vinegars and for black torch singers of the fifties. In other words, we had put sex into mature perspective, hadn't let it overtake our lives. That is what is often said, although the history-minded may note that such rhetoric emerged alongside a renascence of sex clubs, cottaging, kink chic, and enthusiastic tricking on the gym-boy circuit, so conclusions must be drawn advisedly.

My boyfriend and I spent several hours steeping ourselves in the atmosphere of the disco—the tourists dogged with the task of enjoying themselves, the rum drinks decorated with paper umbrellas and precarious beneath the weight of spinnakers of fruit—and then we walked down the strip to the alley where the baths was located. I found him there, in the movie room, watching porno in the midst of a group of men who were watching him. He'd thrown his towel aside and was languidly jerking off—just enough friction to achieve, as it were, Maximum Tumescence in Repose. Later, as everyone knows, he got paid for doing this; at the time, it was just a way to create a scene. Still, he wasn't like most of the men, attractive for one reason or another, who go to public places to put themselves on exhibition. Their displays of dick, body, or prowess are based in hostility; the disdainful rebuff is part of the studied Schadenfreude of the act. His exhibitionism was innocent; anyone who looked might also have touched.

And yet perhaps the act was not entirely without recognition of the commodity exchanges in effect at such establishments as The Steamworks. It would be naive to imagine that it was. But surely there was a time in his life before a marketplace consciousness had taken root, when he experienced the ordinary desire to be loved and touched, but didn't yet understand the means he had at his disposal, if not to achieve his desires, then at least to prove the maxim: "You can never get enough of what you don't really want."

One of the most difficult lessons we learn, of course, is that others are attracted to us for their reasons, not for our reasons. Perhaps he wished other men would seek him out for motives beyond the obvious, though he also, pragmatically, realized the power of advertising. He was, for example, photographed hundreds of times. He never refused an invitation to sit, no matter how unknown, how amateur the photographer. Each photograph was like a kiss, and each kiss was like a promise to remember. And yet imagine the ambivalence: Was he ever unaware of the expectations of the men who invited him into their studios, into their homes, to stand before the camera, that insatiate eye? If none of them actually specified the word "nude" when they asked to take his picture, it was only because to do so was unnecessary.

But, as I say, there was a time before that. When he was fifteen, he seduced a bicyclist who had stopped, during a cross-country road trip, to spend the night at his parents' rural farm. The cyclist was twenty-three, and he fled in horror the next morning after learning the true age of the boy—eager, guileless—who had climbed into his bed long after dark. Later, because all roads lead eventually to San Francisco, or once did, they ran into each other again, and he asked the bicyclist the question that had plagued him for years: "Did you think I was ugly? Is that why you left the next morning without saying good-bye?"

But of course that was not it at all. Fear of arrest was what had sent his guest into the predawn piney woods—for what man sleeps with teenage boys without fearing reprisal?—and it is possible to conjecture that the humiliation and disappointment of that adolescent rejection, for so it must have seemed, were what later caused him to champion the unpopular cause of boy-lovers, although an equally plausible explanation is that he did it simply to be annoying.

Flash forward more than ten years. We're at his brand-new house in a Midwestern state. Say it's located in the lush valleys of Ohio; it isn't, but let's say that. Anyway, the middle of nowhere. Farm country: silos; the sound of tractors in the thick air; the constant buzzing of bees, grasshoppers, other small, flying things. People like to say how quiet it is in the country, but this place is deafening. The insect sounds are a cacophony, especially at dusk; the air is frantic with things that hover and dart. In the bare, vindictive heat of summer afternoons, I sit on the porch, dripping sweat onto the keys of my typewriter. The reflection of sunlight off hundreds of insect wings nags at the corners of my eyes; it's unnerving, as if comets were constantly falling just out of sight.

I stay with him for a month, sleeping in a half-finished loft constructed on the side of the house where the blackberry brambles have all but taken over. There's a door in the room that leads nowhere; you open it onto a drop of fifteen feet. He hasn't gotten the stairway built yet. That's one of the projects we might do together, might not do.

Every morning when I wake up, my first act is to murder hornets. They come in through the cracks in the walls, through the constantly open doors, and agitate themselves against the window glass above the bed. I hate them irrationally, joyfully. I cut off their heads with the smallest blade of my Swiss Army knife, then arrange the severed heads in a line with the miniature pair of tweezers concealed in the knife's handle. Once I'm sure the bodies are dead, I brush them onto a sheet of paper and toss them out the door that goes no place. The heads stay in a row on the sill. It feels very samurai, very *Predator*.

The house is a shrine to eighties porn. Upstairs, the walls are covered with framed photographs of Jon King, Jim Bentley, Al Parker; there's a sculpture made of dildos. Downstairs is an art gallery: oil paintings, photographs, and original drawings by Etienne, Tom of Finland, Philip Core, Marc Chester, a dozen others. The porn-viewing area is built into another loft, with plenty of room to spread out on thick pillows. The video player itself juts into space on a shelf across from the alcove in the loft; you have to lean out over the gap in order to change the tape. Jars and bottles of every imaginable kind of lube fill the shelves, fitted in among the collapsing, disorderly rows of videos—baby oil, Vaseline, KY, Jergen's, and, of course, the expensive name-brand lubricants that don't pretend to be made for anything else. A white terrycloth rag, the kind you can buy in bags of eighty at CostCo for seven bucks, is stuffed under one of the pillows; I pull the rag out; it's stiff with dried cum. In fact, the whole loft smells like cum. And sweat. And him.

I've never gotten completely used to his body odor, which is strong and, now, chemical. I know it's part of what he considers being "natural," but I often wish he'd take a bath, brush his teeth, use a little deodorant. All this is evidence of what he calls my "repression" about sex. I argue that anyone taking six different synthetic drugs manufactured by multi-billion-dollar pharmaceutical companies can't lay claim to nature, but I'm still the only one using the soap.

While I'm visiting his house, we go on a road trip to the nearest big city, where I have a friend. He and I spend the night at my friend's house, on a blow-up mattress on the living room floor. He's a light sleeper and, early in the morning, he's awakened by the sound of my friend throwing the locks on the door and going out. A few minutes later, the sound of the locks again and our host returns, back with the newspapers and coffee from the shop on the corner: enough time for him to arrange his body so that the sheet falls to one side and his cock is exposed, pendant against his thigh. One of the things that's impressive about it is that it's not much smaller when it's soft. Through his lashes, he watches for a reaction. Later he confides to me his disappointment: The guy didn't even look twice.

I'm at his place barely two days when he comes out to the porch where I'm writing. Completely naked, he calls me to the far corner of the deck, where I must stand if I want to see the distant feature he is describing to me: a column of smoke from a far fire rising straight up like an exclamation point against the dull blue haze. I have to lean over to see and he leans with me. His dick rubs against my skin where my leg is bare in my shorts. I haven't started going around naked twenty-four hours a day, the way he does, even when he's working in the yard. He gets into his pickup naked, arranges a ratty towel against the sun-fissured vinyl, and drives to the end of the road where he reaches out the window to check the box for mail.

We're both sweaty, which makes our skin slick in some places and sticky in others: In any case, you're acutely aware of the zones of contact, of having another person's sweat on you. I wasn't sure we'd have sex on this trip, though we always had before. Maybe he wouldn't want to; maybe I wouldn't want to. When he squats down, a perfect plié, his dick as vertical and as exclamatory as that column of smoke, and puts his mouth over the cloth covering my dick, soaking it—then I want to.

We go inside and sprawl on the daybed for a while, letting the sweat evaporate. I play distractedly with his cock, just enough to keep it hard; I bite his nipples and kiss him, thinking of the bleeding gums, for which he's just seen the dentist, thinking of thrush, and I draw his tongue into my mouth. With my free hand, I pull one of his legs across my chest, exposing his asshole, and I tease the opening with the tip of one finger.

After a while I tell him to get on his back. I hawk up a gob of spit, rub the slime around his hole, and shove my cock in. Neither of us mentions condoms. He holds his own legs in the air, scooting his ass against me, soundless except for the rasp of his breathing, which chronic sinus infections render heavy and labored. He starts to fuck his own fist, and I knock his hand away, just to be perverse, just to keep his dick out of it.

Afterward, we doze in a tangle of limbs until he says he wants to do some gardening before the light goes. He gets up, sweaty, slimy, his feet bare, everything bare, and walks through the open door of the room where we've just had sex and into the yard directly beyond, moving from one space to another as easily as stepping across a threshold. I begin to hear the rhythmic *kachunk, sigh* sound that dirt makes as it is dug out of the ground and then slung away on the edge of a spade.

I think to myself: *It's not the same, what we did and what he does. What he did. And let's be pragmatic: It's too late for him to benefit from safe sex. Anyway, he wanted it.*

So let's call it a gray area. You make these sorts of statements to yourself as if sliding a bookmark between the pages of the novel you've been reading, setting it aside for the night with a certain reproachful firmness: *I know there's more to say, but that's all for now.* You make these statements, though the counterpoint of your own experience tells you that there are no gray areas at all in life. Wherever you are, you're standing somewhere.

III.

When he died, was I the only one who wondered whether a cast had been made of his most celebrated feature? I do not raise the question frivolously. Another porn star—one of his contemporaries, in fact—resorted to litigation when he discovered that the company he had engaged to market statuettes and dildos modeled on his own famous attribute had, in an excess of capitalist zeal, added an extra inch to its product. No doubt the beleaguered plaintiff considered the original more than sufficient for the masses or, perhaps like all of us, he just wanted to be loved for his own true self. Penises, certainly, are a matter of pride to those who possess them—more, of course, to some than to others.

Consider the case of another acquaintance of mine, whose equipment is no less substantial for his not being a professional. What I mean is that you would not have seen him on video. He is prevented by his well-paid government job—as much as by his Polish peasant ancestry, which has rendered him unfashionably thick around the middle—from going into film work. He is, nonetheless, extremely popular with the boys he meets on his lunch hours, which he spends in downtown department-store lavatories or in the hallways of construction projects, which his employment obliges him to visit. What his ordinary face and lumpenprole body cannot get for him, a glimpse of his hard dick through polyester blend can, and, though he does not tell the lover with whom he lives about these daily dalliances, he does feel that they provide a balance in their relationship, one unfortunate feature of which is that familiarity and time have rendered the lover immune to the feature that most enchants the lunchtime crowd. Like the porn actor defrauded by callous marketeers, he wants to be appreciated for what he believes is best about himself, and he finds no lack of others who will do so, even if his lover no longer can. It is for this same reason that he keeps his pubes shaved smooth, concerned that an over-bushy pubic patch (another hereditary flaw) will conceal crucial inches.

A casting of The Unit, of course, would have made a unique and befitting death mask and would certainly have gone to the archivists in the end, as did most of the rest of what he left behind—the collection of pornographic art to one foundation, the cartons of correspondence and papers to another. A kind of legitimation at last. During the month I stayed with him, he let me use his computer to finish a project, and I accidentally deleted a folder of outgoing letters. He had hard copies, but my carelessness rendered him sullen and reproachful for days afterwards. He was, at that point, already being shamelessly courted for his collections by more than one concern, and the experience must have been heady. Imagine the sensation as one's ordinary household articles achieve the status of artifacts; he was having people in to make inventories. Perhaps he felt I was being wanton with history.

The scraps and odds and ends, meanwhile, are scattered to a half-dozen lesser archives. San Francisco, I'm told—and one struggles not to be overwhelmed by the irony—got the box of jock straps, greasy Spandex, and strategically torn jeans that were what remained of his sex-performance costumes, a group of items whose cataloging and display will no doubt challenge the skills of whatever archivist is put in charge of them.

The disease gets worse, of course, at first more of a pain in the ass than anything else: less energy, the weight loss, the worry that any cold that lingers may spell bad news. He takes a house in Southern California for a while in order to facilitate trips across the border for a treatment not then (and not ever) available in the United States. He modifies his modes of travel—the constant, horrific sinus infections make flying a torture. But he has always preferred to drive. During the early years of our friendship, in fact—prior to his becoming a personage and when he was still more or less a San Franciscan—his habit was to breeze back into town after one of his extended trips abroad, buy himself a car, and, if the next destination precluded driving, to sell it on his way to the new adventure. He had a weakness for sporty convertibles and famous-name motorcycles, and I heard him bemoan the fact that the mingy monthly allowance permitted by the lawyers who controlled his trust fund rarely allowed him to scrape together enough cash to buy new.

In those years, of course, his itineraries took him largely outside the contiguous forty-eight—southern Europe, Mexico, Hawaii, anywhere there was a reasonable expectation of finding brown boys—and plane tickets didn't grow on trees. He nevertheless traveled whenever the mood struck and returned with the inevitable Polaroids: a hustler in San Juan, a carabiniere who picked him up at the Trevi Fountain. The famous mutual attraction of light skin and dark skin (although, for him, it was largely a matter of *fore*skin, but that's another story); the gay man's reduction of the travel experience to cruising with an accent.

He asked me once whether I thought he was a leech. This was after he had lived in my house for six weeks between trips abroad without once offering to buy supper or pick up the tab for groceries. I was getting sex, after all, though perhaps it is unfair of me to think that he imagined such a quid pro quo. He wasn't famous then; I wasn't yet someone who was occasionally permitted to have sex with a porn star. And yet I can attest, when he became a celebrity—or, I suppose it is more accurate to say, after he was elevated to the ranks of San Francisco's famously indulged eccentrics—that his habit of parsimony did not improve.

During the last years of his life, when people had largely lost interest in watching him have sex, even for the freak-show value, he discovered that they would continue to pay him to talk about it. And so he became a philosopher of sorts—one whose philosophy was to discern what people believed and then to say the opposite. He went, briefly, into journalism, producing first a broadside that directed men interested in anonymous sex to public places where they could find like-minded individuals; the listings were leavened with "true stories" of truck stop sex, "how to" tips for *plein air* encounters, and from-the-field dispatches warning readers away from danger spots frequented by vice cops or fag bashers. A *Green Book* for cottagers.

His timing, as always, was impeccable, given that sex in toilets and parks had never been more popular. He tried his hand at a literary magazine after that, which went almost immediately bankrupt. Nonetheless, the magazines generated publicity—the public-sex guide in particular was widely and passionately condemned, both by the usual suspects among conservative politicians and by homosexual men livid over its affront to a positive gay image—and that was enough to make him both controversial and "transgressive" (a term that was, mercifully, popular for only a moment), either of which, in postmodern queer pop culture, is regularly substituted for quality, originality, or meaning.

The foray into magazines, moreover, earned him a new moniker—"publisher"—bestowed on the basis of approximately the same degree of skill and experience that had preceded the label "porn star," and the two terms became welded together, "porn star and publisher," remarkably like actual credentials. He was also occasionally misidentified as an AIDS activist, an odd term for someone who had never voted and whose hero of political philosophy was Ayn Rand.

What people no doubt meant, of course, is that, like tens of thousands of gay men, he refused to lie about having an AIDS diagnosis, but that, unlike those tens of thousands of others, he sometimes got his picture into magazines. His aphorisms on community, sex, love, and relationships, in fact, were not infrequently quoted in the press; he was periodically interviewed at length on his iconoclastic views; and he became a spokesperson of sorts for the proposition that post-infection sex only got better: Safe sex became beside the point, he explained, once one abandoned all worry about catching "it." There was truth in what he said. The nearly hallucinogenic sensation of bare dick in warm asshole is a secret carefully guarded from the sex police. And yet the smugness of his claims was galling: No one likes the implication that his sexual conduct makes him a safe-sex sissy.

In addition to the interviews, he was sometimes invited to write articles under his own byline on the subjects gay men are believed to find most relevant and compelling—love, AIDS, and tricking, though not necessarily in that order—not because he had anything particularly wise to say about them, but because he was, remember, a porn star and a publisher. (A third credential never appeared in his bio, though it was doubtless how the public, whose tendency to reduce complicated issues to their essence is legendary, most often referred to him: "You know who I mean—he's that porn star with AIDS who has the really big dick.")

During those years, in other words, he made himself a name in the small pond, although, since it is the only pond in which many of us ever swim, dimensions matter less than public relations. The Southern California sojourn, meanwhile, had introduced him and Los Angeles to one another, with the predictable result: He was thin, rich, white, and he fucked for money, which is to say he arrived with a great deal of experience in the local industry. The city that propagandizes conformity but practices depravity ate him up with the proverbial spoon.

Fame, of course, is tedious, or so we are led to believe by the famous; but notoriety can kill you. Some cities—and San Francisco is one of them—make only the latter possible, and yet it was to San Francisco that he returned in the end.

I will admit that the one thing I never understood about him was his ambition—a word whose Latin root refers to the practice of walking among the people in order to court votes. If I had, perhaps I would not have objected that afternoon in the café—that watershed day among the Jurassic ferns and the relentlessly flowering plants—to the suggestion that the possibility of illness was countervailed by the benefits of being filmed having sex. My vision was so narrow. AIDS was not an occupational hazard; AIDS was on the verge of becoming his occupation.

In other words, he wanted it.

Still, I am often accused, passionately, angrily, of failing to appreciate his single most important gift: that he was consistently, in all he said and did, *sex-positive*. That dizzyingly circular term is wary of specifics the way all labels are wary. But he was sex-positive, one gathers, in contrast to the sex-negative people who sermonize against promiscuity, campaign to shut down bathhouses, and wax indignant when exposed to public nudity at parades and street fairs.

Between those extremes, I remain confused where those of us fall who are still dazzled by the complexities of sex; who have trouble distinguishing who is holding the stick of sexual freedom from who is getting beat with it; who, Luddites, cling tenaciously to the belief that what people do with and to one another more or less inevitably implicates a bewildering ethical dimension; who are ambivalent about the practice of making someone famous for a body part.

I am aware that we do not discuss ethics at the dawn of the millennium. We do not discuss morality, either, a topic that reeks of master narratives, the oppression of institutions, and inchoate colonialist leanings. And yet both imply choice, free will, the ability to make manifest that which is quintessential within us. Surely, if it is true that we get the government we deserve, then it must follow that we also get the porn stars we deserve.

What I mean is that I believe two things to be true—first, that nothing happened to him that was not his intention. And, second, that at some point he lost the ability to extricate himself from an irreversible interaction that he originally thought was within his control. We never get enough of what we don't really want; others seek us out for *their* reasons. Such is the madness we endure.

I returned many times to the café where he and I talked that afternoon—with other friends, to engage in other conversations—but only once after his death. On that day, I went alone and waited some time for a moment when, unobserved, I could do what I had come to do. Using the smallest blade of my pocket knife, I carved his name into the soft pine wood of the table where we had talked.

The significance of the act was not, as you might imagine, in leaving his name there; I might have carved anything. Rather, it lay in the fact that the wood, once scarred, could never again be unscarred. We do well to commemorate the points of no return in our lives, the watershed moments when, distracted, we open our hand and the glass falls, never again to be unbroken.

I do not think the owners of the café pay much attention to the condition of the picnic tables on their patio—the tables are, after all, exposed to the elements year round. For that reason, I suspect my marks will stay in place for a while, and you may still read them if you go there.

Lei Pua Kenikeni

For ML: A hui hou kākou

Māpu ʻala hoʻoheno i ka poli
Lanikeha i ka ike a ka maka

I'm ono for teriyaki jerky from the plate lunch truck, but no way Delon's gonna come with. If he doesn't, I won't go. I don't know why. I just feel like having company, I guess. There's no special reason Delon doesn't want to go, but right now he's stoned and the sun feels good and he's not in the mood. Delon's the same as me, though. He doesn't like going anywhere by himself any more than I do. But if I wasn't in the mood, I'd still have to go with him. He'd order me to and I'd go. Sometimes he really pisses me off, but that's the way the cookie crumbles between us. She's the Queen Mother, and that's that.

Laters he wants to bike over to the East-West Center at the U to play volleyball. I'll get my teriyaki jerky on the way. Could be I'll feel like a shave ice, too.

Mostly Delon wants to go play volleyball because of this haole guy who's started coming on Sunday afternoons for the pickup games. Delon says he saw him once at Hula's, so he must be māhū.

Who knows? They all look māhū to me, all these ropy white-boy students who hang around the East-West Center. No sooner they land, they get strung out because they can go around all the time in shorts and two-dollar rubber slippers. They decide they're vegetarians or Buddhists or whatever and they act like the sun cooked their brains. The one Delon likes is that way: too much hair and a pound-puppy grin no matter what you say to him. He just loves how *natural* everything is.

Delon is hoping "natural" means "into brown boys," and the odds are for sure in his favor. There's so many fucking rice and taro queens around this place, you could wind up never getting laid if you didn't like haole boys. I can take them or leave them, except the fresh-off-the-boat ones who catch jungle fever the minute they set foot on this rock. With those ones, I just slide to one side.

By the time Delon finally decides he's ready to go, the beach is pretty much empty. Most of the tribe is already on its way to The Blow Hole for "Cherch," which lasts an hour or two after dusk. By then, the closet cases who have to get back to their wives are on the road and all that's left are tourists and alcoholics.

We pick up our bikes and I get my jerky and a Coke. The sun is beginning its slow curve toward the ocean and it's not hot enough for shave ice anymore. Delon decides he wants a soda, too. On our way out of the beach park, we walk our bikes so we can stay on the sidewalk and under the palm trees with our drinks.

"Oh, looky loo," Delon says, lifting his chin back in the direction of the beach.

"What?" I say.

"Kēlā blondie, 'a'ale ka shirt."

"It's just Jonas," I say. Jonas is a lost Southern California surf bum who washed up on Waikīkī beach without a board. He's famous for coming to the park in a tight blue Speedo and nothing else and doing gymnastics in the sand. I've never seen him go in the water. He's every potato queen's dream, though: pretty face and nice bulge, and then there's all that long blonde hair he throws around and the perpetually semi-stoned glaze on his face. He's always got a few sun pimples across his shoulders, plus the usual splotches of haole rot, but you know—whatever shakes your tree.

If Jonas is sleeping with anyone, Delon hasn't heard about it, which means he isn't sleeping with anyone, most likely. Rumor has it, though, he's being kept by that singer, that guy in the duo that just won all those Hoku awards for their last album. Not the low-rider looking dude from Santa Barbara. The other one, the local guy with the face all kind of uji from acne scars. The bartender at Hula's says Jonas is straight, but all you have to do is look at him. That one's about as straight at the road to Hana. Anyway, it's the same bartender who swears Keanu Reeves used to work there as a bouncer, so whatevs.

"I know it's Jonas, Tina," Delon says. "I ain't blind. But look who's that with him. Christina P, noho'i."

Chris Porte plays violin in the Honolulu Symphony Orchestra. He came here from Pennsylvania uku paila years ago to do his PhD in ethnomusicology, and he ended up taping about 8,000 hours of interviews with Fijians he met through the Polynesian Cultural Center in Lā'ie. In all those months, he tossed back enough kava to float the *Arizona*, but he sure didn't learn shit about Fijian music. Then he graduated and got a job at the HSO. The symphony season here is eight minutes long, though, so mostly he works at the Waikīkī Shell or playing concerts at the Blaisdell. Sometimes Don Ho or Barry Manilow needs a violinist in the band and they call Chris. Anyway, Chris is a big māhū, so if he's with Jonas, that's news.

"Ūi, Christina," Delon calls out, a little louder than necessary, "we're going up to play v-ball if you wanna come."

Chris doesn't make any move to head over in our direction, like I knew he wouldn't. Jonas just stands there looking rabbity, as if somebody just plastered his business all over the front page of the *Star-Bulletin*. "Maybe," Chris calls back. "Have fun!"

As we walk off, Delon grumbles in a softer voice. "The light bulb must of burned out on that one, and she can't find her way out the closet in the dark."

"At least now you got something for the coconut wireless," I say, and Delon just chuckles back in his throat.

By the time we get to the U, the light is soft and the mynah birds are already in the trees. When they first start to mass together in the banyans in the late afternoon, all you hear is noise. They arrive, screeching and whistling and jumping from one tree to another like OCD kids on the jungle gym. But then there's so many of them that the sound starts to flow together into a single stream. The movement slows down and finally stops, and the mynahs disappear deep into the branches. Then it seems as though the trees themselves are droning "ch-ch-ch-ch-ch," calming the air and soothing you for the night.

We play a few games, all very low-key. There's a Chinese doctor from the mainland who works in something in infectious diseases, a couple of Pakistani guys, a Thai chemistry major who once invited us all to his house to eat crab, a really tall, really quiet guy who grew up in Hālawa Housing and now studies butterfly fish at the marine institute out by Sea Life Park, plus five or six others I don't know. A lot of people come only once, but there's a core of us who are here almost every Sunday. There's games on Saturday, too, but that's more hard-core. On Sunday the muffies and the perpetually giggly Japanese girls wearing T-shirts that say things like "Grin! Rocket Danger!" can play and nobody gets a sore head.

When we take a break, everybody just lazes around on the grass, hanging out. "Ūi, māhū," Delon says, coming back from the direction of the public lua on the first floor of the East-West Center dorms. Of course, his haole boy is with him. "You know Scott, yeah?"

"Howzit, Scott." He shakes my hand like all his fingers have turned to noodle rolls and then he plops down behind me, next to Delon.

"I never played volleyball like this before," Scott says over my shoulder.

"How you mean?" I go.

"You know, just so relaxed, no rules or stuff like that."

"We have rules."

"Yeah, I don't mean no rules, I just mean you're all cool, and nobody gets all...." He can't come up with the word.

"Hamajang?" I offer.

"How's that?"

"Anybody wanna grind?" I ask, changing the subject. Scott opens his mouth like he's going to say "How's that?" again, and Delon jumps in: "Eat." Scott starts giggling, "Ahh, ha ha, yeah, eat. Grind means eat! I knew that!" Delon gives me the stink eye, so I quit.

"I got turkey tails and kau yuk and pancit at the house," Delon says. "I just gotta make rice." Every Saturday morning before dawn, Delon goes all the way to the other side of the island and hikes for hours in the mountains above Pūpūkea to collect flowers and foliage, and then he spends the rest of the day and half the night making lei. Then, first thing on Sunday morning, he goes to Chinatown to sell to the shops along Maunakea Street. On the way home, he always buys hella food. I'm tempted, but I know he's just being polite.

"Nahh," I say. "On second thought, I'm gonna hang, maybe go back to the beach for a swim."

"'K'den," says Delon. "Call me, Tina. You know how auntie worries." He kisses me on both cheeks and he and Scott walk off down Maile Way. Before they get far, I see Scott climb up on the handlebars of Delon's bike. Delon tries packing him, but they only get a few feet before they both fall off. They're still giggling even after they turn the corner.

$$\approx$$

A couple months later I'm at Long's in Ala Moana, checking out the specials on the arare and rock salt plum gift packs, when I see Scott coming toward me down the aisle. I need to buy provisions for an ex-roommate whose job sent him to Iowa for a year, where he says he's dying of corn poisoning. I'm wondering how well wet li hing mui will travel and whether I should just stick to dry mango and shredded cuttlefish, and I've just about decided the selection is better at the Crack Seed Center downstairs. Anyway, Scott is pretty far from my mind. Delon doesn't say much about him and, anyway, I'm not that curious.

"Hi," he says, all smiley and friendly.

"Howzit," I go.

"Stocking up?" he asks.

Something about the look on his face makes it too hard to be a bitch, so I just nod and start walking toward the exit.

"Where you headed?"

"Downstairs."

"Right," he says, like I was asking his opinion, which I take to mean that I'm going to be having his company for a while.

I walk out of the store and he follows. "I'm so glad I ran into you," he says. "You've been on my mind lately because there's something I've been meaning to ask you."

"Yeah?"

"Yeah. I mean, you know Delon pretty well, right? You guys are, like, best friends?"

If he knew Delon, he'd know Delon doesn't have best friends. "We've known each other a long time," I say.

"So is he ... I mean, he's kind of difficult, right?"

This is deadly ground. First off, I know I'm not supposed to be discussing Delon with anybody. For Delon, that's as close as you get to a personal commitment—he takes you off the gossip circuit and you're expected to do the same. Never mind talking about him to the guy he's sleeping with. "He has his own way of doing things," I say at last.

"I just feel so, I dunno, not at ease with him," Scott says. Whatever's going on between them, he seems honestly upset over it. "I mean, he tries to do everything for me. It's like he wants to serve me. Plus, he's always making me leis and stuff."

"What kind of lei?"

"The braided kind you wear on your head, or the twisted ones he makes with raffia. He told me the names...."

"Haku and wili," I say.

"Right."

If he's started hakuing lei for this guy, Delon's pretty far gone. "You know how long those take to make?" I ask.

"Yeah, but I mean, he doesn't have to. They're really beautiful and all, but I don't know what I'm supposed to do with them."

"No, I guess you wouldn't."

"I could give them to you."

"No, you can't. You can only give a lei away if you get permission from the person who made it for you. You wanna ask him that?"

"No."

"Anyway, it wouldn't come from you to me with respect, but only 'cuz having them around makes you feel guilty."

"Yeah, I understand that."

Could be he does. We get on the escalator.

"The real problem, though, is that he's so jealous," Scott says. That's true, but no way I'm going to touch that.

"I mean, it's like I'm always failing some test. Like he likes me 'cuz I'm a haole, but then I do everything wrong because I'm a haole. I just feel like it isn't my culture or something."

"It's not your culture," I say, meaner than I want to.

"Yeah, okay, I know, but it's still the United States."

"It is and it isn't." Scott's looking at me like I'm giving him a scolding, which I suppose I am. "Where's your folks?" I ask.

"Colorado."

"Together?"

"Yeah."

"And both of them went to college, yeah?"

"Sure, but...."

"Everybody's the same race, right? And they own their house?" I already know the answer to those, so I keep moving. "Brothers and sisters?"

"One brother, one sister."

"Anybody in your family die of malnutrition?"

"Of course not."

"Delon grew up in a company shack on a sugar cane plantation because his parents worked in the fields. The mom is Filipino and in and out of jail. The dad is mostly Hawai'ian and he's an alcoholic. Delon says he doesn't know where he is. Might be true. He has two dead brothers—one died before his first birthday and the other shot on the street. Nobody went to college. You know Delon speaks Hawai'ian?"

"No."

"You know he teaches hula and that he's got a trunk full of trophies at home from his lei?"

"He never showed them to me."

"Delon doesn't brag. He just is what he is. You plan to live here the rest of your life?"

"Maybe. I don't know. I just thought it would be a nice place to be for a while. It's beautiful. Plus there's no snow."

"Right, no snow. And it is beautiful. A place so beautiful it still has beauty left even after it's been dying for a couple hundred years." We're stalled outside the Crack Seed Center, where I am very deliberately not going inside in the hopes he'll catch a clue.

"So what do you think I should do?" he says.

"About Delon? Break up with him."

"Why?"

"Because in his life, you're a tourist. And tourists always go home in the end."

Scott stares at the sidewalk silently, worrying the front edge of one of his rubber slippers against the cement. His wide, pale big toe looks like the back of a wooden spoon. "I don't even know where that is," he mumbles at last.

"If you don't know where home is, must be you're not there," I tell him.

A few weeks go by, and then Delon calls me up one Saturday night to see do I wanna hang out his place.

"You not making lei?" I ask.

"Gotta be. But jus', you know, come over, talk story. Or watch TV. Nothing special."

It's been choke months since Delon called me on a Saturday, not since he and his haole boy started getting all hot and heavy, in fact. I thought Scott was usually there warming the couch on Saturdays.

"You throwing a party or what?" I go.

Delon pretends he didn't hear. "You know I ain't going no place," he says. "Come whenever."

As I bike to Delon's house I wonder is Scott gonna be there. Delon ignored my hint, so it could go either way. But it's hard to see Delon calling me to hang out with the two of them.

When I arrive, Delon's front door is open for the breeze, and all the lights are on. I can see him in the living room, sitting at one of the two pushed together, fold-out card tables he uses when he's working. There's a box of pua kenikeni right in front of him, and he's stringing lei, but I would of known that even if the room was black as a lava tube. Some people say pua kenikeni has a fragrance close to gardenia or jasmine, but to me it goes way deeper inside than that. When you smell pua kenikeni, a whole long chain of memories comes back to you: who gave it to you the last time and why, and the time before that and the time before that. I lift my hand to rap my knuckles on the door jamb, but Delon knows I'm there. "Ūi, Tina," he says. He doesn't look up from his work.

I sprawl on the couch. There are already four double strands of pua kenikeni looped into U-shapes but not yet tied. Delon has laid them out on ti leaves and misted them to keep them fresh. Drops of water stand on the petals as if it were dawn. Scott isn't here.

"If you hungry, Tina, get plenty ka mea 'ai in the kitchen. Auntie Loke made laulau and she brought some over."

"You ate?"

"When I'm done."

"I'll wait."

"'Kay," but if you hungry, don't mind me. You know you don't gotta ask."

We sit like that for a while, me thinking and Delon working, nobody saying anything. I keep looking for some sign in Delon's face, but all I can see is that he is making lei and he is calm. He's doing what he knows best, and he keeps figuring out a way to go on doing it, no matter the flowers are harder to come by or that a lot of shops have started using farmed flowers now anyway. The mana of what Delon does is all in the invisible work: climbing the trails above Pūpūkea that go up more than a thousand feet, saying the words for picking and gathering, sliding back down over red mud and boulders. All the things that can't be seen or touched when you hold a finished lei in your hands, but they're there if you know.

"Tina, why you staring?" he asks suddenly, not taking his eyes off his work.

"No, naw, I just ... nothing." I know he isn't ever going to say anything to me about Scott if I don't ask. So I do.

"Scott coming by later?" I say. Only because I am watching Delon so closely, I notice that his fingers hesitate, as if they needed reminding of their task, before they return to the gestures that are so like hula kuhi lima.

"He's with Chris," Delon says.

To someone else, those three words might be interpreted to mean Chris had to pick up his results at the VD clinic and Scott went to hold his hand, or about a hundred other things, but not the way Delon says it. Finally, I snap. Scott's not just with Chris; he's *with* Chris.

"Shit," I say.

Later on I'll get the whole hōʻike out of Chris P himself (and in secret because after that both Chris and Scott are forever-and-ever-amen unmentionable): how, the week before, Delon stopped over Scott's place on his way back from the lei stores to leave food and found the two of them having breakfast. At 8:30 in the morning. On a Sunday. With Chris in a T-shirt Delon gave Scott for his birthday.

Right at this moment, though, in Delon's living room, I'm flying blind. When my last boyfriend dumped me, I was feeling so sorry for myself that I ended up in a stall in Hula's bathroom, on my knees, crying and puking up all the alcohol I'd just paid tourist prices to pound down. Delon stood outside, guarding the door until I was ready to show my face again. "Don't worry, Tina," he kept saying. "Just let it out. It's natural." And then he walked with me along the Ala Wai Canal, pushing my bike for me, to make sure I got home. But there was no way I'd ever be allowed to see Delon like that, supposing he ever did get like that. So I'm thinking, I should be pissed, right, 'cuz that isn't fair, and instead I'm getting hamajang about what I can say without stepping in too deep, and then I think: I could just let Delon be. In the end, he knows more about where he fits in this world than anybody I know. And if we joke and call him the Queen Mother, well, he's still the mother, isn't he? And Delon never wonders where home is.

"So ... you guys break up or what?"

Delon raises his eyes toward me. "Māhū, why you always gotta know everything?" That's all the conversation we're going to have about Scott, so fuck it, then. I shut up and watch Delon hold a single, fragile pua kenikeni so gently between his left thumb and forefinger that it will never bruise. With his other hand, he inserts a long needle through the base of the flower and gently slides the blossom down the string to rest against the one that came before it on the lengthening strand.

"That's my favorite lei," I say after a while.

Delon slowly angles his head toward me about an inch, lowering his eyelids slightly. When he wants to let you know you're forgiven, he gets all Japanese.

"Even if they don't last too long."

"He pua maeʻole."

"Yeah, he pua maeʻole." Hawaiʻian songs and chants are full of phrases like that—beauty everlasting, the never-fading flower. But pua kenikeni barely goes a day before the petals turn brown. Of course there's no such thing as a flower that doesn't grow old and, anyway, everything dies. The ocean is dying, this land is dying, the language is dying. Sooner or later even the rock we're sitting on is gonna sink.

"All the more to savor beautiful things, nohoʻi?" Delon says, like he knows what I been thinking.

Whatever Scott came looking for that day at Long's, I still dunno what it was. Pats on the back for sticking with someone like Delon?

Permission to hemo him to the curb? I shouldn't have told Scott to break up with Delon. I wasn't wrong, but that was not my kuleana. I wonder if Delon knows about that, too. Scott could of been dumb enough to tell him.

"Mai, Tina, mai," Delon says, motioning me off the couch. He lifts one of the loops of pua kenikeni, ties the ends so the knot is hidden, and extends the lei toward me in both hands, an empty space filled with invisible work. I lean down as if I were bowing to him, and he slips the lei over my head.

"Smell this," he says. "You'll feel better."

"Thanks," I say.

Those songs—they aren't just about flowers, and I know that. Anyway, even if it's true that nothing is permanent, think how many things last longer than a flower.

What We Lost in the Fire

a novella

"No more war, no more plague, only the dazed silence that follows the ceasing of the heavy guns; noiseless houses with the shades drawn, empty streets, the dead cold light of morning. Now there would be time for everything." — Katherine Anne Porter, *Pale Horse, Pale Rider*

"History's what people are trying to hide from you, not what they're trying to show you. You search for it in the same way you sift through a landfill: for evidence of what people wanted to bury." — Hillary Mantel, *Giving Up the Ghost: A Memoir*

"The contagion despised all medicine, Death raged in every corner; and had it gone on as it did then, a few weeks more would have cleared the town of all, and everything that had a Soul." — Daniel Defoe, *A Journal of the Plague Year*

"Never again leave me to be the peaceful child I was before what there, in the night, / By the sea under the yellow and sagging moon, / The messenger there arous'd, the fire, the sweet hell within." — Walt Whitman, "Out of the Cradle Endlessly Rocking"

"What a horrible kind of travel, that took you only forward into the terrifying future, constantly farther from whatever had once made you happy." — Rebecca Makkai, *The Great Believers*

"I am interested in revealing how Nostalgia—our longing for the passing of what we ourselves have transformed—can function as apolitical memory and in the worst instances, violence." — Will Wilson

"It's not a story about AIDS. It's universal." — Ten thousand novelists, film directors, actors, and playwrights

"I can't change the past, but I don't have to stare at it." — Matthew López, *The Inheritance*

"I came to see the damage that was done /
and the treasures that prevail." — Adrienne
Rich, "Diving into the Wreck"

"In the age of AIDS, gay activists had to invent
a grammar to allow them to speak about their
lives. AIDS sparked a revolution, and so would the
language discovered by the activism it unleashed."
— Benjamin Moser, *Sontag: Her Life and Work*

"There are always three different conversations going
on. The conversation you have with the public, which
is just leading a normal life. The conversation you have
with your doctor or close friends, which is about the
chronic sickness, the everyday symptoms. And then
there's the inner conversation that you have with only
yourself, which is about death." — Micheal Milligan

"Optimism was the fuel we needed to make it this far.
The trick now is not feeling that we were foolish with
our time, or hoodwinked by life." — John Balma

"I grieve that grief can teach me nothing, nor
carry me one step into real nature." — Ralph
Waldo Emerson, "Experience"

"I say there's certain politicians that had better increase
their security forces and there's religious leaders
and healthcare officials that had better get bigger
dogs and higher fences and more complex security
alarms for their homes and queer-bashers better start
doing their work from inside howitzer tanks because
the thin line between the inside and the outside is
beginning to erode and at the moment I'm a thirty
seven foot tall one thousand one hundred and seventy-
two pound man inside this six foot frame and all I
can feel is the pressure all I can feel is the pressure
and the need for release." — David Wojnarowicz

PROLOGUE: WITNESS

And were you there? And did you see it happen? And now: will you testify? Can you call up details: who was wounded and who was lost? Can you bring to mind the color of their eyes and their height and could you say whether it had been warm that day and whether the sky was clear or were there clouds, was it perhaps foggy instead or had night fallen and did you notice the moon reflected in the neon puddles and could you hear singing, could you hear crying, could you hear chanting; was there a St. Christopher's medal or a Star of David around their necks, and did they wear contacts; were they black or brown or pink or something else, do you remember how they kept their hair—long or crew cut or in a Mohawk or a natural—and whether they'd flung a backpack over their shoulders or walked with a book lodged under one armpit or carried a grocery bag in their hands, whether their voices were deep or nasal or whether they had a Québecois accent or sounded like Alabama or Boston, were they short or chubby or muscle-bound or butch or high queens or shrunken as if freeze-dried or several of these at once; and when you saw it happen, were they speaking or sobbing, laughing or pressing their fists against their eyes or moving their lips without speaking, and how are you certain you remember the sound of their voices; did you ask yourself was it the sex, was it the drugs, was it a lying partner or an honest one, a mistake at the hospital, a maculate conception; and do you remember the name of the one who worked with you for two years before someone told you why she called in sick so often; did the perpetrators stop to inspect the damage or did they flee the scene before anyone understood what they'd done, would you recognize them, could you pick them out of a crowd, and could you make a sketch; did you warn your friends about them, or was there no one to blame or did it happen by chance and was there maybe never anyone else there at all; and did you hear singing or crying or chanting; what were the names of the ones who stopped to help and where are they now and why have you not kept in touch; did the others shout accusations and point, did they run through the streets screaming, did they pardon no one and was their anger like the solar wind: too hot for gravity to hold down; in what direction was everyone moving when it happened: were they late for class or walking with the person they loved most in the world or on the way to have sex for the first time with the cutest boy at the bar and look at this diagram and tell me whether it positions them correctly; were they dancing in front of an audience of hundreds or singing Purcell or reading their poetry, and which artist of the last three decades would they have been most sorry to have missed; do you still have the file on your computer where you kept track of dates, the birth dates the death dates the date you found out dates; were they happy before it happened or neutral or indifferent, did they seem to have an air of resignation or guilt or fury, or was there only grim detachment, did they lie alone in beds, waxen and raw, their eyes appalled; were they attended by retinues or were they unaware that others were in the room; was it your job to bring the plastic bag for the head; did bystanders turn away, bent over their own thoughts, or did they put on gloves, cross their arms, and assign blame; were they wearing red ribbons, or did they detour down parallel streets, pretend not to understand the words being spoken, give a tight, embarrassed smile and say "sorry, not today," as they flurried by; did you think you would forget the scene as soon as you were able and never visit there again and did you fantasize about forgetting or rather were you sure the memory would return, day after day, for the rest of your life, and that you would never be rid of it; and did you write names on masking tape to separate all the house keys in your pocket; and what was the soundtrack when the heaving or the silence or the laughter of children outside the window were more than you could bear, Ella or Nina or Billie or Judy; did you think of whom you would tell or how it would be told and when and who would write it and whether anyone would care, and what moments would represent it best, if you were forced to choose only three; or is your mind faithless and imperfect, and do you think it hardly matters anyway, and do your memories make you lonely; were you patient or bored or numb or did you privately wish for them to die faster and did you feel lucky; did you congratulate yourself for being prudent, and was your gratitude unpardonable, and was it your penance to count pills into containers for all the days of the week; did you tell anyone what you'd seen, what happened, what they did, how they took it, how they smelled, the way the sheets were never dry, and could you hear singing, could you hear crying, could you hear chanting; did you worry it might happen to you or were you sure it never would or had you seen it so many times that you no longer cared, and were the perfectly ordinary moments the most harrowing of all: pasta at the kitchen table, sorting the mail, giving him the Arts section first; did it all happen too quickly to follow or did it seem as though it would never end; did time play tricks, did your mind play tricks, did you ever forget what day it was, and did you say you were in a battle, a massacre, a genocide, a war; did you say it was like standing in a hurricane, like an earthquake, did you have trouble standing upright; were you afraid to move or were you certain you could not, did you go through the motions anyway, did you sing or chant or cry, and did you give back rubs the way he loved, pressing your fingertips in and out like typing, and did you ask questions; did you watch the first twenty minutes of the same movie over and over while he fell asleep, did you make schedules, did you bring warm socks, did you read aloud, did you feed the cat?

MICHEAL: 1992

Chaîné. Chaîné. Chaîné. Fast, on a diagonal from up right, deteriorating toward the end. Collapse into a fetal position, then bounce up into a penché. Hold four, then angel arms and arabesque. JD takes my heel and spins. Straighten, forearms up—one palm in, one out. Then elbows angle out and up and deep bend forward, standing on left leg, extended right leg avant. JD will grab the leg that's out and spin me again. This time I fall. Shit. He wasn't ready. I blew the count and got here too soon. Fuck. I'm lousy at counting. Always have been, but now: AZT brain. The infected sinus headache is back, too, a spike between my eyebrows. Hurts when he touches me. Count, damn it. And once more. Chaîné. Chaîné. Chaîné.

Later they take a break. "It's looking good, I think," JD says. "We've still got work ahead, but...."

"There's no ending," Micheal says. That fourth *Lied*." They were doing Strauss's *Four Last Songs*, and they'd choreographed enough on the final song, "Im Abendrot," for a full-length ballet, then kept cutting it back to nothing. They barely had three good minutes, maybe. They needed something like eight.

"We'll get it," JD said, ever the good parent. Three, gruff, reassuring syllables. That butchness some straight men could pull off. Being a dancer had only ever made Micheal more fey, but it made JD a stud. He could tell you things and you'd believe they'd come true, maybe because he spoke so sparingly. Plus shoulders out to here and waist cinched in to there. Lumberjack beard. *If you can pull off a beard, you can pull off my underwear.* Micheal had read that somewhere. No wonder the twenty-something girls in JD's modern dance classes couldn't stay out of his bed.

Thank God JD wasn't Micheal's type, or they'd never have been able to work together. This was the fifth piece they'd made on each other, them and the three women who made up their pick-up dance company. Five On One Hand, they called it. They'd never made a whole piece of duets, but Micheal knows there aren't going to be any more dances, at least not with him. "Performing is killing me," he'd said, joking but not joking. That was probably why they were having trouble getting through the last song. *How tired we are of traveling. Is this perhaps death?* They couldn't finish a piece about death. That was a dance in itself.

For a while after rehearsal Micheal is still "on," still in performance mode. It gets him through. Later he'll suffer the consequences, crash, sob. At work, it's the same: he's chatty, funny, charming, always ready with a quip, through never anything too risqué, never the kind of thing he'd say among gay friends. It was still the East Bay, after all, not The City.

That morning they'd been meeting about the design for the Spring course catalog—spot colors, fonts, images, the usual. "Micheal, given this schedule, when will you need final copy?" Cathy asked. Micheal opened his mouth, swallowed back the sudden rush of saliva, then ducked below the surface of the table to vomit into a waste basket. That shocked them. No one had ever seen him sick before, not in public. Not at work.

He didn't look sick. That's what everyone said. When he ran into people he hadn't seen in a while, he could count on being told how great he looked, as if he'd been away for a week in the Bahamas, as if they'd been steeling themselves for something worse. And then there'd be the confidence, spoken sotto voce close to his ear: "No one would even know you were sick."

He knew, and he knew he didn't look all that great, either. All those years he'd been the guy with the great skin, perfect teeth, beautiful ginger hair, gorgeous legs, and cute ass.... Well, look how that turned out. Sometimes being too popular can kill you. Meanwhile, he was watching his legs deflate in two directions at once: from the ankles up and the hips down. He'd had an intermittent rash for two years, like eczema but not eczema, according to the doctors.

Lately, virologists at the CDC and activists had been locked in another of their internecine battles, this time over the medical definition of AIDS. If the CDC accepted low T-cells as sufficient for diagnosis, that meant he'd officially had AIDS for some time. If they didn't, he officially didn't, at least until he came down with one of the small group of "approved" OIs. "Depending on what the CDC decides," he joked to Kenny. I could be cured overnight! It'll be a miracle!"

He was like a person getting ready to go on a long trip. There was a lot of planning, and then you were gone. No one expected to hear from you; your excuse for refusing dinners, social events, political fundraisers, parties, baby showers was unimpeachable. No one would ask you to fly back from Buenos Aires or Dublin or Miami just for their anniversary. "Oh, well, we'll get together when you're back." The joke was on them. You weren't coming back. It was like that old *New Yorker* cartoon: "How about never. Is never good for you?"

In the mirror in the mornings, he rubbed creams into that once-gorgeous skin, now pocked and rough, and applied concealer to areas that had become permanently discolored. He'd always been a boy who knew his way around a makeup counter. So he had at least one skill that turned out to be useful.

FINN: THE PRESENT

They're in their usual places: she's in her overstuffed wing chair—red leather—and he's on the couch. Not just a metaphor. He could lie down, but they've never talked about that. Do they need to talk about it? She always tells him he can do whatever he wants, even nothing at all, that it's his time.

He tries out nothing at all. The silence drifts like smoke. It isn't uncomfortable, exactly, but it's dull: he feels he's standing in a line that isn't moving. He's tempted to try the whole session like this, to see if he can.

Finally, she says kindly, quietly: "I wonder where you've gone."

To a familiar place, is where. Here, the sadness feels like reflux, a gurgling that moves from his bellybutton to his sternum. Sometimes it's a cramp, sometimes the sensation of being hungry, even when the thought of food is disgusting. It shifts inside him, grasping his heart in its fist. He sighs often, trying to dislodge the restive baby that goes on gestating but refuses to be born. And then there are the crying jags, uncontrollable and often inconvenient. Anything can make him cry now. He goes out, rambles the sidewalks without purpose past pubs and coffee shops and bookstores. At least it's exercise, he tells himself. He doesn't want to go inside any of them because he feels like a tourist in a country where he doesn't speak the language. Every human interaction requires a rehearsal, a consultation of phrase books and dictionaries, the careful construction of a sentence—and then what if they ask a question? He will stand there, mute and uncomprehending, his fluency debunked. Nor does he want to go home where he will only wander from room to room, ferrying objects or papers to a new emplacement and then bringing them back, cataloguing projects he has been meaning to get to and making lists, kindled for a moment by the quickening power of choices but ultimately subsiding into the exhaustion of too many schemes. Often he simply ends up inert on the couch. Clearly, he is not the man for this job.

A lot of gay men his age suffer from PTSD, a version of it. This is what he has read. He doesn't know. He knows he spent much of his late twenties saying things like, "I don't have time to be sad right now," which is what everybody was saying, as people withered around them, one after another, disappearing, briefly, until they reappeared, briefly, as an obituary and a bad photo and a version of the same words in that newspaper font he always thought was so brutal. And then he is suddenly, sidereally, 60 and he finds them all there waiting for him. Not a one of them has stirred an inch. They don't demand anything, and yet here they are, the whole galaxy of them, and this time he doesn't think he can ignore them. He feels it would be disrespectful after they'd stood patiently in place for so long, but what is truer still is that he no longer has the strength to hold them off. He's probably not going to be around all that much longer—either because he'll go through with the suicide he's been keeping in his back pocket for more than a year or because his left ventricle will give out as the cardiologist thinks it may—and he is the only one who can mourn these people. He has to be the one to see to it. So he doesn't mind the sadness. In fact, he relishes this complex stratigraphy of emotions, and he is delighted by the memories, or most of them, and yet he can't help but worry he will never again be anything more than a finely tuned instrument of sadness.

This very day, Sylvester has made him cry. The late Sylvester. An old song from a CD he hasn't played for years. Well, a forty-year-old song. And it's not just Sylvester. Freddie, too, with whom he shares a birthday in September. Definitely Freddie. He's watched that video online at least a score of times, Freddie's last, the one where he sings "These Are the Days of Our Lives." He still had those sly, epicene, Valentino contours, but his gestures seemed truncated, as if his body had been cramped into a small space, and his hair was flat, like trampled grass. Micheal's had been the same, and he'd preferred to shave himself bald rather than have it styled or combed because he couldn't bear to watch it fall out and sidle down the drain. Really, though, Freddie's face was what broke your heart. They'd ruddled up his eyes with mascara and shadow, but, when he sang, every ridge and spur of his skull was visible, the structure of his mandible precise and anatomical beneath the skin. And when he got to that line—"You can't turn back the clock, you can't turn back the tide. Ain't that a shame?"—there was a close-up, and his expression was devastation. The story went around that he'd come into the studio for one single hour that day and recorded the entire album. That was the end of his strength. He died six months later.

*Sylvester's last house was on Collingwood, only a few
doors away from Yossi, but he barely got to live in it. By the
time he moved in, he was already so sick he almost never
went out. During the Castro Street Fair, the year Sylvester
died, they'd stood at 18th and Collingwood, a thousand feet
from his door, and shouted his name, hoping he could hear
from his bedroom. Yossi said he always wished he would
run into Sylvester, just casually, like when he went to pick
up groceries at the Cala, but they never intersected. What
would you have done if you'd seen him? Finn once asked
him. Hugged him, I guess, Yossi said, if he'd have let me.
Sometimes you just want to touch someone like that."*

"Can you tell me?" she asks again, and he still needs a few moments
to answer because he is crying again and cannot speak. He holds up
a finger like a shop clerk with customers waiting: *I haven't forgotten.
Be right with you.* Even in that moment, he can see the humor. But.
The problem is that all he has are small stories because everyone's
story is small, so how can he ever explain how immense they have
grown inside him? She waits, patient as always, and yet he imagines
himself crouched in one corner, watching as a small, gray-haired
woman, calm and attentive on a red leather wing chair, sits in a
room with a grown man—a nearly elderly man, though friends still
call him "middle-aged," as though 120 were a normal lifespan—who
sniffles and wipes tears on his pants, and he is struck once again by
the way that grief is nothing if not relentlessly humiliating.

In fact, he remembers no specific day in the past when he heard
Sylvester sing, or Queen for that matter. Or perhaps only one day.
But when he hears those songs now, projections flicker to life against
the walls of his mind, each image looped to others until the whole
tidal wave comes down and he is beached, gasping.

"There are songs from those days," he tells her, "that are connected
to memories. And hearing them, or even just thinking about them
sometimes, brings up, well, sadness for sure, but not only sadness.
Sometimes they make me smile. It's bittersweet, what I remember."

*And nowhere is safe. In the museum on Sunday: An exhibi-
tion of phantasmagoric textiles and unsettling, grotesque
figures armored in fat tumors of yarn and sequins, kachinas*

*or spirit costumes or soundsuits à la Nick Cave, a riff on the
queer seventies. And over it a soundtrack in the gallery ...*

Ooh
I feel love, I feel love
I feel love, I feel love
I feel love

*... the mechanized, synthesized 128 beats per minute,
the delay calculated in milliseconds and perfect because
no human hand had to keep it up, and he felt a levitation
in his body. A heel jouncing against the parquet, his thumb
and forefinger opening and closing like a heart valve, his
head weaving on his suddenly flexible neck; then he'd notice
he was among staid and sober strangers and he'd stop,
self-conscious, but in the space of a measure it was back,
spilling out through his skin. He saw it then, exactly the
way it was: the heads of handsome men undulating in the
strobing light like buoys on the surface of a night sea, their
sweat streaming down their faces, their teeth glowing blue
in black light. He wanted to hurl himself after them, fling
his arms through the air to gather them in as the music
throbbed, dance with his eyes full of tears, throw his head
back in a poppers trance while the entire earth shrank to
one tiny, rapturous point in space. He wanted to scream
to the gallery: Get out if you weren't there! This was our
music! This was for us!*

"Is there any memory in particular, sad or bittersweet or plea-
surable, that stands out as you're thinking about that music now?"

Of course there is. He has been thinking about the day he went
to empty out Yossi's apartment. "After Yossi died," he says, "everyone was exhausted. We'd been at the hospital for days, but he was
exhausting long before that. He was so angry. He'd have these fits
where he became some kind of dark presence."

*People are such hideous shits, Yossi raged. They've all
abandoned me! I have no true friends. Everyone wanted to
hang around me when I was pretty and sexy and had energy,*

*but now I disgust them and they didn't want anything to
do with me. They don't even try to hide it!"*

*"I'm here," Finn said, and Yossi turned his head to the
wall. Beneath his head, he punched the pillow, humid with
sweat.*

*He'd become brittle and his cheekbones pushed up from
below as if impatient to break through and escape. During
one especially bad week he fired three home health aides,
screaming cutting, unforgivable insults at them as they
fled the apartment. Later, one woman told Finn, "He called
me a fat, wetback whore. I know it's the illness, but that's
too much disrespect." Finn apologized over and over and
then sent her a check for twice what she was owed for that
week. He didn't know what else to do.*

*It was the illness, but Finn had lost all ability to tell
what Yossi could control. So many times he said things
that were so specific and so personal that it was hard to
believe he hadn't been keeping the arrows nocked for years
until being sick gave him an excuse to let them fly. And he
wasn't particularly regretful afterward. "Yossi, you have to
try to be nicer," Finn said. "You need help, and people are
doing their best." Yossi waved his hand. "I'm dying. What's
their fucking excuse?"*

"And we immediately had to organize his memorial and everything," Finn goes on. After that, a couple of weeks went by, while
we all drifted around in that disorienting lull that happened after
a death. You'd been arranging shifts and ticking 'to dos' off lists for
weeks and months, and now you weren't. You'd gotten through the
drama and all that emotion of the finale, which focused you like a
laser and let so much of the bullshit of life just roll to one side. And
then, all at once, the immediacy was gone, and the rest of existence
came back like a freak tide. You called each other up, just to 'check
in,' but what you were thinking was: there's nothing left to do; what
should I do? Anyway, Yossi's mom decided she was ready to go back
to Long Island. She'd been staying with Esta and Carmen, and all that
time, no one had been in Yossi's house. I mean, they took him right
from there to the hospital that last time, when he was in so much
pain, and he never came back. So there was the medical equipment,

too, plus all of Yossi's belongings that needed to be gone through. And I volunteered."

He stands in the tidy, ornate entry porch at the top of the stairs, a key in his hand, staring at the cobalt blue door. Familiar. It's all so familiar. He'd left the key loose in his pocket, apart from the others on his clip, because the key is Yossi's. It doesn't belong with his. There is no one to open the door now, kiss him, tease him about his haircut, tell him to come inside, take the bottle of wine he is holding. He fits the key into the lock, turns it to slide the bolt, then moves to the second lock and opens the latch above. He shoulders the door back and takes a step forward. He had thought going in alone would feel eerie, even frightening, but instead he realizes that the space is merely silent, the air stale and chilly. There is a bad smell, too, which he realizes is coming from vases of decomposing flowers. That is a first task, something to set him in motion, and he carries the collapsed, shrunken arrangements to the kitchen and puts them in the sink. From out of his backpack, he takes the boxes of extra-strength lawn-and-leaf bags that he has bought, opens one, and begins disposing of the rotting vegetation. Festering petals scuttle from deflated stems; the greasy water reeks. Da da da da, snap snap, the Addams family!

The rest of the supplies have to come up from the car: cartons, bubble wrap, labels, tape. He has Yossi's Will, with its list of small bequests, and he decides that will be the next job. Yossi's collection of carnival glass, which is in a breakfront in the living room, goes to his friend, Kenneth. He pads each of the strange and iridescent objects in layers of newspaper until it loses its original shape, arranges them all in a box, then tapes it shut and writes Kenneth's name on one flap. The kitchen utensils have to be packed for Goodwill, much less carefully, who'll also pick up most of the furniture when they come. They're scheduled for late in the afternoon, as are the people from San Francisco Medical Rental, who'll take the hospital gurney, the overbed tilt-table, the IV pole, the wheelchair. The bed pan, whatever is left of boxes of syringes, Vacutainer tubes, alcohol pads, gauze, adhesive tape, and all the other miscellaneous medical paraphernalia are for a group of doctors who take supplies to Cuba. He decides he'll keep Yossi's highball glasses and his ceramic pie pans for himself. That and the blue kitchen table, a gift from McKay that Yossi treasured. Finn had promised to keep it safe.

Then there are the books to tackle, hundreds of them. Most of them go to the Friends of the Library for their annual sale at Ft. Mason, but he's allowed to keep anything he wants—except for the Bloomsbury stuff, which is earmarked for Yossi's friend, Shellye, who also gets the nicely framed portrait of Virginia Woolf, a reprint of one of the photographs Beresford took of her when she was twenty. Shellye is as obsessed as Yossi was. He begins to pull out the Bloomsbury books: The Letters of Virginia Woolf (six volumes); The Diary of Virginia Woolf (five volumes); every one of her novels, some in more than one edition; books of essays, lectures; all of Forster's novels; Leonard's books; large-format coffee-table volumes of paintings by Vanessa Bell, Duncan Grant, Roger Fry; books about the Bloomsbury group; Skidelsky's biography of Keynes (three volumes); biographies of all the principals and most of the hangers-on as well. The box is already full, so he begins to pile the books on the floor at the far end of the hall. He remembers Yossi telling him about the forty-year friendship of Duncan Grant and Vanessa Bell, her marriage to Clive, the cohabitation à quatre, and nearly everyone, except Vanessa apparently, sleeping with nearly everyone; Grant's seduction of one man after another, including the future husband of his own daughter. The way Yossi told the story, it wasn't seventy-year-old literary gossip; it was a soap opera about friends who lived on the block.

"Yossi is gone," he says to the print of Virginia Woolf as he takes it from the wall, and she answers after the briefest pause, as if she had been waiting but was too reserved to speak out of turn. "I do know," she says. "I am so very sorry."

"I don't think it was too terrible," he tells her. "At the end. We were all there, in and out, for most of a week, talking to him, giving him massages, playing gospel music.

His mom sat with him the whole last twenty-four hours. I don't think she left once."

"I should think that would have been an enormous comfort to him," Virginia says.

"I doubt he realized we were there."

"Oh, but of course he must have done. There is so much we fail to understand about human consciousness."

He turns back to the task of the books.

"I wonder if I can tell you," she says, "that I have lately had occasion to speak with Mrs. Elsa Donnelly."

"I don't know who that is," he says.

"No, I suppose you would not. She and her husband built this house in 1891, not long after the cable car line opened on Market Street, and all of Eureka Valley was in the middle of a mad rush of 'homestead fever.' Her husband was a foundry worker. I suppose one could say he died of the foundry. Grinder's rot, the workers called it back then. My point, however, is to say something else, which is that she sends her condolences as well. She knows how much Yossi loved this house."

"He thought it was the center of the universe," he says. He double checks to make sure he hasn't overlooked any of the Bloomsbury material. "Oh, so that must mean they were here during the earthquake," he says.

"Oh, yes. Terrible time, to hear her tell. The house shook like a field mouse harried by a fox, and those are her exact words, but the whole Eureka Valley is built on bedrock, as you know, so they were fortunate indeed. They stayed on for decades after that. Still, I lost two houses to bombs, so I am well aware what it is like not to feel safe in one's home and to live each day against a vague sensation of risk. To think something might come out of the sky and knock the walls flat at any moment."

"Yossi wanted you to go to Shellye's from now on," he says. "It's a good place for you."

"Well, that is very welcome news, indeed," she says. "I shall look forward to it, though it will mean saying goodbye to Elsa. She is quite attached to this house and intends to stay, and of course her husband is here, too.

"Will Yossi be here?"

"He need not be," Virginia says, "and he is not here now. Beyond that, I regret to say, I am not privileged to know."

He needs a break from the library. He picks up an unopened box of lawn bags and heads toward the stairs. All of Yossi's clothes are up there in his bedroom, in closets and the dresser. *Give all that to charity,* Yossi's mother had said. *Unless you want anything. And throw away the socks and underwear. No one needs to wear that.*

"I can see you are much occupied with your tasks," she continues, "so I shan't keep you any longer."

"In fact, if I don't keep moving, I won't be ready when they come for the pickups," he says, "but this has been wonderful, a real unexpected pleasure. Thank you for what you said about Yossi. You've been very kind."

"Not at all," Virginia tells him. "Good day to you."

Once the clothes are done, the only thing left are the sex toys and porn in an army surplus trunk at the foot of the bed, which Yossi called his Hope Chest—*as in let's hope I meet someone who knows how to use these!* The Hope Chest, in fact, is mainly why he's there. No one thought the task of going through Yossi's things should fall to his mother, though she kept saying she could do it, she didn't mind, it didn't bother her, but everyone agreed she shouldn't find the Hope Chest.

He is tempted by take some of the videos home, but then the idea of watching smut that Yossi had watched strikes him as embarrassing, even incestuous. They go into the bag with the rest of the things headed straight for the dump. *Your sex life may be one thing you can't pass on,* he thinks.

The movers from Goodwill come and then another pair from the medical-supply place, and the house, in a space shorter than the length of a single day's light, grows unfamiliar, even anonymous, no longer Yossi's. In every move from one home to another, he has noticed that a time always comes when the soul drains out as if through the hole in the bottom of a killed pot. He has always been able to feel it, always known when his connection to a place he has occupied has flickered and gone out, when he no *longer belongs there. This is what has happened to Yossi's house. He has finished his work, though he still has boxes to deliver, people to let in when they come for what is now theirs, a van to rent for the blue table. But this house is done with Yossi, and he is done with Yossi's house.*

He closes the door, throws both locks, and lets the key fall to the bottom of his pocket. Tomorrow he'll take care of the last few things. As he walks away, a car pauses at the corner. The driver has rolled the windows down, and disco music, rowdy and ebullient, booms from inside. You make me feel mii-iighty real. Even after the car turns out of sight, he can feel the pulse of the bass in his feet. He imagines the vibrations multiplying, increasing in amplitude until they shake the house, the windows and doors in their frames, open cracks in the walls, knock plaster to the floor, send the neighbors screaming into the streets before dawn, panicked and disoriented.

"You remember many details about that day," she says, "but I'm struck that you didn't say how you felt being in Yossi's house. Were you sad?"

"No," he says, "I was never sad. At the hospital, the night he died, his funeral, a year later the memorial on his yahrzeit. I never cried. All I felt that day was that I'd volunteered to do a job, and I was doing it—for Yossi and our friends, and for his mom, so she wouldn't have to."

For those ten years of deaths and marches and unwelcome phone calls and letters he didn't want to receive or to write, he didn't cry. But now he does. Thirty-plus years after it all started, more than two and a half decades since Yossi's death, the sadness has become like breathing—always there, involuntary, whether he thinks about it or not. One day it appeared, and now it is out of his control. Tears roll down his face when he is on the bus, in the middle of meals, at the movie theater. But there were none the evening of Yossi's memorial, none that day on Baker Beach, when they arranged sticks of incense in the sand, and candles that would barely stay lit, and they threw Yossi's ashes into the Pacific, the wind whipping the dust back into their faces. He'd put some aside in a baggie, and the next day he took them to Café Flore and sprinkled them into the wooden planters on the Market Street side of the patio. Yossi had gone there to hold court and watch boys most days of his life in San Francisco, and some of him deserved to remain.

YOSSI: 1982

They are on the quad, east of the brutalist gray geometry of the San Francisco State Student Center building, clustered on the grass like pigeons. Off to the right is the gym and, farther back, the psychology building. To the left is the library. The Student Center was built one year after the student strikes that rocked the campus for five months in late 1968, and the legend was that university president S. I. Hayakawa insisted that it be built on that precise spot to bisect the great meadow that had once existed there and which was the preferred site for giant rallies and protests. Everyone seemed to be certain of this story, but whether it was true or how anyone had come to know it was less clear.

That day they'd won the highest knoll, or a piece of it, a coveted hillock with a shade tree that gave the best view of the plaza outside the SC doors and of the arterial streams of students on the tangle of walkways that ran north toward the deep campus, the dorms and parking structure, the stadium, or back toward the MUNI car stop on Holloway Avenue, to home, to jobs. There were the ones who bent forward as they walked, as if pressed to the earth by the gravity of being there, and the others who moved lightly, even athletically, everything going well, a tedious class over, the sun shining especially for them.

Yossi's group is feeling victorious and celebratory as they eat their bad Chinese food and pizza off Styrofoam containers from the basement food court, falling against one another with laughter, reveling in the warmth of the day and the stories of each other's Brownian lives. Jonah and Masha were already best friends, the kind of friends most people assumed were lovers, especially then, in those days of political bisexuality and the men's movement before it turned reactionary and putrid and lesbianism so radical it meant sleeping with men. But maybe it was really only because they were beautiful and one could imagine them together, wanted to imagine them together, as though when two such perfect people found each other it was a victory for humanity.

Lisa is there, whom Yossi had gone to high school with and whom he'd more or less followed to San Francisco after her year of letters telling him how it was paradise and inviting him to stay as long as he wanted in her Haight Street walkup, where she lived with her brooding, chain-smoking, chronically depressed boyfriend from Holland, the one she'd met during a gap year in Amsterdam. By the time Yossi got there, she'd broken up with the boyfriend, whom she'd taken to calling, in letters to Yossi, the "Dying Dutchman," even though she was pregnant with his daughter, and she'd moved to Orinda with another man, this one more than twice her age, but Yossi and Lisa could arrange their schedules to get the BART together from the East Bay and then rush across the platform to the M train and be deposited on campus in less than an hour.

On the evening when Yossi had finally arrived at the Oakland airport, Lisa had been out of town, and her man had guided him from the terminal down to the BART station and then to a freezing-cold, semi-underground in-law unit where he'd seduced Yossi the very first night. He was forty-five, and Yossi was amazed because he'd never been with anybody so old. Lisa had only laughed when she found out later. "He really does have a thing for boys," she said.

So the four of them are there, along with a guy from Yossi's Gay & Bisexual Literature class on whom Yossi has a secret crush and a woman who is older than them by seven or eight years, Gretchen, who is in an MFA program in dance and who seems both pugnacious and fiercely intelligent. Gretchen is a friend of Lisa's, and she is draped, as she always is, in florid cowls of fabric, membranous or shaggy, and colorful, dangling loops of beads like rosaries, and Yossi finds her daunting. She looks European, Yossi thinks, as if she'd grown up in Paris instead of, as he now knows, the Bywater, but her hauteur is majestic. Part of the strategy for occupying the knoll is to watch for any friends or acquaintances who might be passing across campus and to call them over until, from two, a quorum was gathered, and the right to hold the hill could not be challenged. No one would come and say, "Do you mind if we...?"

Masha finishes her pizza and, flouncing against the lawn, announces: "I'm thirsty." "Here," Jonah offers, holding out the can of Coke he has been drinking from. Masha takes it, holds it in her hand a moment, and then passes it back. "Nah," she says, "better not." The strange thing, looking back on it now, is that none of the rest of them seemed to think that was strange. No one was sure how the sickness was transmitted—at that point, they didn't even know it was a virus. Maybe Masha was right. But Yossi sees the look that passes between Jonah and Masha as the rejected Coke returns, unshared, to Jonah's hand. Jonah's features seem to be wrestling themselves into an expression, and Masha's eyes are too bright.

The moment ends, and Gretchen fishes a bottle of water out of her dance bag. "Here," she says," I haven't opened it yet," and Masha reaches for the bottle, unscrews the cap, and takes a long pull before handing it back, and what they all understand is that Gretchen will later drink from the same bottle without a thought because they were women, because they weren't at risk. This is what they thought they knew then, in the days when nobody knew anything.

THE CASTRO: AUGUST 1993

It is sunny and bright, and they are walking. Shuffling, really, because of the crowd. A flood of people covers both lanes and sloshes up over the sidewalks on the north and south sides of Market Street. The median strips, with their shaggy, incongruous palms in pairs and trios, rise up every few blocks like desert islands, and the marchers fissure, then weave together again as they pass. The surface of the street is buckled by the roots of the trees, ironic because the palms were planted to spruce the city up after the Loma Prieta quake and now they've reproduced the earthquake's effects.

The route is the familiar one. The first march down Market was after the City Hall murders, a candlelight procession that mantled every available space for a solid mile and a half, and after that it became a tradition. But now they walk in reverse: from the Civic Center to the Castro, always in that direction, every year for the AIDS Vigil, the Harvey Milk Memorial March, protests and celebrations, though the celebrations seem fewer these days.

Today, they'd gathered at Dolores Street, closer in, below the old San Francisco Mint, and begun the half-mile walk to the Castro, where a casket waits near the maw-like entrance of the metro station, poised there as though that cavern, that pit would stand in as the gateway to the under-realms.

"I don't feel anything," Finn says, and Yossi extends an arm across Finn's shoulder, cupping the deltoid in his palm.

"You feel everything," Yossi says, "that's different."

Micheal is lagging behind, already winded, but delighted by the sun, by the crowd. He knows they're not there for him and yet, in a way, they are. Finn and Yossi stop to wait for him to catch up. "I hope you guys are planning to carry my coffin to Castro Street," he says when they are together again. "I demand public mourning. No, not just mourning. I want keening. Pay people if you must."

The crowd edges around the small eddy their standstill has created, and then the three move on as well, more slowly now. There's no rush. There are hundreds behind them who still have to get to the plaza where they will stand inside the yellow sawhorses marked "SFPD," and hundreds more are meanwhile being ferried upward on steep, narrow escalators from the deep regions of the metro, and anyway the point is being where they are.

"Cheer up," says Finn. "Maybe we'll see the famous Hot Cop of the Castro today."

"Burn me in the street and eat my flesh!" Micheal says suddenly, loudly, and people turn to stare. "Know who said that?"

"David Wojnarowicz?" Finn offers.

"Nope. It was Jon Greenberg," says Micheal. "He used to scream it in crowded elevators in front of small children."

"That's just crazy," Finn says.

They arrive at the broad, four-way intersection of Market and Castro. They see the rainbow flags and, high on a hill to the west, the three red-and-white spars of Sutro Tower. Later, the fog will shimmer in to shroud all but the tip of the tower, and the antennas will seem like the masts of a sailboat tacking across a lake of pewter-colored spume.

The coffin waits on a bier raised tall above street level, but angled slightly higher at the head so the body is visible. The dead man is wasted, ashy. Alongside, on a podium elevated to the same height, stands a microphone, and another man waits behind it, solemnly, watching the streets fill.

"Moses has come down from the mountain," Yossi says.

"I'm serious," says Micheal.

"I think we can begin," the man at the microphone announces, raising his right hand, palm out, like an announcing angel, like a blessing. "Welcome!" he booms. "We are here today in love and in rage, in grief and in defiance. We are not afraid, and we will not be silent."

"You're serious about people eating your flesh?" Finn says to Micheal.

"I'm serious that I don't want some weepy funeral with organ music and shit."

At the microphone, the speaker's voice is urgent. "This is a public funeral. This is a *political* funeral. Today, we say farewell to our friend, our lover, our son, our brother, Bobby Warner. Today, we carry one of our dead through the streets, and we mourn together."

"I'm so sick of this bullshit," Yossi says. "We have got to do something different."

"Like move to a venue where they serve drinks?" Micheal suggests.

"No, stop fucking around. I mean something big. Something drastic, even monstrous. So many of these bastards deserve to die. Bush, Sullivan, Helms, Cardinal O'Connor, Buchanan, Falwell, Dannemeyer, Lorraine Day, LaRouche...."

"That prick who wanted to tattoo us on our asses," says Finn.

"Buckley," Yossi answers.

"Scott's father," Micheal puts in.

"All our fathers," says Finn.

Yossi is grinding his fist into his hand. "Don't you ever think, if the prematurely dead are vengeful, that we are fucked?" he says. We've turned into a bunch of professional pallbearers. We sit around sewing quilt sections and polishing *BAR* obituaries...."

"Let's write our own obituaries," Micheal says. "It'll be a hoot."

Finn rolls his eyes. "Queen, no."

The man at the podium has been replaced by another. The new speaker wears a black ACTUP T-shirt with a pink triangle and, over that, a black leather jacket studded with brightly colored stickers: Safe Sex Is Hot Sex, Denial=Death, Queer Nation, Fag Power, Dyke Power. "Last October," he begins, "hundreds of people traveled to Washington with the ashes of their loved ones and threw them onto the White House lawn. They went to protest more than twelve years during which our government has mocked us while a genocide is taking place. But we responded with an act of empowerment. Today we do the same."

"What I'm saying," Yossi continues, "is what can they do if a bunch of people who are going to die soon anyway decide to take a few assholes with them?"

"Wait, you mean like kamikazes?" Finn says.

"People who've got nothing to lose," Yossi says. "We've got plenty of friends in that boat."

"I ask that we now observe a moment of silence for Bobby," says the man behind the microphone. He bows his head, and the crowd falls still.

"You're being very intense," Micheal whispers to Yossi.

"Fuck, though," Finn says, leaning close to be heard. "I would do it. I would fucking do it. I don't care."

Their three heads are now nearly touching. "You're saying you'd kill somebody? An actual person?" Micheal says.

The microphone squalls. The man clears his throat and begins again. "And now that we've observed silence, let us be clear why we are here. We are being murdered. Reagan was a murderer. Bush was a murderer. Clinton is a murderer. We are not just numbers. We are people who have lives, who have purpose and careers, who have lovers, friends, and families. Today, we publicly declare our pain, our right to life, and our right to determine our deaths."

"I'm not saying what you should do," Yossi says, "but I'm ready to kill someone. It's not just some war cry. We could do it. Those of us who know we're dying. We could organize it."

Micheal feels a spike of anxiety. "So we just decide who deserves to die?" he says. "All on our own? Us?"

From the platform above the street, the eulogy continues. "Bobby Warner was my best friend for a decade," the man says, "and he knew he was going to die. To the end, Bobby was unafraid of the consequences of his actions, or if he was afraid, he let that fear spur him on rather than stop him from living his life as a full human being."

"I get it," says Yossi, "but what's the alternative? Keep doing *this*? Screaming our throats raw outside the fucking FDA?" Micheal stares at his friend. Finn watches them both, his face mute. "You're the one quoting Jon Greenberg," he says to Micheal.

The man at the podium finishes speaking and steps down. Six men and women arrange themselves around the coffin, three on each of the long sides. They grasp the gleaming wood with white gloves, hoist the box onto shoulders, begin a gingerly choreography down the ramp to the street. The body jounces inside, and a cross someone has placed on Bobby Warner's chest slips into a fold in the upholstery. The crowd surges forward, then stops. A voice begins to chant, "ACTUP! Fight back! Fight AIDS!" and the marchers immediately pick up the call, the spondees like bludgeons, like shields.

"Okay," says Micheal, "okay. I just ... whatever happens, we can talk about it, right? We have time to talk about it. I mean, there's time for that at least, right?"

The procession begins to trickle up Castro Street toward Liberty, where the dead man's family and friends wait in his apartment for the hearse to arrive to take Bobby's body to the cemetery. The street rises slowly but steadily in that direction, and no one hurries. Around Micheal, Finn, and Yossi, the crowd grows denser, funneled from the ample spaces of the intersection into the narrow perimeters of Castro Street, where the police have blocked off the sidewalks for pedestrian use. For a moment it seems as though no one will be able to move at all, that they'll suffocate there in the crush, and then a clot around them breaks loose, and they drift forward on a wave of gentle, inexorable momentum.

MCKAY: 1987

What he knows is that he wants the puppy. He is twenty-six years old, and he has been on his own in this tiny rust-belt town for all the years of his graduate program, but the dog makes him feel ten again, and keeping it is suddenly the sum and the aim of his longing. *How much is that doggy in the window?*

"No, McKay," his mother is saying. "I'm not having a dog in the house. You don't even know if it's house-trained. Best just not to, don't you think? Anyway, you haven't had it long and you aren't attached yet."

She's wrong about that. His master's program is over. His student housing voucher expires in two weeks. He has no job. Everyone he knows is going somewhere: home, to doctoral programs, to get married. That's where the puppy came from: abandoned by someone in a hurry to leave town. So McKay, too, is going home for a while to regroup. He knows his mother doesn't care about the dog except that McKay wants it. All his attachments are suspect, and the only response she knows to them is severity. She'd let him in the house, but she would refuse to *endorse* anything. Her lips thin into a line. When he'd told her he was positive, she shook her head and said two sentences: "I'm already doing the best I can, McKay. You're asking us to accept an awful lot."

His mom had driven out with his sister, Vella, to help McKay pack up his tiny, top-floor room in the Depression-era rooming house on Church Street, just down from the town square with the water tower where he sat on summer evenings. There are oak trees in the yard and peeling green paint on the sills and door jambs and no air-conditioning, though his landlady has lent him a box fan that roars like the ocean. They were kind to come; he is glad for the help, for his mother's ability to organize tasks and move through them, stoic and dispassionate. And yet knowing they were coming, knowing they were on their way, has ignited a kind of dread in him, and their arrival marks the end of something that will never be the same again.

They are crowded into the motel room that his mother and sister have taken for the two of them and his sister's toddler, Evan. The puppy lies at McKay's feet, its chin posed dejectedly against McKay's right shoe, as if it knows it has been turned down. Evan babbles happily to the dog, trying to feed it Ritz crackers, which the puppy licks politely.

"I don't think he likes Ritz, baby," McKay says.

"You like Ritz?" Evan says, cracker crumbs dropping from his mouth like sparse, wet snow.

"I do," McKay answers.

Evan takes the cracker he's been eating and holds it out to McKay. He has already bitten a distinct semicircle out of one edge, McKay notices. When McKay doesn't react immediately, Evan moves closer, extending his arm until his fingers brush McKay's lips. Evan's hand is slimy with saliva, and McKay is slightly disgusted, but he loves Evan and he is touched by the idea that this tiny person, his nephew, wants to feed him. As McKay opens his mouth to bite the cracker, he glimpses his mother's face. Her features seem to be rising all at once, like startled birds. Suddenly, from the opposite direction, Vella's hand comes down over Evan's small fist, knocking the cracker to the floor. "That's OK, Evan," she says. "Uncle McKay isn't hungry now. Anyway, it's time to get ready for a bath, okay? Shall we take a bath, little man? What do you say?" She puts her hands beneath Evan's armpits then lifts him, a lumpy, lubberly bundle, and carries him to the bathroom. The door closes behind them. The lock catches with a soft *shunk*, and McKay hears it as reproach.

McKay's mother is still staring at him, her face closed and defiant. He looks down and sees the cracker lying against the abstract motif of dark orange arcs and whorls on the dark blue carpet. They become the spreading rays of a setting Van Gogh sun, the bitten edge of the cracker slipping below the horizon.

JONAH: THE HOSPITAL

The solitude is greatest at night, but so is peace of mind. Rarely, in the small hours, does anyone demand time, attention, or a pantomime of optimism from him. Granted, the simulacra of hospitality are synthetic (*hospitality hospital hospice*), and everything that Jonah can see from his supine emplacement is temporary, himself most of all. Or, at least, the blanketed hummock of himself that is visible from that position.

Still, a gentleness takes over the edges of things at night. The sharp angles of door jambs and window sills soften; the boxy, uninviting, Scandinavian-knockoff chair for visitors assumes something like a posture of welcome; the huffing, blinking machines become a more reticent version of themselves. Outside in the hall, the sound of footsteps is muffled, and the ringing of phones, which at other times is incessant, pauses respectfully. The lights at the nurses' station dim until the counters are as shadowed as a cathedral altar, though its small glow still looms in the tunnel-dark corridor: a fire-warmed home luminous on one shoulder of the road, off a ways in the distance. The two RNs who work the night shift are subdued; they murmur and move with deliberation, unlike the hustling, giggling squads of the daylight hours. Not that true daylight enters here.

But in his ungenerous bed with its indifferent rails and Bible-thin mattress, Jonah is less and less aware of all this. Tonight and recent nights and fragments of all the other days and nights since he arrived have lost specificity and shift now like glass chips at the bottom of a deep, white well. At least the drugs are good, he joked, earlier, when he could joke, but he hadn't failed to notice that his fully present moments had thinned, that they increasingly resisted his efforts to string them together into the kind of coherent chronology in which this thing came before that thing, and that thing took place on a distinct date from which it did not wander, and none of the things existed in a room of his mind where time constantly shimmered.

He had stepped across a line—one he'd witnessed more than a few friends reach and then surpass—beyond which his dream states remained vivid and his waking states refused to stick, losing texture and context as soon as he closed his eyes.

And when he does close his eyes, the darkness deepens, tangible rather than visible. Of course it isn't visible; it's the absence of sight. This darkness is like slipping into a warm salt sea—it's just that you can breathe below the surface. Once every millimeter of his skin is submerged, the darkness rushes away, eager to occupy other spaces and unafraid of barricades or of coming to an end. Maybe there is no end. Measure the distance across the blackness in this way: in dark years.

But not in silence. A voice is there with him, and images come as soon as it speaks: a bobbing, *Wizard of Oz* head, a towering precipice and a long drop to menacing spurs of rock like punji sticks. That's how much the mind craves geometry and perspective, though these concepts have no function here: enough to assemble them out of nothing.

The voice offers to tell a story, a parable, it says, which means: a mystical resemblance. The parable is about people on an island.

On the island, they forgot it was an island. Or: sometimes they forgot. Other times they could not. When they forgot, the borders surged forward, amoeba-like, on their way to everything. When they remembered, the membranes ebbed, contracted, leaving them *insulāti*—turned once more into an island.

It was a strange island. The edges, which would normally have marked a state change where land met water, did not do so. There was no need to switch to a different mode of transportation at the perimeters: If they had been walking, they could go on walking. The margins were opaque but restless, a drapery rather than a proper coast. Expanding and contracting like lungs, the island could seem as vast as a galaxy or shrink to the size of a zip code. What stayed inside, at all times, were the members of a group that was expected to die.

Beyond the curtain, most people had heard or read something about the island, even if they didn't know anyone there. What they believed about the island and its inhabitants could be anything: that the place was exotic or that it was infernal. That it was a prison or a quarantine or ought to be. That it held evil in or kept salvation out. That it deserved pity if not benevolence. The heavy draperies were impermeable to the mist of sighs and the residues of cremation unless someone deliberately lifted one edge and held it open to force the atmospheres to mingle.

Still, one was either an islander or a mainlander. For the islanders, the island rewrote their existence in a new alphabet that was no one's native tongue, and those Beyond went on throwing and patting their lives into shape with entirely different clay. Even if the islanders had wanted to make something from that ordinary clay, there was nowhere to find it. What they had on the island was strong and indigenous clay, to be sure, but it assiduously refused to assume certain shapes. They were simply not in its nature. Electrostatic bonds would not form; capillary action crawled to a halt.

One thing that could not be made from island clay was an animate being. A man, a woman—a human being, in any case. It was an unnatural rejection of creation because that had always been possible, had it not? From the Qur'an to the Torah to the Christian scriptures, from Sumerians to the Yoruba to the Māori, Incas, Egyptians, Hindus ... gods and humans were made of clay wetted with the water of rivers or seas, blood, spit, semen (the "quintessence of fluid," according to the Qur'an). Adam was made of clay, and would have remained a golem—a mindless, soulless, byproduct of soil—had God not penetrated him to leave the spark of life behind. But the clay on the island could be made into nothing that could serve as protection, salvation, or revenge. If it was true, as the Rabbi said, that the law of destruction was the reversal of the law of creation, why did the failure of the law of creation not mean the reversal of destruction?

Off-island, the water was different, the air was different, and food tasted not quite the same. There were mountains in both places, but when those Beyond climbed their summits and stood atop their peaks, they still could not see the high, green ridges at the center of the island.

How was it possible to live there, knowing the seismic hazards of the island; the molten stone beneath the ground; the spent bodies; the sounds of celebration and of protest; the purposefulness of its inhabitants and the resolve of its mourners; the fury and the havoc; the gestures of poetic madness and divine afflatus—how was it possible to stay there, knowing that off-islanders thought of it, if they thought of it at all, the way they thought of a dam collapse in Uttarakhand, a coal-mine explosion in Laobaidong. Maybe the name gave a clue to the country, but they still couldn't find the place in an Atlas without the index. They were real disasters, of course they were. But also they were not.

And if the island flickered like a mirage for those Beyond, and made them disremember its existence, the people on the island increasingly refused to believe in those on the other side. If they existed, many reasoned, they would act, because how could what was so palpable on the island be invisible elsewhere? The people on the island were sure they were not dreaming, and they were right.

They sang to themselves and each other. They clapped their own hands and waved their own handkerchiefs to try to save one another's lives. They played loud instruments and bellowed out their names and, every once in a while, a sound drifted in from Beyond that might have been a response. Some took this as a sign. *Help is coming*, they said.

Meanwhile, there was the darkness. Warm, peremptory. A blanket, a shroud. A swim in a deep lake on a night with no stars. It could be the void before creation. Jonah's spirit hovers above the waters. *Come in*, the voice says. *Come on in*.

MICHEAL: JANUARY 1992

On the morning of the premiere, Micheal wakes at around ten, scratching. He can see welts on his forearms, his calves, his belly when he lifts his T-shirt. He reaches up to feel his face. Puffy, but maybe without welts. In a minute he'll get up and look, but now he's thinking of how to get through the evening. Could he cover the welts? Could he dance the whole piece without scratching, that was the real question. The itching feels deep; he can't get at it from the surface of his skin. More than scratching, he is pressing his nails into the flesh of his calves, his thighs, hard enough to hurt.

He reaches for the cordless phone beside his bed and pushes the "2" key. JD's number. He won't let the panic get him. All kinds of things can happen before tonight. He can call his father, who'll get him prednisone or something. He's useless as fuck for most things, but he writes Micheal scrips for all the drugs he wants. He's number three on the phone. Thanks to his father, the ever-helpful family doctor who never asked a single question, Micheal has his little stash of Valium, Flexeril, Prozac, and Tylenol 3 that he's keeping for a "bad day." Not even Kenny knows about it. Micheal's secret stage door.

He imagines himself laid out on the bed in something peach, gauzy and Japanese-y. There'd be music playing—Rachmaninoff. Or early Streisand. A queen's end.

JD's gruff hello comes over the line. Micheal has gotten him out of bed. His student Susan is probably there.

"JD, I've got some kind of a rash," Micheal begins. "It's sort of all over."

"Your eczema?" JD asks.

"No, not like that. I'm looking at myself in the mirror now. It's welts. Big, dark red welts."

"Jesus fuck."

"I know."

"Do you feel bad?"

"Well, it itches, but I'm OK otherwise."

"Let me get dressed. I'll be over."

"Yeah, I want you to see, but I think I need to go to the ER and make sure I'm not having some sort of reaction to meds or something, and that'll take a couple hours. After lunch, though."

Micheal can hear Susan's voice in the background. She's asking questions. "Should we cancel?" JD asked.

"Let's wait and see," Micheal says. "It's just ugly is all."

"Yeah."

Micheal hangs up and stands before the full-length mirror. He lifts the bottom of his T-shirt to his chin and shoves down his underwear. He's more blonde than ginger, except for the cantaloupe-colored fuzz on his legs. His light grey eyes still popped, he notices, but the face around them is pallid. The dark welts have missed most of his chest and his ass for some reason, but raised red and violet weals run down his stomach, across his thighs, along his arms. They stand out against the sallow skin like the seams of haphazard upholstery. His cock seems embarrassed against the angry skin.

"Proud flesh," he says out loud. When he was twelve, his aunt had shown him the inflamed incisions from her mastectomy, which the home nurse aide came to scrub with silver nitrate swabs until the blood ran and his aunt cried silently. Proud flesh. *Good name for a dance,* Micheal thinks, angling the blade of his thumbnail deep into the retreating muscle of his left biceps.

When they finally see him in the ER, the phlebotomist greets him by name. He's been there enough that they treat him like junior staff. *You know where the sample cups are,* that sort of thing. He squeezes the green rubber ball in his palm while the tech alternates slapping the inside of his elbow and gently palpating invisible bodies beneath the skin with one gloved finger. And then the hunt begins: the other arm, warm compresses on the insides of his elbows, the back of each hand.

"I've got one here that should work," the tech says. So it was the back of his left hand after all. In a way, he'd come to prefer the hand. It still hurt, but they used a butterfly and a smaller needle, and he had the impression the blood flowed faster.

The tech ungloves and gloves up again. They usually go through at least three pairs with him on a typical draw. Micheal watches a puff of talcum burst into the air as the phlebotomist snaps gloves out of the box; can smell it, dry and sweet against the alcohol scent of the pads the tech is opening one after another as he cleans the back of Micheal's hand with something like zeal.

"Sugar," the tech says, "the next time you see your regular doc, you tell her we're having this trouble finding a vein whenever you come in. It might be time to think about a Hickman."

He must sense Micheal's body react to the word because he lowers his voice and pats Micheal's wrist. "Now I know what you're thinking, but wouldn't you rather not have to keep going through this every time we see you?"

He doesn't know what Micheal is thinking, which is that he'd have a hard time hiding a catheter when he's performing. He's seen people out in public with that strange bulge on the right side of their chests, a raised and inverted V, pressing unnaturally against the fabric of their shirts. The thing was, once you got a catheter put in, you never got it taken out. "It's like the campaign button for death," he'd said to Kenny.

"I'll mention it to her," Micheal says, but he knows he won't. One day they wouldn't be able to get blood at all, not even from his ankles, and then he'd have no choice, but in the meantime he'd rather take the pain of needles, even over and over, and the gauze and tape on a half dozen bloody wounds because at least that way they had to fight to get into his body. They had to break the skin. It wasn't permanent, twenty-four-hour access whenever they felt like taking something out or putting something in.

As he walks out with his bandages and his miniature juice box, he begins his bargaining with God. Today it is this: *Just let me perform the duet with JD*. He repeats the prayer in his head, unsure what he has to offer in exchange.

When JD arrives, Micheal throws off his robe and stands in his dance belt. JD looks him up and down, making a couple of circuits of Micheal's body. "We could change the costume," he says at last. As befit an angel, Micheal was all but nude in the piece—he'd be wearing a gauzy, nearly transparent blouse whose design had been inspired by a classic Greek chiton, sleeveless and loose off the shoulder, above a mid-thigh-length skirt. His legs and arms were completely exposed. Micheal thinks the costume is beautiful. "But I don't think we can cover all of that," JD finishes.

"People will think I have KS," Micheal says. "There's that whole section with blue light ... and some of the welts are so dark." JD is quiet. He is imagining—just as Micheal is imagining—the choreography, movement by movement, moment by moment, and Micheal's marked, alarming body, beaten or bruised or diseased but far from normal.

"Let them," JD says finally.

Let them. And then Micheal sees it, too. The Angel of Death, the final seducer, touched by human sickness. Afflicted but immortal. "JD, that's brilliant," he sighs. "People are going to lose their minds."

NO ONE ORDINARY DIED: AN ABECEDARIUM

A. was a brilliant make up artist, a marvelous cook, a lot of fun, and one of the kindest, wittiest, and most thoughtful people I've ever known. B. was daring, spontaneous, unstoppable, inspirational, compassionate and giving, sensitive, always full of joy, enriched by a lifetime of experiences that most could only dream of. My uncle C. was a literature professor, a connoisseur of wine and French literature, and a beautiful singer with a passion for Schubert songs. D. was a record producer with an uncanny knack for discovering new talent. E. was an ingenious artist who gave us her deeply creative energy through painting, ceramics, sculpture, cooking, and gardening. F. was a celebrated dancer and the choreographer of several smash Hollywood films. G. was sparkling and sophisticated and had a mountain of courage, a wicked sense of humor, and a feisty spirit; he taught me how to see the world. H. was an extraordinary guy—loving, smart, funny, and kind—and there's no one to replace him. My brother I. was a legendary floral designer who brought a flash of lightening to any room he entered. J. was a leading HIV activist, a prolific journalist, and an extraordinary author. K. was a hugely gifted painter with a sharp, critical mind. The world remembers L. as the fearless and original performance artist he became. M. was one of the nicest humans and most loyal friends I ever had; he loved people and they loved him back. N. was a catalyst of creation, the heartbeat of the dance and the music he created. My father O. was an award-winning novelist, translator, and literary critic. P. was a musical prodigy, a genius, an enfant terrible, and a drop-dead beauty who wore his sexiness casually. Q. was an American actor who appeared in countless stage, television, and film productions. R. died after a life dedicated to public service and fighting for the rights of others who had AIDS. S. was a wonderful, intuitive woman who adored cooking, fashion, scuba diving, and photography. T. was an opera lover and a born salsa dancer, and he was obsessed with the diaries of Anaïs Nin. U. was a brain as well as a beauty, a self-taught expert in the arts and Russian history. V. was full of life, irrepressibly colorful, and always brought comic relief to any situation. W. was a talented television producer and later a successful civil-rights attorney in Michigan. X. was a screenwriter, director, actor, and the funniest person I have had the pleasure of knowing Y. was a radiant gay butterfly, a hiker, a proud Black radical faerie, a courageous explorer of the world. Z. was one of the most intensely passionate, charismatic people I had ever known—gorgeously handsome, wickedly funny, and never, ever boring.

FINN: 1995

Micheal was never going to be the one, and they'd known that all along. Yossi got sick too fast ... and the others. Finn still has a respectable number of T-cells—not exactly normal, but not alarming either—and so far, no spots on his face, no patches on his tongue, knock on wood, touch iron, grab your balls. He's lost weight, and the drugs make him feel poisoned, as though his blood, his piss, his cum came out of him glowing like cartoon radioactive waste. Still, in the end: he's the one. Silence=Death, but a big, loud bang could equal death, too.

He's been driving with extra care because he can't risk being stopped. What constitutes extra care is fuzzy, though. He keeps to the speed limit, or a few miles over, so as not to call attention to himself by driving too slowly. On the few occasions when a sheriff's vehicle or the highway patrol pulls up behind him, his body clenches in panic and then he does his best impression of nonchalance. They're probably used to it, he thinks. When you see them, you feel guilty, even if you haven't done anything, so you try to look innocent. Whatever that looks like. A car gets stopped for a ticket, and drivers in every lane suddenly become deeply attentive to the speed limit. For about a mile.

Meanwhile, the trunk is full of things that can't be explained or, more accurately, can only be explained in one way. The hand grenades, the dynamite vest, the rifle and the sniper scope. More than he'll ever need but assembled to give him flexibility at the last moment.

Lately, he's been thinking of things that had never before occupied any room in his mind. His hours of firearm training at the shooting range, then even more hours in the library: field-based analysis for explosive compounds, setting off precision demolitions, explosives for engineers, blast patterns, charge diameter, overpressure, danger area. How much was enough to do the job, but not disintegrate the building around him? How close was close enough to reach the target but avoid accidental victims. Except for him. Though, also, not accidental. Plus, he's always had great beginner's luck, and he only has to do it once.

What it took was fantasizing his own death, forcing himself to go through it, frame by frame. At first, he felt only horror, a recoil that contorted his body into spasms as if he were clawing his way out of physical restraint. He pushed the thought away with his whole will, screamed "No!" out loud, involuntarily, alone in his bedroom.

But then he'd gone back in his mind, inching up on it a little at a time until he could hold the thought for minutes without panic. It was a discipline. And minutes would be enough.

He thought it would be like sudden sleep. That was how McKay had gone, more or less. His doctor turned a small knob near the base of the clear bag that hung above his bed, and, in what seemed like seconds, McKay was transformed. The gasping and panic that had taken him over as pneumocystis smothered his alveoli was replaced by peace. His entire body grew still, and Finn thought that, until that moment, he'd never noticed that McKay had been trying, with whatever strength he still had, to heave himself off the bed with each convulsion of coughing. He would never speak again; that was the bargain. Peace and painless sleep or the ability to say words that no longer mattered to him but were oracles to those standing vigil. What did they want him to say? Something that would help, that would take away their pain?

The doctor watched McKay for a few minutes then said, "I've adjusted his dose to ease his shortness of breath and to dull any pain he may be feeling. The dosage is very important. If I were to turn the valve clockwise, like so, he would receive a larger dose and his lungs would eventually stop completely. He wouldn't feel any discomfort, but he would stop breathing. I just wanted you to know why I've chosen the amount that I have, which is safe and won't do him any harm." He nodded to McKay's sister and smiled warmly at the others standing beside the bed and then left the room.

For a few minutes they all stood where they were alongside the space left by the doctor's absence. In the lull, Finn heard McKay's slow breathing, the ticking and whirring of machinery, the low voices of nurses in the hall. He felt the bodies around him, almost a hum. The silence settled in, impatient to be broken.

McKay's lover, Siddiq, spoke to McKay's sister, Vella, who had sat at the foot of his bed, knitting and silent in the permanent dusk, for more than a week. "Would you like to be the one who monitors McKay's morphine?" he asked. She shook her head. A tear fell into the shallow, scooped-out indentation above her upper lip, and she swatted at it as if in irritation. "It's too much for me," she said. "Anyway, he'd rather it was you," she said, and Siddiq nodded.

Finn was in McKay's room the next night, the night he died. The room was as warm and dark as a chapel. Some of the friends had brought candles, but the nurses had all but thrown their bodies on the first flame, threatening to bar them all from the room for good. So instead they'd gone home and come back with small lamps, which they placed around the room, shrouding the shades with scarves and pieces of colored cloth. The effect was kaleidoscopic and beautiful, like the sun through stained glass on the walls and ceiling. McKay had been sweating so much, even in his sleep, that one of the nurses had pulled the sheet down so that McKay's chest was exposed. You could see it had been a good chest, Finn thought, and then felt queasy. He stood by the bed and took McKay's hand, already cold, and lowered his head to McKay's chest, laying his cheek above his heart. He listened to the slow beats through McKay's skin, counting them while he watched the clock on the wall above McKay's head. Fifty-eight beats a minute. The pauses between beats, between McKay's inhalations and exhalations were long and alarming. A few hours later he was gone. You could call it peaceful.

The death Finn is planning will not be peaceful, and he would see none of what came after, at least he imagined he would not. He'd likely never be sure he'd succeeded, either, but he wouldn't care anymore. His death would bring mayhem, and he's a little sorry to miss that. Maybe he'd linger a moment, long enough to know. His own blood would be everywhere. Did those cells live for a few minutes before lysing? Did the virus? And here was irony. He wanted people to worry, to feel the threat on their skins, to know they'd inhaled his aerosolized blood.

He is about to cross the border that holds his guts in.

Right in that moment, as he is driving, it all seems useless, pointless. Such a small deed, in the context of the billions of people in the world, going about their business, dying, being born, rejoicing, thinking of a better existence or condemned to suffering, an accident of birth, unaware of him and likely uninterested if they were not. It was a tantrum. A fit. It's also a response, he reminds himself, an antithesis. What matters is what comes of it, which is a surmise. *I have dynamite in my trunk and I am thinking of dialectics*, he thinks.

A thunderstorm gets him back in the mood. The day had been clear with a sky an aggressive blue, but it had been hot. "It's got the asphalt bubbling," said a man when he went in to pay for his gas. It was as if there weren't enough words to describe heat. Sweltering, blistering, suffocating, and then you were about done. After driving for six hours, he stops for an early supper at a Chinese buffet in a strip mall, and when he comes out he notices, in this order: the sky has turned shades of deep gray, and raindrops, like small, flung pebbles, are pelting the cars in the lot, ringing off the metal and smacking the windshields like bugs. The storm is so sudden and so savage that he's shocked out of his thoughts by the sight and sound of it, able to sidestep his brooding and walk back into the clarity of what he's come to do.

The truth was, fatigue had been threatening to get the better of him. The sensation of weariness was centered on his sternum, where it pressed in toward his backbone as if wanting him to collapse inward from his center line, and his determination has begun to flag. All of them had worried whether they'd be physically up to it. That was the number one fear or, anyway, the number one calculation. A lot of them were ready to go, but no one was eager to go earlier than was strictly necessary. So they laid it out like military strategists: Rate of decline equals number of days until No Return Point, minus number of days needed to prepare for and carry out the mission, minus two weeks of mandatory Buffer Zone, yielded Latest Go Day. Still, it was only an estimate. Someone who'd calculated an NRP of months could find the whole thing thrown into chaos by a bout of flu or a fungus that decided to bloom suddenly, could wake up blind from a nap or get a call that said a lab result was in the toilet. So anyone could back out at any time—or be backed out. They'd talked about how to avoid getting attached to their individual roles. They had all agreed there was no shame in not being able to continue. And now he was the one.

He has been driving through landscapes that are as familiar to him as his name, and the realization that he can no longer feel them stitched to the edges of his being is troubling. The rigorous lushness of late-summer greenery now strikes him as relentless and overweening. The deer are a nuisance, and their stiffening, distorted bodies at the edge of the roads in the early mornings, their legs akimbo like pick-up sticks, give him a twinge of irritation rather than one of pity; the red velvet mites are menacing in their manic scurrying and leave smears of orange when he brushes them away; the bluebirds and robins and redwing blackbirds, the hawks and buzzards, barely register as scenery. And then came the rain storm, and that could still reach him. He has enough juice left in him to feel small and awed by its force.

So there he stands under the inadequate red awning of the restaurant, half in the rain and half out of it, paralyzed between wanting to be out in the downpour where he can experience everything and wanting not to be drenched to the bone, though the rain is as warm as his skin. All at once, he begins to move toward the car, digging at his pocket for his keys as he goes and pressing the button on the fob over and over to unlock the doors. By the time he half falls, half crawls behind the steering wheel, he is soaked and his glasses are fogged. Crossing fifty feet of parking lot has taken as long as it once did for him to run fifty yards in college, and that was not even ten years back. He'd been so elegantly thin in those days, with stamina to spare. Well, he was skinny again, wasn't he? He sits in his sopping shirt as the rain strafes the windows into opacity, and he thinks about being enclosed in a metal box from which nothing is visible.

The Senator is appearing at a reelection rally at the American Legion hall in Spartanburg. He's on his fifth bid for the senate, and no one expects him to lose. All he has to do is throw out a few "mean-militant-activist lesbians" or "AIDS is God's punishment," and his people all but scuttle up and lick the back of his hand.

It wasn't hard for Finn to get the credentials he needed to walk through the door without anyone giving him a look. The day before, he'd stopped at the Senator's campaign office and asked for bumper stickers and yard signs. A woman at the front desk, who looked like someone who'd sell homemade jam off a fold-out card table during her town's Fourth of July celebration, was so delighted that a nice young man like him was supporting the Senator. She handed over what he'd asked for and more—pamphlets, door hangers, and window signs on stiff cardboard—and told him to come back any time and get more if he needed them and was he going to the rally the next afternoon, and how nice that she'd see him there. "Stop and say hey," she said, and he couldn't look her in the eye.

With the signs arranged for maximum visibility under his arm, he'd walked straight into the already-crowded room. The space was roughly a triangle with the apex sawed off: maybe fifty feet from back to front, but narrowing toward the stage. There, it was perhaps twenty-five across, and the stage slightly less than that. Four rows of folding metal chairs had been set up just below the apron for the fragile and the halt, and, behind them, the standing-room crowd was swelling by the minute. Below the stage and to the left stood a boxy piano and, just in front of it, a small choir of nearly identical adolescents fidgeted, the girls in black shifts and pearls, and the boys looking disreputable and mean in crewcuts and tuxedo shirts and black bow ties. Just beyond, a pack of photographers and camera operators waited. They could walk right up to the edge of the stage to shoot, barely four feet from the podium. The stage was simple and flat, raised less than a yard above the floor, with a curtain for a backdrop and flags at each end: the American flag at one end and the oddly Turkish-looking blue flag of South Carolina at the other. A line of potted palms had been arranged along the length of the curtain, one every few feet, and a green fan of Boston ferns decorated the front of the podium, the kind of narrow, blonde-wood box that's standard in every high-school auditorium in America. Nothing stood between the stage and the first row of chairs.

But there were still too many people, too many chances for someone to react, and he couldn't blend in as an invalid or a reporter. What he needed was to get behind the curtain and work his way to the backstage so that he could stand directly behind the Senator when he got to the podium. The position would be easy to find because it was almost exactly where the two halves of the curtain met. Best would be to shoot first and trigger the explosion at almost the exact same moment. For accuracy, he'd have to walk forward a few feet, pushing one flap of the curtain ahead of him, but that was good. People would be confused by the sight of the curtain billowing forward behind the Senator and that would be the chance he needed. Still, the timing would be split-second.

Now that he knows the layout, he has to get the equipment he needs out of the car. He'll come back in through the back of the hall, assuming there is an entrance there and that it leads to the stage and that he can get through it unobserved. All of that would need to be figured out quickly, or he'd either get caught or have to rethink the whole idea.

A voice asks the room to stand, and the choir runs through a phlegmatic rendition of the "Star-Spangled Banner," but the people put their hands over their hearts, and they cheer when the choir has finished. The choir doesn't move: evidently there will be more singing. A brunette with feathered, Farrah Fawcett hair strolls to the podium and begins to speak, and it's clear that a lot of people are going to come before the Senator, who is slouched in his chair, his bulk spilling over the sides, his folded arms resting on the shelf of his belly. The brunette begins a story about her recent trip to Europe and how all the "everyday, hard-working Europeans" she met loved America and cared about preserving our democracy. Then she introduces another woman, older, severe-looking, and pooched, as a friend of his would have said. She's the chair of the local Republican party, and she, in turn, introduces a thirteen-year-old boy, Billy Winters, who sent a fawning letter condemning communism to the

Senator and has now been invited to read it live at the rally, in front of C-SPAN and all the other cameras.

Besides young Billy, the MCs, and the Senator, there are four other people on stage: the Senator's wife and three others he doesn't recognize, including a black man. Of course there's a black man. They can always find at least one. All of them will speak before the main event. He has time. The room is already so hot that people have begun fanning themselves with campaign placards and door hangers.

He turns to a man next to him, a guy in his forties with a bad beard and none-too-friendly look on this face. He's holding one of the Senator's campaign posters on a wooden stick, pistoning it up and down like churning butter. "Hey, listen, Finn says, "I forgot something in the car. Would you mind keeping an eye on these for a minute?" He lifts his arms to show the bundle of campaign materials. "Sure, sure," says the man, "just stick them here between my feet. I won't be moving much." Finn thanks him and begins to pick his way through the crowd to the door in the rear. He's polite to everyone along the way—excuse me, pardon me, sorry about that—because he figures that'll make him less remarkable than someone who pushed his way out without a word.

Outside, he walks to the intersecting street where he's left his car, partially hidden on the curb side by the trunk of a massive oak whose roots have sundered the sidewalk into a series of gullies and low ridges. The hall has a wide parking lot in front, completely full now, but he'd rejected that immediately. He didn't want someone spying what was in his trunk as he was rummaging around. He's focused now, nervous but not overwhelmed. He knows he has to keep moving forward, one step of the plan and then the next. Working quickly, he removes the dynamite vest and the Israeli Desert Eagle .50 caliber pistol from the trunk, walks around the side shielded by the oak, and puts them on the front passenger seat. He gets into the driver's seat, strips off his T-shirt, and straps the vest snug onto his chest, next to his skin. The vest isn't bulky, but he has to cover it with something thicker. It's so warm out that a coat would seem suspicious, so he pulls on the over-large work shirt he has ready in the back seat, struggling in the confined space to tuck it into his jeans with enough billow that the vest won't be conspicuous. The pistol goes into a backpack. He gets out of the car, makes a few adjustments of his clothes. With luck, the illusion won't need to hold for long.

Both sides of the street are lined with oaks, old and shaggy, and their crowns touch in the middle, forming a kind of arbor. Underneath, in the shade, the temperature is at least ten degrees cooler. He begins an unhurried stroll down the sidewalk, starting on the same side of the street as his car, parallel to the long wall of the hall. He's planning to have a look along the way for doors on the side or at the back. There is a breeze, scant but enough to move the leaves, and the sun falling through the trees shifts small patches of light on the road surface, on the cars parked along it. Squirrels seem to appear with his every step. Fidgety and suspicious, they dive to the opposite sides of the trunks as he approaches and climb as though flying until they're above him, chittering from the high branches.

He spots a door, on the street side, near the back of the building. No one seems to be anywhere near it. He walks further on to make sure no one is at the rear of the hall. There's a low concrete box attached to the building for the HVAC unit, then a strip of lawn and beyond that a privet hedge. The space is deserted. He crosses to the opposite sidewalk and makes his way toward the door. If it's unlocked or can be picked unobtrusively, that'll be half the battle.

He looks toward the street and the portico of oaks. The tiny, oscillating shafts of light quaver lazily, back and forth, moving and jumping against the surfaces they touch. The light is beautiful, and this will be the last time he sees that. Mostly you never know when you do something for the last time. The last time you go to a movie, the last time you drive on a particular road, the last time you kiss someone, the last time you eat a burrito at that place you've loved and gone to for a decade. There has to be a last time. You won't know it's the last time, but it is. McKay in the hospital: his last heartbeat. You couldn't tell it was the last one until no more came. Inside were people in the final minutes of their lives. Or one person, if he were as precise as all his planning had been. Out here was another.

If they knew, what would they do? Where would they go? Would they call a wife, a husband, a parent? Rush outside to see the sun through the oak leaves, pray, hug someone? Scream or cry? If they knew. Because knowing is everything. All in all, he thinks, it's better not to know. Better if it's a sudden surprise—better for the person who's going anyway. The ones left behind would probably prefer the chance to get used to the idea, but that was selfish on their part. They'd get to their own ends eventually, and their perspectives would shift. Everyone's does.

He hadn't noticed the birds before. It's getting on late afternoon, and the starlings are gathering. They haven't yet reached peak racket, but it won't be long. He watches them swoop over the hall, up and around like a ribbon. Calling them happy is anthropomorphization, and he despises it. Better, perhaps, to say that they are being what they are, obeying their faithfulness to the rhythms of light, to the stations of the day, churring for the sake of hearing a return call, for the comfort of knowing others of their own kind are nearby and massing in ever-greater numbers, and that in numbers is safety and common purpose and comfort.

He positions himself to one side of the door frame, opposite the hinges, and crouches to open the backpack. He fits his right hand around the grip of the pistol, still hidden in the open backpack, then reaches above him with his left hand for the knob. It turns, and he eases the door open a crack to peer quickly inside. No one. He lets the pistol fall to the bottom of pack, and he stands. If anyone approaches him, he's going to say someone called him to look at the air conditioning. A tool belt would have been a good prop. Too bad he didn't think of that. He opens the door another couple of feet and steps inside.

YOSSI & THE BABIES: 1994

"Monday Night with the Lesbians" is a tradition, though "Monday with the Mommies" would have been more like it. All the babies had come more-or-less at once, which meant they were toddlers all at once, which meant they were a handful. On Monday nights Esta and Carmen take all the children so someone can have a rest or go back to the office, and then another night the babies go to someone else's house, and sometimes he comes over to help at Esta and Carmen's. Yossi is a constant presence on those Mondays, though, and there is no question that he is the favorite uncle. He lies on his back on the floor, rocking like an overturned turtle, insisting he can't get up, and the girls—they're all girls—climb all over him, roaring like lions or who knew what animal they had in mind and pretending not to want to be captured by The Tickle Monster, who always captured them and wrestled them on the floor until they shrieked and giggled and gasped for breath and, more than once, peed themselves.

Meanwhile, supper was being made in the kitchen, and Finn keeps the babies out of the way so the moms can sip glasses of Johnny Walker Red ("You may have ice; you may not have water," Esta would say), and engage in a few minutes of conversation. Dinner is simple. Two of the largest chickens they could find at the grocery, braised all day in the crock pot, unlimited Tater Tots, a salad or sometimes frozen string beans. Paper plates. Apple juice to drink.

The bravest thing he ever saw, he thought, was the Monday he went to pick Yossi up at his flat for "Baby Night," and he found him in bed, breaded in cornstarch like a cutlet and groaning from an outbreak of shingles. "You need to stay put," he told Yossi. "We'll manage. Don't worry."

"No," Yossi said. "I don't want to disappoint the girls. Just give me a minute to get dressed." It took more than a minute, even with Finn's help. They got Yossi into oversized surgical scrubs that kept the friction to a minimum and a long-sleeved turtleneck to make sure the rash on his torso stayed covered. The girls were vaccinated for chickenpox—Finn knew this because he and Yossi had taken five of them at once to get their boosters—but Yossi still scrubbed his hands and forearms with Phisoderm, and then they went to Baby Night. Yossi lay on the floor and played Tickle Monster, hiding his grimaces behind growls and roars and laughing and smiling and loving those girls as though they'd cured his pain, giving them their Uncle Yossi one more time, at least one more time.

When "Table, everyone!" was called, and the girls gaggled off to wash up, Yossi stayed where he was. He put his arm across his eyes and Finn saw tears slip down his check and into his ear. "Oh, sweetie," he said to Yossi, as he helped him stand, worried that wherever he put his hands would inflict pain.

"Don't say anything to Esta and Carmen," Yossi said. "I don't want them to worry," and Finn didn't tell until Yossi himself was ready to say how bad things had gotten, a few months before he died, and Finn sat with Yossi, Esta, Carmen, a few of the other moms, and Yossi's own mother, who had flown in from the other edge of the continent, and planned the conversation that almost everyone eventually has about someone, but rarely when they are in their thirties: how to tell the children that Uncle Yossi was sick, that they wouldn't see him anymore after a while; and all they could do was put their arms around each other on the living room sofa and sob because never in the history of dying has anyone ever discovered a way to say those things that would not pierce another person's heart and leave a wound and then a scar that would thicken and change the rhythm of that heart for all time.

MICHAEL: NOVEMBER 1993

Before the others arrive, Micheal lowers himself onto the pile of throw pillows he's arranged on the floor to ease the friction against his ischium. The slack flesh on his ass was aiming ever more inexorably for his heels, and his formerly melon-shaped butt was flat, the skin loose and crepey ("A little more and I'll be able to use my butt cheeks for leg warmers," he quipped), so now he depended on extra padding and carried a cushion with him when he went out.

Once Micheal is settled on his makeshift throne, his back pressed firmly against the couch for support, he whistles for Stephen Sondheim, his nasty-tempered Jack Russell terrier, who arranges himself in Micheal's lap. Opening an old-fashioned beauty case he'd found at a thrift store, tooled in fake leather to look like alligator, Micheal begins arranging his pill bottles around him in a semicircle, starting at his left hip and continuing around all the way to the right. Most are the classic, dark amber cylinders pharmacies use, but a few are white, rectangular, and squat. One baby-blue bottle stands out, its wide, black screw cap poised like a shtreimel.

"I want a picture!" Micheal announces, and Kenny goes to fetch the camera from Micheal's bedroom. Stephen Sondheim whines crossly and rises from Micheal's lap to follow him. The dog stands in the bedroom doorway, growling each time Kenny opens a drawer. "You stink, Stephen Sondheim," Kenny says softly, "and you need a bath. But I'm not going to be the one to do it." Micheal had begun finding it exhausting to heave Stephen Sondheim into the tub and, especially, to keep him there long enough to get him clean, and apparently he'd simply stopped trying. *Something else that needs to go on the list of things to do,* thinks Kenny: *Get recommendations for a groomer. Better yet: get a volunteer.*

"Aren't you seeing it?" Micheal calls, not hiding the cranky edge in his voice. He thinks Kenny is sweet and devoted, but when it comes to brains ... he's only Monday-crossword-puzzle smart. Camera in hand, Kenny finally returns to the living room, flanked by Stephen Sondheim, who casts sidelong glances at him all the way back to Micheal's lap.

"Stand behind me on the couch," Micheal orders. "I want one good one from above. I want you to see all the pill caps against the carpet, and then my big, round, bald head in the center of the picture. It'll be like a map of the galaxy."

Kenny takes the shots, perched above Micheal on the couch, then from both sides, then from the front, as Micheal continues to direct. "The next time I get a long-term-survivor interview, I'll give them one of these snaps for the article," he says.

As their friends begin to arrive, Stephen Sondheim glares at each person who comes through the door, baring his teeth whenever someone leans down to kiss Micheal hello. "Maybe I could put him up in your room?" Kenny suggests, knowing that will never happen. The comment is for the guests, the way parents make a show of telling their ill-behaved kids to "stop that" when they're holding a burping contest at the next table in the restaurant: intended to relieve adult embarrassment without affecting the behavior. As the current boyfriend and, as Micheal put it, "the future Widow Gallagher," Kenny has some authority, but never over the dog.

"No," says Micheal, "Stephen Sondheim wants to witness history."

Right on time, Yossi calls them to order. "All right," he begins. "Welcome. As you know, our objective here today is to discuss media and branding approaches, because it's going to be important to get control of our image before the press does. So I'd like to suggest we start by brainstorming ideas for a name."

For three anguishing hours, they talk about the name, considering, occasionally at length, and then rejecting: The Helper Cells, TCellZero, Prophylaxis, GRIDLock—all before landing on Terminal Cause, which had the potential advantage of expanding participation. Anyone with a diagnosis of more-or-less imminent death from any malady could play. Those who were suicidal for other reasons—who had, so to say, a preexisting condition, would be excluded as too unpredictable. They reached a consensus on that surprisingly quickly, mostly because they all knew the rule would be ignored. Someone who'd lost his lover and half his friends before being diagnosed himself was suicidal by definition, but still met the main requirement. "DBL," Yossi had called it: Dead Before Long. Stephen Sondheim was there, asleep at last on Micheal's lap, when the meeting came to an end.

Afterward, Finn gives Yossi a ride home.
"So it looks like we're about to get this off the ground," Yossi says. Finn doesn't answer. He chews the inside of his cheek, and he squirms as much as the seat belt will let him, words churning inside him.

"To be honest, I'm worried about whether we should be doing this," he says at last. "So much could go wrong. The whole thing could backfire and make things worse for other people like us."

"People like us are dying. Badly," Yossi says. Being forced to leave everything you love, everything undone, at 24, 33, 40? Watching your future disappear before you'd even decided what it was. Fading away, turning into a corpse while you're still alive, losing your youth and beauty at the same time you lose control of your bowels. It's not like you haven't seen it. That's what happens. That's what's going to happen to us. What could we do that would be worse than that? Anyway, you were the one who said you were ready to do it! Now you're telling me there's nothing inside you that wants to punch back?"

Finn did want to punch back, but he sees himself punching air. Pathetic as it sounds, stupid and humiliating as the desire is, he wants his death to have meaning. However it happens. *If I die of AIDS, just drop my body on the steps of the FDA.* He wants his dying to shake things up. He wants to spread the worry that something dark and final is stalking them, that any day could be the last. He and his friends live like that. That's the thought that kept pulling him back in, during the meeting, when one of the competing voices in his mind was insisting that he stand up and leave.

"Punch back at who, though?" Finn asks. "I mean, who deserves to die?"

"Take your pick, but Helms is first on my list. God's punishment; 'deliberate, disgusting, revolting conduct'; Mapplethorpe, that bullshit about art that would turn the stomach of any normal person, singing 'Dixie' to Carol Moseley Braun when they got into an elevator together. Fucker is 72 but I bet he's got another decade in the Senate. Mervyn Silverman, that weasel. Reagan's been out of office for years, but that bastard never got what he deserved. Fauci should be on it, or whoever else at the NIH is keeping people from getting into trials. Gina Kolata's probably not worth it on her own, but if there were some way to get her and Randy Shilts together—a sort of anti-hack journalist action. But I wouldn't mind if the two of them worried we were coming for them."

Yossi has thought about this so many times that he has the sensation he's bulleting along a railroad track laid down in his mind. The discussion about "who" tied everyone in knots. In a way, it didn't matter who. They needed to create fear, panic, but the question was especially whose absence would create the biggest vacuum into which, at least as a hope, someone better might step. They had to consider who was racking up more victims, and whether that was because of action or inaction. Action was easier to justify, strictly from a PR point of view, even if the ones who stepped aside or refused to get out of the way when they had the power to help were guiltier in his mind. A consequentialist would say that refusing to take action was still an action. If you poisoned someone's soup, were you more or less of a murderer than if you knew someone else had poisoned the soup but you silently watched the victim eat anyway? Angels? Meet the heads of pins.

At the same time, he doesn't fool himself. A shocking death wouldn't fix everything. And realistically, they'd probably only get away with one. Possibly a second, but also possibly not. As soon as the first one happened, security would be beefed up, public appearances would be limited, though they'd likely do it in some haphazard way. No one would be sure what was happening or who needed protection until the second. Then a pattern would become clear. *How many points determine a line*, Micheal liked to say. That would be the end. So it had to be spectacular because they might not get a lot of chances.

"So much is going to depend on how publicity breaks for us," Finn says. "What public sentiment is. Even how ACTUP chapters react."

"No one is ever going to come out and say they support killing public figures," Yossi sneered. "Nobody. Maybe—and it's a big maybe—someone will write some sort of pseudo-intellectual think piece about what pushed sick people to such extremes. Like dying at 30 isn't extreme enough."

"But we're talking about murder and suicide," Finn said. "That's not exactly 'un-extreme.'"

Yossi pounded the steering wheel with his fist. "We've got a backstage pass to extreme!" he shouted.

It was Yossi's Larry Kramer tactic, Finn thought, and he'd seen him try it before. *The one who makes his point the loudest wins.* He wasn't going to recoil in his seat and shut up, not now. "So, an eye for an eye would satisfy you?" he asked.

Yossi's voice was back to normal. "An eye for a thousand eyes, ten thousand, a million. That satisfies me, yes."

The perverse result and the unexpected benefit, Finn thought. *The liberator and the despot liked the same tactics. You can only tell them apart once the screaming stops.*

MCKAY: 1994

McKay is sitting at his kitchen table, a faux-Victorian with baluster legs that he'd picked up at Busvan for Bargains, unlovely and unloved. He'd sanded and primed it himself, a supplicant to the presence of his long-dead Great Uncle McKay, who made cabinets for a living and whose house was spiced with the scent of linseed oil and shellac. For a finish coat, McKay had chosen what they called Delft Blue in the paint section at Cliff's Variety, but for him it would always be the true color of sky—not the insipid robin's egg pastel people thought of as sky blue, but the indigo that appeared on some few Virginia afternoons of his childhood, when he looked up and raised his arms, ready to be lifted off the ground.

As soon as he moved the table in front of the kitchen window, he forgot he hadn't always owned it. Now the table was a piece of personal history, as if it had been passed down through the generations of his family until his turn had finally come to serve as the custodian for an heirloom. He drank his coffee at the table in the mornings, looking out over the wild and scrubby yard—a city yard, good for a few rose bushes but mostly good for the scurvy raccoons—and the table made him feel unaccountably European.

At ten o'clock, they'd be at the door with his Will and his Power of Attorney and whatever other documents the volunteer lawyer from The HIV Law Project decided he should sign. He wouldn't have agreed except that he couldn't stand his friends bringing it up another time. *Just in case,* they said. *It's good to be prepared.* And now they had infected Siddiq, folding him into their complicity. The drama of it.

He looks down at the jumble of *Acanthus* advancing on the long side of the narrow yard. The wide, serrated leaves shimmer as if oiled.

It's a stubborn plant; no matter what he does to it, it rallies, and so at a certain point he gave up trying to pull it out to make room for the low garden of *Hebe* and *Sedum* he had in mind and began to admire it, out of respect. Together they were soldiering on.

For years he's been sure he was about to die, and it hadn't happened yet. Some of the people he knew actually seemed impatient. They had it fixed in their heads that he'd be dead by a certain point and he wasn't. With each new inexplicable rash or lesion or trip to the hospital, people got their emotions in a turmoil. Then he'd get discharged, and everything was on a plateau for a while, and then it would happen again. He was like the child who cried wolf. And they got resentful. "We bought you a TV set, we gave you money, we cared about you, we chanted Kübler-Ross over you, and here you are, alive five years later, and it's throwing off our programming." When Edmund White kept not dying, a French friend told him, "Mais, Edmund, you made all that up, non? The malady? Good publicité, non?"

For years, he'd refused to hand anyone the power to oversee his death, and he could see they felt cheated. But they were tricksy; they thought they'd still wrestle power away from him in the end. There is no expression of outrage or grief that is not also an expression of vanity.

To be sure, he's had all the usual horrors: diarrhea that seemed to hoover out his innards and expel them into his toilet; weight fluctuations; infected sinuses, pain that scoured his body like a lahar and which came from nothing any doctor could find; fatigue so bad the ten steps to the bathroom might as well have been a free climb up Half Dome, so bad a friend had to come over to dress him. Every once in a while he was sure he could see blotches on his skin. But what did KS lesions look like on skin like his anyway? In the brochures, the arms blotched with brown or violet, the ravaged faces, the sunken, mottled torsos were all ... what would you call it? The boys at Cliff's would have said: parmesan, eggnog, shortbread, toast, heavy cream. In paint, as in life, plain white hardly existed. He wasn't Mediterranean, Eastern European, Middle Eastern. But who knew, really? The whole planet had fucked everybody else at some point or another, the minute they could. Migraines. He'd had occasional migraines for years, but when they came now, they were monstrous and tentacled. The last one had been like being mugged. A pair of hands appeared out of a sunken doorway and smashed him in the forehead with a baseball bat, and the pain seemed both surreal and inadmissible. It could not possibly belong to him, that pain, but if that was true, why was he weeping?

His T-cells have hovered at right around two hundred for years that he knows of. He's probably been positive for more than a decade, though, ever since a sudden and gruesome flu in 1982. His doctors had no explanation for that either, and then it went away, and everyone forgot it happened. Well, he hadn't forgotten.

And then he got tested, and the plague came home to his house. He'd felt the impulse to run, but he was convinced evil did not care where you were. Every destination was Samarra. So in the end he decided to stay in San Francisco, and he'd spent much of the most recent years thinking about when it would be over. About the day his last close friend would die. He read *A Journal of the Plague Year*. He read about the Spanish Flu. He read about the Holocaust and Hiroshima and felt ashamed of himself for placing his convulsed little life in those obscene terms, but he has also begun collecting Godzilla toys. His mini-monsters are a token of the evil stalking the streets—uncontrollable in their destruction, capricious and incomprehensible—but they are also small and plastic and garishly colored and easily breakable. At some point in the last three years of his life, David Wojnarowicz bought a pet scorpion and kept it in a terrarium in his apartment because, he said, he wanted to own death.

He goes to botanicas in the Mission and buys incense and ex votos and red and yellow candles in tall glass jars with pictures of Catholic saints or the symbols of African deities on them, and he has learned how to dress them with scented oils before lighting them; and he reads the words on the sides—*suerte, poderosa vela, abre camino*—and he thinks they sound more effective in Spanish. He buys tapers and pillars and is careful never to blow them out because that is disrespectful, but rather to lick his thumb and forefinger and snuff the wick out between them. He goes to Mission Dolores and steals holy water from the font by the side door of the chapel and keeps it in small bottles stashed around the house.

He feels certain there is something beyond himself—hope, perhaps, or cosmicuniversal compassion—but he has asked nothing of that force because he cannot believe it is interested in the specifics of any single human life. But he likes the rituals of propitiation; he likes imagining mystery. He likes the feeling that comes over him when he sits inside the basilica, which smells of wax and soup. He wishes he could say it reminds him of his youth, but, really, until now he hadn't spent a moment in a Catholic Church since he was four and his mother divorced his father. When she learned they really intended to keep her from taking Communion after that, she left and never went back. Yet he feels at home there—especially when the church is nearly empty and still. Confession hours are good for that; hardly anyone comes. He doesn't go into the booth to speak with a priest but kneels in the pews, his hands clasped, saying over and over under his breath, "I'm sorry, I'm sorry, I'm sorry." He has no other prayers.

"Fuck," he says out loud. Then he shouts it on a steeply rising tone: "FU-U-U-*U-UCK*!" The cat leaps off the table, a spasm of fur and needles, and streaks into the bedroom. "Poor Paka," he says.

More than being sick, more than dying, he resents that his illness has put him at the mercy of the AIDS Machine. It was like a Cuisinart. They crammed you in whole and you came out in shreds. Meanwhile, all around him, people were throwing "we're dying, we're dying, we're dying" into the faces of the public and the media and legislators and everybody else. And once they got everyone to buy into the death cult, the checks started flowing. *We All Have AIDS—If One of Us Does*," went the slogan of Kenneth Cole's campaign for AmFAR, but the four men who appeared—Richard Gere, Archbishop Tutu, Tom Hanks, and Nelson Mandela—didn't have AIDS. *AIDS doesn't discriminate*, that was the message. But AIDS absolutely did discriminate. Still, you should donate to AmFAR or go to Tom Hanks movies or buy Kenneth Cole's shoes or more people would die.

AIDS was paying for everything. Anyone could see it, if they took off their kumbayah glasses. AIDS was the best thing that had ever happened to gay empire building. It was the manna from heaven that financed and legitimized Gay, Incorporated and had created a class of AIDS millionaires, and massive organizations, and infrastructure that pushed the gay movement onto the front page. Woe be unto us; we've been attacked by this terrible thing. Give us lots of money, pour grant money into our community, and we will turn around and go to AIDS Foundation dinners and Human Rights Campaign fundraisers and pour money into your political campaigns, so that you can in turn vote for more money to pour into us. If you were dying, you got patted on the back, and they took care of you. You could even refuse to be afraid of death—heroically, stoically—because death was acceptable when you were living for a cause.

If he's got to die, he wants to do it as far away from all that as he can, away from the marching and shouting, the pious pity and the virtuous mourning, away from the stark, cynical transformation of people into propaganda. As he sits at his beautiful blue table, waiting for the doorbell, he thinks that his ability to choose may be slipping away. When you were queer, they wouldn't let you lead an ordinary life and now queers themselves were determined to keep you from dying an ordinary death. Letting these HIV-project people in is ceding territory, he knows. Still, they're only documents. It isn't like he has some grand estate to parcel out anyway, and the powers of attorney are the important things, especially the medical one. He understands that. If things get bad, all he needs is for his parents to come cruising in from their separate corners of the earth and discover the mutual pleasure of ordering McKay's doctors around or deciding which of his friends should be granted an audience, like they were fucking Steve Rubell outside fucking Studio 54 or something. He'd seen it happen. The Gatekeepers take up their posts, and access to the dying dwindles.

But he isn't dying now, he doesn't think. At least not any faster than anybody else. Which leaves him on the sidelines during the parade, waving his pathetic little "survivor" flag. Ever since he read Michael Callen's book, he's refused to take AZT, and so far: not a single OI. Or not the official ones. He's prophylaxing for everything his doctors can think of, meanwhile, and most of the time, he feels fine. Well, if he's honest, he knows it's just a tiny bit harder to rally after each new KO. That's the truth. Something is shifting under the surface of his life, raising hummocks in the road. He sits and waits, and he thinks: *When will there be time again for beauty?*

FINN: THE PRESENT

He's like a man whose ship has sunk and who washes up on a desert island. Maybe others survived the shipwreck and are alive somewhere, but he can't see them or get to them, nor they to him. What's easy to say now is: there's no community anymore. But even back then, "community" was a word that got pulled out for special occasions, like great-grandma's bone china plates and, especially, the story of how she came to own them—a family legend more than a reality.

Was there community in the bars, in the baths, at the raves? There was something. Yes, there was. In the backrooms, where putting your mouth on someone's cock was an act of resistance and you were all there in mutiny. Whenever they screened *Rocky Horror Picture Show* or *All About Eve*, and everyone knew all the words and recited them out loud. *I'll admit I may have seen better days, but I'm still not to be had for the price of a cocktail, like a salted peanut.* The fact that you knew there was a gay bookstore, which just meant: books about you. On the streets, maybe. Even the faces you recognized but never spoke to. They were the supernumeraries in your grand drama; maybe you were one in theirs, too. At rallies and protests. Standing alongside someone who was fearless, undaunted, the first to lie on the asphalt and be kicked by cops. You talked to people. Strangers hugged you, buoyed you up. They fixed the strap on your backpack; they offered water; they paid your bail; they fucked you. You were in this together. Now we are all in this separately.

How pathetic, going around saying to younger people, "You don't know what we went through." Perhaps he doesn't even want them to know because, yes, some of them are unendurable little twerps, but he has no special need to make them suffer. Your parents keep things from you. And yet they keep nothing from you.

How presumptuous, insisting "we have something to teach you." No one was smarter thirty-five years ago, and he has nothing to impart; he has no wisdom. Or perhaps, only: keep living and something will happen.

But he misses it. The sense that he is where he is supposed to be. Now, he is supposed to be nowhere. He doesn't belong, but he's not sure anyone belongs anymore. Young queers in social occasions look like startled rabbits. They can withstand a minute of conversation before they're back to their phones. It's a strange distortion of what he feels: Whatever he is doing, the past interrupts. For them, whatever they are doing is interrupted by anything happening somewhere else. Either way, the here-and-now is intolerable.

Maybe what he misses is being young. People ask him where he would like to go, if he doesn't like it where he is, and he has nothing to say because where he wants to go is a time, not a place. *The past is a foreign country*, and he wants to return because that is where he was born and took his first steps. When the Plague came, they didn't lose their innocence. They were not innocent. They were voluptuaries. They were freaks and sluts and perverts, which was like having magical powers. Everywhere you went nowadays, the slogan was "Love is love." What about "dick is dick"? What about "sex is sex"? What happened to that?

But cars still roared through the Castro full of angry, often beautiful young men who wanted to beat up a fag because that was the only way they could touch one. The magic didn't protect them from those boys, from the violence that was a form of desire, and it did not protect them from a virus.

He watches and rewatches films about those years. There are so many venues for independents and for TV movies now, or whatever they're called, and everything can be streamed. No need to wait for something to show up at the local art house. It's democratizing, in a way. And with some regularity, some filmmaker or other becomes fascinated with the '90s again. At this point, all the queer films and AIDS documentaries he's watched have modified his logarithm because others like them keep turning up in his suggestions. He says yes to everything. He watches the competing histories of ACTUP (the west coast vs. the east coast, the political strategists vs. the treatment activists) and the internationals (the French perspective, the Irish perspective, the South African perspective). He even watches the terrible romcoms in which HIV is the "obstacle," resolved in the third act; the Broadway plays manhandled into movie scripts; and the cheesy, message-heavy biopics with straight actors getting kudos for playing gay, for dying. He watches eagerly, alone, because he wants silence afterward, not commentary.

Back then, there were no big-release documentaries but, after the idea picked up steam, there were lots of films, lots of TV movies of the week, lots of pretend AIDS: How the plague affected Gena Rowlands or Coleen Dewhurst or Meryl Streep, and the heroic, tragic, heart-rending deaths of Aidan Quinn, or Steve Buscemi, or Ian McKellan, or Mary-Louise Parker, or Ed Harris, scored, if possible, to Maria Callas singing about someone's dead mother, for Christ's sake. And theater. La goddamn AIDS Bohème with a queer drag-queen angel (who dies, but the straight couple doesn't) and the pathos that pays. He wishes Yossi could have lived to see *The Hours*. He would have been quoting lines from it until they begged him to stop.

Anyway, the documentaries are what he keeps going back to. He admires them for their feint at verisimilitude. He watches in high alert, scanning every scene. He still hopes he'll see one and there it will be: the life he lived. But instead, mostly what he gets are new variants on the same two versions of history, which are apparently the only ones anyone knows how to tell.

There's the one he calls "The Wages of Sin," and in that one, sex is dangerous; other men are a menace. They show scenes of gay men on Castro Street or in the Village at demonstrations or Pride Day parades. They are flamboyant, outrageous, dressed in feather stoles or not much at all; they are literally cavorting. There are interior shots of bars: disco balls, drag queens, pounding music, shirtless men, fan dancers, bulging crotches, men groping each other or necking thirstily in yellow-lit club hallways and always men in leather vests, leather caps, as though leather were the uniform of Azrael. Still shots from Studio 54, which, in real life, lasted all of two years, are a favorite milieu-setter. Drag queens and go-go boys in gold body paint. There's Grace Jones. There's Roy Cohn. There's Nureyev and Bowie and Capote. There's Andy Warhol with Liza Minnelli, with Brooke Shields, with Calvin Klein, with Bianca Jagger. Pay attention: Here are all the gays and the secret gays and the gay icons and their enablers. The images are striking in their banality. Everyone seems blinded by the flash, and they are in the midst of speaking, of gesturing at something beyond the edge of the photo. The images are coded, like shots of Hitler fulminating before a crowd, a plane slicing through a tower of the World Trade Center as if it were made of Jell-O, mushroom clouds rising above the sharp, clear line at the end of the sea.

What you are meant to understand is that they are showing the decadence and excess that led to punishment, retribution, just desserts, the inevitable conclusion. Nero fiddled here. Or just the idea that death was already stalking: these silly, thoughtless, sybaritic men didn't know it, but they were already murdering one another. They're stock footage of the catastrophe. What they say is: *This was captured ONLY MOMENTS BEFORE.*

On film, cruising looks trivial. So does dancing or costumes or walking down the street on a sunny Spring day in tight jeans with your hands in one another's back pockets. Kiki-ing on the corners, mugging for the camera, entering a bar with a backward flutter of fingers like Liza Minelli in *Cabaret*. The fact that it all seems innocent and playful is the point. It's like those reenactments of Nagasaki just before the bombs. Thursday rituals; going to school, waiting at the station for the train that carried you to work. Poor fools, they had no idea what was coming. But the viewer does. In retrospect.

The difference, though, is that those "innocent" Japanese did nothing to cause their deaths. They were civilians: mothers, school kids, grandparents, wage workers. There are no innocents in AIDS films. Well, no innocent queers, anyway. Everyone was asking for it. Maybe they didn't know how bad it would be; maybe they didn't deserve such pitiless retribution. But they did something to get it: their "lifestyle," at the very least. Their dirty, dirty sex.

And why not say the obvious, for what little good it would do? Straight people "flaunting their sexuality" at a frat kegger, in Las Vegas on St. Patrick's Day, at Mardi Gras, at a bachelor party was their straight pride parade, complete with dress-up and outrageousness and show-us-your-tits excess. But it never stuck. Those were people being people, good clean fun, blowing off steam on a holiday. Gay men were never just people being people; they had no good, clean fun.

So that is one story: How AIDS exposed the sickness at the heart of male homosexuality. The "practices" people couldn't even imagine (*What do they do in bed, anyway?*). Or maybe they could imagine. "There is not one single case of AIDS in this country that cannot be traced in origin to sodomy." Jesse Helms said that in 1988. The villains who pulled others into the darkness and exposed them on purpose, but still: no innocent victims. No one could do all that and expect to get off scot-free. AIDS was the logical end of that road. The wages of hubris demanded to be paid. It was all very Greek.

They would never say, or most of them, that they'd always found gay sex distasteful, but how easily they slipped into a clucking, paternalistic disapproval. *Terrible, what's happening, of course; a huge tragedy; I've been to so many funerals; you can't imagine how many friends I've lost. But maybe they should have taken things a bit more seriously, hm? I mean, there's also a question of personal responsibility. It's one thing to have gotten it before anyone knew, but after the mid-'80s? Those people knew, and they didn't stop.*

But maybe some didn't know. Maybe some were being lied to by their partners. Maybe some had accidents. Maybe some couldn't take precautions because that would have meant admitting ahead of time what they wanted to do. Maybe some were too terrorized to get tested. Maybe some tests were wrong. Maybe some thought they were too young or too old or too rich or that their skin was too white or not white enough. Maybe some just came to the end of their ability to live in constant fear. Maybe some had decided that everyone would get it and there was no point in trying to escape. Maybe they believed what they'd been told: they deserved it. Maybe some thought having HIV made them special. Maybe they were in denial, the way people are about cigarettes or that long series of after-dinner cocktails or how much butter they put in their food. Maybe your mind can become a prison, and the walls have no windows.

And then there was "The Gift." The Gift was worse than the Wages of Sin because it spent the dead as the price of enlightenment. *Yes, we lost a lot of people*, went that version, *but we also learned something*. About love. About community and sacrifice. About helping one another. About the families we choose. About how precious life is. We're stronger now. *It's a remarkable success story*.

The men and women in the documentaries are trying to tell the truth just like Finn is trying to tell the truth, but he thinks it isn't working. All the words are an excuse for there being no words, yet he still longs to be connected to a largeness, to the words that call things into being. Adam named the animals, or so goes the legend, and they became real. People all over the planet had invented chants and songs to explain the world into existence, one plant, creature, mountain, constellation at a time. This thing existed before that thing. There was an order. Let there be light. First the light, before all else. And these are all stories about the past, about how the world ended up the way it is, and yet there is no song of uncreation, of things passing out of existence, of three-dimensional absences forming like the empty, untouchable fruit of a tree whose branches, laden with shadow, droop low, lower, felled.

No one asks Holocaust survivors what they learned in the camps, but men like him are expected to have learned love or patience or how to approach death or let go of anger or build community or the importance of friends, and anyway, it's all over now and we survived, and so everyone gets to go home with a tune he can hum and a cozy thought about the bravery of others, and that is the saving grace. It's beautiful because it's sad.

But it wasn't a book or a movie or, god forbid, a musical. There was no message, no moral, no blessing in disguise. Whatever people got out of it, whatever they're left with, if they're still alive, has nothing to do with anything. It's accidental and random. It's about them, not about that. Not about the ... death. The Plague, the Purple Monster, the Tragedy. Not about how America confronted an epidemic or pretended it wasn't happening or how some people defied the powers that were indifferent to them and occasionally won a victory.

You woke up to that reality everyday. And that cowed you or shaped you or energized you or beat you down, but it didn't matter because there were always more days—until there weren't. No one could keep track of it all—the part that was friends and caretaking and personal loss and Day-Timers with funeral dates and the part that was political and huge and angry and demanding and seemed cathartic at times and a useful channel at times and at times was part of the burden because of the never-ending stream of everything has gone wrong and may never be fixed and the sky is endlessly, constantly falling and the part that was an erotic kermesse of fierce, indignant, beautiful paladins.

Is this where he should talk about the fun? The way the terror brought things into focus, made colors more vivid. Sunny days were crisper. Joy was more overwhelming. Romance took place in CinemaScope. The intoxication of sex with hot men you'd been arrested with but whose last names you never knew; the parades and dates and demonstrations and cruising and concerts that were electric and sensuous and galvanizing.... God help him. How could all of that coexist? *Witches can be right, giants can be good.*

Is this where he talks about the way it *looked*? Because it had its own aesthetic. That time of do-it-yourself graphics and of pop-up galleries and of seeing, suddenly, that things never before considered art actually *were* art had formed an unmistakable visual landscape. The signs and symbols and stickers and posters on light posts, bank walls, subway cars, baby-poop-green postal relay boxes, on every urban surface were a response to—or, no, the child of—the New York graffiti artists who, though they didn't seem to know it, were already coming to the end of their moment when AIDS hit. And then AIDS did hit and there was a renaissance: "LIFE IS CONFUSING AT THIS POINT. SAMO©." Keith Haring in the subways with his radiant babies and then his last major work, a wrap-around wall of totemic, splooging cocks in the bathroom of the LGBT Center in the West Village. He was already calling it "Once Upon A Time." It was 1989. *We die. They do nothing.* David W. on the lower East Side with his boy on fire. Gran Fury's *"Read My Lips"* or *"Men: Use Condoms or Beat It!"* Boy with Arms Akimbo's SAFE/UNSAFE campaign and the schoolmarmish face of Jesse Helms. Elaborately Xeroxed DIY collages, the dramatically kerned all-caps of Queer Nation, clockable from two blocks away. The word "queer" everywhere, as if it had been washed in HIV-infected blood and emerged as a word for warrior. *Diseased Pariah News.* Blow Buddies. *Fuck you, faggot fucker.* Everything yearned to be reclaimed and sometimes barely kept apace of the forces that held the hateful old meanings in place. A fucking blizzard of red ribbons: the one Elizabeth Taylor wore to the Oscars in 1992, the one somebody else not gay wore to the Tony Awards in 1991, the one somebody else not poz wore to the MTV Movie Awards in 1992. And now the ACTUP posters rest in archives in protective, acid-free sleeves, safe from your contamination. When they appear, they are behind glass, the way, back then, you saw your friends in hospital rooms. Then and now, you put on gloves to handle those objects, if you're allowed to handle them at all. That's an irony. Retrospectives occasionally take place where orderly and beautiful museum labels get the dates wrong or the sequence of events wrong or someone's name wrong, and you pay money to get in, and everything is clean and straight-edged and the only thing missing is the truth of it.

That was the last genuine grassroots movement in America. He's not counting hashtags or one-day marches of millions who disappear back behind their screens until the next one or online petitions or periodic convulsions over whose lives matter. The end was in sight in the '90s when AIDS activists started showing up on the boards of pharmaceutical companies. They were working from the inside, they said, but what became apparent was that, if they maneuvered in the belly of the beast, it was because the beast had swallowed them.

Still ... Hell hath no fury like a twenty-something WASP queen whose world order is being attacked with hand grenades. All their lives, they've heard nothing but that they were special. Do you want to be the one to tell these best little boys in the world that they're not going to grow up to be comfortable and bourgeois stock brokers, lawyers, CEOs with bright futures? That they can't do something or have something or be something? That they wouldn't have healthcare?

Promises had been made! They weren't taking no for an answer! In their deepest hearts they were apoplectic with indignation that someone, something would say no, wouldn't like them, wouldn't be charmed, wouldn't see things their way, wouldn't call an old school chum for them, wouldn't at least get out of the way. They were pissed, honey, and it's only 'cuz they came from power that they could talk to power.

So the middle class white boys were the ones crawling up Mount Suribachi on their hands and knees. And they got shit done. Mostly for themselves, but, in fairness, they dragged a lot of people along with them who would otherwise have stayed invisible. Not everyone by any means. That's why poor black trannies and Dominican street kids on the New York docks didn't get nothing and weren't ever gonna have nothing. They've got no political consultants who went to Oberlin working for them. No New York marketing experts film students NYU or MIT math majors Mensa members from Brown dropouts from Tufts who made it in tech children of lawyers and successful painters or famous playwrights managers of major publishing companies who have drinks with agents and have the *New Yorker* editors in their Rolodexes.

But you couldn't get too caught up in the big picture, how much went on out of the light, the whiteness and classness of it, the conspiracies that seemed more than plausible: a plan to exterminate gay men or black people or poor people or the entire Third World; activists who were moles; an invented virus; cures that were being deliberately withheld; cures you could only get if you knew someone, though that didn't always work out. Just ask Rock Hudson when Ronnie stopped taking his calls. Corporations were evil. The government was evil. AIDS, Inc. was evil. Or they could be. Not all the time and not in every way, but always, at any rate, obtuse and self-interested and tardigrade and inscrutable.

Anyway, evil was a familiar presence. You lived with evil and, to your surprise, this could actually be done. Evil came at you from the mailbox or from a phone call, or from the newspaper or even casual conversation. Evil was everywhere, so it didn't matter how it got to you. The point was: it couldn't be avoided. So many people tried. The couples that suddenly escaped to Guerneville or Hemet or Chico, as if they'd caught the Underground Railroad. They went antiquing or visited farmers' markets; they acquired dogs named Darwin or Charlie. And then they died.

The monsters were awkward and bungling and wobbled over life like Macy's parade balloons. If you went to the store, you felt they were there, ready to ambush you, so you were alert, you searched for allies on the street, caught their eyes, signaled them in the code you both knew. You had to stick together. *Demons are prowling everywhere / Nowadays.* If you made it safely home, that was a victory. So many people thinking about their own deaths in one place at one time thickened the air.

What it really was like was being alive. There was no order, no strategy, no sense of how he was moving through stages or how today was affecting him. No sense that he was acquiring knowledge or engaged in a deeply meaningful apprenticeship. His experience was an electric, filamentous farrago of all that, like the inside of a fig. *The way we live now.*

He's envious of people who narrate their existences, who start sentences with words like "I'm the kind of person who...." because they know what kind of person they are. People who can identify a character arc, a narrative theme, who have an analysis that put events into an order. Who can look at their lives and talk about the phases they've gone through, are going through now, were about to enter; who could imagine their everyday lives into some sort of chapter structure, where there was a beginning and an end, the movement through the pages had a purpose; there was rising action and then a triumphant climax. "I'm in a very vulnerable period," a friend would say, and he wouldn't know what that meant. Well of course he knew what vulnerable meant, but how it could be the theme of a period, or how long a period was, or how you knew when it started or ended—all that remained opaque. How did people find a place to stand that offered such an unimpeded view?

It made life easier, he guessed, seeing it not as one haphazard, inexplicable mass of unclassified events, but something with plots and through lines and its own internal logic. Where there were lessons to be learned, and you knew which lesson was being presented at any given time and you didn't mind that it was painful because you were on a path that led to revelation. "Living intentionally," he'd heard it called. Which presumed you had some intention. He didn't. Well: he had the intention to pay his rent, go on waking up in the morning as long as possible, to get through each thing that was asked of him or that had to be done or that he'd chosen to do, at the time prescribed for it. He had the intention to go to brunch with Randy on Sunday. He had the intention to go to Italy in the Fall, gauging that precise moment when fares were low but the weather hadn't yet turned dismal and rainy. He didn't know how to have intentions grander than that. He didn't know how to get them all to line up and march in a single direction.

Here is what happened: People's friends and lovers and siblings got sick, turned into frail, scarred mummies before their eyes, and died. No one could process all the information, though some bent themselves to the task, becoming the cenobites of a hermit order whose sunna and Talmud were *JAMA, The Lancet, PI Perspective, MMWR, AIDS Treatment News*; they appeared at conferences and demolished the tables of the Pharisees, screaming the Seven Woes: *You blind guides! You strain out a gnat, but gulp down a camel.*

Hundreds of writers and artists disappeared before they were forty. Photographers, writers, dancers, poets, and filmmakers and singers and choreographers until it seemed extinction had come for the sublime and the beautiful, for irony and wit. For rage and mordant humor. And as they dissolved, so did a generation and a half of critics, of people who went to the theater, the ballet; who were thinkers and philosophers, who read books and talked about them; who took movies seriously. How could art even continue to exist when there was almost nobody left to love it? How long before there would be another Foucault another Peter Allen another Alvin Ailey another Robert Ferro another Essex Hemphill another Gia Carangi another Willi Smith another Joffrey another Mapplethorpe?

They took the ones who loved theater, who loved ballet and who went to lectures and gallery openings and attended poetry readings and black-box plays, and experimental performance art at WOW, La Mama, at the 92 Street Y, at PS 122, at Judson Church; at Fort Mason, at Theatre Artaud, at Z Space, the Women's Building, 848, Highways and others flung all over the country, wherever queer people congregated; they took almost all the designers, almost the entire cast of *Boys in the Band*, they took the critics and taste-makers, the newspaper arts columnists, the artistic directors and the casting directors, the curators, the ones who wrote books and essays about art and culture that you maybe hated but talked about for years, the ones who had twelve versions of *Tosca* at home, the ones who saw subway graffiti and DIY posters wheatpasted to the walls and recognized them as something to which attention must be paid, the ones who risked their lives to be the first in the South of Market or Alphabet City to see some new performance piece they'd heard must not be missed.

All you could compare it to was a natural disaster: It came, it hit, it flew down the mountain at the speed of a car on the freeway, it blew in, it made landfall, it fell from the sky, it surged across dry land, it touched down, it engulfed them. Or an unnatural one: from the bell tower above a public square, someone picked them off, one by one. Not randomly, but with vicious purpose. Yes; you needed metaphors. So much of art was trying to find a way to tell the story in other words.

And art had recovered after a while. More or less. Or anyway, its broken, orphaned foster child had grown up. But was anyone making anything dangerous anymore? Anything edgy? Anything *queer*? Did anyone care? He's thinking of the day he and Micheal went to see *Bram Stoker's Dracula*. Sitting in the third row, they'd gasped at the same moments. The scene when Jonathan Harker is traveling to the Count's castle for the first time: the train, the blood-smeared sunset outside the windows. Gary Oldman's outrageously campy, queer-as-fuck Dracula; the ludicrous orgy-pile scene. Michael grabbing his arm with delight in the dark. Not even Keanu Reeves and his grotesque accent could ruin it. Had anything since ever been as unselfconsciously excessive and campy? The film, yes, but also the delicious, unaccountable experience of sitting beside someone from home, who *knew*, who was a master at picking out subtext because he'd always had to exist as subtext; who, like him, lived for experiences that were *ravishing* in a way real life never was.

And it did not mean anything.

He knows what an absurd, grotesque thing that is to say.

But he doesn't mean unimportant or trivial. He means: It is what happened, the way everything is always happening, all at the same time, everywhere. Nothing was the *real* tragedy; nothing was the minor one, least of all to the people who were standing right there as it unfolded. What he went through ... he wants to understand its human position. Was that Auden? He means to stake out some small piece of high ground between despair and romanticism where he can stand.

What people say is that they thought they were going to die all the time, but the truth is: he never did. He couldn't imagine being sick, permanently sick. He couldn't imagine dying. Not from a disease. Or at all.

He recognizes a few people from San Francisco in the documentaries, but every queer man around him who is of a certain age was there then, too. When he sees them, he can't help himself: He expects there to be camaraderie, or at least a look of recognition. A nod. *Yes, we are veterans of the same war.* He looks for it. And at the same time he isn't sure he can bear men like that, meaning men like him, if these are the conversations he is forced to join. The lesson of "the gift." The recitation of things learned, the words like "purpose," the ones who say they are grateful. The fantasy about how their friends would all have been brilliant, happy, would ultimately have come fully into themselves, would have accomplished impressive things. They'd be writing, making dances, painting, changing our understanding of art, uncovering history, righting wrongs, standing in front of the camera, at the front of the parade, in front of the barricades on the courthouse steps. And that is why it is such a tragedy, such a shame, such a loss because. If only.... *We are blessed to be alive because so many of our friends are not.*

There was another of his failures. He does not feel blessed. He does not want to be blessed or grateful or lucky. The fault was in the fucking language. That's what trapped you. Every word contained its opposite, so every word was wrong. If you were spared, someone was condemned. If you were lucky, someone was cursed. If you were blessed, someone else was damned. Metaphor distorts whatever it tries to depict, which is another way of saying that metaphor is, unpreventably, fiction.

What if their dead friends, his dead friends, had done nothing special with their lives, only lived and worked and fallen in love and broken up and voted and bought groceries and talked about music videos over drinks or at the café or in the park and made babka and cruised in seedy places for anonymous sex and given up their gym memberships and watched the grey hairs grow in and grumbled over the cost of car insurance, abandoned the idea of owning a house, groaned in the mornings when they awoke with hot spikes in their backs, read books and eaten and shat those meals away, hated their jobs and buried their parents, and sometimes navigated days in which they did all of this despite a bone-deep mourning that seemed as though it would uncouple their molecules and heave them into space?

Why does no one talk about this? he wonders. Instead, the past becomes a lineage of aphorisms lined up like a rack of thrift-store suits: at least they had become spiritually mature, learned about love and letting go and opening their hearts and the preciousness of life and how nothing is promised and everything changes, your pain is universal, so breathe deeply into your heart chakra, let us pray, let us take a moment of silence, let us send healing energy, om shanti. No, thank you, fuck you, no.

In the documentaries, he listens to the interviews of men and women who are still here: survivors, nurses, mothers, someone who worked in a hospice and saw 365 people die, one for each day of a year, a man who owned the most famous flower shop in the Castro, the one he'd heard called "Exotic Plants in Bondage," and he remembers the man's store and his extravagant window displays; but what the florist man remembers is how many funerals and memorials he sent flowers to, how people would come and ask for flowers and they didn't have money and he'd make up bouquets for them anyway; and he tells a story about a man who used to ride past on a bicycle every day and wave and then started rolling by in a wheelchair and then he stopped coming altogether, which means that one single day was the last time he ever went past the flower shop, but of course the florist didn't take notice of which day that was.

He remembers the florist above all the others because he seemed to be saying something that was closest to Finn's experience. You got used to the diminishment of things until that became normal and you didn't notice that something was wrong, sometimes, until a long time afterwards.

He saw the world end thirty-seven years ago, but he kept waking up and the world was still there, or something that was so similar that it could fool you, and that was confusing and not entirely welcome, and he kept going, as did all the others, wondering what it had to do with him anymore. Their suffering flensed them like whales, bleached them white in the sun, turned their eyes inward, rendered their skin transparent. Their anguish was epic. But now these men, these people in the documentaries, the writers and speakers and commentators, these bloggers and pundits, they talk as though it all happened to a proud and primitive civilization whose glyphs we can only partially translate, as if grief and sadness were a costume they could take out of a box on the day of the annual commemoration and then put away again because they had Gotten On With It.

He has not gotten on with it. For him, the past still lives in a theater that is never dark, and onstage the play goes on and on forever and you can get a ticket any time and the seats for viewing the carnage are all ninth-row, center. And the actors are so young, and they are so angry. They deliver long soliloquies about rage. Everyone is dying, and no one cares, they say. But "no one" doesn't mean literally no one, because, truth be told, the caring was crippling, and anyway it's a kind of primordial wail, pathetic in the original sense of the word, from the hearts of people who don't want to die, who don't want their friends to die, at least not so soon but they can't work out an alternative; and a scrum of doctors and nurses and hospice workers stumble through the theater, dragging their feet up and down the aisles, onstage and off, climbing up to the empty balconies and then down again, wailing and flagellating themselves like penitentes because they have nothing to offer but different brands of death.

One character is a twenty-seven-year-old guy who says he doesn't think he can make it to the bathroom and he's not being a drama queen because he shits himself, right there onstage, in front of everyone. A scene (many scenes) is set in a hospital where a hot pink placard hangs from the door handle and everyone knows what that means, and the characters struggle to put on moon suits that seem made of super-absorbent paper towels. Visitors take a break to go out to the vending machine next to the nurses' station, ten minutes at most, and, when they come back, a new Kaposi's sarcoma lesion has bloomed, a character sticks out his tongue to reveal the white, furry maculae of thrush that wasn't there before. In one sex scene, a handsome lawyer says, "You probably shouldn't even be kissing me," and his partner takes his face in his hands and kisses him again, and then again, harder, and keeps kissing him, and he says, between kisses, "I am not afraid of you."

There are suicides: Staten Island, a parking lot in Honolulu, a home in the Los Feliz Hills because the characters can't tolerate their meds, can't stand the pain, want to have at least one victory over the disease by finishing themselves off first. There's a character who catches a cold and dies fifteen minutes later. AZT timers go off over and over again during the play and everything comes to a stop while water is brought so someone can swallow pills, grimacing, and as he does so, an actor declaims articles from *SPIN* magazine and the *New York Native* about how AZT is Agent Orange for PWAs, and crew members dressed in black construct General Idea's AZT sculpture on stage, painstakingly mounting 1,825 blue-and-white fiberglass capsules on the walls as three fake baby seals are set adrift on ice floes made of sheets of polystyrene foam, and two of the three members of General Idea are dead now and one is a survivor.

There is a brief pause for a set change. The lights go down almost all the way, leaving a glow like twilight, and the ushers come through the aisles and point at people, and the people simply disappear. A booming voice begins from the back of the house: "Oh, they're all very convincing. Because they've rehearsed it so many times over the years." The speaker floats in the air, his round, grizzled face now sharp, his scowl contemptuous between setaceous brows arranged like a cornice above his broad drinker's nose. "And this figure of 700,000 deaths from AIDS! Ridiculous! There was no AIDS. No 'syndrome.' They died from destroying their immune systems with all the sexual diseases they contracted, from ingesting vast quantities of drugs. There was no overall government policy to kill homosexual men. It's the great gay deception! If there were, they would have been killed and there wouldn't now be so many survivors." And it is clear what has happened because, yes, of course, there was always going to be a David Irving for AIDS.

But the audience continues to dwindle. The ushers take anyone who seems even vaguely hopeful; they take anyone who is in love; they take anyone who protests the barking man who hovers over the audience like a doughy grey chandelier.

And then the Denier disappears in a flash of blue light and is replaced by the Affirmer: the doyen of AIDS, the master quilter, the mariner solely because of an accident: he lived to tell when so many people didn't. He stepped into a vacant niche and thrived, like mammals after the asteroid. His history had become *the* history, and his "rime" had so many meanings: a thick white frost; a fissure; the crust that dries on the surface; even a reckoning, according to one definition old a thousand years. "You have to understand that we were in funerals every day," he says. "In our address books, we had entire pages where every name had been crossed out." He deploys that monstrous "We" with the air of someone who has invented a language, as if it were the only one in which the story could be told, and he has chosen himself to tell it.

A spotlight falls on eighteen-year-old Ryan White, who stands behind a screen in a corner of the stage, illuminated in crisp shadow like a wayang puppet. "I never owned an address book," he says. The light waxes as if dawn had arrived, and Simon Nkoli, Arthur Ashe, and Michele de Marco Lupo stride in from the wings. "Three hundred sixty-five funerals a year?" says Nkoli. "Who did that?" and Ashe nods. Lupo sneers: "I caused funerals. I didn't attend them," and his voice is sinister. The spot narrows, leaving them in darkness, until it comes to rest on a metal easel where a sympathy spray of white roses spells out "WE."

In the next scene, they tell stories. The first is about an afternoon two men spent sitting in the garden, having lunch on the deck, talking as if nothing were wrong. They discuss prophylaxis for tuberculosis over salad, wondering whether they've killed themselves with sex, and yet the man who is not infected still wants the man who is sick. Yes, because of the stubble on his chin, the fur on this forearms, his lush ass, but also because he is temporary and precious. The first man wants to say this but does not because he worries the second man will think his desire is charity or pity or fetishism when really it is perfectly ordinary lust. He thinks he will kiss him, but stage hands suddenly come and swaddle the second man in Saran wrap, like a transparent mummy. His eyes are visible, and his nose is uncovered for breathing. They put a sign around his neck that says "At Your Own Risk," and they hand the first man a scissors. *Decide*, they say, *decide, decide, decide*, and the etymology of the word appears in the supertitles: to murder one of two.

The other stories are about narrow escapes from towns in places like Iowa, Kentucky, Texas, but also the southwest corner of Oregon, the Central Valley, the Finger Lakes region of New York, so they could be free to live and love. Not that anyone lived freely. Not that love existed without qualification. Authorized, perhaps, was a better word than free. They created their own families onstage. They knew how to spell the "Barbra" in Streisand and the one in Stanwick, the "Bette" in both Midler and Davis and how to pronounce them; they debated whether Sondheim's greatest show was *Into the Woods* or

Company; they had Helen Morgan recordings that no one has. She begins to play in the background: *Don't ever leave me, now that you're here. Here is where you belong,* and she drank herself to death two months before Pearl Harbor and there are no survivors.

The scene that follows is all about obituaries. *He was 37 years old. He was 41 years old. He was 26 years old.* The obituaries are in the *Bay Area Reporter*, but also in *Dance Magazine* and the *New York Times*, where the tortured phrasing and the dissembling become legendary: the rare blood disorders, the liver failures, the bone marrow disease, the sudden hospitalizations for exhaustion, and the cancers: all those generic, euphemistic, useful cancers. The actors bring out lists of the dead and read their names, and the names are meaningless if you don't know the people; they might as well read a phone book, and yet the actors go on reading the names, and all that matters is the sheer ponderous mass of the list, and the audience-participation activity is: make your own list and no one has any trouble getting started.

Then there's a vaudeville-style entr'acte. Someone who looks like Redd Foxx in drag as Joan Rivers tells AIDS jokes. "If we can put a man on the moon, we can put a man with AIDS on the moon. And then someday, we can put everyone with AIDS on the moon." "What's the hardest part about having AIDS? Convincing your parents you're Haitian." It ends with a song: "I hate to tell you, boy, you have AIDS. / You got the AIDS. / You may have caught it when you stuck that filthy needle in here. / Or maybe all that unprotected sex which we hear. / It isn't clear, but what we're certain of is that you have AIDS. / Yes, you have AIDS. / Not HIV, but full-blown AIDS." *Family Guy* from 2005. Seth MacFarlane, always pushing the envelope. Isn't it great how he can say just anything?

At the beginning of Act II, the curtain rises on an empty stage, as wide as a football field and so deep the far end is no more than a distant grey vanishing point. There are TV monitors in tiers on each of the walls and fixed to both sides of black-metal racks that run the middle of the stage lengthwise like grocery store freezers. An announcer's voice tells the audience to leave everything at their seats and walk onstage. *In the event of an emergency evacuation, leave all your carry-ons behind.*

The screens come on all at once. There are thousands of them, and each one shows a different scene. What they show is everything in the world. MTV videos. Commercials for Shake 'n Bake. A man walking his dog. A woman driving over the Bay Bridge at rush hour. People studying quietly in a library. A soccer game. A high school band rehearsal. Two people in face masks, beaming and sweaty as they hold up a brand-new baby. Funerals. A family doing the shopping together and the man, to make the kids laugh, reads the labels on cans out loud in a squeaky, cartoon voice. A museum tour: the Pre-Raphaelites. Parades: Macy's for Thanksgiving, St. Patrick's Day, Pride. Germaine Greer is lecturing about "intromission." A kid is holding up a bodega on Avenue C at gunpoint. Eight people follow a tour guide through a sandstone grotto in Arizona under an orange light that seems made of swatches of sun. A woman whose long, black hair is matted with sand body surfs at Pololū. The 1st Battalion Welsh Guards march like wind-up toys outside Buckingham Palace, their Dr. Seuss bearskin caps pulled down nearly over their eyes, the straps barely held in place by their lower lips. A man stands at the paint-chipped bars of a prison cell, staring onto a concrete corridor; his face, like everything around him, is a shade of rust. At the back loading dock of a warehouse store, employees carry boxes from the depths of an eighteen-wheeler that dwarfs them. Planes drop bombs. Two men in a park play chess at a faded gameboard painted into the surface of a concrete table. A figure in a pale lavender cardigan scans the bookstore shelves for items on a list. In a movie theater, hundreds of people laugh and cheer Bette Davis as she files her nails and calls her husband's house a dump. A couple searches Expedia for flights they can afford that would take them to Oaxaca. A group of men and women in filthy uniforms pull recycled jars and plastic bottles from reeking bins and toss them into waiting receptacles according to color and material. A student who is worried about getting to work on time waits in the maddening crawl of a line to register for classes at the university. The ones who fell to earth.

There is infinite time to see all the videos, but it requires an active parceling of attention. Otherwise, it is what psychosis looks like. You can always go back to a video you like, or shift to a different view if you're bored, or never move at all. People in wheelchairs, with canes, pushing IV poles, trundled along on stretchers, gasping for breath, wander up and down the aisles. Some fall and are carried away. Some seem to get stronger; they kick their walkers to one side and keep moving.

Act III opens with a house being burned down in Arcadia, Florida, because three hemophiliac kids with HIV want to go to school and their parents sue the district and win, and then other parents pull their children out of class, and the family's house is firebombed and they flee into the night like it's Beirut, and two of those boys are dead now and one is a survivor; and then it is still Florida and the ghost of Kimberly Bergalis appears from Ft. Pierce to sing a duet with the dentist who may or may not have infected her but no one will ever know for sure; and then believe it or not it is still Florida, and this time it is a town called Belle Glade and people insist that mosquitoes are transmitting the virus and from the front of the stage the cast releases thousands of them into the theater and chaos and terror follow.

YOSSI: OCTOBER 1994

Jonah died a week after Halloween, and during that week his friends learned a few things. Such as: It was a bad idea to take Polaroids of the Castro Halloween Street Party and then rush back up Potrero Hill to show them to Jonah in his hospital bed. In his room, they situated themselves around him, waiting for him to laugh, so they could all laugh, as he slid the photos from the top of the stack to the bottom, ready to be praised for their thoughtfulness. And then, all at once, all of them together, saw what he was seeing: the way the tipsy, over-the-top revelry—the leering werewolves in hot pants, the coquettish Reapers, the gym boys in jock straps, their faces made up like alebrije skulls—began to look like a cruel parody on the theme of death. How so many of the men in the photographs would be gone by next year, faded out of frame like time-lapse photography, and they were muzzled by their palsied, gauche cheerfulness, mortified to be healthy, to be able to go home, mortified, most of all, to stand there watching, as though catching Jonah in the act of dying was like catching him masturbating.

At Jonah's memorial, his best friend, Masha, is the first to speak. She stands quietly at the lectern for a moment, looking around at the gaudy beaux-art excess of Herbst Theater, and then she speaks. "We're here tonight to remember Jonah," she begins, "to celebrate our good fortune in being part of this large group of friends, family, and colleagues; to give one another the gift of our memories. And, yes, we're here to cry. You all know Jonah from different worlds. Some of you knew him as a dancer and choreographer, some of you knew him as a party-giver extraordinaire, others of you knew him from his tireless work to give artists with AIDS a venue and a voice. Tonight all those worlds come together in a place that Jonah loved and where he never once missed a chance to hear his beloved Margaret Atwood speak."

The crowd in Herbst waits politely for Masha to go on. Masha takes a deep breath and begins again. "Not long before Jonah died, we had a conversation about regret. And I asked him about his. This is what he told me. He said, 'I fucked my way through San Francisco, and the only thing I regret is all the beautiful men I'll never have time for.' In fact, if you were a friend of Jonah's," she said, "you knew that Jonah loved men. Legions of men."

That gets a big laugh. You could call a dead guy a slut and it wasn't an insult.

When Jonah was dying, some baleful urge came up in Yossi, during one of those last nights at the hospital, to remind Masha of that day on the grass at San Francisco State. The memory had putrefied in him during the days and hours of vigil, and now it made him angry, vindictive, as though she'd brought the disease down on Jonah, on all of them, that day by refusing to share his food, by seeing him—all her gay friends—as a danger. She'd opened the door to the possibility; she'd been the anti-Eve: her betrayal of Jonah took the form of the food she had been offered and refused to eat.

Jonah's room was the last in the hall, and just beyond his doorway was a sort of vestibule with a green leatherette banquette, two unnaturally orange chairs, and a haggard *Ficus:* a mini-waiting room. Toward the end, they were taking turns in Jonah's room. They lounged on the banquette or on the floor of the vestibule (Masha had brought a beach blanket and a plastic pitcher that she could fill in the bathroom to water the *Ficus*) until it was time to stand beside Jonah for a few minutes, hold his hand, speak to him as though what he had was amnesia and not AIDS. "*Hi, Jonah. It's your friend, _____. Remember?*" They said it even though they knew Jonah wouldn't respond now, that there'd be no rally.

Masha was with Jonah, but she'd be out soon. He'd ask her about it now, get it out in the open. The day with the soda. See how she'd defend herself. And instead Masha came back to the vestibule weeping, and he couldn't confront her, but when she'd stopped sniffling, she said, "You know, I've been wondering," she said. "How come you and Jonah were never lovers?"

> *Because he found Jonah's energy jangly and frenetic. Because he sensed Jonah was at heart a diva, and he didn't want to bed a diva. Because Jonah was too beautiful. Because he knew Jonah slept with everyone but attached himself to no one. Because of the New Year's Eve party when Jonah had slipped his tongue inside Yossi's mouth as they were all kissing each other at midnight, and Yossi pulled back in shock to see Jonah smirking at him.*

"I dunno," he said. "Incest taboo? You know how it is. Other gay men are either tricks, sisters, or competition."

Masha nodded but didn't speak, and they sat for a few minutes like that, and then Esta came down the corridor, and her partner after her, and they were all laughing and joking as they always did, and Yossi realized what a shit he was for blaming Masha for anything in the first place. This happened over and over: your rage was exultant to have found a target but then all at once you realized it was the wrong target, and you had to take it back, every bit of it, rewinding the whole matted skein where it had unraveled, and holding the bundle again in your own arms where it was heavy and the fibers turned into nettles against your skin. That was why there was so much screaming at ACTUP meetings and out in the streets. All that fury, needing to land somewhere. All those Furies, swooping down on bat wings and latching onto anyone who deserved punishment, but mostly those who did not.

MICHEAL: OCTOBER 1987

Micheal is stationed on a wide strip of white canvas that extends before him and into the distance like a Wyoming ranch road. He wears a nametag that identifies him as an official volunteer, and he carries a box of Kleenex. At the check-in tent, below the tables they assembled just after dawn, there are cases of it. Around him, people are walking, stopping, pointing, smiling. Most of them are in pairs or groups. They lean their heads against one another, dab their eyes, hug, walk with arms wrapped tightly around each other. They stop to take photos; they get down on their knees, their faces in their hands, weeping. They're not supposed to touch the sections, but they do. They caress them, really, running the tips of their fingers along the fabric, the appliqués, the sewn-in objects: shirts, teddy bears, leather vests, photographs, even, on one, a tiny baggie filled with cremation ashes. Their fingers move so gently over the surfaces that they could be stroking the face of a newborn.

The squares in every color run from the foot of the Washington Monument to the edge of the lawn in front of the Capitol building. Earlier, before the official opening, Micheal took his turn going up in the cherry picker, and he could see that the white central walk-way curved gently as it neared 3rd Street at the U.S. Capitol end of the Mall. It was an accident, he imagined. The Mall doesn't run precisely west/east but rather shifts north at a gentle angle, and it is just slightly wider between Madison and Jefferson at the east end. A matter of some .0001 degrees of latitude or about eleven yards. When they calculated the layout of the quilt, they probably imagined lines in perfect parallel. Anyway, the unintended curve is perfect. Now it looks like a path worn across the earth by the passing of human feet and not the perfect product of geometry and landscaping.

He doesn't notice the man coming up on one side until he throws his arms around Micheal's neck and hangs there, sobbing, inhaling with deep, ragged gasps and then keening as he sinks, and Micheal sinks with him, to the ground. The man wails and his body shakes, his shoulders pistoning. He seems unaware of Michael—unaware of him as a specific person, that is—as though he knew only that he needed a human presence, the nearest buoy in the sea. He is fastened to Micheal as though Micheal is fastening him to life.

Micheal is terrified. What does the man want? Michael isn't trained to help beyond giving logistical information or discreetly proffering a wad of tissues. He isn't trained at all, in truth. They had a volunteer meeting about it: Dealing with grief. But it was surprisingly cursory—"Just be there for people"—and no one men-tioned anything like this. He has a mental image of what it looks like when someone "breaks down," and he supposes that is what is happening to this man, but what if it gets worse? Then he thinks: What could happen, realistically? Would the man start screaming? Would he run, crazed, over the quilt and off into the crowd on the Mall? And then: Maybe he had the means to kill himself, a gun or a knife in his backpack. Having been chosen, was Micheal now responsible for this man's well-being? He sees himself wrestling a knife from the man's hands as others rush to help. The fact is: Michael does not personally know a single person who has died, but he has kept this illegitimating truth from the other volunteers, from anyone at the project.

As suddenly as the man appeared, another volunteer kneels beside them on the walkway, sandwiching the crying man between him and Micheal. He puts an arm across the man's shoulders, pulls him close. Across the back of the man's head, he winks at Micheal. He leans close to the man's ear, almost as if he were about to kiss his neck, and begins whispering. Micheal hears a few words, but feels embarrassed, as if he has intruded on a couple's intimacy. After a few minutes, the man's breathing slows and his shoulders stop heaving. The other volunteer sits up and asks, in a voice accented with Texas, "Is anyone else here with you today?"

"A friend," the man answers as though each word is pain. "But we got separated. I don't know where she is."

"Okay," the volunteer says, and Micheal stares at the two of them. "Why don't we walk over to the check-in tent? We can sit down there in the shade and get you some water and I'll bet your friend wanders over before long to find out where you've got to. You could probably use a rest from the quilt anyway."

The man nods.

What's your name, brother."

"Corey," the man says.

"Rigo."

Micheal and Rigo rise together, supporting Corey between them, and they walk slowly to the tent, shielding him with their bodies from the other sections of the quilt, the other visitors, the general mourning. When they get there, they find chairs for Corey and for themselves, and they sit in a triangle just beyond a corner of the tent, in the shadow of an elm. Corey tells his story, a story that Micheal hasn't yet learned by heart, and no more than a quarter of an hour passes before, just as Rigo predicted, Corey's friend comes asking after him, and Corey stands and throw his arms around her, crying again, but this time his sobs are no longer corrosive and violent.

When the two walk away, after hugs and thank-yous, Micheal is left with Rigo. They sit again, looking at one another then looking away, suddenly shy, until Rigo leans over and kisses Micheal on the mouth. He puts one hand in the hair at the nape of Micheal's neck and pulls him into his lips, and it is a long kiss. "You are too cute to be out in public," he says to Micheal when they stop, and Micheal blushes, or he thinks he blushes but anyway he feels himself simultaneously contract and expand and he stares at the ground.

"You were so good with him," Micheal says, and Rigo shrugs. "I'm an ER nurse," he says. "That was nothing."

They walk back toward the quilt, ready to take up their positions again, and Micheal says, as casually as he can, "Shall we stick together? Just in case someone else needs you?"

"Sure," Rigo says, and he puts his hand in Micheal's. Micheal knows they will spend the rest of the day clinging to one another, touching like starvelings; that they'll have supper later, after they've helped close up the quilt; and that, later still, they will have the kind of goatish, all-devouring sex that's only possible with someone you've just met, whom you barely know, who is both an enigma and a blank screen on which you can project the full-length feature of your imagination. They will kiss until their saliva has dried up, swarm over one another until their skin is raw, and the sounds their throats make will be an echo of Corey's sobs; and they will go again and again because as long as they concentrate on the parts that are hard and those that surrender, the parts that are bony and the spongy places in between, the parts that are wet with sweat and those whose softness is like overripe fruit, the havoc will stay outside and the misery will have no power over them, over anyone they love, over the entire godly creation.

FINN: THE PRESENT

He sees Micheal now, and he hears him, and that has been going on for months. At first, it was nothing more than the sensation of glimpsing him out of the corner of his eye, as if he had caught the back of Micheal's bald pink dome as he disappeared down the hallway, or he'd look up from his seat in the rear of a crowded bus and feel sure that Micheal had just climbed on from the front, his bobbing face blocked by all the people standing in the aisle with their backpacks, their puffy winter coats quilted like corn cobs.

He has no sense Micheal wants to tell him anything specific. No message from beyond the grave. It isn't a Marley's ghost sort of thing.

The experience isn't frightening, as if Micheal could ever have pulled off being a baleful presence. He just seems to want to be around, on the edge of things. It took a while before he started hearing Micheal's voice as well. Just Micheal, talking. Not speaking to him specifically, but mid-phrase, as though it were a cocktail party where the disjecta of conversation levitate above the buzz, or one of those long phone calls they used to have after Micheal moved away for a while to live with a boyfriend, and they'd get on the phone to narrate their days like live-streaming. Did he know that verb then, "live-stream"? They'd keep it up for two, three hours while they were cooking or folding clothes, or they watched TV together or read books to one another. Literal salons across physical wires, planted in the earth. Michael paid for most of those calls, but Finn's sense of honor meant that he tried to put them on his bill as much as he was able. He'd had to budget for those conversations, he remembered. What an irony that just when long-distance phone calls became free, no one wanted to talk on the phone anymore. If they'd been free then, Micheal would never have put the phone down. He loved the phone. He would call anyone. He called Liz Smith at the *New York Daily News* once, and got her on the line on the first try.

He's stretched on the therapist's sofa—he's started lying down for his sessions, even though he has to force himself each time not to think about the hygiene of it, all the other people who use that couch and probably cry and snot all over it, and which end do they put their shoes on, anyway—and there's that pause that always starts the session while he prepares what he has to say. She encourages him to say whatever is in his head, to let the stream of consciousness flow, but that happens rarely. His stream of consciousness is fairly heavily curated. As it is, he has to ratchet down the drawbridge, hulking on its rusted chain, and try to make contact with his, so to speak, inner conversation. All of this takes time. Out her windows is a magnificent view that is slowly disappearing, blocked by new apartment and office buildings, one column at a time as if someone, in boredom, in distraction, were inking in all the free spaces in a newspaper crossword. Even over the course of the eighteen months he's been seeing her, the change is obvious, but he looks out because he can still see a piece of the Bay, the container ships and ferries, the sky and, sometimes, the hills to the northwest.

In one way it seems they've known each other for decades, because she knows all his stories, or a lot of them, and so it's as though she'd also been around for most of the lifetime in which they had accumulated. At this point some of the memories don't seem like his anymore anyway. They're a story he knows, like the plot of a novel, but the possibility exists that they happened to someone else. Or never happened at all. Then again, he doesn't know any other stories.

At least she's old enough to remember the time he's talking about; he doesn't have to explain everything to her. She'd lost friends; she'd said she had, and she remembers the celebrity deaths and the significant events and, most important of all, the general way that reality, for them, was infused with an awareness of what was taking place in the world or, in the United States or in eleven major cities in the United States with the occasional heartbreaking story of tragedy and prejudice and unforgivable human behavior in the middle of Montana or in a county at the corner of Arkansas. He doesn't have to explain the Zeitgeist to her, the time ghost.

She knows a lot about Micheal of course, about Micheal when he was alive and he and Finn were friends. She's heard all the good stories. Now he doesn't even need to say "my friend Micheal"; he just says "Micheal," and she knows. And then Micheal is there in the foreground, supine on the window bench, where she has arranged attractive but worn cushions that look like they've come from a thrift store and are probably meant to seem homey. If they were too new, people might resist the urge to lie on them or hug them to their chests, as he sometimes does. Micheal is slouching seductively, his right hand languid over his crotch, and Finn instantly knows he's pretending to be Truman Capote in that famous 1947 Harold Halma book-jacket photo.

Hi-how-are-you-what-are-you-doing-what's-going-on? Micheal says. It was the way he'd started every phone call.

"Would you like to lie quietly for a while?" the therapist asks, and Finn nods.

> *I've been thinking about when I was making that piece with JD, Four Last Songs? Micheal says. About how everybody who saw it was convinced it meant something different. I mean, I was dealing with stuff about having AIDS, and*

JD was dealing with that because he was dealing with me, but he was also mourning the death of his mother, which had just happened. But people thought it could be about cancer, or maybe we were father and son, and there was a woman at one performance who said it spoke to her about surviving the Holocaust. Did I ever tell you that? What does it mean, what does it mean, what does it mean? Everyone needs a metaphor. "No great tragedy can be understood except through metaphor." Somebody said that, I think. Maybe Susan Sontag. Maybe it was me. Anyway, everything depends on your stage of life when you experience something. My stage of life now is that there are no stages of life, and honestly, it makes things a lot simpler.

Why are the dead always so fucking cryptic? Finn asks.

Micheal giggles. Why are the living always so fucking literal?

"I guess I'm hoping someone will tell me everything's all right," he says to her.

"That what's all right?"

"The story of my life. What I did or didn't do. And dying, I guess. I mean, not that I'm about to die or anything, but maybe that I'll mind less when I do. That what happened and what I did will be enough. That I'll be ready or prepared or something."

"Tell me what being ready or prepared means."

He already knew a version of the answer because he had experienced it once. He'd prepared himself; he'd gotten ready, made peace, or whatever the cliché was. He wasn't at peace that day, but maybe he'd made peace with not being at peace. He had assented.

Yeah, and it was a drag thinking about it all the time, wasn't it? Micheal says. My whole life turned into getting ready to die and how much time did I have left, and how much needed to be done first, but at the same time acting like I wasn't going to. And everybody wanted me to be a fighter. "You're going to beat this!'" they'd say. These fucking healthy people. Jesus. Sometimes I read things on the treatment-activist message boards that threw me down a hole for days. They were amazing people but it was either

nothing is coming down the pipeline that has any promise
and we're doomed or else someone had heard about rectal
ozone therapy or detoxifying drugs to cleanse your mucus
membranes or write a letter to your AIDS and tell it what
you like about it. You couldn't believe any of it, but you
wanted to. Desperately. And I'd think about all the things
that were going to go on without me—my friends' birthday
parties or JD rehearsing for other performances with other
dancers or the new person who would be at work, sitting
at my desk—and it would just infuriate me. You know,
that last day, when I passed out on the bathroom floor on
New Year's Day and poor Kenny was trying to drag me to
the bed and call 911 at the same time and was screaming
my name.... I just wanted to tell him to calm down. That
it was finally happening, what we always knew was going
to happen. I wasn't mad or frightened. I was ... relieved. It
didn't feel like such a terrible thing.

"It's hard to think about being alone when it happens, and it's embarrassing to imagine that someone who doesn't even know you might wind up having to take care of things. All the shit people leave behind. And maybe little, private things that were meaningful because they were attached to some part of your life, but then you die and any connection to the arc of your history is cut, and when someone else fishes those objects out one by one, they seem tacky and pathetic and trivial. It makes me want to just get rid of everything now, strip it all down to nothing, like a monk, and practice letting go while I still have a choice."

"I think the question I would ask is, what is the point of gathering things around us that we love and that mean something to us if not to enjoy them while we're still around to do it? Getting rid of everything sounds like a punishment."

She's not bad, Micheal says.

"Anyway, the thought of trying to organize something like that is so overwhelming that I doubt I'd ever do it," he tells her. What he means is: *again.* He knows he sounds petulant.

"So you feel you should prepare yourself but you also find the idea too disturbing to think about?

"I guess."

"I know it's difficult to speak about this without what seems like bumper-sticker philosophy, but does it help at all to know that this is a worry for everyone? Some people meet it head on and some refuse to think about it at all, but there is literally no one alive who knows how to do this well or correctly or painlessly. For each one of us, it's going to be the first time. And for our friends, too, with us. And if they have to clean up our natural human mess and disorder, maybe it will be meaningful and important to them to do it for us. Perhaps the way it had meaning for you to be the one to go through Yossi's apartment."

"But what's the alternative?" Finn says. "Not doing anything, refusing to think about it so that it's all emergency and panic when it finally becomes imminent?" She absorbs that in silence.

> *It's the inevitability, Finn says to Micheal. Most everything that happens in life can be fixed or rearranged or taken back or survived at least. Nothing is as bad as you think it's going to be. Except for that. Or maybe some alternative solution exists, if you think hard. You move to a new town, or you quit your terrible job or you fucking go to therapy and find a way to live with what's happening, and it softens or shifts or....*
>
> *Honey, don't I know, says Micheal.*

"Everything is all mixed up," Finn says. "My father's death when I was a teenager, the decade of dead friends and lovers, my divorce, friends who've died recently just because they've gotten to the age when people get cancer or have heart attacks. It all feels like the same big mass. I can't even tell what I'm mourning anymore. Or if I'm mourning myself, my own personal, solipsistic Goldengrove. But when I'm gone, they'll all be gone, too. I'm the only one who remembers my conversations with Micheal. I'm the only one who remembers cleaning out Yossi's apartment. No one else on the entire planet has those memories. If I'm alive, all that still exists. And then it disappears for good.

"Living with the thought of that loss sounds unbearable," she says.

"And yet I'm bearing it," he says. "I don't stay in bed all day or drug myself. I go through my days. I come here. I go to work. I deal with the pain. I'm not a cripple."

So anyway, yes: He was moving toward the end. He's old enough to die. And things were going wrong, a little at a time. Nothing dramatic—yet—but still. He had six medications to take every morning, not nearly as many as Micheal was taking, but the concept was the same. The pharmaceutical industry was keeping him alive. There was no forever anymore, not that anyone had forever, but there was also no use pretending that it didn't feel that way at one point—that time spread out ahead of you beyond what you could imagine, which was the same as forever, but now his end was finite and foreseeable, no longer too far off to imagine. That was a big difference. He had—he probably had—more time to think about what was coming than Micheal had had when he found out he was sick ... or Yossi, or Jonah ... and in the meantime he had nothing specific or galvanizing to help him focus his rage, his sense that he wasn't ready, that it wasn't fair, that it was too soon. That is, it wasn't too soon, actuarially speaking. But there was no ACTUP for aging.

And he knew, and Micheal knew, if Micheal could be said to know things anymore, that he was going toward it mostly alone, not surrounded by friends as Micheal had been. In one of her novels, Sigrid Nunez wrote that "the only thing harder than seeing yourself grow old is seeing the people you've loved grow old." But maybe there's one thing harder than that: *not* seeing the people you've loved grow old.

And, in fact, virtually none of the brilliant, out-of-proportion queens he'd come out with were still around, the ones with whom he'd imagined his transubstantiation into a battle-hardened old queer, who were intended to stick with him through their trite and predictable dilapidation. They'd sit in cafés and cackle over cute boys who looked through them as if they were made of cellophane. They'd go to the ballet and the theater and critique the shows at SFMOMA and talk about how they'd never again done anything as great as Avedon's *In the American West*; they'd bitch about the *Glee*-ification of the American musical; they'd say that pop culture had never been more vulgar and less fun. They'd emphatically state that art was over, that camp was over, that the novel was over, that travel was over, that irony was over. And don't get them started on music. They'd speak rigorously and precisely about things that were of no importance to the billion-footed, but which were the things that gay men magnified. With them, through those dilations, they beglamored and transformed their existences. *Mary, it takes a fairy to make something pretty.*

He'd be alone because most of his friends hadn't made it this far and then he forgot to make new ones or he forgot to know how to make new ones or it was too painful to make new ones, or everyone's lives fragmented and spiraled outward like galaxies as though they could no longer stand to circulate too closely to that nucleus. He knew he'd never go back to San Francisco again. He'd visited once, fifteen years back, and spent the whole time outrunning ghosts on the street.

"This makes you angry," she says.

"It makes me furious. It's not fair. It isn't. I know there are so many people in worse shape than me. But I still say it isn't fair. It wasn't fair to them. It isn't fair to me.

> *Welp, says Micheal. Not to put too fine a point on it....*
>
> *Listen, I'm thinking ... I want to tell her about my ... aborted mission. Do you already know all this? he asks Micheal.*
>
> *Nah. You don't turn into a clairvoyant or anything. I mean, I did notice you weren't dead because I'm clever that way, but I just thought the idea had petered out.*
>
> *Yeah, sort of. She is going to have such a reaction.*
>
> *I'm quite sure she will, Micheal says.*

"Let me ask you a hypothetical question," he says to her. "Suppose you had a patient who was involved in something criminal a long time ago, but no one was hurt, and suppose that patient told you about it during a session, would you be obligated to report to someone?" There was probably no statute of limitations on attempted murder. Especially not when it was a public official. And not for a murder that was seriously premeditated. And what did he know? Was it a federal crime, given that he crossed more than a few states to get there? Did it matter that the public official had been dead for over a decade? Could he get charged under the Patriot Act, even though it happened long before there was a Patriot Act? They could probably do it. He'd probably stand trial in the south, too, which, ciao bello.

She suddenly looks alert. "Did this involve children?" she asks.

"No." He hadn't seen any children there, unless you counted the choir members, but in any event: that isn't what she means.

"And you say no one was hurt. Does that mean the crime was never actually committed?"

"It didn't ... take place. It would be more a 'conspiracy to commit' kind of thing."

"How long ago would this hypothetical crime have occurred?"

Finn thinks, does the math in his head. "Twenty-five, twenty-six years ago."

"What would make this patient want to tell me about it now?"

"Maybe because he's never talked about it with anyone, even though it sent his life in a completely different direction. And maybe because he's getting older and has started weighing things."

"Is there any chance this crime could still take place? In other words, if I'm understanding the hypothetical, there was a plan to do something twenty-five years ago that was never carried out, but might my patient or someone he knows potentially revive the plan and carry it out now or in the near future?"

"No," he says. "No one else is left who.... There would be no point...."

"I think this falls into the realm of a judgment call," she says after a pause, "though my very strong inclination, if things are as you describe, would be that it would not be reportable." The smile she gives him is contained but warm.

"Right," he says. And then he starts. "Everyone had died," he says. "Yossi, Micheal, McKay.... Micheal had some kind of seizure at home on New Year's Day, we never knew exactly what, and he didn't last twenty-four hours. But Yossi lingered on until Valentine's Day. I don't know what it was with the holidays. Terminal Cause had already more-or-less disintegrated. That's what we called our group. There were only a half-dozen people who'd stuck with it anyway. Me, Yossi and Artie, Michael, McKay, Jonah. They were all gone. Kenny was still alive. He still is. I Google-stalked him not too long ago. He apparently ended up back in Columbus, where he and Micheal were from."

Death in Columbus is redundant, says Micheal.
"Buffalo."
"Tomato, tomatoh."

He goes on with the story, right up until that afternoon at the American Legion hall in Spartanburg. And he stops there, where the skewbald light through the oak branches had stopped him a quarter of a century earlier. He can't say why he didn't keep moving toward the stage. He'd come that far; it was literally a matter of feet, of minutes. Instead, he turned back to the side door, opened it cautiously, looked outside. The angle and shade of the late afternoon sun seemed painted on, and the flecks of yellow light that dropped down through the oak leaves jittered like bumblebees.

He gets back into his car and drives away in a state of what he will only ever think of as shock. The hair on his arms is greasy with sweat. He rolls the windows down to feel the air on his skin and slows to look at trees; at houses, the ones that are stately and set back from the road, surrounded by green space and held in by white vinyl fencing or the ones that are pinched together in coveys, spindly and weary, at the edge of an isthmus of sidewalk; vultures picking at a carcass in the shallow ditch at the side of the road and rising with an ill, peevish grace when he passes; a snapping turtle blithely risking death to cross the highway; the blaring signs of gas stations and fast food joints, clustered around the exits like SEM images of the virus. He drives through the night and into the unearthly hours, and when he gets near the Mississippi, he turns north onto the 55, which the map tells him will take him to the Memphis-Arkansas Bridge. He doesn't expect the pedestrian walkway below the road surface, but he takes it as a sign. He turns off his headlights and eases the car down into the parking area at Crump Park.

There isn't much traffic above him on the highway, mostly long-distance truckers. From the park, he can hear their remote rumble on the asphalt. He isn't sure whether his car is visible from up there, but he doesn't plan to waste time anyway. Everything except the vest fits into the gun bag from the Army surplus store, though now it's heavy as fuck and bulges strangely. He hoists the strap over his shoulder, picks up the vest, and starts toward the low cement wall that leads to the walkway over the river. Halfway across,

*he stops and drops the vest over the railing. He waits a few
seconds, then hefts the gun bag up and releases it into the
black air. He's already moving back toward the car when he
hears the splash. No one seems to have noticed him at all.*

But still. Why had he turned back at Spartanburg? He's had more
than half his life to hold that question up to every kind of light, to
give his sleep to it. Twenty-five years more than them. Is he glad
to be alive now, because of all the things he would have missed
if he hadn't been around? He's been to a dozen weddings of men
in couples and women in couples, and who thought that would
ever happen. He's married himself, for God's sake. Well, he was.
But when they'd gotten married in New York, their best man was
a straight friend of Finn's from high school because no gay man
that he'd known in New York had survived, no long-time friend
was left from those days. So even at his wedding, his old friends
loitered, a gallery of cut-out spaces.

There is the thing, and then there is the story about the thing.

Michael has changed positions and is now standing at the far end
of the office looking out across the Bay. He seems to be staring at
Alcatraz Island, visible to the northeast, gray on gray, its chimney a
slender finger pointing at a cloud.

> *Do you have an opinion? he asks Michael.*
> *I know you want me to have one, Michael says.*
> *There's no one else left to ask.*
> *Oh, bitch, I don't know, Michael says. I'm just a dancer.*
> *You know dancers have a reputation for being stupid.*
> *You mean like "dancers are cattle."*
> *I've always refused to believe Balanchine ever said that.*
> *Before I left, I was so angry all the time, Finn says. It
> was clean anger, though. Now I'm angry all the time, too,
> but it feels messy.*
> *Did I ever tell you about the time our house burned
> down? Michael asks.*
> *God, no.*
> *I was 9 or 10. Right around in there. Me, and my sister,
> and my parents had all gone out to the movies, and when
> we came back it was gone. We never did know exactly*

what happened. Later on the insurance adjuster said they could tell it wasn't arson, so they paid. That night, we just stood there, looking at the house, fallen down on one side, black water gushing down the driveway and out into the street, the ruts from the fire trucks in the yard, soggy as a swamp. Some of our neighbors came out of their houses and brought us towels and toothbrushes.... One woman carried over a full service of plates for eight, still in the box, and sat it down in front of my mother. They'd leave something and then hurry back indoors. I guess a few of them patted my mom on the shoulder, but nobody said anything.

What could they say?

Exactly. But I didn't know that until years later, that there was nothing to say. Anyway, we went to live in my grandparents' house for a while. My mom was crying all the time, and my dad would try to console her but then get frustrated because he couldn't make her stop. It was a crazy time before we got back into another house. Just as if ... everything was tainted, and nothing you could do was normal. I remember kids at school gesturing at me and whispering, and I knew they were saying, "That's him." People stared at me with this kind of pitiless curiosity, as if they were trying to figure out whether you could tell by looking. What a person looked like whose house had burned down, I mean. I remember yelling a few times, "I don't look any different than before!"

But it's true what they say: you do just sort of start over. You get some sheets because someone gave you a mattress and then some pillows and then some curtains and a lamp, and then something to put the lamp on, and pretty soon it looks like a bedroom. Except there's nothing in it that's been there as long as you can remember. For a while I told myself it was like staying in a motel and that sooner or later we'd go back home. And then I stopped minding so much.

I think my mom never fully got over it, though. She spent the rest of her life—well, the rest of my life—talking about what we lost in the fire. If she was slicing bread, she'd say this knife won't hold an edge, it's not as good as the one *we lost in the fire. If we went to a mall, she'd look in some shop window and say, "You see that sewing machine? They're asking a lot more for it than what I paid for the one we lost in the fire." When I was 19, I needed my birth certificate to apply for my first passport. I asked her where it was, and she said, I can order you a copy, but we lost the original in the fire. She couldn't stop bringing it up. She seemed to be able to find a way to work it into every conversation. Right after it happened, she said it so often that I started to think she meant that everything—the knife, the sewing machine, and all the other things we didn't have anymore—was still wandering around inside the fire, not knowing how to get back to us. Not destroyed, not gone, but literally lost in the fire.*

One day she said, just out of the blue, "I woke up wanting to look at your baby pictures and I can't because they got lost in the damn fire!" And I realized she was mad at the fire. It had ruined everything. It stole her memories. It made her afraid to leave the house. It made her refuse to let us get a pet because, she said, what if something happened and it was trapped in the house? She dated things "before the fire" or "after the fire." The "conflagration," she called it. And she never stopped thinking about why it happened. One night, it must have been at least two years later because I remember we had been in the new house for a while, I heard her and my father fighting, and at the end he yelled at her, "Goddammit, Evie, there was nothing wrong with the wiring!" And she said, "Shhhhhh!"

So you're saying her anger was clean or messy?
I think it started off clean and then it got messy.

Finn's therapist shifts in her chair. He notices, when she speaks, that her voice is less sure than he's used to. "There's so much in that story we could talk about," she says.

Honestly, I never thought anyone really intended to go through with it, Micheal says. I thought we needed to say we were going to do it because we felt so helpless, and it

was a way of feeling ... dangerous. But you know, just as
performance art. Really, the whole idea always struck me
as so ... Old Testament.
  You've changed the subject, Finn says.

He isn't sorry there had been no violence that day in Spartanburg, no explosion, no panic, no death. With each year that passes,
the guilty thought that he had dishonored his friends grows more
feeble. But he has also lived long enough to know that the world
wallows in premeditated havoc: 9/11, Utoya Island; Mumbai; Paris;
the deaths by cop; the massacres week after week in movie theaters,
in malls, in nightclubs, in places of work, in churches, in schools, in
schools, in schools. Virtually no horror show had failed to materi-
alize, somewhere, at least once, and each evil leaves him careening
into the dark backward of the universe. Each time he feels less able
to think beyond formulated phrases: Sorry for your loss. We must
stand against hatred. They can never defeat love. We must not live
in fear. We are all one. We remain united.

And yet no horror ever united everyone, not really. No evil was ever
the last straw, the one that finally razed the drawing board of existence.
It was just the one that came before the next one. The bodies in stacks
didn't move people to take action together, to march, to fall down in
the streets and block bridges at rush hour, to break into buildings and
scream into the faces of CEOs, to throw bags of pig blood at politicians.
Not anymore. Instead, everyone seemed inert with shock, torpid with
pain, squeezed between some vestigial, last-century longing for contact
and the insurmountable certainty that contact was obsolete.

His reaction to that was confusion, dismay at the relief of inaction
and his tacit collusion in it. Before, they worried that the world was
ending and insisted that it must not. Now, people see the world is
ending and exhaust themselves documenting and amplifying every
individual moment of collapse and malfunction and rupture. They
seem almost cheered by the mounting evidence: it's nearly over.

Spartanburg would have been a pivotal moment. A Senator, probably his wife, too. In 1995. Assassinated by an "AIDS victim." That's
what the papers would write. He can't justify his mind at the time
except to say his friends were dead and there were walking skeletons
in the streets; people's raving, spotted loved ones died in narrow,
sweat-soaked beds with metal rails; politicians speechified about

mandatory testing and money still did not come and a cure did not come; and something had to be done. So he had done something: he had become a jihadi.

> *How can anyone become so radicalized that killing people becomes an answer? Micheal says. He flaps one hand in the air as if fanning away smoke. Rhetorical question, he adds.*
> *People are allowed to defend themselves, Finn says. We're back in the same place now, only worse. It's not just urban queers, it's entire races, entire religions. If people felt a reasonable threat of death or injury at home, they'd be entitled to meet force with force, to not retreat if attacked. That's what all these "stand your ground" laws say. In the end, it boils down to philosophical definitions: What's reasonable? What's a threat? What's life-or-death? What's home? But who's not thinking that today? The sense that, in desperation, someone in power needs to die because the poison is accumulating too quickly to be cleansed by the normal processes, if those still even exist. And how long must you wait to react? Everyone's wondering that, too: How will I be able to tell when it's the last moment to act before it's all too late? Waiting is probably the whole problem. Maybe I waited too long.*

In fact, what force *was* more powerful than the impulse against fracturing the most basic tenet of human coexistence? *You shall not murder.*

Finn has some insight into the answer, though it wasn't what anyone wanted to hear. Maybe he even understands modern-day kamikazes better than most people.

It starts when your people are being herded toward extinction, when hopelessness whittles your worldview to a single sharp point. It digs in deep when wrongs accumulate so egregiously that the sustained absence of punishment for them can only mean that the universe has tilted off its axis. Killing does not beget killing then, it is an expiatory offering; killing begets equilibrium. It coheres in the certainty that, in the forge of such miscreated realities, the purpose of your life has been annealed to its essence. It starts in observing others who are living as though your tragedy means nothing and coming to believe that their nonchalance is criminal and that none of them is innocent.

"I think what it all comes down to," he says to his therapist, "the stupid banal not deeply psychological reason is: I stopped believing it was my fate. I didn't think it was wrong. I still don't. I just thought it was … like Chekhov's gun. Or I mean the opposite of Chekhov's gun. If there's a rifle on the table in the first chapter, who says you can't decide not to fire it before the end of the book? I realized I could have gone through with it and I would have gone through with it, but then … as if I could reduce all those years and everything we lived through to a single gesture, to the death of one man. One vile, evil, gangrenous man, but still just one. It was almost like admitting he was more powerful than all of the rest of us put together, living and dead. People who've lost the plot of their lives, their last hope is to find meaning in death. And in those moments behind the stage, I was asking myself, *Is this my meaning*?

So I drove away, and when I got home I almost literally went straight to the airport, and I moved to Europe for five years. I didn't just leave my old life behind; I pretended it had never happened.

*T*hat day he walks out of the therapist's office and realizes it is for the last time. They've been together for a year and a half, according to his insurance billings. That seems like long enough for him to reasonably expect to be getting better. The fact was, he could talk about it for the rest of his life, and he probably will, but he knew he was done with the red leather wing chair, the slow extinction of the view out her window.

He was sad. He was full of regret. He was alarmed by aging. At times his memories were dark, and he thought he couldn't bear them. But none of that needed to be cured. Mourning isn't a sickness. There was nothing wrong with him.

Or, rather. Everything was wrong, but it was the wrongness of losing a limb, being mugged, watching your house burn to the ground. What was left formed a keloid, repaired itself around an absence. Some things that are broken cannot be fixed, but you keep them anyway. The cells in his body, each on its own timeline, had died and been replaced several times over. The skin that had touched dying friends, that had pressed against other skin, humid with sex—that was long gone. His body, the physical body he had now had, in reality, not even been there.

He has read that people who have been shot and live sometimes, years later, develop lead poisoning. The bullet fragments in their bodies are often left where they are, unless they threaten a major organ, because to cut them out would be more traumatic to the body than the bullets themselves. It's a common medical practice, a standard emergency-room protocol. This is what the article says.

At the bus stop he observes the people waiting with him; the ones on the sidewalks trying to weave an invisible tunnel through the crowds, the men in suits, the women in gym shoes they hide in their bags when they're in the office; the small group of homeless men and women clustered around the McDonald's takeout window. The glass on the window is as thick and impenetrable as the glass he'd encountered at the post offices in Italy, as though the postal workers lived in imminent physical danger of attack from their patrons. You spoke through a small hole in the bottom, slightly larger than a deck of cards, meaning you had to bend awkwardly to make yourself heard. Otherwise, it was a dumb show.

They order their coffee and their \$1 hamburgers, thin and flat, through the slot and food is pushed through another window that opens on the server's side, and then swings around to be opened for the customer. They pay in coins, counting them out and handing them over with rabbinical seriousness.

He has bullets in him. Fragments small as sawdust, too dangerous to remove, and they leach their poison into his blood every day in micrograms. They would for the rest of his life. In the mass shootings, in the massacres, he had been wounded, he had been poisoned. But he had not died.

When the bus comes he waits his turn to heave himself on board like cargo and finds his favorite seat open, the one just at the buckle, so that he is shifted in a slow-motion Tilt-A-Whirl every time the bus makes a turn.

He'd told her he hated the burden of carrying memories that were his alone and that would end with him. But now he thinks: Maybe they should end. Maybe that is the point. That a clean place might exist when they were gone where something new could be made.

And in the meantime, *What is this little guy's purpose in the world?*

He is by far not as sharp as he once was, and his memories tend to form long, kinked chains that come apart in random places and then link together again in unexpected shapes. Some of them have turned entirely into emotion, the specificity of details lost. *Memory is the key to everything*, he'd once heard the poet Howard Moss say, *but it brings with it nostalgia, which must be outgrown.* And here he is, aging and sentimental and his community now is the weepy old, and he is still here to do a job. *If you are unable or unwilling to perform these functions, please ask a flight attendant to reseat you.*

The parts that people think were the worst weren't the worst. The worst didn't come until years later, sometimes decades later, as time drifted along, carrying you away from then and from them, farther every day. They never changed, but you did, until you felt as if they'd no longer know you now, though you knew them, stopped, as they were, where they'd left off. Time could do that: render people strangers all over again. But the memory of your own self in those years is just as foreign. Who was that person? You remember places, fragments of conversations, certain boyfriends, a few rituals and habits, and that kitchen, infested with roaches and hardly big enough for a table and chair, where you watched a black-and-white TV atop your refrigerator, back in the days when you hardly ever watched TV. You saw the Pope arrive and kiss an "AIDS sufferer" at Mission Dolores—a four-year-old child who got HIV from a transfusion, of course, but still. The Pope said God loved everyone, especially those who were sick. No condoms or safe-sex education allowed, but still. And he'd likely cribbed the gesture from Princess Diana, who'd shaken hands with PWAs at Middlesex Hospital in London five months earlier, but still.

You saw the earthquake—well, the aftermath, once the electricity came back on. You saw the collapsed Cypress Street Viaduct, fuming smoke and dust and the final exhalations of people who died in their cars, crushed between the layers of roadway, and after that you'd never drive through a tunnel or beneath an overpass without anxiety. You saw people chipping at the Wall with hammers, and now you can buy those fragments on eBay, encased in Lucite, for fifty dollars.

He is still here—wrapped in rainbow-colored flags, awash in rainbow-colored credit cards and rainbow-colored crosswalks and rainbow-colored bagels, stupefied by the 13,505 days since then, give or take, and gleesome over the forms of his kind that were everywhere now onstage on television in movies in books in music on the covers of magazines on the nightly news on his phone in his head, streaming viral mainstreamed ubiquitous emblematic diagrammatic anamorphous, imitating him and meaning him and always missing something and yet they existed, and that was not a thing to be taken lightly.

YOSSI & YOUNG TOM: 1991

His mind is not still when he begins kissing Tom—Young Tom, as he's called. Yossi had wanted to fuck him the first time they'd met at a party. Five feet two, a sweet-faced, muscle-bound fireplug of a blonde boy out of a Catalina Videos fantasy. Tom seemed permanently, amiably stoned, hung out in the Castro, was often at Café Flore in the mornings, could occasionally be found at the Midnight Sun on a Saturday evening, wearing a leather vest, bare-chested beneath, a nucleus orbited by a dense cloud of acolytes. Was he someone's boy? Was he a Top? Was he hung? Did he have a job?

The Castro was full of guys like him. There was the one who materialized suddenly, prefabricated, like a Tom of Finland tableau vivant: one knee up against the light pole; leather jacket thrown over his shoulder and held in place with two fingers; a jock strap and nothing else beneath; cruising, eternally cruising, his fat wad of cock like a redwood burl. They appeared and then withdrew into some empyrean abode; they were décor, mise en scène; they were mirages and apparitions.

Yossi had flirted with Tom at the party and invited him home to smoke weed, after which nothing happened. A week or so later, he'd found Tom standing at the bus stop outside The Elephant Walk, tilted against the wall like a stepladder, illustrating the word "louche." Yossi asked him home again to get high and, that time, Tom fell asleep on the floor.

Tonight was try number three, and Yossi decided not to wait for what, under normal circumstances, would have been the usual cues of acquiescence. After they'd smoked and Tom lay half-reclining on the couch, smiling his sappy grin, his eyes slitted like a satisfied cat's, Yossi leaned over him, slid his hands under Tom's wife-beater, and began to lift it gently over his head. Tom raised his arms like a child. "You feel like getting fucked?" Yossi asked, reaching for the top button on Tom's 501s. Tom lifted his hips to help Yossi wriggle him out of his jeans. That was the answer.

Tom had one of those skinny, mushroom-headed dicks, and for the rest of the sex he had remained not so much passive as inert. He didn't move, though he allowed himself to be positioned, and his limbs stayed where they'd been put, like a Gumby doll. He barely made a sound and kept his eyes semi-closed and that distracted grin on his face. He never got fully hard and he couldn't come, though Yossi worked at it for a while.

Afterward, they lay on the bed as Yossi ran his hands over all those stately muscles, traced a finger along the raised vein that rode Tom's biceps like the Great Wall of China. Tom put one hand underneath his head, and Yossi immediately reached up to play with the tuft of fur under his arm. Tom had magnificent armpits, important nipples. The parts were perfect, but they'd been constructed around a hollow. All that gorgeous real estate with a sinkhole in the middle of the property. *That was damn lousy sex*, Yossi thought.

So this was also the San Francisco Miracle. Tens of thousands of young men came to the city to be gay, and Yossi had joined the river flooding west: from Riverhead in the figurative crotch of Long Island to, as he said, the literal crotches of the Castro. They came for freedom, to escape angry or intransigent or Bible-banging families; they came to be themselves. That was the sanitized version, anyway, and it wasn't untrue, only partial. Because they also came for sex—for the *promise* of it. That's certainly what he had come for: to ogle men and "thing" men and suffer painful crushes and bed amazing beauties and sniff out sex in the air like petrichor. To flirt on the street and hold hands in public and make out at the movies and squeeze a dozen dicks and asses in the semi-darkness of a backroom and then go home and put on a suit and go to work the next day. Harvey Milk once said to Jimmy Carter's sister, when she told him Jesus could cure his homosexuality, "I'm surprised you shook my hand, because you never know where my hand has been." If he was debauched, it was a debauchery of his own design and choosing.

Yossi's roommate in his first weeks in San Francisco had been Rodney, a tall, grizzly bear of a leather Daddy who'd once advised him, "Why would you bother to go to bars when you can walk down the block to mail a letter and find someone to have sex with before you get back?" But that was Rodney, not him. Yossi had never been that confident. And he couldn't pull off being anybody's daddy. True, though. There were men everywhere, looking. They weren't necessarily looking for you, and you weren't necessarily looking for them, so it could be fraught. Yet it was everything to find those men who were looking for you at the same time you were looking for them. Not a needle in a haystack. More like a rake in a haystack.

The one thing no one ever told you was that sex you'd come looking for was often so bad. Forgettable, depressing, boring, alienating, even humiliating. What they didn't tell you was how many men were insanely bad at sex, their neuroses blooming the moment they got their clothes off; their dicks like stricken animals flushed from their dens, their bodies battlefields. Escape to Oz was meant to end the pain, but couldn't erase its effects, which lived on in the skin. Few managed to make it to the city of refuge undamaged.

If he felt trauma, maybe it was all the nights he'd spent propped against the rail in a smoke-filled bar, knowing he'd tear his clothes off the minute he walked in his own front door again, alone, and throw them on the floor, disgusted by the smell of cigarette smoke. It was the smell of wasted time, of the pettiness of desire, a reproach that had seeped into the fabric. He has wasted so much time. Why couldn't he talk to people? He was paralyzed. He's still paralyzed.

Masha was right. Jonah had loved legions of men. How many was a legion, by the way? You could think of it as counting coup. Content to know that someone you wanted, wanted you back. It was exhilarating but, if he was honest, the sex itself sometimes ruined it. Reciprocated desire was often enough, an end in itself. Once you had proof the other guy would have sex with you, going through with it didn't always matter. Actual sex was all logistics and unspoken undertones and a sphinxian etiquette. Still, what you said to friends was that you'd "had" someone; you never said if the sex was bad or if you felt lousy afterwards. In fact, you almost always implied that it had been hot—no, incandescent, you hinted salaciously. You let the other person fill in the blanks.

The blanks. He'd slept with five hundred men at least, and he remembered perhaps a dozen of them. The rest were the blanks. Was that a good statistic or a pitiful one? People would be disgusted by how much sex Yossi had, was having, planned to go on having as long as he could. The usual people, obviously, the "family values" people, the people who hated queers, prostitutes, and junkies; the ones who were delighted by the idea that "promiscuous" sex could kill and for whom the idea of men fucking was loathsome; but now even other gay men, other emissaries of the San Francisco Miracle, who sneered about sluts and people who couldn't control themselves and how some had brought the plague upon themselves. How could he still think of sex the way he did before? They'd shuttered the bath houses, closed down the piers. For public health. But also to end the open depravity. It was for someone's protection, even if not for his. In their place were jerk-off parties and fishbowls of condoms and sex-club monitors paid to interdict penetration.

Once he'd gone to a play and there was the line, "Some men would have sex in a burning building," and he immediately thought of a Linda Pastan poem: "It is forbidden to touch a dying person unless the house is on fire, the rabbis wrote." And the counterpoint: "But aren't all our houses / burning?"

And then he met Artie. During his months with Artie, who was deaf, they spent a lot of time with Artie's deaf friends and with hearing friends who could sign. Yossi had learned, too—well, he had learned enough to follow along, to form simple sentences. He knew how to curse because Artie delighted in teaching him the most vulgar signs. At dinners or at drinks parties, even with rooms were full of people, the main sounds were the crackling of hands that darted in the air like bats at sunset. There was often laughter, too, alongside staccato, aspirated syllables of speech.

Of all his remarkable features, Artie was proudest of his hair. Glossy, black, and soft, it fell just beyond his shoulders. He parted it in the middle and, when he spoke, he reached up to tuck wayward strands behind his ear. Rarely did he pull his hair back or restrain it in a ponytail. Artie's friends had given him a name sign: The right hand raised to the right ear, the fingers slightly curled, and then a backwards flick and a quick, campy toss of the head. That was his name in sign. Not A-R-T-I-E, but a coy mime that captured and parodied Artie's pride in that beautiful hair.

And what was the point of getting tested then? What would he do any differently if he knew, Yossi asked as his friends rolled their eyes. Because he lived in fear anyway; he lived as though he were positive anyway. Yossi shared bites off a plastic fork with a friend who lay in his hospice bed anyway, bringing it to his lips after him because that was solidarity, even though the terror told him to fling it down. He couldn't help feeling it, but he could master it. He used condoms and was careful about "body fluids" and tried to make love anyway as though nothing was wrong and he kissed Artie anyway as though he was certain spit didn't count, forgetting that he knew dozens of clinical details about bleeding gums, microabrasions, probabilities. He refused anyway to think of Artie's cum as poison.

And yet Artie had infected him. There, that was a truth to put alongside all the others. And then Artie died, and it was tough work to be angry at the dead. But really it was more that other people expected him to be bitter when he wasn't. Artie was the sexiest boy he'd ever been with, and Yossi couldn't get enough of him, his smell, the way he seemed to slip through the world like an otter, silky on the surface, quick, elemental. Artie seduced people just by existing. Yossi thought it was in his face, that being deaf had taught him to animate his expressions, to create an entire vocabulary of eyes, mouth, the angle of his chin. What could make Yossi angry at the chance to have lived with that, to have Artie love him, fuck him, hold him, eat breakfast with him, kiss him, tease him, his face turning to laughter when Yossi mastered the sign for "Asshole!"

When Artie started having a cough that wouldn't go away, his doctor had tested him. She was a kind woman whom Artie had seen for years. She'd treated him for *Giardia* and crabs, and she was the only lesbian to whom Artie didn't mind telling the truth about his sex life because she never gave the merest indication she disapproved or was disgusted. He'd come home and told Yossi, and the next day Yossi had gone to the free clinic in the Castro for his own test.

During the intake, one of the things his case worker asked was how many sex partners he'd had. He didn't keep count, Yossi said, and the case worker smiled. "Probably half the gay men who come here say that," she said. That made Yossi snort. They were the ones like Jonah, like him, who had slept with legions, and it wasn't that they didn't keep count—they'd lost count. The day his results were ready, a nurse had called him into a room to speak with the counselor, who placed a folder on the desk. "Do you have any questions before we look at your tests," he asked, and Yossi held back the urge to lunge, to shriek like an animal. Were they supposed to chat? Was there any question other than the obvious one? "Just the results," Yossi croaked.

And now: He was poz, and even if he had sex with someone who was like him, there was still judgment. The papers, your doctors, your friends with their treatment-newsletter subscriptions and their ACTUP meetings, they harped on about STDs, co-infections. That was it: people were always *warning* you about sex. *You could die,* they said, as if otherwise you never would, as if celibacy were the secret fountain of immortality.

No one ever told you either that sex could be the antidote to fear or how much brokenness you could encounter in it without dying. No one ever asked whether you were getting what you wanted or, if you weren't, how you could. No one ever wanted to know what it meant to you, and maybe you never even thought about it. Did you think about what food meant to you? He and Jonah had talked about sex a hundred times, but they'd never asked each other these questions. And yet you could barely walk down the street in the Castro now without some bright-faced twink shoving a clipboard in your face and asking you to take the "Safe Sex Pledge." Jesus, they were earnest. *What for?* he wanted to say. *So I won't get "it"? Too late. Anyway, we're already all infected. We're all going to die. Or most of us are. Legions of us. Yes, actual legions.*

About the Author

Wendell Ricketts is a writer, editor, and translator. He was born on Wake Island, an atoll in the middle of the Pacific Ocean, and raised in various small towns on Oʻahu, Hawaiʻi. He is the editor of *Everything I Have Is Blue: Short Fiction by Working-Class Men about More-or-Less Gay Life* and of *Blue, Too: More Writing by (for or about) Working Class Queers* and the translator of *The Wrong Door: The Complete Plays of Natalia Ginzburg*. His fiction and poetry have appeared in *The Long Story, Blithe House Quarterly, James White Review, POZ, Salt Hill, Blue Mesa Review, Mississippi Review, modern words, Harrington Gay Men's Fiction Quarterly*, and various anthologies.

Also from FourCats Press

How to Read a Photograph: Frame and Focus (Carolyn Whitson) — A vocabulary and a procedure for training the eye to see photographs but also to understanding how photographs have trained our eyes to see the world.

Blue, Too: More Writing by (for or about) Working Class Queers — Twenty writers speak meaningfully—in short fiction, memoir, performance pieces, and prose poems—about queers in and from the working class.

The Book of Singloids (Stefano Tartarotti, Roberto Corda & Roberto Frangi) — A comic strip about nerdiness, friendship, sex, love ... and other maladies of the human condition.

Cher Upon A Midnight Clear (Matteo B. Bianchi) — How do adults know when something is for boys and when it's for girls? For eight-year-old Luca, it's a mystery, but who does a child turn to when he can't even count on Santa Claus?

Twenty Cigarettes in Nasiriyah: A Memoir (Francesco Trento & Aureliano Amadei) — The November 2003 suicide bombing of an Italian military base in Iraq left twenty-eight dead and scores wounded. Amadei, gravely injured in the attack, reflects upon the circumstances that took him to Iraq and on his role as a reluctant "Hero of Nasiriyah."

Heterosexual & Homosexual Identities: The Normalization of Sexual Relationships (John P. DeCecco & Michael G. Shively) — A sweeping critique of writing on sexual identity and the processes that have contributed to the toxication and detoxication of "homosexual identity."

www.FourCatsPress.com